.the
missing
HUSBAND

AMANDA
BROOKE

HARPER

Harper
An imprint of HarperCollins*Publishers*
1 London Bridge Street
London SE1 9FG

www.harpercollins.co.uk

A Paperback Original 2015
2

A catalogue record for this book
is available from the British Library

ISBN: 978-0-00-751136-5

Set in Sabon LT Std by Palimpsest Book Production Limited,
Falkirk, Stirlingshire

Printed and bound in Great Britain by
Clays Ltd, St Ives plc

MIX
Paper from
responsible sources
FSC **FSC™ C007454**
www.fsc.org

To my mum, Mary Hayes

'Gone – flitted away,
Taken the stars from the night and the sun from
the day!
Gone, and a cloud in my heart'

—Alfred Tennyson

1

It wasn't the bright flash of light or the soft hum of the extractor fan that raised Jo Taylor from her slumber but the darkness that returned to the bedroom after David slipped into the en suite and closed the door behind him. Keeping her eyes firmly closed, Jo listened to the shower lurch into life. The gentle drizzle of water was replaced a moment later by a thunderous downpour as her husband stepped beneath it. He began to hum softly but then stopped himself, continuing the rest of his ablutions in silence.

Jo wriggled her fingers and toes but resisted the urge to stretch her stiffened limbs. She didn't want to alter her position and let David know she was awake. Carefully, she lifted her head an inch off the pillow and checked the alarm clock. It wasn't yet five. Through the gloom she could see light and steam leaching out from beneath the bathroom door. A shadow flickered as the shower switched off, making her start, and she dropped her head back down. As she listened to him brushing his teeth, she snuck her hand up to her face and raked her fingers through her fringe until it fell perfectly straight across her brow. If she was going

1

to pretend to be asleep, she wanted to look good, angelic even. She settled back into her pose and didn't move again.

She could still hear water falling, but this time it was the sound of rain ricocheting off the window in a vicious spray of bullets. Jo squeezed her eyes shut and savoured the warm hug of her duvet. Unlike David, she wasn't prepared to go out into gale force winds at such an ungodly hour – but he already knew that.

Yes, she felt guilty, of course she did. David's fifteen-minute walk to catch a train at West Allerton station on this cold and miserable October morning wasn't going to be a pleasant one, especially when it was only the first leg of a long and tedious journey from Liverpool to Leeds for an equally long and tedious day's training, after which he would face the same epic journey home again. She had made the trip herself and didn't envy him. But when he had asked her for a lift to the city centre so he could catch the Leeds train direct from Lime Street Station she had refused. She wasn't going to change her mind and she didn't really need to feign sleep; it was just easier that way.

Remnants of their argument trickled into her thoughts and she tensed her statue-still body. It hadn't been a blazing row but rather a slow burning battle of wills. That was how their marriage worked, and for the most part, it worked well. They both had strong opinions and Jo didn't like backing down or admitting it when she did, but David was exactly the same. It was a game they usually enjoyed, but not this time. This was one that had been rumbling on since Jo's thirtieth birthday over eighteen months ago, although the latest argument had begun only the night before when she and David had arrived home. He had pulled into the drive and switched off the engine before leaning in to nuzzle her neck. Remembering the warm touch of his lips, Jo's skin tingled now as it had then.

'What are you after?' she had asked.

David cupped her face in his hand and guided her lips towards his. He kissed her before replying. 'Who said I was after anything? I was simply overpowered by a desire to kiss my wife.'

He let his thumb trail across her mouth. She bit it. 'No, David. What are you after?'

The beginnings of a smile made David's face twitch. He wasn't expecting her to resist when he asked for a lift to the station, or as he put it, 'one tiny favour'.

Before answering, Jo took his hand from her face, kissed his palm and then pushed it away. She was trying not to let her disappointment sour the mood. The way she was feeling lately, she had wanted him to look after her, not work her. 'There's nothing to stop you taking a taxi,' she said, her clenched jaw pinching her words.

'But you could drive to Lime Street and back in thirty minutes,' he had said, trying to coax her. 'You wouldn't even have to get dressed.'

'Or I could stay in bed and get some much needed beauty sleep.'

'You couldn't *get* any more beautiful.'

Jo refused the bait. 'If it's the cost you're worried about then I'll pay for the taxi myself.'

'It's not the cost. I just thought it would be nice to snatch a few extra minutes with my *beautiful* wife rather than some grizzly old taxi driver.'

'I can assure you I would be just as grizzly at five o'clock in the morning.' Jo shifted in her seat and tried to pull her coat around her but it didn't quite reach across her expanding girth. She was trying to make a point but it was far too subtle and completely lost on her husband.

'You mean even more grizzly than you are at five o'clock at night?' he asked looking at his watch to make the point.

'It's six o'clock, David and the answer is still no.'

The little spat could have ended there and would have if David hadn't made the mistake of stepping on to dangerous territory. 'It's not like I'm off for a weekend with the boys,' he said. 'I'm going on this training course so I can provide a secure future for my *family*. I thought that was what you wanted, Jo.'

She narrowed her eyes as she analysed each and every word. 'Ah, yes, of course; this is all about what *I* want.'

'You, me, us – it's the same thing, isn't it?' he demanded, his words choking the breath out of him.

'Is it?' she asked, wanting his reassurance, but her plea sounded more like a challenge and that was exactly how David reacted to it.

'You tell me, Jo. Isn't that how you justified it to yourself when you took all those life-changing decisions on *our* behalf?'

The question had hung in the air and the argument had stalled, leaving an uneasy silence between them that had stretched towards the dawn of the new day.

Beyond her closed lids light flooded the room, followed quickly by a cloud of warm, soap-scented steam. The light dimmed as David closed the door, leaving just enough illumination to pick out a shirt and suit from the wardrobe. Jo listened to him dressing but it was only when he slid

4

his tie beneath the collar of his shirt that she felt his eyes on her. She hadn't moved and had kept her breathing slow and steady, unlike the stampede of emotions rushing through her mind. Guilt was edging to the front.

Jo didn't want to let the argument drag on. She wanted David's arms around her so she could feel loved and protected, now more than ever. He was the love of her life and even though she sometimes wondered why on earth he put up with her, she knew he loved her too.

They had met ten years ago when Jo had been taken on as a graduate at Nelson's Engineering, a large-scale construction company where David was working as a trainee project manager. Jo outwardly cringed whenever he told people how Nelson's had *cemented* their relationship, but the pun was delivered with a twinkle in his eye and, as always, she could forgive him anything. And she was the first to admit that Nelson's had given them a good foundation for their life together. They both had flourishing careers in the company, Jo in human resources, David in project management and they had progressed up the career ladder in perfect symmetry, one spurring on the other to face the next challenge. At thirty-one Jo was now a HR Manager and David a Project Team Leader. The seminar he was attending in Leeds was part of the next goal he had set himself with Jo's encouragement: he was training to be the trainer.

But in the last couple of years their seemingly perfectly parallel lives had started to diverge. Jo had an absolute conviction that they still wanted the same things; it was just the timing that had gone awry. Aware that petulant silences would do nothing to help them get back on track,

Jo's pulse quickened and her muscles tightened as she willed herself to move – but she was too stubborn to give in.

Jo kept her eyes closed as the weak gloom from the en suite was snuffed out with the flick of a switch. She heard David's socked footfalls reach the bedroom door. He was leaving and she was consumed by an irrational sense of panic: she didn't want him to go.

David paused at the door as if he had heard the silent plea that had sliced through the shadows deepening between them. He crept towards the bed and, without saying a word, leant over and kissed the top of her head, his fingers gently sweeping across her fringe.

'Bye, Jo,' he whispered and then, before straightening up, he placed a hand on the duvet over the unseen swell of her stomach and the baby she was carrying. 'Goodbye, little FB.'

She willed herself to peel back her eyelids and look at the man who was her soul mate, the man she loved with all her heart and for a fraction of a second she thought she might. But she kept her eyes closed, her breathing steady and when at last she allowed herself to speak, David was long gone.

'I love you,' she whispered, the words falling into the empty room.

2

By the time Jo was ready to leave for work, the sun had begun its sluggish ascent and grey light bled through the stained glass panels of the front door leaving multicoloured trails across the timbered floor. The only item of furniture in the hallway was a shabby chic dresser and Jo checked her reflection in its large oval mirror. She pulled her ponytail tight at the base of her skull and smoothed the poker-straight fringe that cut a sharp line just above her eyebrows. Her glossy auburn hair shone despite the dim light which was making the rest of her features look distinctly ghoulish and she had to resist the urge to switch the hallway light back on to chase away the shadows.

Adjusting an aquamarine silk scarf around her neck, Jo tried to reassure herself that she looked perfectly present-able. The grey cashmere coat had already seen her through a couple of winters but it was as immaculate as ever and would have seen her through this one – if it still fitted. But at five and a half months pregnant it was now snug around her chest and gaped open at her midriff.

She had once imagined that she would be wearing

maternity wear within moments of that sacred blue line appearing on the pregnancy test, but then she had also thought that when she did take the test, David would be looking over her shoulder with eager anticipation. As things turned out, he hadn't even been there. Jo had taken her time revealing her pregnancy – and when she had told her husband, he had been stunned and angry. She had reluctantly accepted that it would take time for him to come around to the idea, so hadn't rushed out to buy maternity clothes to flaunt her delicate condition. But every time she thought he had taken a step forward he somehow managed to take two steps back. She placed a hand protectively over her stomach.

'How are you doing down there, FB?' she asked softly, using the nickname David had come up with for her bump only recently. It had been a tantalising glimmer of hope that he was ready to accept that they were going to be parents – one that he had snuffed out again last night. 'I bet you're glad you didn't have to go out into the storm this morning, aren't you?' she went on. 'I can't believe your dad even thought to ask.'

Jo suspected that David still preferred living in denial. That was why it was taking him forever to get around to clearing the second bedroom in preparation for a nursery and why he expected his pregnant wife to get up in the middle of the night to drive him to the station. It was ironic, really, because it had been David who had first devised their family plan.

'How many children do you want?' he had asked her.

Jo was lying on a sun lounger at the time, listening to the waves crashing on to the shore of a tiny Grecian island as David rubbed suntan lotion over her body in slow sweeping caresses. 'Where did that come from?' she had asked with a laugh that made her perfectly flat stomach wobble beneath his wandering hand.

'After two years, it's a bit late for a honeymoon baby but still . . . that biological clock of yours is ticking away. I can hear it.'

'That's probably just my arthritic knees clicking now I've reached the advanced age of twenty-six.'

David had continued to rub the lotion into her skin, his fingers moving in sensuous arcs. 'This has nothing to do with getting old and everything to do with the way you go all gooey-eyed when you see a baby.'

'And what about you?'

'Oh, you go gooey-eyed over me too.' He had waited for the smile on Jo's face to broaden then said, 'We were watching you at breakfast. You couldn't take your eyes off that little boy sitting with his mum at the next table.'

'We?'

'There was a little old dear sitting behind us. She collared me later and patted my hand. "Give that woman her babies," she said.'

Jo had giggled. 'Are you sure she wasn't the one who wanted your babies?' She had paused then as she met his eyes. He was serious. 'Two. I want two babies, David. A mini me and a mini you, but only when the time's right.'

David had leaned back and nodded slowly, his fingers hooked under his chin and his thumb resting on the prominent groove in the middle of it while he remained deep in thought. He had then proceeded to explain the plan he was hatching in a way that only a project manager could, with timelines and milestones and of course, deliverables. He had started off by listing all the other goals they had set themselves. There were qualifications to excel at and promotions to secure for both of them. 'I'd say we'll be ready in four years' time,' he had concluded.

'Ah, when I reach the big three-oh.'

'Which still gives us plenty of time to practise.'

David had resumed massaging her sun-kissed skin, and Jo had to put her hand over his before his roaming fingers breached public decency laws. 'Let's go back to our room,' she had said with a contented smile, no doubt in her mind that the future laid out before them had been set in stone.

That long-forgotten smile made a brief appearance as Jo picked up her handbag and slung it over her shoulder, but the pull of material across her chest was tight enough to constrict her breathing and she sighed in frustration as she was reminded how easily David had discarded their plans. She had been the one to pick up the pieces and glue back together the life they had planned, the one she was convinced would make them happy – if only David could remember it was something he had wanted too.

The rain was torrential as she drove the twenty miles to a building site north of Southport for her first meeting of the day. The foul weather had snarled up the traffic and as soon as she realized she was going to be late, Jo telephoned Kelly. She didn't want her over-eager assistant starting the meeting without her. Kelly was in her early twenties and had worked as Jo's assistant for three years but while she had acquired an unrivalled knowledge of policy and procedures, she still had a lot to learn.

'What have I missed?' Jo panted as she shook the worst

of the rain from her umbrella before leaving it propped up next to the Portakabin door. She had to strain her ears to hear Kelly's reply above the cacophony created by the rain hammering against the metal roof and a radio blasting out from the room next door.

'Only the offer of a cuppa.'

Kelly was sitting at a table with her notepad at the ready. Even from this distance, Jo knew that the neat script on the open page was a list of the key points for the meeting. The air of professionalism Kelly was trying to project was lost slightly by the mounds of coffee-stained paperwork scattered across the table in front of her, which from recollection had a Formica top.

To say Jo liked order and cleanliness was an understatement and she tried not to notice the mess as she slipped off her coat and pulled self-consciously at her navy blue Jasper Conran dress. It had a bias cut that was meant to be forgiving but not enough to cope with her ever-growing bump.

'I think I've doubled in size overnight,' she said.

'That dress must be two sizes too small now,' Kelly said helpfully as she absentmindedly ran a finger down the row of buttons on her cream satin blouse, which fitted her trim figure perfectly.

'Thanks, Kelly, you certainly know how to make a girl feel better.'

'You're pregnant, for goodness' sake; you're allowed to be fat.'

Fortunately, Jo knew Kelly well enough to know that her bluntness wasn't ill-intended but the comment still stung. 'Like I said, you know how to make a girl feel better.'

Kelly mumbled an apology and a frown creased her brow as she returned her attention to her notepad while Jo pulled her ponytail tight and tried to flatten her damp fringe, which had surrendered sleekness to frizz thanks to the atrocious weather, unlike Kelly's short-cropped hair, which had been gelled to within an inch of its life.

As Jo approached the table, Kelly crossed and uncrossed her legs. The hem on one of her trouser legs was unravelling and her colleague's imperfections should have made Jo feel a little less shambolic, but the mud-spattered flap of material only served to irritate her. Hesitating before she took a seat, Jo glanced towards the door that led to the kitchen. 'I could do with a coffee right now to warm me up.'

Her words were drowned out by a loud burst of music and laughter as the internal door opened. Jim's arrival was accompanied by the smell of bacon and toast.

'I'm already one step ahead,' he said, holding up three mugs that slopped about as he moved. 'Coffee, milk, no sugar.'

Jo was only drinking decaf these days but didn't want to appear rude. Besides, she could do with just a little caffeine to liven her up so she took the proffered cup and wrapped her hands eagerly around it. She tried not to notice the brown staining on the inside of the cup above (and undoubtedly below) the steaming liquid. 'You're a mind reader,' she said.

'I caught a glimpse of someone running across the yard under a frilly umbrella and guessed it wasn't one of my lot.'

'There are women working here too,' Kelly reminded him evenly.

12

'None that need umbrellas on a building site,' he said, matching her tone. 'And if you and Jo fancied getting your hands dirty and wanted to go beyond this cosy little office, you'd be kitted out with hard hats and hi-viz jackets too.'

Jo met the foreman's gaze and gave him a silent apology. Jim was in his late fifties and had worked all over the world for construction companies, big and small. But where Jo recognized his wealth of experience, her assistant was more preoccupied by his occasional lapses in political correctness. Kelly's years of study had given her strong principles as well as making her something of a bureaucrat. She looked on managers like Jim as dinosaurs and it was a view that Jim wasn't afraid to reinforce, if only to wind her up.

'Shall we get started?' Jo asked.

Kelly's response was to look at her watch and then over to the internal door where the sounds of muffled music and laughter could still be heard. She opened her mouth to say something but Jim beat her to it.

'Some of us were here at half six,' he said. 'Some of us need a bit of drying off and a hearty breakfast before resuming our labours.'

'I wasn't going to say anything.'

'Then I apologize.'

Jim sat down next to Jo. Rather than find a clear space he balanced his mug on a relatively level pile of paper.

'Simon Harrison,' Jo began, as if the uncomfortable exchange hadn't happened, 'has been on sick leave since 24 June. He's been declared fit to return to work next week so we need to decide what adjustments if any can be made.' She then went on to discuss possible options, and while

Kelly chipped in with the occasional suggestions and cited precedents, Jim was more than happy to make it as easy as possible for one of his most experienced bricklayers to resume his duties.

'We've six brickies on site so it shouldn't be a problem offering him a phased return; the lads have been sharing the load for the last four months anyway, so a few more weeks won't make that much difference.'

'But what about Simon's duties?' Jo added. 'Mental health issues don't disappear overnight and even if it isn't the same site where the accident happened, it's still going to be tough for him.'

The accident in question had occurred the year before and for one of Simon's workmates it had been a fatal one. A cable snapped, equipment dropped on to scaffolding and a man had fallen to his death. The subsequent investigation had found no evidence of negligence or human error, which had made it all the more difficult for Simon to accept. Freak accidents couldn't be predicted or avoided and there-after he had seen danger around every corner.

'I was thinking about that,' Jim said. 'We're at a pretty high level in the construction right now but I could start off a ground-level job ahead of schedule.'

'That's bound to make things easier for him,' Jo agreed with a satisfied smile. In her experience, meetings like this didn't usually go so well. Too many of the managers she dealt with would prefer to ignore the problem or, worse still, look for a quick fix. They expected their staff to get on with the job or leave; it was as simple as that. Jo's role was to find a way forward, one that satisfied the company's needs as well as the employee's and Simon Harrison was a competent and experienced worker so it made good business sense to retain those skills. These were all the arguments that, for once, she didn't have to use and she was glad for it. Her mind wasn't as focused on the job in hand as it should be.

'Will Mr Harrison's colleagues be supportive?' Kelly asked. 'Mental health still carries a stigma.'

'My team are like family, they take care of each other and they'll look out for Simon.' There was the merest hint of a smile when he said, 'I can't promise there won't be some mickey-taking, though.' As if on cue, there was one final burst of laughter as Jim's 'family' left to start work again. A distant door slammed and the only sound to be heard now was the incessant drum of rain on the Portakabin roof.

'We have procedures to deal with that kind of thing,' Kelly said.

'I know, but Simon wouldn't expect or want to be treated differently and if anyone does overstep the mark then I'll be the first to let them know. And if by some miracle that doesn't work then you have my permission to use your "procedures".'

Jim and Kelly locked eyes and Jo was about to intervene when her phone began to ring. She scrambled around in her bag as she apologized for the interruption. It was David.

She had told him she had a site meeting that morning; it was, after all, the reason she had needed the car. She wondered if he had forgotten or, more likely, he hadn't been listening at all. Trying not to let her annoyance get to her, she took some satisfaction in knowing that at least he had made the first move to break the stalemate. She wasn't sure if she would have answered the call even if she had been on her own, but she wasn't so she didn't hesitate in diverting the call to voicemail. She would talk to him later after he had stewed in his own juices a little longer.

When Jo looked up from her phone, Jim winked at her; Kelly had her head down and was skimming through her notepad. The confrontation had unsettled her assistant far more than the veteran. But despite her frustrations with Kelly's attitude at times, Jo was responsible for her and felt obliged to come to her rescue.

'Sorry, where were we? Look, Jim, we appreciate that you're more than capable of handling discipline informally but as you well know, even the informal stages are in our procedures.'

'Of course,' he said then waited for Kelly to raise her head. 'Procedures are there to protect managers – isn't that what you lot keep telling us?'

There were tentative smiles and the remainder of the meeting continued to a swift conclusion. Jo didn't even have time to drain her coffee for which she was grateful. She hadn't been looking forward to uncovering the murky stains lurking at the very bottom of her mug.

The sound of rain hitting the roof had stopped but if Jo imagined she could dispense with her umbrella then she was sorely disappointed. The drizzle fell in rolling waves that were as wet as the ocean.

'You need a new coat,' Kelly said as they stood beside their cars, which were parked next to each other on the mud patch that served as a car park. She was staring at the gaping hole through which Jo's stomach protruded.

'I know, I'll get round to it.'

'There are a couple of spare waterproof jackets in the office if you don't mind the Nelson's logo. I'm sure one's a large size. It'll do for now if you want.'

'Maybe,' Jo said with a note of irritation that had nothing to do with Kelly reminding her again that she was as big as a house. 'Or maybe David will finally notice and take me on a shopping spree.' Her umbrella was doing little to protect her from the vaporous drizzle that defied gravity and swirled around her. As she dipped her head against the worst of it she caught sight of Kelly's trailing hem, which was now caught in a stiletto heel.

'Shall I see you back at the office then?' Kelly asked.

'I was going to suggest we have lunch on the way back but then I wasn't expecting the meeting to end so quickly or be so easy. I should have known Jim wouldn't need convincing.'

'I hope it's all worth it in the end. I still think there's a chance this Mr Harrison is only setting us up for a claim somewhere down the line. It's too easy these days to convince your GP that you're having a breakdown so you can get signed off work and then wait for a big payoff when your employer loses patience.'

Jo winced and she wasn't sure if it was the sight of Kelly's hem being buried in the mud or her assistant's cynicism. 'I don't think Simon has anything else in mind except putting the past behind him and getting back to a normal life as soon as he can,' she said, thinking back to the handful of welfare visits she had made. She knew Simon quite well but had barely recognized him. He was haunted by memories of the accident and his misery had been excruciating to watch. 'If it turns out he isn't genuine

17

then I think it would pretty much destroy my faith in humanity.'

Kelly shifted from one foot to the other, digging her heels deeper into the mire. 'It's not like you to be so defeatist. Are you all right?' she asked.

Jo put a hand against her back as she stretched her spine and pushed her bump out even further. 'Oh, just tired I suppose. David was up at five this morning and I didn't get back to sleep. And for the record, I'm not being defeatist because I know Simon Harrison will not let me down,' she said purposefully. 'Now, let's get out of this rain and back to the office. We can always do lunch later.'

Kelly was the first to leave the car park and although Jo started up the engine, she didn't drive off straight away. She placed her mobile into its hands-free cradle and dialled into her voicemail. As she waited for David's message to kick in, she flipped open the mirror on her sun visor and concentrated on flattening her fringe, which was all frizz and damp curls. She stopped what she was doing when she heard the tone of David's voice: it was as foul as the weather.

'So you're still not speaking to me then?' he asked before releasing a long sigh of surrender. 'You're so damn stubborn.' There was another pause as he considered what to say next. 'You want things your way and you want them now. Well, you may not believe me but I have been thinking about the future. In fact, I haven't been able to think about anything else, and you're in for one hell of a shock Jo, because I've been making plans.'

Jo raised an eyebrow. 'Oh, really?' she answered as if he was sitting next to her.

'And before you say it: yes, really,' David added. There was another pause and another sigh. 'I'd better go into the seminar now but I'll see you later. Assuming you want me to come home, that is.'

Jo's response was as petulant as her husband's. She stuck her tongue out at the phone, which had fallen silent. It didn't make her feel any better and she frowned at her reflection in the mirror, not liking what she saw. David had accused her of being stubborn and in fairness she could offer no defence because it was her obstinacy that prevented her from phoning him straight back. She was always too quick to put up defences and impossibly slow to pull them down again, a replica of her mother, some said. In contrast, her dad was warm and compromising, traits that he had passed on to her sister. Not that Steph considered herself lucky; she complained that she had also inherited his sluggish metabolism.

Jo snapped shut the mirror and returned the sun visor to the upright position then tried to find a comfortable position behind the steering wheel which was getting perilously close to her expanding girth. She found the lever on the stem and adjusted the wheel a fraction to give her baby more room.

'There you go, FB. Is that better?'

There was a strong flutter that could have been either a kick or a punch and she rubbed her stomach contentedly as she wondered what David had meant about making plans. His comment was meant to keep her guessing – he was intent on playing with her as much as she was playing with him – and it was working. Had he been working up ideas for decorating the nursery? Did he have a long list of baby names? Or maybe he was thinking further ahead, about what school their child would go to or how long they should wait before baby number two? Basically, she thought wryly, any acknowledgement *at all* that they were having a baby would be a good start. David's stubborn refusal to discuss any of these things so far had gone way beyond playing mind games.

'Don't worry,' she said to her baby as if he or she were wondering the same things too. 'We'll get through this. We just have to hold our nerve and get your dad so riled up that he'll be desperate to do anything not just for me but for you too. So he's making plans, is he? Well, I've heard that before and I'm not taking the bait. It's time he stopped planning and started *doing*.' That was, after all, what Jo had done by getting pregnant in the first place.

When she looked up, the windscreen had completely misted over and she found herself settling her vision on a spot just beyond the grey shroud, casting her mind towards the future. A shudder ran down her spine when she couldn't quite place David there but the premonition was countered by another baby kick and she pushed the unwelcome thought to the back of her mind.

Switching the fan heater on to full blast, Jo waited for the grey veil to lift. She wished her obstinacy could be vanquished as easily but she had spent months being understanding and patient. David needed to know that the time had come for him to step up to the mark, so she refused to phone him back and instead drove off, secure in the knowledge that they had all the time in the world to make amends.

* * *

Back at her desk, time slowed down to a snail's pace, and each laborious tap of the keyboard echoed off the walls of Jo's office. Unsettled by the sound, she stopped what she was doing and tried to collect her thoughts. She turned her back on the glass partition that separated her from the main office to gaze out of the eighth floor window with its panoramic view of the Liverpool waterfront, but no matter which way she turned, she couldn't shake the feeling that she was the one on the outside looking in.

In reality there was only one person she felt disconnected from and she checked her phone again. It was one o'clock. David's seminar would have broken up for lunch by this time and she willed him to phone. She was ready to speak to him now but she needed him to want it more. She reasoned that he was best placed to know when he had a free moment, so although her finger stroked the soft, supple buttons of her mobile, she refused to dial his number. Was he doing the same?

'Here,' Kelly said as she marched into the office giving Jo a start. 'If Mohammed won't go to the mountain, then . . .' She dropped a packet of sandwiches and a carton of orange juice on to Jo's desk. When she saw the way Jo grimaced, she added. 'You need to eat something. You have to look after yourself, not to mention whoever's in there.'

Jo put her phone face down on the desk before idly rubbing the rounded stomach which Kelly had just pointed at. 'Sorry about letting you down for lunch.'

'That's all right; I'm trying to drop a dress size by Christmas anyway.' Kelly put her hand on her hip and tried to pinch at the excess fat she imagined had wrapped itself around her body while she wasn't looking.

'You don't need to lose weight,' Jo protested.

'Neither do you,' Kelly answered. It was her turn to grimace. 'You do know I didn't mean to suggest you were fat before, don't you?'

Smiling, Jo said, 'Yes.'

'So eat.'

'I will,' she said while playing with the corner of the plastic container without actually picking up the sandwich.

Kelly wasn't convinced. 'It's still not too late to go out for lunch if you fancy a breath of fresh air.'

Jo glanced out the window and dared Kelly to follow her gaze. From this vantage point, they could see the riverfront where angry waves were being smashed against the promenade by gale force winds. 'Not that much fresh air.'

'Or maybe go somewhere for a break and a chat?' The question was tentative. Even though Jo had taken her under her wing, she wouldn't describe Kelly as a close friend. When they did talk, it was usually Jo offering advice or guidance and on the rare occasions when she had a problem to talk through, she would be the one to initiate the discussion just as she would be the one to figure out the way forward. Kelly's inquiry was at best a prompt to see if Jo needed a sounding board. 'Are you sure everything's all right, Jo?'

'Probably,' she said. 'I'm in a weird mood, that's all.'

'It'll be your hormones. When my sister was pregnant she blamed everything on them.'

'So what was my excuse before I got pregnant?' Jo asked but didn't dare wait for an answer. 'Now, have you drafted the Simon Harrison letter yet?'

'Sorry, I've been digging out personnel files for Gary's meeting this afternoon.'

It was Jo's turn to follow Kelly's gaze towards the open plan office where Gary was peering over his PA's shoulder as she typed away furiously. He looked up and caught them watching him. When Jo scowled he lifted up his hands by way of an apology. As Head of HR, Gary was her immediate boss but he wasn't beyond reproach for commandeering her assistant's valuable time.

'He's known about that meeting for three weeks and he still leaves everything until the last minute,' Jo said, still glaring at him. He winked; she smiled. All was forgiven. Gary might be disorganized but he was good at his job and with twenty years' experience on her, he was a great mentor who would be the first to admit he could learn a thing or two from her organisational skills.

'At least it's Jeanette's turn to be harassed now, so I can get on with the letter. I'll have it finished by the time you've finished your lunch.' Kelly raised an eyebrow, daring Jo to recognize the veiled threat.

'Thanks, Kelly.'

Left to her own devices, Jo made a start on her sandwich but the bread lodged in her dry throat. She told herself she was being ridiculous. Someone had to be the bigger person; David had tried to make the first move so why couldn't she?

'You are such a child, Joanne Taylor,' she told herself. 'Stop sulking.'

She picked up her phone and dialled but the call was immediately put through to voicemail. Jo hung up, not sure what she should say. She couldn't stop thinking about her husband's mysterious plans and was desperate to know what they were. Her obstinacy was showing again but this time it was working in David's favour – she wasn't going to give up that easily. She had started to compose a text message when her mobile burst into life.

'David?'

'No, it's Lauren,' came a cheerful, almost lyrical voice.

Lauren was Jo's favourite and only niece and, at fifteen years old, it was unlikely to be a social call. 'What are you after?' Jo demanded.

'Who says I'm after anything?'

'What are you after, Lauren?'

Lauren sighed heavily and Jo imagined her raising her eyes to the heavens. 'I've been picked for the Christmas pantomime.'

'And?'

'I need to design and make my own costume.'

'Good luck with that,' Jo said dismissively.

'Jo . . .'

'What?' Jo asked, tapping her keyboard loudly to let Lauren know she was busy and in no mood for playing games.

'I was hoping my most favourite, most talented aunt in all the world would help me. Mum's hopeless at that sort of thing,' whined Lauren as the child within let herself be known. 'Please, Jojo.'

'I presume by help you mean that I do everything and you take the credit?'

'Thank yoooooo!' Lauren squealed.

Jo was laughing too much to point out she hadn't agreed to help yet but they both knew she would. Lauren was right: Steph would be hopeless.

With the arrangements made and the call ended, Jo sat staring at her mobile. There was another matter that took precedence over any school production. She was going to take her time composing a text message to David and she was going to make every word count.

The message had been exceptionally long in its early drafts but by the time Jo was ready to press send, it was direct and to the point.

Sorry, hope you didn't get too wet.
Will pick you up from Lime St if you want.
What plans?!!?
J x

Her finger hovered over the send button as she recalled lying in bed that morning listening to him leave. They were at loggerheads with each other but Jo had never lost sight of the one thing that still held true. She inserted a new line.

I do love you.

Rather than wait for an immediate response, which was unlikely given that David would be engrossed in his seminar again, Jo slipped her phone out of sight in her handbag. Even without knowing his reaction, the act of sending the text message alone gave Jo a sense of release and the impetus to focus fully on her work for the first time that day.

'Ready to sign these?' Kelly asked. She slipped into the office while Jo was poring over the draft minutes of a meeting she had attended the week before, and when Jo looked up, she was surprised to discover the office awash in artificial lighting. Outside, sullen clouds had drawn a steel grey curtain across the sky, bringing a premature end to the day.

'What time is it?'

Handing over a folder, Kelly said, 'It's gone five. I was planning on leaving soon if that's OK?'

'Yes, of course. I should be going too,' Jo said, opening the folder and skimming through the letter Kelly had prepared for Simon Harrison. She had already seen the draft and made a few corrections and the version in front of her was almost perfect except that there was a comma where there should have been a full stop. She glared at the offending punctuation mark and willed herself to let it go. She needed to leave soon so she would have time to call in at the supermarket on her way home to pick up ingredients for the special supper she was planning for David.

'What have I missed?' Kelly asked, picking up on Jo's inner turmoil.

'Full stop,' Jo said regretfully, pointing out the error.

'I'll be two minutes.'

Jo pulled the folder out of Kelly's reach. 'Oh, no, I'm the one being picky. I'll pull the file up and amend it myself. You go.'

Kelly feigned an objection but didn't put up much of a fight. She had her coat on and was waving goodbye by the time Jo had sent the amended letter to the printer. It was a two-minute job and in no time at all Jo was pulling on her own coat. Only when all her work had been dispensed with for the day did she allow herself to check her phone. Her heart fluttered a little when she saw the message alert.

No need for a lift. Will make my own way.
Phone about to die so switching off.
D x

It was impossible to gauge from his pithy reply if his refusal to accept a lift was due to his own stubbornness – he could be guilty of that too – or because he was trying to make amends. She would also have felt better if he had said he loved her too but all of that didn't matter: they were reaching a turning point; she could feel it.

3

The normally harsh street lighting along Beaumont Avenue had been muted by an undulating mist that was hopefully the last damp remnant of the day's storm. The headlights of Jo's car picked up a golden river of sodden autumn leaves that flowed along the tree-lined avenue, leaving no distinction between grass verge and pavement as she pulled into the drive.

Their house was a traditional 1930s semi with an imposing black-and-white facade and it had been a little worn at the edges when they had first moved in five years earlier. Cutting off the engine, Jo did her best to ignore the shadows that obscured its newly restored splendour and concentrated instead on the warmth borrowed from the subdued streetlamps and the turning leaves.

The autumnal hues had given a false sense of security and the biting wind took her breath away as Jo scurried from the car to the front door. The stained glass window had given up its rainbow colours for the softer reflections of orange and gold but Jo was more intent on getting inside the house than marvelling at the beauty of its external features.

The central heating was already on but it wasn't until Jo had switched on every light on her way through to the kitchen that she felt at home. It drove David mad when she left so many lights blazing, especially when the fuel bills came in, but while Jo accepted they could perhaps be more efficient, it was a luxury she was willing to pay for. A house full of light and warmth felt like a welcoming embrace and she had absolutely no doubt David would be glad of it tonight.

The kitchen had once been long and narrow but they had knocked it through to the adjoining reception room to create a space that felt open and modern. The grey and turquoise colour scheme in the newly installed kitchen had been extended into the dining area where Jo dropped her handbag before setting about unpacking her shopping. She had almost two hours to prepare dinner and get ready. Plenty of time, she told herself. And then the phone rang.

'Hi,' Steph chirped. 'Are you busy?'

Jo scanned the counter where she had just lined up all the ingredients for a steak and ale pie. 'Sort of. I'm in the middle of cooking supper,' she said, hoping her sister would take the hint.

'Oh, well I won't keep you then.'

Jo couldn't ignore the disappointment in her sister's voice so she propped the phone under her chin and set about preparing the meal. 'It's all right; I can multitask. What's up?'

'Nothing, I was only phoning for a chat. How are you feeling? Still tired?'

Jo had been surprised how exhausting being pregnant could be. She had presumed she would only start to feel tired once her bump had grown to mammoth proportions but she had felt completely drained even before she knew she was pregnant and she had been struggling to recover her energy levels ever since.

'I thought I was getting over that particular hurdle but today has knocked the stuffing out of me. It didn't help that David was up at five. If I'd known I wouldn't be able to get back to sleep again then I could have avoided the argument and given him a lift.'

'Have you two been winding each other up again?' Steph asked. 'There are better ways of adding spark to a relationship than arguing, you know.'

'This was more of a quiet rumble actually.'

'So you gave him the silent treatment,' Steph surmised. She was three years older than Jo and had a lifetime of experience of her sister's surliness. 'You're not a moody teenager any more, Jo. You've got some growing up to do before you're ready to be a parent.'

'I know,' Jo said impatiently. She had said the same thing often enough to David.

'I can't believe you can troubleshoot for a living and yet be completely incapable of applying those same skills to your marriage.'

'I know,' Jo said again. Tears threatened, although they had more to do with the onion she was peeling than anything else. Jo was used to Steph pushing an issue to its limits; it was an annoying habit akin to picking at a scab that should be left to heal – although once in a while it proved good medicine, cathartic even. But today it felt more like picking a scab. The healing process had barely started. She tried to regain control of the conversation. 'David's on his way home from Leeds and I'm cooking him his favourite meal. I think we're ready to sit down and start planning properly for the baby.'

'At last! So you're finally working together. Maybe you are both learning,' Steph told her in a tone that ought to be reserved for the primary school children she taught but Jo couldn't blame her sister for taking the moral high ground. She had been happily married for fifteen years to her first love and whilst she and Gerry had their disagreements, she never let the sun go down on an argument, unlike her sister. Jo had often said the key to Steph's successful marriage was her ability to wear anyone into submission but in truth, she was as considerate as she was persistent.

'So is it only my welfare you were concerned about or is there something else I can help you with?' Jo said, eager to draw the conversation to a close. She could see her reflection in the glossy kitchen unit and her hair was sticking up at all angles. There was still so much to do.

'No, nothing.'

'Fair enough. You can rest assured that I'm fine and dandy. Now, could you please leave me in peace so I can get on with my cooking,' Jo said, then casually added, 'I expect you've got a lot to do too. Wicked Stepmother costumes don't make themselves, you know.'

There was stony silence at the other end of the phone and then, 'Bloody teenagers. So I suppose you already know what my next question will be.'

Jo tried not to let her smile reveal itself in her voice. 'Not really. I can't imagine what you would be asking of your little sister who's been complaining of exhaustion.'

'But you've just said you were fine and dandy!'

Jo yawned.

'Don't do that, you'll get me started,' Steph said immediately stifling a yawn. 'You will help, won't you?'

'Of course I will.'

'But only if it's not too much for you and of course I'll do what I can to help.'

'I'll do it.'

'Not that I can do much – you're the creative one – but I can sew on buttons, cut things out, that kind of thing. And I'll do all the running around . . .'

'Stephany,' Jo interjected, 'I said I'll do it.'

'Thanks, Jo. And in return I'll give David a ring to tell him he had better start fussing over his wife and the future mother of his children or he'll have me to answer to.'

'Erm, I don't think so. I can manage my own affairs, thank you very much! I'll come over at the weekend and we can start planning the costume but for now, will you please let me go?'

With the call ended, Jo tried to concentrate on the pie she was making, but a frown furrowed her brow as the conversation with her sister played over in her mind. Jo was the first to volunteer her services for most things, to the point that it was almost expected of her, and she genuinely didn't mind. She rarely felt put upon so her refusal to drive David to the station had come as a surprise to both of them. But it wasn't the lift that had got to her; it was the principle. Steph was right, all Jo really wanted was for David to fuss over her. Of course she couldn't tell him that because she had been the one who had elected to become pregnant, not him, but that didn't stop her wanting to be cosseted like any other pregnant wife.

Jo looked at the neat piles of perfectly cubed vegetables she was still in the process of preparing and then at the illuminated clock on the microwave. She worked out that if she left now there was just enough time to collect him from Lime Street Station, but before she could give into the impulse, she visualised David walking into the house where the welcoming aromas of crisp, golden pie crust would give him his first embrace, quickly followed by another from his adoring wife. The hug would be all the more appreciated after a long walk on a cold, dark and miserable night. Her mind was settled.

4

Jo swirled the contents of her glass and watched it bubble and fizz. Not for the first time, she wished it were wine rather than the sparkling water that was meant to settle her stomach, which was also fizzing and bubbling. She glanced up at the clock above the fireplace. There were no numerals on the timepiece, just a collection of silvery shards arranged in a starburst effect, the longest and sharpest marking the quarter hours. After years of practice Jo could tell the time to the exact minute and it was now showing ten minutes past nine.

She had already gone through a mental calculation of what time she had expected David to return home. He had texted to say his train was due into Lime Street at ten past seven and she knew it would have taken less than an hour to complete the rest of the journey home. She had already checked online and there was no reported travel disruption – and even if he had missed the connection to West Allerton, he would have taken the bus or even jumped in a taxi. She couldn't think of a single scenario where he wouldn't have made it home by now.

She had lost count of how many times she had tried to phone him but that didn't stop her picking up her phone and trying again. She pressed redial and, as expected, David's mobile went straight through to voicemail. He had said his phone was almost out of charge and that he would be switching it off to conserve the last dregs of power, but while that might explain why he wasn't answering, it didn't explain why he wasn't home.

'Hi, just wondering where you are,' she said having decided to leave a message this time. She kept her tone light but didn't doubt that David would recognize the strain in her voice. 'Can you give me a call and let me know what's happening? That offer still stands if you want me to pick you up.' She paused, unsure how to end the call. 'I love you,' she whispered even though her traitor fingers had cut off the call the moment she recalled his earlier omission of any such sentiment in his text.

'Oh, FB, when will we ever grow up?' She gave her bump a gentle rub that gave her, rather than the baby, some much-needed comfort. 'We're like big kids. *I can't say I love you because it's your turn to say it next,*' she added in a childish voice. 'But he already knows I love him, just like I know he loves me.'

She was getting tired of the games they played. What used to be playful battles over who could remember the details of their first meeting or their first date; who could find the best surprise gift; or who could prove they loved the other more; had taken on a more serious tone of late. She wished this silly spat over a stupid lift to the station had never been started and she was annoyed with herself as much as she was with him.

Jo returned her gaze to her drink while her ears strained for the sound of approaching footsteps or the jangle of keys in the lock. All she could hear was the background music that she had already turned down until the three tenors had been reduced to the faintest warble.

Draining her glass, Jo stood up and switched off the music before heading back into the kitchen. She couldn't drink any more sparkling water, so she washed and dried her glass then returned it to the dining table where she had laid two place settings. The crystal candelabra had sparkled an hour ago but the candles had burned themselves out and the romantic ambience she had been trying to create had lost its appeal, as had the pie, which was slowly drying in the oven. She wasn't sure she could face food now; her stomach was knotted up with nerves. Or was it anger? She wasn't sure how to feel and wouldn't know until David arrived home safely and explained why he couldn't have warned her he was running late.

During her absence from the living room, the minute hand of the clock had sneaked past the hour but there was nothing Jo could do except resume her vigil. Each time she blinked, she could see the ghostly impression of the starburst burnt on to the back of her eyelids.

For the next hour and a half Jo remained in the living room. If this was David's idea of punishing her he couldn't have planned it better. Jo hid her insecurities well but they were there and they tormented her now. Only a single lamp glowed in her self-imposed prison, its light too weak to reach the shadows into which she had crawled and was determined to remain until her husband appeared. Other than the torturously slow progress of the hands around the clock, the only other movement in the room came from the rhythmic strum of Jo's fingers on the armchair. Occasionally the glare of headlights swept across the window blinds, causing the strumming to halt and Jo's heartbeat to quicken. But without fail the car would continue on its journey, taking with it the hope that a taxi was about to pull up outside and put her out of her misery.

When her gaze could be drawn away from the clock, Jo stared at the two phones she had placed in her lap: one her mobile, the other the house phone. She was using her mobile to dial David's number at regular intervals, listening only long enough for the automated announcement to kick in advising her to leave a message. She didn't. She hung up each and every time before waiting precisely ten minutes until she allowed herself to repeat the process.

Jo hadn't yet decided what she would use the landline for. She wanted to phone someone but didn't know whom. She had gone through her address book on her mobile but dismissed every one. Right now there was only one person's voice she wanted to hear and no one else would do, not family or friends and, God forbid, not the emergency services. If there was the possibility that something awful had happened to David then, she reasoned, it wasn't yet real and it wouldn't be real until she told someone. She and David lived an unremarkable life; nothing bad had ever happened to them and as long as she didn't let her imagination run wild, it wasn't happening now. Telling someone would be like taking a pin and bursting the protective bubble she was desperately constructing around herself.

And then the phone rang.

Her mobile shone through the darkness and the warm rush coursing through her body took Jo's breath away. She squeezed her eyes shut but it was too late. She had seen the caller ID and the spark of excitement was cruelly extinguished.

Jo's tone was flat as she answered the late night call from one of her oldest friends. 'Hi, Heather.'

'Sorry, I've only just seen your missed call and thought it must be important for you to call so late. What's up?'

'What missed call?' she asked but was already working it out for herself. 'Oh, sorry, I must have pressed a button by mistake when I was going through my address book.' Jo's mouth was dry as she spoke, a stark contrast to the tears stinging her eyes.

'I didn't wake you up, did I?'

'No, I'm waiting up for David.'

'Out on the town, is he?'

'He's been in Leeds all day,' Jo replied, leaving a pause to summon up the courage to say more but Heather was already talking.

'I've just got back from London. I was only away one night but Max acted like I'd been gone a month,' Heather said of her six-year-old son. 'He's been clinging on to me for the last couple of hours so this is the first chance I've had for some peace and quiet. I'm sure Oliver's been winding him up just to put pressure on me to travel less. It wouldn't cross his mind that my earnings from these sales trips mean I don't have to squeeze him for every penny he's got.'

As Heather launched into complaints about her ex-husband, Jo's eyes returned to the clock. The longest hand was creeping towards ten past eleven – the next ten-minute marker for phoning David. 'I'd better go,' she said, interrupting Heather mid-flow.

'Is everything all right?'

There was a pause. In the fifteen years they had known each other, she and Heather had taken it in turns to be the shoulder to cry on. It was only in the last year, while Heather was going through a bitter divorce, that Jo had found it impossible to confide in her friend. She hadn't been able to share her worries about the direction of her own marriage because in comparison, her troubles had been trivial. They didn't seem trivial any more. 'I don't know where he is, Heather.'

'David?'

Jo told her what time David was supposed to have arrived home and left her friend to draw her own conclusions.

'He's probably met up with Steve and gone for a drink,' Heather said. 'I know what you're like, Jo. Stop thinking the worst!'

Jo shook her head. If David had gone out with his brother he would have called her from Steve's phone. Heather wasn't the only one who knew how much of a worrier she was. 'I'm sure you're right, but can I go now? He might be trying to phone as we speak.'

Heather wasn't fooled by Jo's quick acceptance but she didn't think for a minute that her friend's concerns were warranted. Jo, on the other hand, wouldn't rest until she heard David's voice and she cut off the call to Heather before she had even finished saying goodbye. She made the call to David with only seconds to spare.

The automated voice grated on her nerves and Jo cut

that call short too. Leaning forward in her chair, she closed her eyes and put her hands over her face. Her bump was substantial enough to make her attempt to curl into a ball uncomfortable. She wished she could hold her baby. She wished she could fast forward four months to the moment David could share in the miracle growing inside her, to a time when they could heal the rift between them, but for now her arms were empty and the only thing she could feel was the pressure on her bladder. She hadn't dared go to the toilet in case David turned up because she wanted to be there when he came through the door as she knew he would; he had to. Heather's theory about his whereabouts wasn't the only one Jo had explored. There were a myriad other explanations which could have delayed him, the majority of which involved nothing more than mild inconvenience and Jo had practised her response to each of them.

He could have lost his wallet and might have decided to walk the eight miles home from the city centre. That would take a good few hours, in which case he should be walking up to the door right about now . . .

The travel information might be wrong. The train could have broken down or been delayed by a fallen tree, in which case he would be arriving home right about now . . .

He could have met an old friend and gone for a quick drink, in which case he would be arriving home . . . right about now . . .

Or he could have had enough of his interfering wife who thought she knew best. He could have tired of all those idiosyncrasies he had said he found sweet, such as her obsession for neatness – in which he case he would be coming home . . . right . . . about . . . never.

She shook her head. Kelly was right, her hormones were playing up and she was definitely overreacting.

But why hadn't he phoned to say he was delayed? Even if his mobile wasn't working, he could use a pay phone or work his charm on someone to borrow theirs. And if he didn't have cash he could reverse the charges.

To break the monotony of going around in circles, Jo replayed David's voicemail message from earlier that day and listened to every nuance in his voice, analysing everything he said and didn't say. When that didn't settle her mind, she looked at the last text message he had sent. It was even shorter than the one replying to Jo's earlier message.

On train home.
Arrive Lime Street 7:10 p.m.
D x

He was rushing with his texts because his battery was low and his battery was low because it hadn't been charged the night before. But if Jo hadn't been sulking like a child, she would have made sure that it had a full battery. David relied on his wife's obsession for detail to ensure that both of them were ready for anything.

But as time ticked by and it became less likely that David had been held up for some simple reason, Jo was anything but ready. As long as something too awful to contemplate hadn't happened, and she prayed it hadn't, then there was only one other explanation left.

David had chosen not to come home.

And if Jo was being perfectly honest, that was the real

reason she hadn't been prepared to pick up the landline and phone for help.

At eleven thirty, Jo's urgent need to relieve herself forced her into action. She went upstairs to the bathroom as fast as she could and only just made it. The near miss made her angry with herself. She had become paralyzed by a fear of the unknown, compounded by the theories her mind was conjuring to fill the torturous gap in her knowledge. David was only a few hours late and there would be a rational explanation. She simply didn't know what that was yet.

Rather than return downstairs to be held captive by the ticking of the clock, Jo slipped into the spare room they had made into a study. She sat at the desk, switched on the laptop and began browsing not only the rail network sites she had checked before, but local traffic and news reports that might mention disruptions or serious incidents. The search was fruitless, but enough of a distraction to have eased her anxiety a little. The reprieve, however, was short-lived and her stomach lurched the moment she walked back into the living room. Both hands of the clock were pointing north.

Jo paced the floor as she tried again to reach her husband. The automated voice had the same effect as someone scraping their fingernails down a blackboard and made her shudder. There was nothing else for it; she needed to hear a human voice.

She picked up the landline and dialled, only to be greeted by another automated voice not too dissimilar from the one that had been taunting her all night. A scream began to build at the back of her throat, tearing at her vocal chords as she listened to the answering machine message. She came close to releasing it when the message cut off.

'Hello?' asked a groggy but blessedly familiar voice.

'I'm sorry, did I wake you?' Jo whispered.

'What's wrong?' Steph asked, ignoring the question and reacting instead to the unmistakeable catch of emotion in her sister's voice.

'I don't know.' The words had started off so strong but then quivered over trembling lips. 'I don't know where David is.'

'What?'

'He was supposed to be home at eight.'

There was a groan as Steph rolled out of bed. 'What time is it now?'

'Quarter past twelve.'

'And he hasn't been in touch to say—'

'Nothing. I've been phoning him constantly but it's going through to his voicemail.'

'Oh.'

Jo bit her lip. It wasn't the response she wanted to hear. She could already imagine the scenarios being played out in Steph's mind; they had played out in her own on a continuous loop all evening. 'I'm scared, Steph,' she managed to say in a broken whisper. Her hand flew to her mouth but it was too late, the first sob had escaped. Tears welled in her eyes, blurring her vision as she stared at the living room clock, its lethal shards blunted but not obscured.

'There'll be a reason.'

'I know, I just wish I knew what it was and I hate to

say it but right now I don't even care how bad it is. I *need* to know.'

There was the sound of soft footfalls, the creak of floorboards and the occasional click of a light switch as Steph made her way downstairs. 'It'll be all right.'

'Will it?' Jo asked, preparing to grasp even the most tenuous thread of hope.

'Have you thought about phoning the police . . . or the hospitals?'

Steph's words were soft and gentle but they stabbed fear into Jo's heart. 'No, I don't want to look like a complete idiot when David turns up alive and well.'

The pause that followed was excruciating. 'Steph?'

'Could your argument last night have been more serious than you thought? Have you checked his things?' she said. 'Is anything missing?'

It took a fraction of a second for Jo to catch up with Steph's train of thought. She laughed nervously. 'I think I would have noticed if he'd packed a suitcase before he left this morning,' she said, immediately dismissing the theory, not because she didn't think it possible but because it was perhaps the most plausible – and that terrified her. She glanced towards the stairs, measuring the need to check his closet against her fear of what she might find. She tried to corral her thoughts. 'Do you think I should phone the police?'

'Maybe. Do you want me to come round?'

'No, Steph, it's late and blowing a gale again outside. Besides, you've got work in the morning.'

'It's not as if I'll be able to get back to sleep now.'

'But you have Lauren to look after,' Jo protested, even while hoping deep down that Steph might overrule her.

'That's what husbands are for.'

Steph didn't need to be in the same room to know that Jo had flinched at the remark.

'Sorry,' she said.

'It's all right. I'm sure we'll laugh about this tomorrow. Now please, go back to bed. Keep your phone under your pillow if you have to and I'll call you as soon as he turns up. And he will,' she added as if the words alone would make her husband materialize.

'I wouldn't want to be in his shoes when he does,' Steph offered with forced cheeriness.

Left to her own devices, Jo stared at the armchair she had been glued to for most of the evening. She couldn't sit and stare at the clock any more but needed to keep herself occupied. Unable to resist the urge a moment longer, she rushed back upstairs to satisfy herself that David's clothes were still in the wardrobe. They were, but the sight of his things only made her long for him more. Desperate for any kind of reassurance, Jo slipped back into the study to check one more thing. When she couldn't find what she was looking for, the theory she had hoped to dismiss took on a life of its own.

Jo went through every drawer and file, not only in the study but in every other possible hiding place. Her search for the missing article was methodical and she left the paperwork in a tidier state than she had found it, but by the time she reached the kitchen there was nowhere else to look. Refusing to think about what that might mean Jo began clearing away the uneaten dinner.

She carefully wrapped the dried-out steak and ale pie in foil before gathering up the hardened bread rolls and throwing them in the bin along with the side salad that had been left to wilt on the dining table. The plates were returned to the cupboard and the cutlery back to the kitchen drawer, which Jo couldn't bring herself to close again. Forks lay across knives and a couple of teaspoons were peeking out beneath half a dozen soup spoons. The disorder in the drawer set her already frazzled nerves into a fresh jangle, but at least this was something she could fix. As Jo removed every item from the drawer, an image of David standing behind her, came unbidden. He rested his head on her shoulder, the warmth of his sigh caressing her neck. His breath smelled of coffee and dark chocolate from the cake she had made him for his birthday.

'What are you doing?' he asked.

'Tidying up your mess.'

She was grouping the stainless steel soldiers into regiments, laying them in tight formation. Knife-edges facing left, fork tines pointing upwards and spoons – well, they simply spooned.

'There was nothing wrong with it.'

'I *need* to tidy it,' she persisted. She could feel the anxiety constricting her chest although it had been there long before she had opened the drawer. It had been building ever since she had missed her last period and she was now about to miss the next, but she wasn't ready to tell David yet. It was still early days and anything could happen, or at least that was the excuse she was using to put off making her announcement.

'And what exactly do you think would happen if, God forbid, you threw the cutlery into the draw and left things where they fell?' he asked.

46

Jo's eyes narrowed in concentration as she tried to apply David's logic. Perfectly ordered cutlery wasn't going to have even the slightest effect on his reaction when he found out what she had done. 'Nothing,' she offered.

David kissed her neck, unaware of her deceit and simply enjoying the sport of challenging his wife's compulsions, which had been increasing of late. 'Make a mess. I dare you.'

She leaned back against the man she knew so well and felt their bodies meld into one. He was going to love the idea of becoming a dad once he had got over the shock, she was sure of it. Putting aside her troubles for another day at least, she let a soft laugh tickle her throat as she picked up a single fork and turned it on its side.

'Nah, not good enough.' David leaned over and when the thunderous clank of metal subsided, the drawer was in more of a mess than ever.

'I'm going to make you pay for that,' Jo warned but David was already wrapping his arms around her and pulling her away.

The sound of their laughter faded and Jo's eyes began to sting as she stared unblinking at the cutlery drawer where the tight formations had been reformed. 'What was the worst that could happen?' she asked herself, but without David holding her, she shrank in terror from the answer.

Quickly closing the drawer, Jo pulled up her sleeves and set to work scouring the grey granite surface of the kitchen counter until it sparkled. Next she mopped the floor, not limiting herself to the porcelain tiles in the kitchen but moving on to the timbered floor in the dining room, even moving cupboards to reach hidden nooks and crannies.

And she didn't stop there. She swept the mop in wide, purposeful strokes out into the hallway and then continued through to the living room.

The smell of industrial strength bleach had completely obliterated the more homely smells of cooking. It had started to burn the back of Jo's nostrils but she couldn't, *wouldn't* stop. She returned the mop to the store cupboard under the stairs and picked up a duster and a can of polish. In no time at all, the black marble fire surround in the living room was so shiny it reflected an image of the clock she was refusing to look at. She was in the process of polishing the coffee table when there was a knock at the door.

Not daring to consider who might be calling at half past one in the morning, Jo's heart thudded against her chest as she rushed out of the living room. The hallway lights reflected brightly against the glass panes in the front door but she could still make out a vague silhouette. Unconsciously, Jo checked for the outline of a helmet or the reflection of a hi-viz jacket. Relieved that it wasn't a policeman calling, she flung open the door expecting to see David standing there, looking sheepish and apologetic. The realization that it wasn't David hit her with the full force of a body blow. Her knees buckled and she dropped to the floor.

'I can't bear this any more, Steph. Why is he doing this to me?' she sobbed.

The tears that came wracked her entire body; Jo had never known pain like it in her life. She had thought she had experienced heartache and grief before but everything else paled into insignificance. The loss of grandparents, the demise of a beloved pet or the kind of teenage angst she thought she would never survive couldn't compare. Even the sudden death of David's dad after a massive stroke two years ago hadn't felt like this. But why was she even thinking of it as grief? What was she grieving for?

When Jo felt able to lift her head and face the world again, she was hunched up in the armchair in the living room, still clutching the yellow duster she had been holding when she answered the door. It was sopping wet with tears and there was the taste of beeswax in her mouth. Steph was perched next to her, rubbing her back. Jo sniffed and tried to give a watery smile, taking in Steph's anxious face.

'Sorry about that.'

Steph smiled back and, as she did, the tears in her eyes reflected Jo's own. 'It *is* allowed, Jo. It might not be like you, but normal people do this all the time.'

Jo prided herself in being the staunch one; hard as nails Steph might say and often did. But it didn't mean she didn't care or feel things just as deeply as anyone else. And what she needed to feel right now was her baby move. She placed a hand on her stomach, worried that her histrionics might have harmed him or her.

Steph noticed her concern. 'Is everything all right?'

Jo's hand paused as she felt a soft but unmistakeable kick. 'Yes, we're fine.'

Not giving her sister time to enjoy even a moment's relief, Steph asked, 'Did you phone the police?'

'No,' Jo said quickly as she rubbed her eyes, which were dry and flaky. Her tears had stopped flowing long before she had finished crying. She stared hard at Steph as she built up the courage to speak again. 'His passport's missing.'

Steph's laugh was more a result of shock than amusement. 'You think he's gone on the run and left the country?'

'We would have been on holiday in America now if . . . If I hadn't been pregnant.'

'That's still a pretty big conclusion to jump to. He's only been missing a few hours, Jo. Maybe he's gone to his mum's or maybe he's with Steve?'

If it turned out that David had left her then Jo didn't think for a minute that he would turn up on his brother's doorstep. Steve's six-year marriage to Sally was hanging by a thread and if anyone were about to leave their wife then Jo would have laid bets on it being Steve. No, Jo thought, if David had gone anywhere, it would be to his mum. But if she phoned Irene and David wasn't there then she would be drawing her mother-in-law into the mix and Jo wasn't ready for that yet. Irene had once been a formidable matriarch but the death of her husband had affected her deeply and Jo dreaded to think how she would handle this latest development. Steph was right; it had only been a few hours. 'I'll speak to them tomorrow if I need to.'

'So phone the police then.'

Jo shook her head. 'Not yet.' She had to swallow hard before she could get the next words out. 'But could you check the hospitals for me?' she asked.

Unable to listen as Steph made the call, Jo escaped to the kitchen. If David hadn't willingly left her, if he had become embroiled in some major incident, then it would have to be something serious enough to prevent him from phoning her during the six hours that had elapsed since her marriage and her life had been suspended. If he hadn't physically been able to get a message to her, then surely by now someone would have been able to identify him and . . . Jo's brain disengaged as the images she had unwittingly created in her mind became too much to bear. She began mopping the floor for the second time that evening.

'No news,' Steph said without ceremony when she arrived in the kitchen.

Jo halted the mop mid-stroke. She tried to let out a sigh of relief but it felt empty. She was completely drained and couldn't muster the spark of hope she had hoped the news would bring.

When it was clear that Jo wasn't going to move or respond, Steph continued, 'And I hate to say it but you might not find out anything else tonight. Maybe we should get you to bed.'

'I couldn't . . .' began Jo but she didn't resist when Steph pulled the mop from her grasp and guided her up the stairs. The tiredness that had blighted her pregnancy was a blessing in disguise and for once she didn't fight her exhaustion but let it swallow her up whole.

5

If there was a moment when Jo woke up and thought it was David lying next to her in bed then she must have missed it. Her sister hadn't left her side all night and the reward for her efforts was an elbow in the ribs as Jo scrambled around to find her mobile, which had slipped from her grasp while she slept.

Her eyes were still bleary but she could see enough to know there were no missed calls or messages. The slithering fear that had begun to wrap itself around her the night before tightened its grip around her chest, but it was the violent lurch of her stomach that sent Jo flying out of bed and into the bathroom where she dry retched into the toilet bowl. She kept one hand over her abdomen in a vain attempt to settle the baby who objected to being jostled about, its kicks making her stomach flip all the more.

Her body shook violently and she swallowed back the bitter taste of bile before turning to her sister who had followed her into the en suite. 'What time is it?'

Steph held out a glass of water. 'Almost seven.'

A second later, the radio in the bedroom burst into life.

Jo often woke up just before the alarm and despite the traumas of the night before her body clock was ticking along as if nothing had happened. She clung on to this fragment of normality as she stood up and took a sip of water.

'I'd better get ready for work.'

'You are not going in, Jo.'

Jo chose to interpret the command as a question. 'Of course I'm going in. What use am I waiting around here?'

'But . . .'

'David is due in work too. I'd rather be there in the same building waiting for him to arrive than phoning his office every two minutes and annoying everyone.' Jo sensed another 'but' coming and quickly added, 'And you have to go to work too. I'll be fine, Steph. I have to be.'

'And what if David doesn't turn up?'

'Then I'll phone his mum to see if he's there. And if he isn't,' she continued, predicting Steph's next question, 'then I promise I'll phone the police.'

'Let's hope it won't come to that.'

Jo bit down hard and let the pain in her lower lip focus her mind on something other than the possibility that she might have to face another night like the last one. 'It won't,' she said. 'Now, can I have some privacy? I need to get ready.'

It was only when Jo had closed the door that she dared to look in the bathroom mirror. She recalled her haunted reflection the morning before when she had stood in the hallway draped in shadows. The shadows were there again but this time no amount of downlighting could dispel them. She hoped she was doing the right thing. She prayed

David would turn up at work and put her out of her misery but more than anything, she hoped and prayed that he wasn't lying in a ditch waiting for her to come to his rescue . . .

'You look absolutely awful,' Kelly said.

At times like this, when Kelly failed to apply any kind of internal filter before speaking, Jo would often suggest a more diplomatic turn of phrase or, if she was in a less forgiving mood, provide a sharp retort. But today Kelly's remark barely raised a ripple in Jo's consciousness. 'Can you cancel all of today's appointments for me? I'm going to spend the day in the office catching up on paperwork.'

'OK,' Kelly said but didn't move. She was waiting for further explanation.

'My first meeting was for nine so you'll need to get a move on,' Jo persisted. She was holding Kelly's gaze but she sensed her assistant was concentrating more on her bloodshot eyes than the warning glare she was giving her. 'Kelly?'

Finally on her own again, Jo turned her attention to her computer screen and the time-management system that was busily registering the arrival of staff in Nelson's Liverpool office as they swiped in. David Taylor's time log showed that he had left work on Tuesday night at 17.38 but she already knew this because she had left with him. She closed her eyes as she recalled David next to her in the car as they pulled up outside the house. She could feel his breath on her neck as he leaned in to nuzzle her. She could recall the sensation of his lips brushing against her neck then gently pinching soft skin between his teeth.

'What are you after?' she whispered as if he was right there next to her.

Squeezing her eyes tight, she willed the tears not to fall again. If only she could go back in time she would agree to give him a lift; in fact, she would say yes to *anything* David wanted if only he was there next to her. But when she opened her eyes and checked the information on the screen, her husband remained frustratingly out of reach. Tuesday evening was the last recorded event. Wednesday was blank because he had gone straight to Leeds and then there was Thursday. So far it too was blank. Jo refreshed the screen, hoping that a series of digits would magically appear. The screen didn't even flicker.

To compound her misery, Jo forced herself to open up her calendar. She stared at an entry at the beginning of that week. It marked the start of what was meant to be an amazing two-week adventure across America. David had sent the invitation months earlier and had even attached an itinerary: if things had turned out differently, they would be in San Francisco now. She hadn't accepted the invitation but neither had she declined it. She hadn't wanted to crush one of David's dreams, not when her own had just been conceived, so the appointment was left pending.

Closing the calendar, Jo checked the time log again, her hope rising only to drop to earth again with a thump. The log hadn't changed. Unable to concentrate on anything else she stood up and gazed out of the window. The previous day's storm had returned with a vengeance and battle-grey clouds thick with rain smeared the horizon. Completely immobilized, Jo lost all sense of time and drifted back to her last evening with David, desperate to recall every detail.

She tried to remember the very last thing she had said to him.

After the initial war of words in the car she had said less and less, each syllable too much of an effort. After months of being patient and understanding, she had had enough and it was time for David to accept once and for all that they were having a baby. He had been excited about the idea of fatherhood once and she had caught glimpses of that excitement in recent weeks, but the irrational fears that had made him want to postpone their original plans were still there and she was at a loss as to how to break through them.

She could see herself standing in the living room. 'I'm tired so I'm going to bed. That's what happens when you're pregnant.'

By all appearances, her husband was engrossed in a TV programme and didn't respond.

'You can't make me feel guilty for ever, David,' she said as her parting shot.

Her remark hit its target and he turned to face her. 'I don't want you to.'

'Then what *do* you want?'

The pained look on his face softened and there was a twinkle of mischief in his eyes. 'You'll see.'

His smile had done nothing to improve Jo's mood and she had stomped upstairs to bed without a second glance, unwilling to engage in a game of cat and mouse. But that was exactly what it felt like now and David's last words cut into her heart like jagged claws.

You'll see.

What did that mean? Was he trying to prove something and if so, why be so cruel?

When the phone rang, jolting her back to the present, the rush of adrenalin made Jo's heart thump painfully against her chest.

'Hello?' Her voice shook and by the way the phone rattled against her wedding ring, so did her hand.

'Hi Jo, it's Jason.'

'Hi,' she replied, already trying to think of an answer before David's colleague had even asked the question.

'Erm, David was meant to be in a meeting that started ten minutes ago and we were wondering where he is.'

'Me too.'

There was a pause: Jason was clearly thrown by the remark but then said, 'Jo, is everything OK?'

She took a deep breath that was meant to compose her but her words still trembled. 'I don't know where he is, Jason. He didn't come home last night from Leeds. Well, he didn't come home to me. You wouldn't know . . . Is there anything he said . . . ?'

Jason and David had worked in the same office for several years and spent most of their working lives together, so if David had been planning something, he might have confided in his colleague.

'Jesus, Jo, I'm sorry but no, I never saw this coming. You think he's left you?'

So far the only person Jo had told was her sister, but if David had left then she would have to face that particular shame at some point. Not just yet though, and not with someone she barely knew. 'I don't know. What other explanation is there?'

Before Jason had a chance to come up with his own theories, Jo quickly continued, 'Look, Jason, I don't know what's happened yet, but it looks like he's not coming into work either. I'll put in a request for emergency leave on his behalf and hope that he gets in touch soon. In the meantime, if you hear anything – the minute you hear anything – promise me you'll let me know.'

'Of course, Jo. Of course I will.'

Unwittingly, Jason had forced Jo to accept that David wasn't going to show up any time soon, and the sense of despair was crushing – but a sudden spark of anger kept Jo's mind focused enough to write the email to cover her errant husband's absence. If David was doing this deliberately, then he was going to feel her wrath. As soon as she pressed send, Jo picked up the phone again. She had no idea what she was going to say beyond the opening line.

'Hi, Irene. It's Jo.'

Her mother-in-law wasn't used to receiving calls from her daughter-in-law without good reason, especially not at ten o'clock in the morning on a weekday, so she was immediately on the alert. 'Hi, Jo. Is everything all right?' she asked.

Irene was in her late fifties and had devoted much of her life to being a wife and mother. The sense of purpose that came with the role had diminished once her boys had left home and then disappeared completely when her husband had died. Her grief had eased over the last two years but it was the change in circumstance that continued to affect her deeply. She was searching for a new role in her family's life but had lost confidence and needed constant reassurance from her sons, which frustrated Jo because she knew her mother-in-law was far more capable than she gave herself credit for.

When Jo didn't answer her quickly enough, Irene added, 'Is the baby OK?'

'Fine,' Jo said, momentarily taken aback. She had become attuned to her baby's movements and normally kept track of them throughout the day but since leaving the house the only time she had thought about little FB had been to consider the role it played in her husband's disappearance. These were not pleasant thoughts. 'I was looking for David.'

Irene took a moment to respond as if she didn't quite understand the question. 'But why would he be here?'

Jo was finding it hard to breathe. The last shred of hope had been viciously snuffed out by Irene's gentle words. She gulped for air. 'He didn't come home last night. I don't know where he is.'

'Have you phoned the police?' Irene's soft voice had developed a distinct wobble.

'No,' Jo said as if she was pleading with Irene not to open a door that would allow a pack of wolves to rush in and tear her life apart.

'Are you at home? I'll come over.'

'No, I'm at work.'

Irene spluttered her reply as if she couldn't quite comprehend what she was hearing. 'He could be lying in a ditch somewhere and you've gone to work?'

Jo put a hand over her face, rubbing her forehead then massaging her temples as she tried to push that particular scenario from her thoughts. It was an impossible task. 'I didn't know what to do, what to think. I was hoping that, wherever he'd stayed last night, he would turn up here today.'

'Oh my God, I feel sick. He wouldn't disappear without

telling you, without telling me. What's happened to him, Jo? Where's my son?'

Jo pursed her lips as she considered telling Irene about the missing passport but Irene would snatch at the ray of hope in a way that Jo couldn't; he wasn't abandoning his mother, only his wife. Before she could say anything, Irene made the decision Jo had been putting off. 'The police have to be told. I'll do it.'

'No, I will,' Jo said quickly. She had already looked up the number for the local police station and knew it by heart now. Her fingers played with the buttons on the telephone base as she imagined making the call that terrified her most.

Glancing up, Jo caught Kelly watching her from the open-plan office. She had twisted her seat around so that she could keep Jo in her sights. They made eye contact and Kelly quickly looked away. A second later, Gary appeared in front of her office and was reaching for the door handle.

'I'll do it from home, Irene.'

'When, Jo? You can't leave it until tonight.'

'No, I'll go home now,' she said as Gary stepped through the door.

He waited for Jo to finish her call and then said, 'What's going on Jo? I've had a call asking me what to do about a certain member of staff going AWOL.'

For a moment, Jo didn't know what to say, then blurted out, 'David didn't come home last night.' She paused, and looked searchingly at his face, as though her mentor and friend could provide answers, but he looked dumbstruck. 'Is it all right if I go home?'

Gary's eyes narrowed as he considered his reply. She

60

knew how his mind worked. He wouldn't be wondering whether or not to agree to her request but deciding whether to say yes and take a step back until Jo was ready to talk, or probe a little further. 'Take the rest of the week off if needs be,' he said at last. 'I'll work with Kelly to reorganize your diary but phone me if you need anything or if you think you'll need more time off next week.'

'Thanks, Gary,' Jo said, trying not think of the possible reasons why she would need more leave the following week.

She held her composure, but only until Gary had left the office. She started swallowing back air in desperate gulps as she scrambled for her mobile and dialled. Tears stung her eyes as she waited impatiently for the recorded voice to stop prattling on so she could leave a message. 'I don't know where you are but you're scaring me, David,' she said. Her fingers dug into the hard, uncompromising plastic of the phone that refused to let her make contact with her husband. She released a sob of frustration. 'I love you and I'm sorry. I'm sorry for everything and I'll do whatever it takes to put things right.' She looked down at her bump. '*Anything*. Just come home. Oh God, please come home, David. I love you so much and this is killing me!'

She hung up and held her breath, refusing to let the tears fall, but when she tried to stand, she was hit by a wave of dizziness that turned her legs to jelly and then they buckled. Collapsing back on to her chair, Jo bent over and tried to put her head between her legs or as near as her pregnancy would allow. She thought she heard the door opening again but the sound was all but drowned out by the whooshing of the rising blood pressure inside her head. After a few minutes she sat up to find Kelly standing there.

'I'm here to make sure you go home. Gary's orders,' she said.

'I'm going,' Jo agreed and was thankful that her training was finally paying off. Kelly didn't ask any more questions.

6

There was no warm glow to greet Jo this time when she turned into Beaumont Avenue. The incessant rain had beaten the golden carpet of autumn leaves into a sodden brown mulch, but on a positive note, the bad weather had forced Jo to concentrate on the road, giving her brain a temporary reprieve from thoughts which would otherwise paralyze her with fear. But she couldn't escape them for ever and as she pulled into the drive she knew she was about to face her fears head on. A familiar car was parked outside the house and through its steamed up windows she had spotted Irene and David's brother Steve.

'Any news?' Irene asked, already at the side of the car as Jo opened the door.

Jo shook her head. 'Let's get in out of the rain.'

The house felt empty and abandoned despite the stampede of footsteps and flutter of coats that dripped puddles on the hallway floor. It was almost eleven but the daylight refused to step over the doorway and lights were flicked on as they trudged into the kitchen where Jo switched on the heating and then the kettle.

So far no one had broken the silence. Her in-laws had only just entered this nightmare but already had that same haunted expression Jo had seen reflected in her bathroom mirror. She wondered if they too had convinced themselves that their worst fears wouldn't be realized unless they were spoken aloud.

'Coffee OK for everyone?' Jo asked. 'I'm afraid it's only decaf.'

Two heads nodded. Steve had taken a seat at the dining table but Irene stayed close. While Jo absorbed herself in lining up three mugs in a perfectly straight line, each one equidistant and with handles pointing to the right, Irene found the teabags.

'So it's tea then?' Jo asked.

'Hot, sweet, tea. That's what's needed,' Irene said.

Jo considered reminding Irene that she had stopped drinking caffeine while she was pregnant and that included tea but it didn't seem so important any more and the two women continued the seemingly complicated task of making the drinks without another word.

When Jo passed a mug to Steve she couldn't look at him. He was younger than David by a couple of years but he had the same bright blue eyes. His deep brown hair was cropped in a similar style too, long enough to run your fingers through but only just. David's features were perhaps a little rounder and the dimple on his chin more pronounced. Of the two, Steve was arguably the more attractive but where Steve was the charmer, David was the joker who could raise a smile in the darkest of hours and right now that was what they were all missing.

'So when exactly did you see him last, Jo?' Steve asked, as the silence became too much to bear.

Guilt leaked warmth across Jo's cheeks as her mind replayed the moment David had leaned over to kiss her goodbye while his stubborn wife feigned sleep. 'He left for Leeds early yesterday for a training course. He texted to say he was on the train home and it was due in at Lime Street around seven. The battery on his phone was running out so we didn't talk and – and I didn't hear from him after that. He was going to get another train to West Allerton but I've no idea if he did . . . I don't know where he went . . . I don't know where he is.'

'I haven't seen Dave since the weekend but he seemed OK to me. I've checked with all our mates and no one else has seen him either,' Steve said, answering the question that Jo hadn't asked. 'And I've tried phoning him, but no luck.'

'Something's happened to him,' Irene said in a tone that wouldn't be denied. 'I know you're scared but I can't believe you didn't phone the police last night. They should already be looking for him. You need to phone them, Jo. Now!'

Jo's body was so tense that she was barely able to nod, but when she saw Irene reaching for the phone, she quickly said, 'I'll phone from the living room.' She didn't want anyone listening in when she confessed to the police that she had misplaced her husband, but as she slipped out of the room Irene was right behind her.

Jo stared down at the phone standing to attention in its cradle while her hands wrapped tightly around her mug of tea which she was loath to put down.

It was Irene who eventually picked up the phone, but

even she seemed frightened to hold it and quickly offered it to Jo. 'Do you know the number for the local station or should we just dial 999?'

'I've got the number.'

Jo pressed each memorized digit slowly and deliberately. It was delaying the inevitable, but unlike the fruitless calls to David, this call was answered almost immediately.

To her surprise, Jo's concerns weren't instantly dismissed although she did have to explain her situation three times before she was put through to a Detective Sergeant Baxter who made a formal record of her call. She spent much of the call reassuring the police officer that her husband was bound to turn up eventually. In fact if Irene hadn't been standing next to her, leaning in so close that Jo had to fight the urge to push her away, she might have asked him to close the enquiry there and then. DS Baxter agreed that in all probability David would return of his own accord, but in the meantime he took down all the relevant details.

As well as the basic information about David and his last known movements, DS Baxter asked Jo some necessary but intrusive questions about the state of her husband's mind, their marriage and any particular stress points in their lives. Her answers weren't as open as they could have been, not with Irene listening to every tremulous word that reverberated in Jo's mind like a nail being driven into a coffin. The best she could hope for was that the casket contained her marriage and not her husband.

'He's taken his passport?' Irene asked when Jo replaced the receiver.

Jo nodded.

The sigh of relief was accompanied by a 'Thank God,'

but when she saw the look of dismay on Jo's face, Irene added, 'Sorry, I just mean it's a possible explanation. However irresponsible and – I can't believe I'm saying this of David – however heartless it would be of him, it's better than considering what else could have happened. But I can tell you this much, Jo, he'll be getting a piece of my mind when he does come home.' Irene sighed and shook her head. 'But right now I'd—'

'Forgive him anything?' Jo offered in complete agreement.

'Are they sending someone round?'

'Yes, later on this evening, assuming we still haven't heard anything, and I've got a number to ring if David does show up.'

'Right,' Irene said, nodding her head, letting the news sink in.

Jo had been dreading the call, afraid that the police would simply dismiss her concerns but terrified that they would convince her that something bad had happened. What DS Baxter had actually told her was that they would be taking David's disappearance seriously, but to hold out hope that the call had been unnecessary. She should have felt relieved but instead she felt a crushing sense of anti-climax. What was she meant to do now? David was still missing, now it was simply official. She couldn't move forwards and she couldn't travel back in time; she was caught in limbo.

Irene took Jo by the arm and led her back into the kitchen. 'I'll make us another cuppa,' she said.

Jo didn't argue when Irene yanked a half-full mug of tea from her grasp – her mother-in-law clearly needed to keep busy, and if making a fresh brew that no one wanted was Irene's way of coping then so be it. They would all have to find their own ways of coping over the next hours, days or, God forbid, longer.

Turning her attention to another of Irene's errant sons, Jo asked, 'Where's Steve?'

'I heard him go upstairs; he probably nipped to the loo.'

When Jo stepped into the hallway, she stopped to listen. There were no signs of life and judging from the grey light glancing off the walls on the landing the bathroom door was ajar. There was only a slight hesitation before she began to climb the stairs. She might have to accept that very soon every inch of her life would be scrutinized but this was still her house and no one, especially Steve, had the right to poke his nose in her life.

Jo didn't trust her brother-in-law at the best of times. Steve had relied on his charm a little too much to get him through life. The twinkle in his eye which said 'I know you want me,' had fooled some women but not Jo. She preferred the brother with the mischievous smile and eyes that simply said, 'want me.' And she had wanted him. She still did.

However, despite their differences, the two brothers were as thick as thieves, as David had proved some five and a half months ago. A picture formed in her mind of David in the living room. April sunshine streamed through the window, warming his face and softening the frown furrowing his brow.

'I can't believe you've just done that,' she had stammered, looking from her husband's face to the phone still in his hand.

He ran his fingers through his hair in exasperation. 'What did you expect me to say?'

'I don't know, David. Perhaps tell Sally the truth?'

'He's my brother, Jo.'

'And I suppose Sally is only his wife,' Jo concluded.

'She phoned on the pretext of offering me and Steve a lift on Saturday but you know as well as I do that she was only checking up on him. And I didn't lie; I will be with Steve and I'm happy to be the designated driver.'

'But unless I'm very much mistaken, you've been designated to drive to the races, *not* the golf course,' Jo said as she continued to glare. 'Why the lie?'

'You know what Sally's like. She's counting the pennies and wouldn't approve of him throwing money away on the horses.'

'Counting the pennies so she's not left destitute when Steve leaves her high and dry,' Jo countered. She watched David draw a breath and knew what he was going to say so added, 'And yes, he would do that. You know it's only a matter of time before their marriage disintegrates and you're not helping.'

'He's my brother, Jo,' David said again.

'And you'd cover his back no matter what.'

'Yes, I would.'

'Including lying to his wife?'

'Well, yes, if I was forced to.'

'And would he do the same for you?'

'Yes!' David said with a passion that vanished once he saw Jo's eyes widen. 'I mean, no! There's nothing I'd ever do that would ever, *ever* require Steve to lie for me. Not ever, Jo.'

He was half-laughing while Jo remained grim-faced. She had cornered him on purpose so she could enjoy watching him squirm, but her thoughts had been drawn to her own deceit. She was feeling distinctly uncomfortable and didn't know what to say. She hadn't exactly lied to David. She had told him she was getting impatient to start a family and he knew her well enough to know that she would take matters into her own hands. If he asked, of course she would tell him she had come off the pill. If he asked . . .

'You are the most important person in my life, Jo,' David continued. 'More important than any other living being, including myself.'

Jo caught the twinkle in his eye that dared her to want him. Resuming their game, she glowered back.

Unabashed, David turned his attention to the mantel-piece, his eye drawn to the long silver tray holding three church candles of varying heights. He reached over and nudged the tray off-centre then looked back for Jo's response. He was going for her Achilles heel.

Jo's eyes narrowed as her discomfort returned, only this time it was caused by three blocks of wax that were out of alignment.

He pushed the tray an inch further and her patience along with it.

'Stop it,' she warned, but a smile was now pulling at the corners of her mouth.

'Come here and say that.'

The memory was strong enough to bring another smile to Jo's lips as she reached the top of the stairs. They had enjoyed making up after the fight and if Jo wasn't very much mistaken, it had been the night she had conceived.

David's art of seduction may not have been textbook, but it had worked. Refocusing on the present, her smile faltered and when her stomach lurched she did her best to ignore her baby's kick. She had been the first to breach the trust in their relationship, so wouldn't David be justified in breaking it completely? Would there be any making up this time or had he had enough? Was he using his unconventional powers of seduction on someone else at that very moment? Unwilling to contemplate the answer, Jo concentrated her mind on the brother she could hear scuttling around in the study.

'What the hell?' she began, leaving it to Steve to finish that particular statement. He had heard the door opening and was jumping back from the desk even as she entered the room.

'That was quick! Did you phone the police? Any news?'

'Not really, they're sending someone round later,' Jo replied but wouldn't be distracted. 'So?'

'I thought there might be something here, some clue to suggest he's gone away of his own accord. Have you checked the wardrobes? Is anything missing?'

'You mean you haven't gone through my knickers drawer yet?' she asked, raising an eyebrow. The comment broke the tension and she relaxed a little. 'I've done this already, Steve, and no, nothing is missing.' She held back from telling him about the passport because the last thing she needed was someone else rejoicing at the possibility that David had deserted her. She still couldn't believe it of him, not really, and yet she wouldn't consider anything else. Her eyes darted to the world map that was David's pride and joy as if it could provide the answers. It covered almost one entire wall and was peppered with a dozen green pins marking all the places they had been and a scattering of red ones to pinpoint destinations that David still planned to visit. The pin piercing the 'San' in San Francisco burned red, searing Jo's conscience.

'I've gone through every drawer, every file, even the ones on his computer but there's nothing.'

Steve shook his head. 'There must be something.'

'I know everything there is to know about David.' The statement was meant to give her courage but instead it knocked Jo off kilter. They lived and worked together but there was a healthy degree of separation too. Right now it felt like a chasm. 'Or at least I thought I did.'

Steve came forward and without invitation wrapped his arms around her. She wanted to push him away, still annoyed that he had invaded her privacy but her need to feel a pair of arms around her was too strong. She closed her eyes and tried to imagine it was David holding her but as she inhaled, the tenuous connection was severed by the pungent smell of another man's aftershave. Repulsed, she pulled away.

'We'll find him,' Steve promised. 'Let's go downstairs, shall we, before Mum thinks we've gone missing too?'

'I'd prefer it if you asked before rooting through my things next time,' Jo said acidly in case he was under the impression he was forgiven.

'Sorry, I was just so desperate to find an answer. I can't sit back and do nothing.' They were heading downstairs now and as they reached the bottom, Steve stopped her in her tracks. 'Why didn't you phone the police straight away, Jo?'

'Sorry?'

'I mean, if it was me, the first thing I would have thought was, and I hate to say it, that something bad had happened. You were expecting him home and he didn't make it. What did you think had happened if you didn't think it was something bad?'

Jo looked at Steve as she considered her answer. His face was the picture of innocence but she didn't doubt he had his own suspicions. 'We had an argument on Tuesday night.'

'About?'

'Something and nothing. I wouldn't give him a lift to the station, that's all,' she said although she was beginning to believe that less and less.

'Something and nothing,' Steve repeated as if he was getting a feel for the words.

She had no idea how much David had told Steve about the surprise pregnancy and the friction it had caused in their marriage but she knew from experience that they would protect each other to the hilt. 'Unless you know otherwise, Steve. If you have even an inkling of why he would do this deliberately then please, *please* tell me,' she begged but Steve was already shaking his head. He reached over to give her arm a reassuring squeeze.

'I'm sorry, I'm as much in the dark as you are, but I will say this: I don't believe for a minute that Dave would ever leave you, certainly not like this and that's a hard thing for me to say because right now I'd rather believe that he had. It has to be better than considering other possibilities. No offence meant.'

Jo cleared her throat and gave him a weak smile. 'None

taken.' The deep breath she took tasted of buttery pastry. 'What in God's name is your mum up to now?'

The dining table had been set and three plates of warmed up steak and ale pie awaited them along with replenished cups of tea.

'Irene, I'm really not hungry.'

'You need to keep your strength up, if not for you then for the baby.'

Jo wanted to say she didn't care. Nothing else mattered except finding David but she kept her voice level and said, 'Thank you, but what I really need is some sleep so I can gather my strength for the police interview later.'

'But . . .'

It would never cross Irene's mind that Jo wanted to be left in peace. If there was a family crisis then the Taylor family pulled the yarn of their tightly knit family tighter still. It was Steve, on his best behaviour now, who took the hint. Jo could almost forgive him his previous indiscretion as he now persuaded his mum that they could make better use of their time by conducting their own investigations. Steve wanted to walk the route that David would have taken home so they could check for any signs that he might have been there. What those signs might be Jo didn't dare imagine but she was glad of the reprieve.

'OK, we'll leave you to it, Jo,' Irene agreed. 'Once I've seen you clear your plate.'

'Irene, really . . .' Jo began but then pulled herself up short. There were tears welling in Irene's eyes and in a matter of seconds she was a wreck. Her sobs were heart wrenching and she grabbed hold of Jo and clung to her for dear life.

'I want my son home,' she cried. 'I want him home safe. I've lost Alan – I won't lose David too. It isn't going to happen. I want this to be over – now!'

Jo had comforted Irene often enough in the long painful days after her husband's death but as she felt the trembling, limp body of the widow in her arms, she knew she didn't have the strength to help her now. Just the sound of Irene's sobs was sending her emotions into free fall. She was being sucked back into the dark abyss she had struggled to emerge from the night before. She simply couldn't bear to go through that again and looked imploringly towards Steve. He pulled his mum off her.

'We'll leave you to get some sleep,' he said.

Irene was still sobbing but managed to say, 'We'll come back later when the police are here.'

'I'd rather you didn't, Irene,' Jo said, looking again to Steve for support. Her in-laws would begin to dissect her marriage soon enough and if she had to reveal more to the police – if she had to reveal everything they'd been through in recent months – then she didn't want them there. 'Right now all they need is for me to give a statement. Steph promised to come over when she finishes work so I'll have someone with me, but I'll be the one doing all the talking. I think that works best, don't you?'

'Jo's right, Mum. Look how upset you are now, it's not going to be easy tonight and like Jo says, she'll have her sister there for moral support.'

Except for the occasional hiccup, Irene had regained her composure. 'Tell them to check the airports. If he's taken his passport . . .'

Jo cast her eyes down to avoid the look Steve was giving

her. She felt guilty for not telling him when, in the absence of any other evidence, he had been taking her side, but then guilt was something she was more than used to.

'And they'll want to speak to me too,' Irene continued.

'They can do that later,' Steve said, scrutinizing Jo's face as if that act alone could help locate his brother. 'Let's just take it one step at a time.'

Irene nodded. 'And David could still walk through that door at any moment.'

And it was to the front door that they all headed, each one peering longingly through the stained glass window for a familiar silhouette. But when the door was pulled open, the step held no greater treasure than sodden autumn leaves that squelched underfoot as Irene and Steve said their goodbyes.

Jo's blouse was still wet from Irene's tears but her cheeks were dry as she watched them drive off. She closed the door, sealing up her home and containing the emptiness that filled every corner of the house, mirroring the growing void inside her. She returned to the kitchen where three plates remained untouched at the table, the steak and ale pie congealing and cold. Picking up a plate, Jo had to stop herself from launching it against the wall. She didn't have the strength to face an afternoon clearing up the mess and she knew she wouldn't be able to leave it. Instead she had to satisfy herself with hurling the uneaten dinner into the kitchen bin, the plate included and to the accompaniment of a choked scream. The second and third plate followed in quick succession, her scream louder and more satisfying each time, heightened by the sound of china shattering into smithereens. It reminded her of her life.

7

'I have quite a list of things I'll need from you,' DS Baxter warned after Jo had taken him through David's last known movements. 'A couple of recent photos, a list of friends, family and any other useful contacts, and details of his employment, his mobile phone and his bank accounts so we can access them. I know it's a lot but just as soon as you can manage.'

Jo reached over to a small table at the side of the sofa and picked up a wad of papers and a holiday brochure. 'I think I have most of that here,' she said handing over everything except the brochure, which she rested on her lap. 'I've also included all the details of the course David attended in Leeds. He was the only delegate from Nelson's but the course coordinator should be able to provide you with a full list of delegates.'

DS Baxter was occupying the armchair where Jo had kept vigil the night before and she was more than happy for someone else to take her place. The policeman was younger than she expected; his deep voice over the phone had suggested a heavy smoking and careworn detective but despite the receding hairline and deep-set laughter lines, the man in front of her looked the right side of forty still. He scratched at his five o'clock shadow and looked quietly impressed as he leafed through the collection of papers. He glanced briefly at the brochure on her lap then said, 'Thank you, we'll start making some preliminary enquiries and check CCTV footage at the train stations and local area.'

'OK,' Jo managed to say.

'We probably won't need to investigate too deeply. There's usually a perfectly natural explanation for a grown man to go missing and more often than not they turn up of their own accord.'

'I hope that doesn't mean you won't be taking this seriously. My sister needs answers,' countered Steph who had so far been sitting quietly next to Jo. 'She's five and a half months pregnant and this kind of stress can't be good for her.'

'What do you mean by a natural explanation?' Jo asked.

With Steph's words still ringing in his ears, DS Baxter gave Jo an apologetic smile but he spoke bluntly. 'There are people who simply choose to step out of their lives and for a variety of reasons. Even our closest family members are capable of surprising us, no matter how well we think we know them. I can assure you we will be taking this seriously and we will investigate, but I have to warn you that if all the evidence then suggests David elected to disappear, I'm afraid there's not much more we can do.'

Jo made a point of swallowing hard as if she had a raging thirst. 'I think I could do with that cup of coffee you offered,' she said to Steph. 'Are you sure you don't want one, DS Baxter?'

The policeman sat back in the armchair. 'Please call me Martin,' he said, 'and yes, I think I do. Milk, one sugar if it's not too much trouble,' he said, offering a smile to Steph as she stood up.

Jo watched her sister leave the room and held off speaking until she had closed the door. 'I've gone through every possible reason why David didn't come home last night and I keep asking myself the same question that I know you're asking yourself right now. Has my husband left me?'

'Is it possible?'

Jo played nervously with the corner of the holiday brochure. 'I met David when I was twenty-one, a week after starting at Nelson's,' Jo began, choosing to concentrate on the birth of their relationship rather than what might turn out to be its death throes. She briefly closed her eyes as the memory of their first meeting came to mind. She had been a fresh-faced trainee, sitting meekly in the corner of what had been her first professional meeting. David admitted later that he hadn't even noticed her until she interrupted him mid-sentence to announce he didn't know what he was talking about. In truth, she hadn't been quite so abrupt, but the story was all the better for his retelling. 'I'm not sure if it was love at first sight but it didn't take long for both of us to realize that we were soul mates. We married three years later and have spent the last seven years building our lives together.' She paused as she saw the flicker of a thought cross Martin's face. 'What? You think this is the dreaded seven-year itch?'

'It happens more often than you'd think,' the policeman said and probably wasn't aware that his thumb stroked the flesh around the third finger of his left hand where perhaps a wedding band had once been. 'Given that he didn't go to his family, is there anyone else he could have turned to?'

'You mean was he having an affair?' Jo had questioned her entire belief system in the last twenty-four hours but in this one regard she had come back with the same answer time and time again. She shook her head and said, 'No, I won't believe that of him, not David. And apart from the fact that I trust him implicitly, we work together. Yes, he goes out with his friends and his brother, but I really don't see how he'd have the opportunity, not without me knowing or at least suspecting.'

'You understand why I have to ask,' Martin said by way of an apology.

'Of course. You're not asking anything I haven't already asked myself. We were happy.' The use of the past tense had been an unconscious slip and one that frightened Jo and made Martin raise his eyebrows so she hurried on, 'I'll admit it hasn't been easy of late but I've never doubted my love for my husband and before now I never doubted his love for me. I questioned why he loved me often enough, but I never doubted it.'

'What do you mean by that?'

'David and I are complete opposites. He's spontaneous, daring, a bit of a risk taker while I'm more measured, less impulsive. He adds the colour to my black-and-white world while I . . .' Jo's mind stalled as she tried to think exactly what it was that she added to David's life. Why had he put up with her?

There was an uncomfortable pause and Jo imagined the

policeman losing interest in the case by the second. She had spent the last twenty-four hours searching for answers and was slowly and painfully coming to the conclusion that David must have abandoned her, and now she was convincing Martin of the same thing.

'You said there have been issues recently. Was there something in particular putting a strain on your marriage?'

Jo lifted the brochure up but only enough to hide the gentle mound of her stomach. 'As my sister was keen to point out, I'm pregnant. We'd agreed to start a family when I was thirty. It was David who came up with the plan but then he is the planner – or at least that's what's written on his job description,' she added bitterly. She was repeating a well-worn argument that was no stranger to those same four walls. 'And me, being the one who follows policies and procedures to the letter, I thought once we had a plan we would stick to it. I was looking forward to being a mum. I really wanted to start a family with the man I loved.'

Her voice softened as the dream she had spent years creating came so vividly to mind. As if sensing her excitement, FB made her stomach flip; then the colour faded from her imaginary world. 'But David changed his mind and at first I couldn't blame him. He was affected by his dad's death quite deeply and I didn't push, but after a year of prevaricating, I told him that I'd had enough. I didn't exactly tell him I was coming off the pill, but I didn't say I wasn't, either.'

'So he wasn't happy when you told him you were pregnant?'

Jo's laugh was hollow. 'It was more a matter of him

being in shock and OK, maybe a little angry too. He didn't agree with how I'd gone about things, but he didn't blame me either.'

'It sounds like you wanted different things,' he said.

'No, I think we wanted the same things – just at different times. He wanted to see more of the world before settling down, that's all. If things had gone his way then we would have been in America this week.'

'Ah . . .' Martin said and took the brochure which Jo was finally ready to relinquish.

'I'm finding it impossible to believe that he would hop on the next plane to America,' she said, 'but there are pages torn out, pages that David was poring over just before I dropped the bombshell. And now I can't account for where those pages might be or, more importantly, his passport . . . It doesn't look good, does it?'

'It's one line of enquiry,' Martin agreed but wouldn't commit himself further. 'So tell me more about how things have been lately. Was he getting used to the idea of becoming a father?'

'He was more subdued than anything. It was as if he wanted to be excited but was afraid to be,' Jo said hesitantly. 'But then I wasn't much better. I felt guilty about trapping him – if you can trap someone you're already married to.' Her voice tightened as she finished her sentence and she looked away, out of the window, blinking back tears.

'So you would have told him about the baby around five months ago?'

Jo's guilt was showing on her face when she turned back to Martin with a wavering smile. 'I took my time telling him, so it was more like three or four months ago. Still enough time to plan his escape, do you think?'

Rather than answer her, he pursed his lips then said, 'Had anything happened more recently that might have made him want to up and leave now?'

The hairs on the back of Jo's neck stood on end as she felt another layer of her life being stripped away. 'David came with me for the twenty-week scan a few weeks ago and I thought we had reached a turning point. He had even come up with a name for my bump.' She patted her stomach and didn't give a second thought to the blush rising in her cheeks. 'We'd started calling it FB. Don't ask why, because I don't think even I followed his logic.' There was a brief pause for a smile that didn't quite reach her eyes and then she added, 'But anyway, when we got there for the scan, all David wanted to know was if I would be able to travel on a long haul flight.' There was still a note of disbelief in Jo's voice. 'He was still more interested in going ahead with our holiday than he was about becoming a father.'

'You argued about it?'

'Not as such,' Jo said. 'I didn't tell him how annoyed I was although I'm sure he picked up on it. I was still trying to be patient and understanding, but the comment festered, I suppose. Then, the night before he left for Leeds, he asked me to get up at an ungodly hour to give him a lift to the station. I'd been waiting and waiting for him to accept this pregnancy and our baby, to start fussing over me, and this was the final straw. What annoyed me most of all was that he couldn't understand why I was so upset with him for asking for the lift.' Eyes stinging with frustrated tears, Jo put her hand to her temple as if she could ease the pain of the memory.

'How bad would you say the argument was? In the heat of the moment insults and allegations are often the weapons of choice and the cracks in a relationship can be blown wide apart. Is there anything you might have said which could have tipped David over the edge, if he *was* contemplating leaving?'

Jo had a feeling that Martin was talking from experience. 'No, nothing like that and I know it sounds like our relationship was on shaky ground, but it wasn't, not really. He loved me. *Loves* me.'

Martin pretended not to notice Jo wince at her use of the past tense again. 'Was that the last time you spoke together?'

'Yes, although he did leave a voicemail message.'

Jo tried to keep her hand steady as she held her mobile in the palm of her hand and switched to speakerphone. The ever-present knot in her stomach tightened a little as she prepared to hear David's voice echo off the living-room walls for the first time since their argument.

Having heard the message countless times before, Jo knew every word and every sigh by heart but it was her analysis of those sounds that constantly changed.

'So you're still not speaking to me then?' he clipped. The hiss from the sigh he released sounded taut with exasperation now, rather than the resignation she had first heard. 'You're so damn stubborn.' There was another pause and the sound of movement. David was running his fingers through his hair. 'You want things your way and you want them now. Well, you may not believe me but I have been thinking about the future. In fact, I haven't been able to think of anything else and you're in for one hell of a shock, Jo, because I've been making plans.'

The tone of voice was familiar; it was the one he used to tease her. It ought to have sounded playful and full of promise, but as Jo looked towards Martin, they both heard only the threat.

'And before you say it, yes really,' David was saying. There was another pause. Was he waiting for his wife to read between the lines? 'I'd better go into the seminar now but I'll see you later. Assuming you want me to come home, that is.'

After the message ended abruptly, it was Jo who spoke first.

'Do you still think it's worth exploring other lines of enquiry?' she asked weakly, unsure how she wanted Martin to answer. Did she prefer to hear confirmation from a third party that her marriage was indeed in tatters or, worse still, for him to tell her there was a real chance that David was at the bottom of a ditch or floating in the Mersey?

'At this stage, yes.'

The policeman looked around the room then shifted uncomfortably in his seat. 'I can't believe how spotless your house is,' he remarked. 'There's a strong smell of bleach . . .'

Steph re-entered the room, moving so fast that the two cups in her hand slopped over her hand, but she seemed not to notice the scalding liquid as she glared at DS Baxter. 'I hope you're not suggesting for one minute that my sister had anything to do with David's disappearing act! She's bared her soul to you, for God's sake!'

Jo gasped as the implications of Martin's comments hit her. She wasn't sure what surprised her more, the realization that she was one of the lines of enquiry or the unabashed look on the policeman's face. Martin might not be the worn-out detective she had imagined but he clearly had enough years of experience to remain open-minded, if not a little cynical. What didn't surprise her was the fact that Steph had been eavesdropping, but with her whole life about to be brought under scrutiny, her lack of privacy was something she was going to have to get used to.

8

The pencil moved across the page in long, sweeping curves, softly sighing as the figure began to take shape. Next came a series of scratches that brought the drawing into sharp focus and Jo refused to let anything else invade her thoughts. It was Saturday and David had been missing for three days and no one, not even the police had found any trace of him yet. It was as if he had been erased off the face of the earth and while Jo was tempted to summon him back into life with the sweep of a pencil, she was determined to remain grounded. She was forcing herself to carry on as if her life hadn't been shattered.

'How does it look so far?' she asked with as much enthusiasm as she could summon.

'Shouldn't a wicked stepmother have a fancy wig or a big hat?' asked her niece.

Jo and Lauren were sprawled out on Lauren's bed with paper cuttings scattered around them for inspiration. Before replying, Jo settled her gaze on her niece's flowing locks. 'We could always get your mum to style your hair into a beehive – she's good at that sort of thing.'

'Do you think she would let me dye it? I was thinking maybe blonde.'

'Who ever heard of an evil, *blonde* queen?' Jo said, then picked up a cutting from a magazine and wafted it in front of Lauren. 'Red hair is most definitely on-trend.'

'Yeah, and there I was thinking you'd cut out pictures of models with red hair deliberately,' Lauren said. 'I don't care how on-trend it is, I'm fed up being a *ginger minger*.'

Jo reached behind her head to grab her ponytail. It was long enough to swipe across Lauren's face. 'And is that what I am?'

'You dye your hair.'

'Only because I had the misfortune to be born with boring brown hair like your mum,' Jo explained. Lauren's ginger gene was rooted in her dad's side of the family.

Lauren's lips tightened to a thin line and she chose not to deign her aunt with a response. The fifteen-year-old liked to act as if she had a fifty-year-old head on her shoulders but that was often the point, it was only an act. Lauren's maturity was like a new outfit she was struggling to grow into.

Jo stood her ground. 'I'm in no mood to argue, Lauren,' she warned. 'We'll add a headpiece but that's as far as I'm willing to go.'

Rather than a counterattack, Lauren dropped her head and a flush rose in her cheeks. 'Are you sure you're up to making it now?'

Jo tapped a pencil against her chin as she took another look at the design she and Lauren had been working on. She had a flair for creativity that was distinctly underused in her choice of career. She might create policies and procedures, rules and regulations but even deciding which font to use in her reports was beyond her control; Nelson's Engineering had set rules on branding. That was why she always jumped at the chance to put the creative skills she had acquired from her mum to good use whenever she could. 'You've given me harder projects in the past,' she said, deliberately misunderstanding her niece. 'The owl and the pussycat costume was a particular challenge.'

Lauren had been seven when Jo had dressed her up as a black cat and built a cardboard boat complete with owl to hang around her middle. She had won first prize at the school fete, but the memory wasn't enough to raise even a smile. 'That wasn't what I meant. Mum said we could hire something from a fancy dress shop.'

Jo failed miserably at her own attempt to smile, managing only to make her chin tremble. She swallowed hard and willed her emotions not to give her away. 'What else do I have to do Lauren, except wait for news?'

'You have the baby to look after.'

'Oh, little FB doesn't need any help from me right now.'

'FB?'

'It's the name we gave my bump,' she said, but was already regretting her slip. The family hadn't known about the pet name, and she wanted to keep some things sacred, even from them. '*Don't* tell anyone.' When Lauren agreed, Jo moved on quickly. 'The thing is, if I don't have something to occupy myself then I'll go crazy. You're my therapy, Lauren,' she told her niece with a hint of desperation. 'So, how about deciding on the colour. The outfit that is, *not* your hair.'

* * *

Jo would have liked to have spent the entire day absorbed in the design of Lauren's costume but this temporary distraction couldn't keep her cocooned for ever. Her niece began spending more time on her phone messaging her friends than helping, and Jo found herself doodling rather than concentrating on the costume. When she realized she had filled an entire page with spirals that followed her train of thought in ever-decreasing circles, she knew it was time to go.

Her back ached almost as much as her heart when she went downstairs to find her sister.

'I've made lasagne for tea,' Steph said. 'And there's tiramisu for afters to keep with the Italian theme. It's a Nigella recipe that I've been meaning to try for ages.'

'Oh,' Jo said. She looked at her watch and was surprised to see it was already gone five. She didn't feel hungry, despite not eating properly for days. And even if she wasn't sick with worry, she was too full of self-loathing to enjoy a meal while her husband was missing. 'Sorry, Steph, I wasn't planning on staying for dinner.'

Steph stopped what she was doing and released a puff of air, directing it upwards so it lifted her fringe and cooled her brow. She looked as if she had just finished an intense workout but the jog pants and trainers had never seen the inside of a gym despite her New Year's resolution ten months ago to lose two stone. Steph put her hand on her hip, smudging chocolate custard on her T-shirt in the process. 'I had a feeling you'd say that. You have to eat, Jo.'

Try as she might, Jo couldn't accept Steph's concern with the good grace it deserved. Her nerves were in tatters and it was too exhausting being polite all the time and with her sister, she knew she didn't have to be, so she didn't hold back. 'For God's sake, what is the sudden obsession with people wanting me to eat? Irene turned up yesterday with a chicken casserole as if filling the house with David's favourite foods will make him magically reappear.' She stopped and took a ragged breath, punctuating her next words with vicious jabs to the kitchen counter with an extended finger. 'Well, it won't. *It won't*. I tried that on Wednesday night, remember?' Realizing she was on the verge of losing control, Jo pursed her trembling lips.

'I'm thinking of you, not David,' Steph said patiently. 'You're the one who loves Italian. David's more a meat and two veg kind of person, isn't he?' She waited for Jo to nod and then said, 'Please stay.'

Jo shook her head. 'I should be home in case . . .' she started but couldn't finish. Such hope was beginning to feel futile so she tried to find another justification. 'I wouldn't want Irene thinking I was out on the town enjoying myself.'

'She wouldn't think that, she knows you're as worried about him as she is.'

'She probably thinks it's my fault and I wouldn't blame her if she did.'

'It's not your fault, Jo.'

'If David left me then, yes, Steph, of course it's my fault!'

'Not for the way he's done it! Leaving you like this is unforgivable,' her sister said, the last word a snarl.

'Unless it wasn't his choice,' Jo said, immediately leaping to David's defence. 'What if he's hurt, or been kidnapped by the Mob, or abducted by aliens . . . none of that makes it his fault.' Jo pushed her fingers hard against her temples.

These were the kind of thoughts that had made her head spin for days and once they started she couldn't stop. The spirals she had been drawing in Lauren's room danced across her vision and a wave of dizziness crashed into an equally powerful wave of nausea. She could taste the vomit burning the back of her throat and had to stop herself from gagging when she asked, 'What if he's lying in a ditch somewhere? What if, while everyone is cursing him for leaving me, he's actually *dead*? What if he died loving me, which I know he did – or at least I thought he did? I'm not ready to start hating him, not until I'm absolutely sure I shouldn't be grieving for him, so please don't expect me to.'

When Steph put her hand on her shoulder, Jo shrugged her off. Any act of kindness now would tip her over the edge. 'I don't know what to do, Steph. I don't know how to feel,' she said in a hoarse whisper.

'I wish I had the answers for you, Jo. And I wish there was more that I could do.'

Jo slowly pulled back her shoulders and looked at her sister. Both were amazed that Jo's eyes were still dry. 'You're doing as much as you can, as much as anyone can,' she said.

'Well, I hate to add to your woes but Mum phoned while you were upstairs. She suggested coming down to keep you company.'

The colour drained from Jo's face. She had already spoken to her mother and, with more strength than she thought she possessed, had assured her that she was coping. 'Please say you talked her out of it.'

Steph smiled. 'She didn't take much convincing, actually.

With Dad still away in France she would have had to close up shop and you know how she hates doing that.'

Their parents had moved to the Lake District ten years earlier. Ray was in the antiques business while Liz spent her time reclaiming and renovating the so-called junk her husband couldn't sell. She had built up quite a reputation, but then it was a vocation that suited her frugal yet creative personality perfectly. Together, they made the perfect team and their antique-come-craft shop in Kendal had gone from strength to strength. It was also an arrangement that suited their two daughters who loved their parents dearly but preferred to keep Liz's sometimes-overbearing nature at a distance. What Jo needed was time to work out for herself how she was supposed to feel and how she was meant to move forward before her mother waltzed on to the scene and told her what to do, which would probably involve hanging David out to dry.

'I suppose I'd better phone when I get home,' Jo said and made a move as if to leave.

'You're not going right now, are you? Gerry will be back from the shops soon; he can give you a lift.'

'I walked here and I can walk back. I need all the fresh air I can get after being cooped up at home for days,' Jo insisted but then followed Steph's gaze out the kitchen window. It was already getting dark and home was a good two miles away. 'At least it isn't raining.'

'If you have to go then you're not going empty handed. I'll put the lasagne in a container and if you can wait two minutes I'll knock up a mini dessert too.'

'Do I have a choice?' Jo said raising her eyebrows but not an objection to taking home the food she had no intention of eating. Steph's mothering was a much-needed balm and by far the better option to the smothering she would receive from her real mother.

'No, you don't. I know it's hard but you have to look after yourself, Jo. Think of the baby.'

Jo's hand was already resting on her bump. 'I am trying.'

'I know, and I'm going to help as much as I can. For a start, we need to do something about your coat. You're going to freeze to death in that thing you came in.'

The showerproof jacket in question offered little protection against the elements, less so because Jo could no longer fasten the zip, so she didn't argue when Steph said she could borrow her duffle coat which was two sizes bigger. 'And let me know the minute you get home.'

'I will.'

'And make sure you keep to the main roads. Don't go taking any short cuts in the dark.'

Jo nodded obediently, but like a naughty schoolgirl, she had her fingers crossed.

True to her word, Jo texted Steph to say she had arrived home safely, but it was the text itself that held the lie. She had made a slight detour and was standing outside West Allerton station with a good fifteen-minute walk still ahead of her. The route home was a well-known one because she and David had often caught the train here, usually when they were off out for a night on the tiles. Walking to the station was never a problem but on the way home she would complain drunkenly that they should get a taxi. Sometimes she won the argument but more often than not David used his powers of persuasion to convince her they could walk.

'So you're really going to wimp out on me?' David had asked when she rested her head on his shoulder and looked up beseechingly as their train approached the station.

Jo groaned dramatically and lifted up a foot to reveal a very high and particularly beautiful strappy sandal. 'My feet are killing me,' she said. 'And look, I've chipped a toenail already.'

'But think of all the fun we'll be missing. It's a lovely summer's evening and the stars are out. I could pick out all the constellations for you.'

'I know you make them up, David,' Jo said as he pulled her to her feet.

'I think you're scared I'll challenge you to a race again and you'll lose . . . again.'

Jo wouldn't look at him as she waited for the train door to open. Choosing her moment carefully, she grabbed his arm to steady herself and quickly pulled off her shoes. 'You're on,' she said and made a run for it through the half-open door before he knew what was happening.

The memory of David giving her a piggyback halfway home was one that would have had them in fits of laughter but Jo wasn't even smiling now. She kept her head down as she put one perfectly booted foot in front of the other. But if David had walked along the same cracked pavement on Wednesday evening then his trail was as invisible as the man himself.

Walking downhill from the station, Jo's steady pace belied her racing pulse. So far she had left it to others to retrace David's steps and she hadn't intended on making the trek herself, not today. It had only been when she had stood in front of Steph, defending her husband, that she felt compelled to follow him home, but when she reached a narrow path that led away from the main road, she came to a juddering halt and questioned her sanity.

There had been only a handful of occasions when David had been brave enough to tell Jo what to do, but he had been very firm when he had told her she must not, under any circumstances take this shortcut home in the dark when she was on her own. Not that he would heed his own warning, Jo thought as her coat snagged on the overgrown brambles that partly obstructed the entrance.

The only light to guide her came from the rear windows of houses running along one side of the path while on the other she glimpsed distant floodlights from the railway track beyond a high mesh fence and an equally impenetrable wall of tall trees. Both sources of light were too far away to offer any real illumination and, barely able to see where she was going, Jo stumbled over potholes a couple of times.

She wished she had brought a torch, but then wondered if she would have had the courage to use it. The path was less than ten feet wide in parts but much wider in others and there were plenty of places to hide her worst nightmares. Without warning, an image of David's dead body lying in the undergrowth flashed in front of her eyes. Her heart was pounding and she felt hot and clammy in spite of the cold weather. She wanted to unbutton her coat but instead wrapped her arms around herself, drawing herself and little FB in together, against the unknowns that lurked in the dark.

Common sense told her that those particular fears were unfounded. Even though the police were still deciding whether or not it was necessary to conduct a fingertip search, DS Baxter had assured her that his officers had carried out a thorough search of the area already and had found nothing untoward. Which beggared the question, what on earth did Jo think she was trying to achieve? A little peace of mind, she hoped.

At the halfway point she came to a large clearing about forty feet wide. There were vague outlines of perhaps half a dozen boys playing football, their dark hoodies all but obscuring their features in the dim light. It was only the glow from a couple of cigarettes that gave some away.

A football shot past her and clanged noisily against the mesh fence and a moment later a boy ran over and retrieved it while the others looked on. All eyes were on her. She wanted to give them the benefit of the doubt and told herself that they were halting the game to let her pass, but fraught nerves allowed darker thoughts to seep into her consciousness. She quickened her pace only to stumble and, reaching out blindly, grabbed hold of the metal fence, making it rumble angrily. One of the boys passed a remark in a low voice, inaudible to Jo, and a couple of the others laughed.

Jo felt a sharp sting where the rusted mesh had scratched her but she was more concerned with the panic bubbling up like lava from the pit of her stomach. If David had been with her, they wouldn't have given the boys a second glance and his absence weighed heavily on her chest. For a moment she couldn't catch her breath and her lungs began to burn.

'Are you all right, love?' the boy holding the ball asked.

He was about Lauren's age and it was entirely possible that they went to the same school. The deliberate thought was meant to calm Jo but her body had a mind of its own.

'Yes,' she gasped, with what little air she could squeeze from her lungs.

She managed to collect herself and, placing a protective hand over her bump, scurried past as someone accused the boy of fancying her. An argument broke out but their voices quickly receded into the distance and she focused on reaching the end of the path. With a cry, Jo burst out of the shadows on to a brightly lit road only two streets away from home. She tried to catch her breath and slow her pace but fear continued to prick the length of her spine. She had an unshakeable conviction that someone was stalking her and kept looking behind until eventually she couldn't resist the urge to run. She must have looked a sight as she hung on to her bags and her belly for dear life but she didn't care.

A gasp of relief burst from her lungs the moment she slammed the front door shut and pressed her back against it before sliding down on to the floor. The quick gulps of air slowly amassed enough breath to let out an anguished sob. The sob caught in her throat as the sound of the house phone ringing cut through the darkness.

'It's looking like he's left you then.'

'Thanks, Mum, that makes me feel a whole lot better,' Jo said, her hand on her chest as she tried to remember how to breathe. She was still letting the disappointment sink in that it hadn't been David. Even a call from the police with news of a sighting would have been more welcome, but on a positive note, a conversation with her mother was guaranteed to rile her enough to put the fight back in her belly.

'Sorry, love, I don't mean to sound blunt but even if he did turn up now with his tail between his legs, it's been three days without so much as a word. I don't know about you but I won't forgive him for what he's put you through.'

After picking up the phone, Jo's subconscious had guided her to the armchair that had the best view of the clock above the fireplace. 'We all do things we regret, Mum,' Jo said, unsure if it was a dig at her mother for her own past indiscretions, or a reminder that Jo carried her own guilt. 'And right now I'd forgive him anything if only he'd come home safe – and I would expect you to do the same.'

There was silence on the other end of the line. They would have to agree to disagree so her mum changed tack. 'Have you checked your bank? You have a joint account, don't you?'

'There's nothing wrong there. It hasn't been used since last weekend.' Jo withheld the fact that they both also had separate accounts. They each contributed to the joint account to pay all the household bills, but their salaries were paid into their own accounts to be used for their own pleasures and shared luxuries. While Jo's savings tended to be spent on more homely pleasures like a new kitchen, David's money had funded their holidays and satisfied his wanderlust. She didn't have access to that account but she imagined it would be enough to keep her errant husband in food and shelter for a good few months if that was his intention.

'Put a block on the account if you can,' Liz warned. 'Or better still, empty it before he does.'

'Mum, I'm not about to draw battle lines until I know there's a war to be had.'

Liz's breathing quickened, giving away her agitation. 'Well, more fool you. Maybe I should come down and help for a while.'

'There's nothing to do, honestly. Steph is looking after me just fine.'

'Change the locks too,' her mother blurted out.

Jo welcomed the rising anger that formed a barrier against the tidal wave of fear that had carried her home. 'At what point did your beloved son-in-law become the devil incarnate? I may not be in a position to argue against the possibility that David has left me, but I don't and won't believe that he would leave me destitute.'

'Your dad's back on Wednesday so if David hasn't appeared by next weekend, I'm coming down. No arguments, Joanne.'

Jo didn't argue. Next weekend was a whole week away, and judging by the last seventy-two hours, that was an eternity. When she finally got her mother off the phone, Jo couldn't draw her eyes away from the starburst clock, its sharp points stabbing at her heart. She didn't know how she would get through the next hour let alone the next seven days.

When the phone rang again a few minutes later, Jo was holding two small batteries. She let them roll off the palm of her hand and into the waste bin and, as she took the call, glanced up only briefly at the clock which was now frozen in time at ten minutes past seven.

'Steve's been interviewed by the police again,' Irene said before Jo had a chance to say hello.

David's mum had been following the police investigations obsessively. She hadn't waited for DS Baxter to contact her but had turned up at the police station with Steve on Friday morning and by all accounts it had been Irene conducting the interrogation. After years of being lost in the wilderness, her mother-in-law had found a new purpose in life: to find her son or at least find out why he had left. That ought to have comforted Jo – she wanted someone to keep the police on their toes, but it was making her uneasy. When Jo and David had announced that they were having a baby, they had told everyone how it had been a surprise to both of them. It was only a matter of time before Irene discovered who she could blame for David's disappearance.

But that was for the future. In the present, Irene told her that Steve had been asked to return to the police station, only this time without his mum.

'Have they come up with something new, then?' Jo asked but without any real hope. She wasn't surprised the police would want to speak to Steve without Irene shadowing him and didn't suspect any ulterior motives. They would get a far better insight from David's brother without his mother there to monitor any revelations, but if that had led to any significant development, Martin Baxter would have been in touch with her by now.

By way of an answer, Irene asked another question. 'Did the police ask you about David's state of mind?'

'Yes, sort of,' Jo replied, slightly taken aback by the question. 'I told them he wasn't happy because I'd refused to give him a lift to Lime Street.'

'But did they ask you if he was depressed?'

Irene spoke so softly her voice was slurred and it took Jo a moment to realize what she was asking her, or to be more precise, what the police were considering. Her grip on the phone tightened and she became aware of a pain in the palm of her hand. 'No, not really. They asked me some general questions about David's health and his state of mind but I didn't think it was something they would pursue,' she said as she tried to think back to the night before last when she had laid bare the faults in her marriage to DS Baxter. She had thought the conversation had led them both to the conclusion that David had walked out on her; but had it been leading the policeman down another route?

'Do you think he could have been so unhappy that he would . . . ? You know . . .'

'No, Irene,' Jo said quickly. 'No, it never entered my head; not once. He wouldn't. He *loves* life.' Jo stopped to take a breath and in that moment an internal voice asked if he loved life quite so much after she had clipped his wings. She pushed the thought away and tried to sound convinced as she said, 'He wouldn't give up without a fight, Irene. Not David.'

'I keep asking myself if there was something he said, some kind of hint he might have dropped that might explain what was going on inside his head.'

Jo squeezed her eyes shut. Stop this, Irene, she pleaded silently. Stop giving me new ways to torture myself, new ways to blame myself.

'I try to remember,' Irene continued, 'but my heart's pounding so hard I can't hear his voice any more. Only endless questions.' On the other end of the phone there was a series of thumps and Jo pictured Irene banging her palm against her chest. 'Questions, questions, questions. No answers.'

The slur in Irene's voice had become more pronounced and only now did Jo realize that her mother-in-law had been drinking. She wasn't a heavy drinker by any stretch of the imagination although she did like a nightcap these days to ease her loneliness as she adjusted to life without Alan. It was apparent that her usual tipple had been more generous and earlier than usual.

'It's good that the police are considering every possible option but David wasn't suicidal, Irene. I won't even consider that possibility.' Irene started to say something else; something that would pull Jo down into the murky depths of her despair where she imagined finding the bloated body of her husband after he had jumped into the river; so she cut in quickly, 'Why don't you have an early night and I'll speak to you tomorrow?'

'There's no point; I can't sleep. I won't be able to rest until we've found him.'

'Try,' Jo pleaded, as much to get her off the phone as anything else. 'And I really should go. I don't want to keep the line busy in case someone's trying to get through.'

It was a trick Jo had been using for two days and, for the time being at least, it still worked and she managed to persuade Irene to hang up. When she replaced the phone on the receiver Jo considered unplugging it. She'd just about had enough for one day, but there was no real choice, not when the next call might be David.

Her thoughts and emotions had been spinning faster and faster since leaving Steph's and now they were no more than a blur. The only thing that did come into sharp focus was the smear of blood on the handset. She checked the palm of her right hand and saw that it was grazed and muddied with a mixture of dried blood and rust. From her hand she looked up at the frozen hands of the dial. There was blood on the clock too and on the wall. She hadn't even noticed that she had cut her hand on the rusted fence in the cut-through.

When she moved, everything appeared to be in slow motion including her thoughts. Her steps were measured as she headed to the kitchen to clean her wounds. The antiseptic stung but it was a pain she welcomed because it was something she understood and she focused on it until it blocked out everything else.

Like the silent clock on the wall, time lost all meaning for Jo and the next thing she knew she was in her bedroom. She pulled the plug on the alarm clock on her bedside cabinet without bothering to check the hour. It would have surprised her to see that it was approaching morning, with only a few hours until sunrise. Lying on her back as she waited for sleep, Jo asked simply, 'Where are you, David?' then strained her ears as if waiting for an answer. The silence was deafening.

9

When Jo awoke on Sunday morning, consciousness arrived in the form of a series of thoughts, each one adding a leaden weight to her chest. Her misery was crushing and yet she still managed to drag herself to the bathroom in time to throw up. After dry retching for five minutes, she straightened up and looked at herself in the bathroom mirror. She barely recognized herself in the dim light borrowed from the bedroom. Her face was gaunt, her long hair dull and greasy and her fringe stuck out at all angles. To accessorize the haunted look she had carried through to a fourth day, her eyes were framed with dark, puffy bags. Jo leant forward until her head was resting on the bathroom cabinet. The cold surface of the mirror soothed her throbbing forehead. 'I want to go back,' she whispered. 'I want to go back and make it all better.'

As if her words could weave magic, Jo sensed David standing behind her. She closed her eyes and time slipped seamlessly back to what had been little more than a month ago although it was starting to feel much longer. Immersing herself in the memory, she felt her husband place his hands on her hips and then pull her close. She could feel his body pushing against hers and she pulled herself up until she was leaning back against him.

'Hello, beautiful,' he whispered into her ear before nibbling her lobe.

Jo could feel her body responding to his and she reached behind her, grabbing his bare legs and pushing him against her. She groaned as she felt his hands sliding over the smooth material of her satin camisole, touching her breasts and then roaming ever downwards. Her skin tingled as his hand followed the rising curve of her stomach without any sign of trepidation. He wasn't frightened any more.

Her pulse raced with excitement as she put her hand over his to keep it there. She held her breath and a second later David jerked his hand away with a gasp.

'Did you feel that?' he asked.

Jo took hold of his hand again and pressed it against her abdomen. 'That's your baby.'

David rested his chin on her shoulder. She could feel his breath warm her neck as he laughed.

'I can't believe it.'

Jo was tempted to point out that he'd had plenty of opportunity to acknowledge the changes in her body and accept there was a baby growing inside her but she didn't want to sully the moment. 'And next week we get to see him or her,' she said, referring to the appointment for her twenty-week scan.'

'Wow,' he said and then dropped his voice to a whisper. 'Hello, little FB.'

She let go of his hand and tried to turn around to see

his face but David wanted her to stay where she was. He was waiting for the next kick. 'What did you just say?' she asked.

'Nothing,' he said innocently.

'Yes, you did. You just called our baby FB, didn't you? What does it stand for?' She felt him shrug so she pushed back hard against him. 'Tell me!'

'It's, erm, silly. It stands for . . . Fur Ball.'

'We're having a baby, not a fluffy animal!'

'Really?' He grinned at her in the mirror. 'OK, OK, and I know it's not an obvious comparison, but babies are cute and cuddly too, aren't they?'

Even though Jo wasn't convinced he was telling her the full story, she was simply relieved that he was starting to connect with their unborn child. With a contented smile spreading across her face, she went to place her hand back on top of his, but it wasn't there. The vision froze until another well-aimed kick from a tiny foot completely shattered the image she had conjured and Jo's eyes snapped open to face reality. Her forehead was still pressed against the mirror and she was looking down at her hands gripping the washbasin, her knuckles as white as the porcelain. She barely had the strength to lift her gaze and confirm that the en suite was as empty as she feared.

'You *were* ready to become a father, David. Maybe you still wanted to give me a hard time about it, but you *were* ready to accept we were having a baby,' she whispered, painfully aware of the implications of what she was saying. She suddenly felt queasy again. 'Please don't be dead, David. Please, I beg you. I know you were scared about being a dad but now I'm terrified that you never will be.'

Jo's knees started to buckle as she gave in to the need to sob. Keeping her grip on the washbasin, she went with the fall, hanging her head down between her outstretched arms and letting her tears drip on to the tiled floor. 'I'll forgive you anything, David. Anything! Just please, please, please don't be dead!'

At some point later, Jo became aware of the dull ache in her knees and her back, and found herself curled up on the bathroom floor. As her surroundings returned to her consciousness, so did the memories of the night before. She unfurled her hand. There was a scab forming on her wound but it was the overwhelming sense of panic she had experienced on her fraught journey home that still felt raw. She could recall the phone calls from her mum and then Irene but no memory of what happened next. She rubbed her fingers together as she tried to work out why they felt so sore. It was only when she detected the faint smell of bleach that she realized it was chemical burning. She knew without a shadow of doubt that when she went downstairs, the kitchen would be pristine.

With no control over David's whereabouts, Jo was determined to cling on to the few things she did have control over. While she was at home, she had nothing to do except wait but if she could just get through one more day then maybe she would feel strong enough to return to work. If she could make it to her desk then she could at least have part of the day where she could pretend everything was normal still. It was a minor goal but one that gave her the impetus to drag herself up off the floor and get showered and dressed although she was under no illusions; it was going to be another very long day.

Jo watched her computer flicker into life as she sat in the study preparing to discover what kind of future awaited the wife of a missing person. She already knew David's employment at Nelson's was hanging in the balance, but from the list of search results coming up, that would be only the beginning of her problems. The first site she opened provided a wealth of statistics. It didn't so much give her answers as give her odds, but they provided at least one glimmer of hope and a reason to dismiss the growing fear that David was dead; only a fraction of one per cent of missing persons were found to have died and even though 95 per cent of those were adult males, David didn't match the other high risk profiles. He didn't have existing mental health issues and she refused to believe he was suicidal. So in all likelihood David had elected to disappear . . .

Pushing back against the chair, Jo put a little more space between herself and the computer screen. Was that hope she felt? Was she seriously wishing that David had left her? Of course it was better than David being dead but a husband abandoning his pregnant wife was not cause for celebration. She spread both hands over the growing mound of taught flesh across her midriff.

'So tell me FB,' she said softly. 'Which would you prefer? That your daddy abandoned you or that he didn't live long enough to see you born into the world?'

In the absence of an answer, she listened to her body, which ached from her toes, along her spine, right to the top of her skull, the deepest concentration of pain pooling in her heart. She stretched her neck and looked up at the map on the wall. It was a monument to their life together with a cluster of green pins around the Mediterranean and a thinner scattering further afield. Until she had met David, Jo hadn't been much of a traveller. It wasn't flying that bothered her but the stress of preparing for every eventuality, from delayed flights to missing passports. It negated any benefit in getting away at all, especially when Jo spent most of the holiday worrying about catching the flight home.

To remedy his wife's anxiety, David wouldn't allow Jo to become involved in any of the arrangements. He didn't even tell her the times of the flights. He had the plan and she followed it. It worked so well that David became more and more adventurous. She could clearly remember the time he had announced they were going somewhere a little more exotic than they were used to. How could she forget?

'Vietnam?' she had stammered, still blinking in disbelief at the piece of paper she had pulled from inside the card. It quivered in her hand.

David, lying next to her in bed, had leant over to kiss her on the cheek. 'Happy birthday, sweetheart.'

Jo was still looking at the list of instructions he had given her that would take them halfway across the world but it was the timeline rather than the destinations that had occupied her thoughts. 'In six months' time?'

'It's a bit more expensive than our usual trips but I've been saving up especially.' He had wrapped an arm around her and slid down the bed so he could take in the look of astonishment on his wife's face. Tears had sprung to her eyes.

Jo had blinked them away. 'But wouldn't the money be better spent on other things?' she had asked.

The meaning had been lost on him. 'No, I want to spend it on you. I love you, Jo.'

Despite herself, Jo had felt goose bumps prick her skin. She would never tire of hearing him say that. 'But I'm thirty, David.'

'I know.'

'What about our other plans?' She had waited then for the look of recognition on his face and when it hadn't appeared she was forced to be blunt. 'What about having our baby, David?'

For the first time, he had looked a little less comfortable. He had rested his head on her stomach without taking his eyes from her. 'Isn't that all the more reason to get in some heart-stopping holidays now, while we still can?'

'Some? Has this got anything to do with that map you've put up in the study?' Jo had tried to keep her tone light but the sense of disappointment had been crushing.

'There's so much out there to see. African plains, rainforests, ancient worlds . . .' David's eyes had lit up as his imaginary globetrotting trailed a blaze across his mind. 'Life's too short, Jo.'

Those simple words had wormed their way into Jo's head and left her body with a sigh of resignation. David's dad had died only the month before and it was hardly surprising that his own mortality should be playing on his mind. 'There are no guarantees in life, I know that,' she had told him. 'But you were the one who planned out our future, and you were the one who worked out when we would be ready to start a family. I bought into that and I want a baby, David. *Our* baby. I thought you did too.'

'Yes, I do. Eventually.'

Jo had looked into his eyes and couldn't bring herself to crush his dreams, not while he was so fragile. She stroked his hair and did her best to soak up his enthusiasm for the holiday of a lifetime. One holiday, she had told herself. She wouldn't be so malleable if he tried this again.

Jo's eyes stung now as she stared at the green pin dotting the 'i' in Vietnam. There was no denying she had some good memories of that trip but she hadn't been sorry to put away her passport. The baby chose now to give her a kick, reminding her exactly how she had drawn a line through his travel plans – a blue line that was meant to bring them more joy than any breathtaking vista – or so she had thought. She pulled herself upright so she could face the computer again.

The next site she visited described in detail the kind of financial and emotional limbo the partner of a missing person could face for years to come. As she continued to read, the guilt that had plagued her for days began to recede. She had committed some selfish acts, putting her needs before David's, but she would never inflict the kind of torment he was inflicting on her now. David *was* alive, he *was* being unimaginably cruel and when the phone rang, Jo was more than ready to direct her growing fury at him.

'Hi, it's DS Martin Baxter,' the policeman said with exaggerated friendliness to counter Jo's harsh greeting.

'Have you found him?' Her heart was pounding; something that happened so frequently that her ribs permanently ached.

'No, but I would like to call around to the house if that's all right. I can give you an update and we can talk about the next steps.'

Her lungs deflated and her shoulders slumped. 'Of course, anytime.' The anger had disappeared as quickly as it had arrived. Only desperation for news remained.

'How about now?'

'Oh, OK,' Jo said realizing that the call had uncovered yet another aspect of her life over which she had no control.

'And I'm afraid I'll be coming mob handed. As I think I mentioned to you the other day, we need to carry out a search of your house and garden. It's nothing to be alarmed about, just standard procedure,' he said, clearly recalling the earful Steph had given him.

'I understand,' Jo said and she did. But that didn't mean she was happy about it when four police officers marched into her home and invaded her privacy half an hour later, giving her more reason to hate her husband – if only she would allow herself that luxury.

'We'll try to make this as painless as possible,' Martin said, 'but just so you know, we may need to take some things away, particularly anything we can get a DNA trace from, like a razor?'

Jo nodded. All of David's things were still there awaiting his return.

'Good. I'll give you receipts for anything we do take and while we'll try not to disturb things too much, I can't promise that you won't notice we've been here. And you're perfectly within your rights to watch as these guys carry out the search.'

'I'd rather leave you to it but if you have to go into the garden can you try not to bring half of it back into the house with you?' she asked as they all followed her gaze to the faint trail of footprints that had already been left in the hall. A long thin shadow crawled across the floor towards them as someone else appeared at the door.

'Looks like I arrived in the nick of time,' Heather said. Tall, blonde and willowy, her friend oozed confidence as she lifted her chin and looked down her nose at the boys – and one girl – in blue. She and Jo made an indomitable pair under better circumstances but today Heather would have to be strong enough for both of them. Jo had called in reinforcements as soon as she had taken the call from DS Baxter and Heather had been more than happy to have something real to offer her friend rather than false hope and platitudes.

'This is Heather,' Jo said, catching the smile on her friend's face and making it her own.

Martin was next with the introductions. 'This is Mary Jenkins. She's a family liaison officer,' he said as a young policewoman stepped forward to shake Jo's hand.

'Perhaps we can give you an update while the search gets underway,' she said.

'Don't worry, Jo, I'll keep my eye on this lot,' Heather said, casting a warning glare at the unfortunate policeman who met her gaze.

Martin wasted no time setting up a laptop on the dining table where Jo and Mary joined him. He began by explaining the positive sightings they had uncovered and asked Jo to pick out David from a series of CCTV recordings, some in Leeds and some in Liverpool. She was able to confirm from the grainy images that David had reached Lime Street station on Wednesday evening and had managed to catch the connecting train. The very last image was at

20.06 at West Allerton Station. David could be seen zipping up his waterproof coat with the distinctive Nelson logo on the lapel, apparently preparing for the walk home.

'I don't know what that is,' she said, pointing to the large carrier bag he was carrying.

'We're going to collect statements from everyone else who attended the seminar. One of them might know more. It looks like he went shopping but there are no bank or card transactions that day to help us which brings me on to the next piece of information we've uncovered.' Martin placed a printout in front of Jo. The uppermost page listed transactions from David's personal bank account. Along with the payment of his salary into the account and a standing order transferring money over to their joint one, there was a long list of cash withdrawals.

'Two or three weeks ago, your husband started withdrawing cash, £300 each time. It amounts to £3,000, which as you can see, pretty much cleared the account until his wages went in. Were you aware that he was taking out that much cash? Do you know what it was for?'

By the tone of Martin's voice, he wasn't expecting Jo to have an immediate answer and waited patiently for her to draw her own conclusions. It didn't take long and Jo's mouth went dry, making it difficult to speak. Mary fetched a glass of water for her and when Jo took a sip her teeth rattled against the glass. 'It was the money he had been saving up for our trip to America. Part of his dream to travel to all four corners of the world,' she said eventually.

'Until you became pregnant.'

'This proves he's left me, doesn't it?'

Martin had the good grace to leave a pause even though the answer was glaringly obvious. 'It's certainly a strong suggestion that David was planning something, but he hasn't used the account since he went missing. And I'm still concerned that your husband's movements followed a predicted route until he was fifteen minutes from home. For the moment at least I'd like to keep all lines of enquiry open.'

Like a ticker-tape parade, Jo could see each and every one of those lines of enquiry swirling around her.

David had left her to start a new life.

He had suffered a nervous breakdown and was hiding somewhere, unsure what to do next.

He had had some awful accident and was lying dead or unconscious somewhere.

He had been abducted and the kidnappers would be in touch very soon to ask for a ransom.

He had been assaulted and killed.

He had killed himself.

He had left her to start a new life.

He had left her to start a new life.

Jo struggled to concentrate as DS Baxter went on to explain what else they had uncovered. She could hate him now and she didn't have to feel guilty. About anything.

'From most of the interviews we've undertaken, it still feels uncharacteristic for David to walk out on you like this.'

'Most?' Jo asked, surprised that she had the wherewithal to pick up on the subtle nuances of the policeman's words.

'His brother has said that David was, if not unhappy, then deeply unsettled by the news that he was going to become a father. He seems to think it's entirely plausible that David could have run off to escape his commitments and to see through his travelling plans.'

'Steve said that?' Jo's voice took on a higher pitch, and she shook her head, unable to quite believe what she was hearing. Steve had told her in no uncertain terms that David would never leave her. 'I don't believe him,' she managed to say but then her eyes were drawn back to the bank statements laid out on the table in front of her.

'We've checked telephone records too,' Mary added, perhaps to coax Jo out of what could only be described as a stunned stupor.

'Yes, sorry,' Martin added and produced a computer print-out. 'We've got a list of numbers and names and I'd like you to cast your eyes over it and let me know if anything jumps out.'

Jo took the list. 'There's nothing since his text to me on Wednesday evening?'

Martin shook his head and then waited patiently while Jo pored over the list that was now trembling in her hand. She could see her own number and a lot of other calls she would have expected: to his mum, Steve and Sally, friends and colleagues. Then she tapped a finger against one particular name. 'Simon Harrison,' she said.

'You don't recognize the name?' Martin asked eagerly.

She gave him an apologetic look, sorry that this wasn't the next big clue he had been hoping for. 'Yes, I do. Simon works for Nelson's, and David has known him for years; he lives nearby and while I wouldn't say they're close friends, Simon has had a bad time recently and David went to see him, to let him know his mates at work and

117

in the pub were all thinking about him. He was like that. It's hard to believe but my husband is a good man. Or at least he *was*.'

Martin cleared his throat before explaining what would happen next. 'David has been missing for more than seventy-two hours now which means his disappearance has been reported to the National Crime Agency's Missing Persons Bureau and his details will be added to an international database. Not that we have any indication that he's left the country. He certainly hasn't boarded a flight for America.'

'I suppose that's something,' she said with just a hint of sarcasm.

'And I have to be honest with you, Jo. As much as I'd like to pull in extra resources to carry out a fingertip search of all the potential routes that David might have taken home, I can't justify it given the evidence we've uncovered so far. My next plan of action, therefore, is to engage the public in the search. I want to hold a press conference and I need you there.'

'But what's the point if he's left me?' Jo asked, too exhausted to keep afloat all other possibilities. What little strength she had was being used to hold back angry tears.

'The point is that it's too early to jump to any conclusions,' Mary said. 'Our main concern is that your husband might not be in the best frame of mind at the moment. We need to let him know that you're looking for him and even if we can't convince him to come home we might at least be able to persuade him to get in touch. We'll have a helpline in operation so that if he is out there but not ready to speak to family, he can talk to someone else.'

Jo put her hands over her face. She pressed her fingers against her eyes to staunch the tears, pushing so hard she could see stars. 'I can't believe this is happening to me. I don't want to do this, I really don't.' In one final gasp, she added, 'I just want things to go back to how they were.'

Mary Jenkins put her hand on Jo's back but Jo recoiled. She didn't know this woman and the woman certainly didn't know her. What the police officer saw was a trembling shadow of the person Jo had been four days ago.

'Sounds to me like you're the one jumping to conclusions,' Heather said from the doorway. She was being tailed by two policemen who Jo assumed had had enough of rooting through her underwear. Her friend gestured towards them. 'They just need to do a quick check of the garden and then they'll be leaving.'

No one dared to disagree with her.

'Thanks, Heather,' Jo said and relaxed a little when she took a seat next to her.

'So from what I've just heard, you think David has run away and is too frightened of Jo to get in touch.'

Heather was looking at Mary but it was Jo who answered. 'He withdrew £3,000 from his account before he disappeared, Heather. He's not frightened of getting in touch, he just doesn't want to. I pushed him into having this baby and now he's had enough. He's had enough of me,' she blurted out. 'I knew it was too good to last. I'm surprised he put up with me for as long as he did.' Jo quickly clamped a hand over her mouth to halt the tirade.

'He didn't *put up* with you, Jo, he loved you. He still loves you,' Heather said, putting her arm around Jo and steadying the worst of the tremors running through her body. 'I'm the expert at spotting a man who has stopped loving his wife and I'm telling you now, David adores you.'

'So you think something happened to him then?' Jo asked with a note of desperation. Her mind was playing a game of ping pong with the possible scenarios and it was making her head spin.

Heather didn't sound her usual confident self when she replied. 'He wouldn't put you through this deliberately.'

'Which is all the more reason to make a public appeal,' Martin said. 'It's a way of getting a message to David about how this is affecting you and the rest of the family. And even if that message doesn't get through, we're appealing to all members of the public. We want people to know that we're concerned for his wellbeing and for yours too. Hopefully someone will come forward who had contact with David after he left the station, a taxi driver perhaps.'

'When?' she asked with growing dread as she imagined laying her soul bare in front of gawping strangers. 'When do I have to do it?'

'We should be able to schedule something for tomorrow. Mary can help you prepare a statement to read out and meanwhile we'll start contacting the media and spreading the word across social networks.'

Jo had no choice but to agree, which also meant that she wouldn't be returning to work tomorrow, but then she had been foolish to think she could reclaim even a small part of her old life. With a heavy heart, she looked out of the kitchen window where she could see a policeman opening up the shed at the bottom of the garden. David claimed it was his shed even though Jo did most of the gardening while her husband concentrated on growing a collection of tools. He spent more time oiling and sharpening the scythes and secateurs than he did using them and she had teased him that he ought to have bought toy ones rather than the real thing for all the use he made of them. Was he being childish now? Was he attention-seeking? No, she told herself, that wasn't the David she knew and loved. But while the pain she felt reminded her that she still loved him deeply, she had to accept that she didn't know him any more.

10

Through the multicoloured panes of glass, it was impossible to make out the features of the woman who had just rapped on the front door but the shock of platinum blonde hair shone like a warning beacon that Jo recognized at a glance. Already disappointed that the caller wasn't her husband, she faced greeting someone she could do without seeing right now. However, her shoulders slumped only briefly and by the time she opened the door, her head was lifted high and she wore the smile on her face like a mask.

'Oh, my poor, poor girl,' Liz cried, dropping shopping bags on to the floor as she stepped into the house to give her daughter a hug.

'You should have warned me you were coming down.'

'What, and have you or Steph find more excuses to keep me away? Your dad is due back later tonight so he can keep the shop going for a change. When Steph mentioned that everyone would be here tonight, I had to come and see for myself how you were coping.' Liz pulled away to have a better view of her daughter. 'And from the look of you, not very well at all. You look awful, Jo. Have you been to see the doctor yet?'

'Yes and she's signed me off for two weeks,' Jo replied solemnly. She had tried to argue with her GP that her state of mind would not improve being cooped up at home with nothing to do except wait for news, but the doctor had insisted and Jo hadn't helped by bursting into tears. She had no choice but to accept that she wasn't ready to return to work. Her entire life seemed to be in the hands of others now and the arrival of her mum would only add to her subjugation.

'Did she give you anything?'

'Medication? No way. I'm pregnant, remember.'

'I'm well aware of that, Joanne. It makes this whole sorry mess all the more heartbreaking. I don't know how you're going to manage. I've been reading up on this kind of thing and it doesn't look good.'

Jo held her breath and tried to count to ten, only managing to get to three before her mum found more words of balm. 'If they don't find a body then you'll be left in financial limbo for seven years. Seven years, Jo.'

'Yes, we know all this.' Steph came out from the living room to rescue her sister. It was Wednesday afternoon and for the last three days, Jo hadn't had a moment to herself. David's disappearance had made local news on Monday evening following the press conference and various interviews with the media and despite Jo's initial reservations about Mary Jenkins, she would have been lost without her. She had been there to hold Jo's hand through the whole process and eventually, Jo had been ready to grasp it. The information released had focused on the concern for David's welfare and so far there was no suggestion, publicly, that he might have planned his disappearance in advance. The withdrawal of cash was information that hadn't even been shared with the wider family yet. Jo had wanted some breathing space to come to terms with the news and find her own theories before being bombarded with everyone else's.

'She won't be able to access his bank accounts or even sell the house until the police get their finger out and find out what's happened to him,' Liz continued.

Steph closed the living room door and lowered her voice in the vain hope that her mum would realize they could be overheard. 'The whole point of putting Jo through this media circus is to get some answers, or better still, get David home again where he belongs,' she said. Liz looked as if she was about to say more but Steph didn't give her the chance. 'Jo, why don't you go and make Mum a cup of tea?'

Steph gave her sister a look that promised that by the time she returned, their mother would have been better advised on how to comfort her youngest daughter. The last thing Jo needed was someone reminding her that the nightmare she had been plunged into could endure for years to come. If David had vanished without a trace then she was well aware that she would have a very long wait before there could be a presumption of death and only then would she be able to take control of his finances and manage his estate. Up until that point she couldn't even do something as simple as cancel his mobile phone contract.

Jo had armed herself with all kinds of information including websites and support groups that would help her through the legal and emotional maze while Mary Jenkins had tried to reassure her that it was too early to resign herself to a life living with the unknown. Mary regurgitated some of the statistics Jo had already come across but quoting odds wouldn't solve her problems. Only tracing David would allow her to face the future, even if that was a future without him.

After only one week, Jo was already willing to accept that David had left her. She had even reached the point where she felt ready to face the news that he had killed himself or died by some other means; willing to accept *any* answer as long as it was a definitive answer and not an endless stream of questions.

By the time Jo had made the tea, her mum was ensconced in the living room, squeezed in between Irene and Steph on the sofa. Lauren was sitting on one of the armchairs which left only one seat for Jo, the one she hadn't wanted to sit in tonight of all nights. She looked up at the starburst clock which Irene had helpfully found batteries for after noticing it wasn't working.

'I don't think she should be on her own tonight,' Liz was telling Irene.

'You're not staying here, are you?' Jo asked, almost slopping the cup of tea as she passed it to her mum.

'You've still got a guest room, haven't you?'

'Yes,' Jo said, her jaw clenched as her mum scored another direct hit on her emotions. She had been dropping hints for David to turn it into a nursery for the past month, but he had said he needed time to come up with ideas. There had certainly been enough money in his account for lavish plans but it would seem that David had had another purpose for his cash all along.

'Good.'

Jo took a breath to say more but then there was another knock at the door. She should have learnt by now not to build her hopes up, it was probably only Steve, and yet her pulse raced to a different conclusion, as it did whenever there was a knock at the door or the telephone rang.

'Sorry we're late,' Steve said, 'Luke was playing up.'

Luke was Steve and Sally's four-year-old son and he was part of the reason Jo had become so broody, but then David had been just as besotted when his nephew arrived into the world. 'Where is he?' Jo asked, preferring to direct the question to Steve's wife, Sally, rather than the man who had sworn to her that David would never leave her only to tell the police an entirely different story.

'He's with my mum,' Sally said as she stepped into the house to give Jo a hug. Despite her petite frame, her embrace was fierce. 'I'm so, so sorry, Jo. I can't believe this is happening.'

'Me neither,' Jo said as she was released from Sally's grip, only to find Steve ready to wrap his arms around her. She tensed up. If David could be this cruel then she held out little hope that his brother would prove to be the better man and tell her why he had suddenly changed his view about David's disappearance. What did he know now that he didn't know then? She waited until they were both slipping out of their coats before she said, 'Although, Steve seems to think it's entirely plausible.'

Steve looked from one face to another as the two women waited for an answer. The way he ran his fingers through his hair was achingly familiar and forced Jo to look away.

126

'I'm just as flummoxed as everyone else,' he began. 'I can't believe Dave would put you through this.'

'But?'

'But he didn't want to be a dad yet, Jo. You know that.'

It was the first hint that Steve knew how their surprise pregnancy hadn't been as much of a surprise to Jo as she had been letting on, but before she could say anything, Sally cut in.

'Only because he'd been listening to you droning on about it being too much like hard work,' she said. 'Don't listen to him, Jo. Hard work or not, David adores Luke, more than Steve does sometimes, and when he comes home – and he will – he's going to make a great dad. He wouldn't abandon you or the baby you're carrying.'

Jo wasn't sure what was worse, hearing those convinced her husband wasn't capable of walking out on her or those who added weight to the evidence that he had. She was saved from having to agree or disagree with Sally's optimism by Irene's voice.

'Is that you, Steve?' she called. 'The news will be on soon!'

When Jo returned to the living room, everyone shuffled around to make space for the new arrivals. Lauren lifted her eyes briefly from her phone as she found a place to sit on the floor before leaning back against the mantelpiece and resuming her texting. Sally sat down on the vacated seat and when Steve propped himself on the arm of her chair, she moved away slightly as if she didn't want to be near him. It was clearly going to take more than a family crisis for the warring couple to present a united front. Jo returned to the armchair that had imprisoned her exactly one week ago.

'I was just telling the others that I've come bearing gifts,' Liz said, delving into one of her shopping bags. 'I've been putting my time to good use while your dad's been away.'

'Wow, that's gorgeous,' Steph said as her mum unfolded an exquisite handmade quilt and bumper set. It was made from a patchwork of pretty patterned squares in shades of yellow that ranged from summer sunshine to buttery cream.

Despite her mum's various failings, she was an accomplished crafter with a good eye for colour and detail. Unfortunately, Jo wasn't in the right frame of mind to appreciate her efforts and couldn't quite mirror her sister's enthusiasm, not with Steve's words still ringing in her ears. 'Yes, it is,' she managed.

'I'm not treading on your toes, am I? Did you have something else in mind for the colour scheme?'

'No, do what you like in there.' After months of growing excitement, Jo couldn't bear the idea of bringing her newborn baby home to what could be an empty house. She couldn't face it.

'Great, because I called into a couple of the charity shops on Allerton Road on my way over and I've picked up a few bargains. This mobile is brand new and still in its box and the sunflowers match perfectly with the appliqué on the quilt, don't you think?'

Liz showed off the mobile which had dangling bumble bees chasing after half a dozen bright yellow flowers with even brighter smiles that matched the ones Liz forced from everyone in the room except Jo who could manage only a grimace.

'The news is on,' Irene announced, cutting through the polite murmurings over the baby things.

The next hour was spent glued to the TV as they waited for the public appeal to air on one channel before switching over to hear the same report from a slightly different angle. They were still broadcasting the statement Jo had read out, her voice catching on her direct plea to David to come home. The second news report included brief interviews with friends and family and, as they watched Irene break down in front of a reporter, the sound of her sobs was echoed in the room and continued long after the programme had moved on to another report. Liz patted Irene's hand but raised her eyebrows as she cast a glance towards Jo.

'Time to switch it off, don't you think?' Steve said.

Jo tried to nod but her body was so tense that she could barely move. She had sat through the same news items for three nights running now and there was nothing new to report. Their efforts to entice David home again had so far failed and Jo had had enough.

'A week tonight he was on his way home,' Irene sobbed as she took a tissue from her pocket and blew her nose. 'Oh Jo! If only you had gone to collect him from the station, we wouldn't be going through all of this.'

'I did offer.'

Irene stole a glance towards her daughter-in-law as she bit her lip but it was too late to take back the accusation. 'I know, I didn't mean to blame you, Jo, but if only we could put the clock back,' Irene said and even Jo couldn't resist the urge to follow her gaze towards the pointed shards of the clock. 'Where would he have been right now?'

Jo's jaw clenched and the tendons in her neck pulled taught. Her lips cut a thin line across her face and when she closed her eyes she could see the ghostly image of a starburst. She squeezed her eyes tighter still and then saw only red. 'I don't want to do this, Irene. I don't want to relive last Wednesday night – and I certainly don't want to torture myself with what might have been if I'd made different choices.'

'How's half term going?' Liz asked her granddaughter after an uncomfortable pause. 'I hope you're not spending all your time on that phone . . . Lauren?'

Lauren looked up, only vaguely aware that her name had been spoken. 'Did you say something, Nan?'

'Lauren, for God's sake put that thing away,' snapped Steph. 'Your family need your attention now, not your friends.'

Her daughter huffed. 'I'm not talking to my friends as it happens. I'm on Twitter, helping with the campaign to find David.'

'How in God's name is twittering, or whatever it's called, going to help?' Steph asked.

'Well, the police think it will. I'm asking loads of famous people to retweet the appeal. Someone somewhere might see it who knows something.' Lauren jutted her jaw in a gesture that reminded Jo so much of her own determination – or should that be arrogance?

When the two became ensnared in a staring competition, Liz interjected. 'So how are you getting on with the Wicked Stepmother costume, Lauren? Jo?'

Irene blew her nose, more loudly this time. 'How can you expect Jo to think about such things at a time like this? I know life goes on but how can we even look to the future until we know where David is? He's out there somewhere and life can't go on for us, not until we find him.'

'Yes, I know that, Irene, but Jo needs something to distract her. She'll drive herself crazy if she has nothing to do except sit and think about what your son has done to her,' said Liz sharply.

'Mum's right,' Jo said, the statement surprising her almost as much as it did her mother. Jo didn't want to be consumed by the black hole that had appeared in her life. She wasn't Irene; her husband hadn't died, or at least . . . 'What if he doesn't want to be found?' she asked.

'He loves you, Jo, you *and* the baby,' Irene said weakly.

Jo was shaking her head. With each passing day, another layer of emotion had enveloped her like a shroud and she didn't know from one minute to the next how she would feel. At that moment it was a smouldering anger, which couldn't be directed at the one person who deserved it most and was burning through her veneer of civility. All it would take was one misplaced word and she didn't care if it was laced with accusation or quilted in comfort.

'He *loves* you,' her mother-in-law persisted. Jo's eyes snapped across the room to Irene's other son. 'That's not what Steve thinks and I'm starting to think he's right! What if David's been planning this ever since his wife came off the pill without telling him? What if he thinks he shouldn't have to take responsibility for the baby his wife chose to have when he'd said he wasn't ready? And what if he's been withdrawing lots of cash for weeks so he could pull off this little vanishing act?' Her eyes shot back to Irene. 'What if your son was sitting in front of a TV tonight watching his family breaking down in front of the TV cameras and still didn't have the courage to tell me to my face that he'd had enough?'

In the awkward silence that followed, Jo's ears strained for the sound of footsteps at the door but angry words couldn't conjure up David, just as gentle words had failed before them. Jo had endured a full week of misery and there was no sign that it would end any time soon.

11

Staying at home waiting for news that never arrived was torturous, pure and simple. When there were people around, Jo had been desperate for them to leave and eventually they had. Her mother went back to Kendal, to run the family business that needed to thrive more than ever while her daughter's finances were in such dire straits. And, with a distinct lack of news, everyone else had no option but to return to their normal lives too, or in Irene's case, to keep her own vigil should David decide to turn to his mum rather than return to his wife.

But when Jo found herself on her own, it was even worse. She had nothing to do but keep her house obsessively clean until it was hard to believe that anyone lived there at all. It had been years since she had been allowed to indulge freely in her compulsions but it was a preoccupation that brought her a measure of comfort as long as she felt able to control it and not the other way around. After two weeks, however, she could feel that balance of power slipping away from her.

Her life had been put on hold. She couldn't go back, she

knew that, but she was struggling to see a way forward either when there were so many unknowns. The only thing she could do was sift through the wreckage and pick up the scraps of her life that still survived, and she tried to view a return to work as a positive move as well as one of necessity.

The night before she was due back was a restless one. At one point she didn't think she would sleep at all but in the next she could feel herself waking up. She heard a noise and when she recognized it for what it was, it made her blood run cold.

She kept her eyes closed as she listened to the shower running. When the noise stopped and the door opened a cloud of warm steam wrapped around her, making her skin tingle. She held her breath and a moment later felt David's warm lips on her forehead sending an electric current through her body and making her eyes snap open. Grey light filled the empty room and when she turned her head towards the bathroom door, it was slightly ajar, leaching dark shadows rather than clouds of steam.

Sitting up in bed, Jo looked at the clock, which she had been forced to plug back in the night before for fear of sleeping in. It was five to seven. Her body was working to a practised routine even while Jo's conscious mind had spent the last two weeks learning new ones, like cooking for one person, shopping only for herself, and watching whatever she wanted on TV – not that she could concentrate long enough to take in a storyline. Was David doing the same? And was he hating it as much as she was or had he embraced his new life?

It didn't take Jo long to shower and dress but she put off

looking in the mirror until she was in the hallway, ready to leave – and then she came face to face with the image her colleagues would be presented with. She had hoped to see a little of her old self staring back at her so she could face their awkward looks and questions and had even dyed her hair an extra bright shade of auburn the day before to deflect some attention away from her pale complexion. Her fringe was perfectly straight with a radiant shine but it framed a set of eyes that were gaunt and would fool no one.

Her grey cashmere coat was no longer snug across her chest because, unsurprisingly, Jo had lost weight in the last couple of weeks but it gaped open at her middle that little bit more. Trying to ignore the reminder that little FB's arrival was getting ever nearer, Jo pulled at the red chiffon scarf draped around her neck in an attempt to hide her ill-fitting coat but it wasn't long enough. She tried to tell herself it would do but then, with a sigh of resignation and a clatter of keys, she pulled the scarf from around her neck and opened a drawer to reveal a selection of gloves and scarves folded in neat piles. She knew if she didn't leave soon she would become tangled up in the school run traffic and it would take twice as long to get into the city centre, but she had to get her appearance right. She rummaged through the contents of the drawer until she found what she was looking for, a long green woollen scarf that David had bought her last Christmas for their trip to Iceland. She shoved the rejected red scarf in the drawer and slammed it shut, leaving a single beaded tassel poking out.

Jo wrapped the woollen scarf around her neck and let it hang in front of her protruding stomach. She was finally ready to face the world and grabbed her handbag before heading for the front door. She switched off the hallway light but as her hand touched the doorknob she was already slowing to a stop. Rather than open the door, she released a sigh that ended with a curse. The colourful smears of light seeping through the stained glass brought enough daylight to cut through the gloom, trailing along the hall and guiding Jo's eyes towards the dresser.

She couldn't see the chaos inside but the red tassel bleeding from the drawer taunted her. If David had been there he would have grabbed her by the coat sleeve and yanked her out of the house and she would have forgotten about it by the time the car pulled out of the drive. But David wasn't there to keep her eccentricities in check and so she pushed him from her mind as she emptied the contents of the drawer and began to neatly fold each scarf as if that act alone would help get her life back in order.

'I'm so sorry I'm late,' Jo said as she rushed into Gary's office. She hadn't had a chance to switch on her computer or catch up with any of her colleagues although in fairness that had been deliberate. The sympathetic looks had been painful enough.

'You're not late, Jo. You're just not ten minutes early like you usually are.'

'Sorry,' she repeated.

By the look on Gary's face he was about to ask how she was coping but the door opened before he could draw breath and Jeanette swept in. 'Here, you can at least find time to have a cup of coffee even if you can't stop to say hello. And yes, it is decaf.'

'Thanks, Jeanette,' Jo said, taking the proffered mug with

surprising gratitude. It was the first time in a long time that someone hadn't forced strong, sweet tea on her.

Gary's PA looked as if she was about to leave but then put her hand on Jo's shoulder. 'You're doing great.'

Jo attempted a half-smile, which trembled with the effort.

'Now, where were we?' Gary said when they were alone again.

'Look, I can't deny things are difficult at home but I'd like to get back to my job as quickly as I can. I don't want any special treatment, I just want normal. I want *busy*.'

Gary sucked the air between his teeth as he picked up a folder from his in-tray. It was a personnel file and Jo didn't need to guess whose it might be. 'So what's the decision?' she asked.

'I'm sorry, Jo but we don't really have a choice. Until David's whereabouts are accounted for, we have to assume he's elected to walk away from, amongst other things, his job. He's in breach of contract and payroll is in the process of working out his final salary payment.'

Jo had expected as much. Nelson's was used to dealing with transient workers and she had dealt with countless cases herself. 'I understand,' she said.

'All I will say is that I am truly sympathetic to your circumstances. The company owes you its loyalty, and David too. The post isn't going to be filled overnight so if he does turn up and there's a satisfactory explanation then there's always a chance you can both recover from this.'

Jo could almost have laughed if she hadn't been so terrified that she might then cry. 'If he has a good explanation then I'd love to hear it.'

*   *   *

Jo spent the rest of the morning going through her emails, a mundane task at the best of times but today she found it therapeutic. She was in the process of reorganising half a dozen meetings when Kelly crept into the office.

'How's it going?' she asked.

Jo accepted Kelly's concern in the spirit it was given, although the pity in her assistant's voice grated on her nerves. 'Fine.'

'Don't go pushing yourself too hard, you've the baby to think of, remember.'

How could I forget? Jo thought but said, 'I'll manage. There's a bit of catching up to do but I'm getting there.'

'I haven't done anything glaringly wrong while I've been covering for you, have I?' Kelly said with a confident smile that suggested she held no doubts.

Again, Jo tried not to let her irritability show. While her assistant's need for reassurance wasn't unreasonable, it was ill-timed and her role 'covering' for her was somewhat overstated.

'Gary and I are very grateful for your help,' she said, through gritted teeth.

'Did you notice?' Kelly said. When Jo looked nonplussed she tipped her head towards the coat stand. 'I managed to get you issued with a coat.'

'Yes, I was wondering where that came from,' Jo said without looking over. It was olive green with the Nelson's logo on the lapel and reflective strips on the sleeves. Most employees had to make do with the Day-Glo yellow jackets for site work so these coats were like gold dust, but Jo didn't feel particularly fortunate. The last time she had seen someone wearing this type of coat was on the CCTV footage

DS Baxter had shown her of David's last movements at West Allerton station, and she didn't so much feel as if she had gained a coat but was reminded that she had lost a husband.

'You'll probably swim in it, but at least you'll be able to fasten it up. How about you try it out? We could always go out for something to eat.'

'I'm really not that hungry,' Jo said, grimacing at the idea of lunch, especially lunch with Kelly.

'By the look of you I'd say you haven't been hungry for weeks but if you don't fancy eating out, you at least deserve a break,' Kelly persisted. 'You can't hide away in here all day.'

Jo didn't have the energy to argue but fortunately she didn't have to. Over Kelly's shoulder, she had noticed the welcome arrival of a friendly face.

Heather popped her head through the door. 'I'm not disturbing you, am I?' she asked. 'I thought you might like to pop out for lunch.'

'I'll leave you to it then,' Kelly said but loitered a little longer as if hoping for an invitation.

'Thanks, Kelly, and thanks for organising the coat for me,' Jo said then felt obliged to add, 'I promise we'll do lunch another time.' She was trying not to let the relief show.

'How about Chinese?' Heather asked.

'Wherever you fancy,' Jo said, more interested in the company than the food. She picked up her bag and mobile and was even ready to slip on her newly acquired coat when her phone rang. The number wasn't one she recognized which meant she couldn't ignore it. 'Sorry, I'd better get this.'

Rather than providing her with new information, the caller confirmed something Jo already knew. It was one of the midwives at the health centre checking up on her. She had missed both a hospital and an antenatal appointment in the last two weeks. Jo tried explaining that she had been busy but it wasn't necessary: the midwife had seen the news report.

'It's my first day back at work today and antenatal clinics are the last thing on my mind,' Jo said when the midwife suggested she call into the clinic later that day.

'If you're back at work then it's even more important that you find time to look after yourself,' the midwife replied curtly.

'So people keep telling me,' Jo said with a sigh and then tried to make vague promises about calling in soon but the midwife was insisting on seeing her that week. 'OK, Friday then.'

'And don't miss this one,' the persistent midwife said.

'I won't,' Jo promised then cut off the call as quickly as she could.

'You've missed an appointment?' Heather asked.

'Or two,' Jo confessed. She watched Heather's jaw drop and then said, 'For goodness' sake don't turn into my mother; I have enough earache from the real one. I'm only five months pregnant. There's still plenty of time to get my head around what to do about the baby when the dust has settled around the disaster area that's become my life.'

'You're six months pregnant, Jo.'

'Really?' Jo turned to the calendar on the wall to check for herself. It was 4 November and her baby was due at the beginning of February, three months away. For a moment she didn't think she was going to keep down the contents of her empty stomach as it did a somersault.

Was it possible to feel even more guilt? Her baby deserved better. It ought to be nurtured and brought into a world where it would find two joyful parents eagerly awaiting its arrival. But its father hadn't wanted it and now even its conniving mother couldn't bring herself to think about it without feeling sick with dread. What had David reduced her to? She had tried so hard not to hate him in the last few weeks and was surprised at how deeply her loathing for her husband now burned.

12

The light from the back of the house stretched out over the glistening patio but no further and Jo needed a flashlight to find her way across the damp, squelchy lawn. She came to a halt when she stepped on to the jagged concrete edge of foundations to an old outbuilding David had demolished a couple of years earlier. It was wide enough to provide a solid base for the new shed with a fair amount of working space left for other projects. David had talked about building raised beds for Jo to grow herbs and vegetables and had even suggested a hen coop. As Jo surveyed the scene of chaos in front of her, she still didn't know if he had been serious. She knew less about her husband with each passing day.

'Are you sure we should be doing this?' Lauren asked.

'Of course,' Jo said as the flashlight traced the outline of the huge pile of wood David had amassed over the summer while replacing some fencing. 'It's Bonfire Night and what better time to have a fire at the back of the garden without half the neighbourhood objecting?'

Lauren dropped a black bin liner on to the ground. Jo did the same.

'Won't it be too wet to light?' Lauren asked, still un-convinced.

Jo pulled open the shed door and picked up a petrol can, which was at least half-full. 'Now don't think for a minute I would normally condone this but needs must.' Jo was trying too hard to sound confident as she contradicted the internal voice in her head which was telling her it might not be one of her best ideas. She had actually told David off when he started building the bonfire, warning him it was too close to the shed and that they should hire a skip for all the rubbish instead. But David had insisted he would be careful and she had trusted him. She had *trusted* him.

Jo took a couple of T-shirts from one of the bin bags and shoved them between planks of wood at the base of the wood pile. Lauren followed her example and took out a suit jacket. 'Are you sure?' she asked again.

'I'm not burning everything, Lauren. I've had a clear out and this stuff would all be thrown out anyway. It's all right, honestly.'

Thankfully Lauren didn't question why it was only David's belongings that Jo was about to burn, including the pile of holiday brochures he had been hoarding. Jo didn't know what she would say if Lauren did ask, not because she couldn't justify her actions but because she didn't want to face the humiliation of admitting there was little doubt now that David had left her. The evidence was irrefutable. It was there in black and white and it was in David's handwriting.

Since discovering David's passport was missing on the night he failed to come home, Jo had gone through every-thing in the house with a fine-toothed comb, and not only once but time and time again. Even last night, after a long and tiring first day back at the office she had been compelled to search for clues, the action replacing another insidious compulsion to scrub and polish until her nostrils burned with the smell of bleach.

She had started by going through his wardrobe yet again, but that had proved as fruitless as ever so she had turned her attention to the chest of drawers. She searched every item of clothing, every pocket and any other hiding place she could think of. She had found what she was looking for tucked inside a pair of socks. Except it wasn't what she had been looking for – it wasn't what she had wanted to find at all.

The note was a half-written letter that had been screwed up and then perhaps hidden away quickly from prying eyes. There was no way of knowing when David had written it, but she guessed it would have been shortly after she had told him her good news. The letter was in her pocket now and she had already memorized every venomous word that had not only obliterated her wavering hope that David simply needed some space and time, but had poisoned some of her most precious memories like the one of him putting his hand on her stomach and feeling little FB kick for the very first time. And to add insult to injury, the letter wasn't even addressed to her. Apparently she wasn't that important in his life.

Dear Dad,

I can't believe it, I really can't, which is why I think I have to write it down otherwise the news just won't sink in.

Jo's pregnant. I'm going to be a dad!

I'm still in shock. Seriously, I wasn't expecting this at all. She came off the pill without telling me and apparently she's known for weeks that she was pregnant, but hadn't had the courage to tell me. She even pretended she'd had PMT the other month to stop me getting suspicious. Why did she do that? What the hell was she thinking? How could she make that kind of decision without me? What does it say about us, what does it say about me?

It doesn't matter now, I suppose, what's done is done and I keep trying to imagine what it will be like this time next year. Am I going to be like you, Dad? Am I going to spend the rest of my life relying on documentaries on TV to show me the world instead of going out and experiencing it for myself? I wanted to wait. I wanted some more memories under my belt to keep me smiling while I'm changing nappies and wiping snotty noses. I didn't want my kids ending up like me, being a fucking burden to their father. A Fucking Burden!

There had been a brief moment when Jo had read the first lines and her heart had soared, she had thought she was about to be vindicated. She had thought David was describing his joy but it had been a cruel ruse and, even as his initial words lifted her up, the next paragraph sent her plummeting to new depths. The letter had broken off abruptly and she supposed she should be grateful that she hadn't been subjected to even more of her husband's diatribe.

She had sat on the bed, sobbing, staring at the letter

145

long after the tears had blinded her. She had been brought down as low as she could possibly get, or so she believed until another thought struck her. She had wiped her eyes and glared at the last two words he had written and her misery was compounded. Fucking Burden, he had written. FB. Fucking Burden – not Fur Ball . . .

And that was why she was burning his clothes. She was terrified of finding another note but that wouldn't stop her continuing the search, and that was when she had come up with a simple solution. She wouldn't need to check jacket pockets ever again if they had been reduced to ashes and so she had stayed up until the early hours removing David from her life as ruthlessly as he had removed her from his. And she had sobbed as though her heart would break the entire time.

'Stay as far back as you can,' Jo warned as she turned up the sleeves of her newly acquired coat and began pouring petrol over the rags and rolled-up magazines they had already poked into the wood pile. She was grateful for Lauren's presence; it forced her to act calm and collected; only she could hear the scream inside her head.

Jo wiped her hands with a rag but the cloying scent of petrol was too strong to be whipped away by the biting wind. 'I think it would be safer if we stood upwind,' she said and guided Lauren to the furthest reaches of the garden. 'Ready?'

Holding the rag at arm's-length, Jo set fire to it with a gas lighter. Flames licked gently around one leg of the boxer shorts but suddenly the whole garment was alight and she let go of it reflexively. Still several feet from its intended target, Lauren quickly picked up an old fence pole and used it to fling the flaming rag towards the bonfire. The whoosh of hot air made them both step backwards and the ensuing heat forced them to retreat further until they had their backs pressed against the fence at the end of the garden.

The seemingly benign pile of damp wood roared into life and Jo marvelled at its beauty, which had immersed the rest of the garden in flickering, golden light. She turned to Lauren whose face glowed orange and her flame-coloured hair shone. Her niece's eyes were wide with wonder.

'I didn't expect it to take hold that quickly,' Jo said. She had a smile on her face as she basked in the warm glow from what was, effectively, the incineration of her marriage.

'We should have brought some potatoes to bake.'

Jo looked at the narrow gap between the shed and the bonfire. She could just make out the lights from the kitchen beyond the wall of fire. 'Maybe we'll wait for it to die down first,' she said as she looked deeper into the dancing flames, which seemed determined to draw David back into her life despite herself.

She stamped her feet and almost expected to feel the crunch of snow. Above the crackle of burning wood she could hear fireworks whizzing above her head and, although she knew she was in Beaumont Avenue, she could just as easily have been in Iceland, enjoying another of those life-affirming trips that David was intent on fitting in before family life clipped his wings. This one had been last New Year and was meant to celebrate Jo's thirty-first birthday but, try as she might, Jo hadn't been in the mood to celebrate.

The memory couldn't be eviscerated as easily as David's worldly goods and she heard his voice first . . .

'Dance with me, Jo,' he had called to her.

'I'm too tired. If we're going to be climbing glaciers tomorrow then I'm going to need my beauty sleep.'

'We'll have plenty of time to sleep when we get back home to tame, old England. Dance with me, Jo.'

'Dance with yourself,' she had shouted and through the red and orange ribbons of fire, she had watched in disbelief as her husband began to waltz around the bonfire, arms clasping an imaginary partner, chin lifted. She had laughed when he had sneaked a hand down to squeeze the behind of the invisible woman, but as he moved towards her, she was already digging her heels into the snow.

'You can be so stubborn sometimes,' he had said when he was close enough to whisper in her ear.

Jo had held her tongue even though she wanted to remind him of how magnanimous she was being. The year in which they were meant to start a family had come and gone and, other than the occasional reminder to her husband that their family plan had been postponed rather than cancelled, Jo had ignored the ache in her arms to hold their baby. She had supported him as he came to terms with his father's death and silently watched the world map in the study fill with red pins.

She had pushed him away. '*You* dance.'

'Stubborn,' he had repeated.

'Yes, and I don't know why you put up with me,' she had said, knowing why he did.

David knew she did too but had said it anyway. 'Because

I love you, Jo Taylor. I love you, I love you, I love youuuuu,' he had sung as he danced away from her.

Jo had felt a flutter of excitement as she watched him. If she was being forced to postpone having a baby for the sake of a holiday, then she should at least be enjoying it. She had raced after him and leapt on his back bringing a yelp of surprise from both of them. He had held on to her and twirled her around as they laughed together . . .

The laughter Jo was trying to recapture caught in her throat. She still loved David – her heart wouldn't be told otherwise – but her hand was reaching inside her pocket to touch the evidence that suggested he might not feel the same. Unable to bear the presence of the damning letter for a moment longer, she took out the crumpled piece of paper and flung it into the flames where it was hungrily devoured. She wished she could destroy the memory of his words as easily. She wished she could have just one more chance to talk to him, to remind him how much they loved each other, and to find some way for them both to make amends for their mistakes.

As Jo stared into the flames, the wind changed direction and clouds of black smoke billowed around her. Jo's eyes were streaming as she tried to summon her husband again from amongst the dancing shadows. To her surprise, she saw movement then blinked, not trusting what she was seeing. When the smoke began to clear, Jo's heart leapt.

'Did you see that?' she asked Lauren, gripping her niece's arm tightly with one hand and pointing over towards the house with the other. She was sure it had been the silhouetted figure of a man walking past the kitchen window.

Lauren followed Jo's gaze but the wind had blown new

life into the flames and the gap between the shed and the fire had been reduced to nothing. 'See what?' she asked, wincing a little as Jo's grip tightened.

The reply came from the far side of the garden and cut through the November night.

'Jo? Are you there?'

'David!' Jo cried and lunged forward. She used her arms to beat a path through the flames and almost made it past the bonfire unscathed until the lingering vapours of petrol caught light on her coat sleeve.

Jo waved her arm frantically but only succeeded in helping the fire catch hold. Flames sucked the oxygen from the air as she stumbled on, more desperate than ever for David to be there to catch her. The searing heat and smell of burning polyester choked the breath out of her lungs. As she gasped for air, panic bloomed in her chest and she was sure her heart was about to explode. Darkness began to creep and then coursed across her field of vision and the last thing she saw before she passed out was a man's face looming over her.

The acrid mix of smoke and petrol seeped into Jo's consciousness and triggered flashes of memories so bright they burned the back of her closed lids. She took a gasp of air that tasted of oily soot. Her stomach churned and her eyes flickered open.

'Are you OK?' Lauren asked.

Jo was lying on the sofa and she quickly checked her right arm, which had been engulfed in flames. She wasn't wearing her coat now but her jumper felt rough where the wool had scorched. The skin on her hand felt tender but miraculously she had avoided any serious burns. Her hand moved across her abdomen. There was no pain there, but neither had there been any hint of movement since she had come round. The gentle kick that came a second later should have given her some comfort but it only succeeded in making her stomach lurch. She looked up at Lauren whose face was streaked with soot and tears but it was the face of the man who had come to her rescue that played on her mind. She willed herself to resurrect each and every one of David's features from the ashes but it was hopeless. 'Where's Steve?' she asked.

'He's trying to damp down the fire. We weren't sure if we should phone for an ambulance.'

'Have I been out long?' Jo was heaving herself up and ignoring the speckles of light that threatened to return her to darkness.

'Only a couple of minutes,' Lauren said, but her words caught in her throat. 'I was so scared, Jo. You were on fire and I couldn't get to you and then you fell. Do you think FB's OK?'

Hearing that name was like being stabbed by a red-hot poker. 'Don't you ever, *ever* let me hear you call it that again!'

Lauren blinked in shock and her lip trembled furiously. 'Sorry, Jo. I didn't—'

'No, *I'm* sorry, Lauren. I'm so sorry. It's not your fault,' she said, but the sight of her niece's tears was bringing Jo's roiling emotions closer to the surface and the scream she had been stifling since finding David's note was getting difficult to hold back.

She tried telling herself that she had to withhold judgement

151

until she knew exactly what had happened to David, that there was always the possibility that something bad had happened and she would be wracked with guilt for thinking the worst of him, but it was too late: she had already burned that bridge – the ashes were still smouldering in the back garden.

Her body started to shake as if it were a pressure cooker waiting to explode. 'I've had enough,' she hissed as she scanned the room for something on which to direct her fury.

There was a gasp as Lauren was pushed unceremoniously to one side and Jo's heart pounded as she snatched up a framed wedding photograph. It crashed into the wall but the sound of breaking glass was impossible to hear above her screams.

'You bastard! You selfish, heartless bastard!'

Jo's eyes were wild with rage as another picture-perfect image was sent flying through the air, crashing against the mantelpiece.

'Why didn't you have the guts to tell me to my face that you didn't want to be here any more? Why couldn't you have the balls to pack a bag and leave me crying on the doorstep? What did I do to make you hate me so much that you would put me through this? Isn't it enough that I have to lose you? *How could you be so cruel?*' Her last words tore from her lungs with a howl of fury as she ripped the starburst clock from the wall and hurled it towards the door. Steve only just managed to dodge the missile as he rushed towards her. For the second time that night, he made a grab for his sister-in-law, only this time she was far less malleable. He did his best to calm her but he was reluctant to put up much of a fight against a pregnant woman no matter how much she hit him.

'Please, Jo, it's all right. It's going to be all right,' he was saying over and over again, but Jo wasn't listening. She was too busy fighting him off as she searched for something else to smash into smithereens.

The battle of wills might have continued indefinitely if Jo hadn't seen Lauren flee out of the room in terror. She thought about what her poor niece was being forced to witness, and it was that, along with the sound glass crunching underfoot and the mess she would eventually have to clean up, that brought her back to her senses. With one final shove, she pushed Steve away. Her body heaved as she tried to catch her breath between sobs. 'Why can't I just hate him, Steve?' she asked when she could talk. 'I can't go on like this! I need to know why this is happening.'

'I don't have the answers, Jo. I wish I did.'

Jo shot Steve a look but he wouldn't hold her gaze. 'Don't you?' she snapped. 'You changed your story pretty fast when it came time to speaking to the police! What convinced you that David might have left me? Have you seen him, Steve? Have you heard from him?'

Fragments of glass were ground further into the floor as Steve shifted from one foot to the other. 'I promise you I've not seen or heard a thing,' he said. 'If you'd told me straight off that he'd taken his passport, Jo, I might have thought differently from the start. It's pretty damning evidence that he planned to leave, don't you think? He was finding it hard getting his head around having this baby, and you know how obsessed he was about seeing the world.'

153

Jo shook her head, trying to make sense of a problem she had tackled a thousand times in the last three weeks.

'He's probably on one last jaunt but he will come back, just give him time,' Steve added. 'And until then, I'm here for you, whenever you need me. We all are.'

'I'm not sure your mum would agree. I don't think she's forgiven me for my little outburst the other day.'

'She's not used to David being the black sheep of the family and she's struggling to hear anything bad said against him. And she needs her remaining family around her now more than ever. So do you, Jo, especially if David doesn't show up by the time the baby arrives.'

She squeezed her eyes shut so she didn't have to face the future. When that didn't work she opened them again to find Steve watching her. 'You can do this,' he said.

Jo was shaking her head as she sat back down on the sofa. 'I wish I had your faith. The truth is that I'm not going to be able to make ends meet when there's another mouth to feed. I don't have access to the little money that's left in David's account and my savings won't go far.' Jo brought herself up short, aware she was focusing on the finances as if David's value in her life had only been a monetary one.

'Have the police frozen his account then?'

'Not at all,' Jo said with a laugh that held traces of her previous hysteria. 'There's no sign of foul play so all of his accounts and assets remain his for the taking. I'm sure they think he's holed up with another woman somewhere. Maybe he is. Maybe they've run away together.' She looked to Steve again for hints of deceit. He was so similar in looks to David that it hurt. She had assumed that was where the similarities had ended but now she wasn't so sure. How ironic that the irresponsible, undependable brother should be the one who had remained by her side.

'If he'd been up to anything like that then I'd know about it. He wasn't, Jo.'

'And you don't know why he would withdraw so much money?'

Steve was shaking his head as Lauren reappeared at the door. She handed her aunt a cup of tea that was no doubt strong and sweet.

'Sorry if I scared you, Lauren,' Jo said softly.

'Again,' Lauren added. 'It wasn't the kind of firework display I was expecting, that's for sure.'

'I'll make it up to you,' Jo said. 'I promise.'

'I just wish things could go back to the way they were.' Lauren's voice shook and she made the mistake of trying to smile but only succeeded in toppling fresh tears.

Jo wanted to offer some sort of reassurance but couldn't bring herself to lie, not even for Lauren's sake. 'There's no going back,' she said, bringing forth an image of the funeral pyre in the garden. 'Not now.'

13

Jo made a concerted effort over the next couple of weeks to prove that her breakdown on Bonfire Night had been a one-off. She had temporarily lost control but she was back in the driving seat and there was no reason for Lauren to worry and certainly no reason for her to say anything to Steph.

'Lauren, why don't you see if you can find some gold trim for edging the hem and sleeves?' Jo said. They were standing in the middle of a maze of tall metal racks, each piled high with folded sections of fabric of all shapes and sizes. 'We'll need about four metres.'

Excited that her costume was starting to take shape, Lauren didn't argue and promptly forgot to adopt her teenage slouch as she skipped down the aisle and out of sight.

'Do you want to look for anything else while we're in town?' Steph asked.

'Like what?'

'A new coat for one thing,' Steph said.

Even though she could only fasten the top button now,

Jo had reverted back to wearing her grey cashmere coat after ruining the one from Nelson's. She had apologized to Gary but felt too ashamed to ask for a replacement. 'I'm not paying out good money for something I'll hardly wear – and besides, Mum said she'll keep her eyes peeled for a bargain for me,' she answered.

'Well, what about baby things, then? You're going to have to start preparing for his or her arrival sooner or later.'

'I *am* getting prepared. Steve's promised to paint the spare room and Sally's digging out some of Luke's old baby stuff for me. So there you go, I'm all sorted.'

Steph snorted. 'I think you're in for a shock.'

Jo didn't share the joke. 'Life has been one big shock, Steph, and I don't exactly have the money to splash out on anything new. Once this baby's born then any spare cash I have left is going to have to cover childcare. I've been working out the figures and I won't be able to afford to take more than twelve weeks' maternity leave. I can't downsize because I can't sell the house without David and so I have no choice but to live beyond my means. It's a complete mess.' As she talked, Jo was systematically picking up and refolding scrunched-up pieces of fabric, creating neat piles from the chaos.

'I could always help look after the baby in the school holidays,' Steph offered. 'I know it's going to be a struggle at first but the baby will start nursery in a few years. It's not for ever.'

'No, it'll just feel like it is,' Jo said, wondering at what point everyone, herself included, had started assuming David's disappearance and the mystery surrounding it would drag on for years.

The police were continuing their investigation but hadn't come up with anything new. They couldn't even explain what might have been in the carrier bag David had had with him. It could have been wads of cash at the ready for jumping on a plane, or perhaps a house-warming present for the new woman in his life – some champagne glasses to toast their new start; nothing would surprise her any more.

Jo took a step away from Steph and the conversation that was making her uncomfortable, and peered over the metal racks to see if she could spy Lauren, her hand going to the small of her back as a twinge flicked down her spine. There were plenty of people milling around on this wet and windy Saturday afternoon but no sign of her niece's distinctive ginger locks.

'How's work going?'

'Blissfully normal,' Jo said, returning her attention to the piles of fabric. 'Or at least, as normal as it can be while I'm waddling around reminding everyone that not only am I an abandoned wife but an abandoned mother-to-be. I swear the next person who gives me that simpering look of concern is going to get a smack in the mouth.'

Steph pulled a face to hide any telltale signs of compassion that might offend her sister. 'Missed any more antenatal appointments lately?' Her hand reached out to pat Jo's bump but Jo sidestepped the touch and ignored Steph's furrowed brow.

'Unfortunately my midwife is almost as much of a nag as you are, so no, I've been good.'

'And you're doing OK?'

Jo glared at her sister whose eyes were brimming with sympathy. 'I'm. Fine.'

'All right, I get the message,' Steph muttered. 'Now, are we looking for fabrics fit for a wicked stepmother or are we here to reorganize every shelf in the shop?'

Jo replaced the piece of fabric she had been holding, now neatly folded. Steph gave a nod of approval and, as they continued down the aisle, Jo kept glancing over the top of the racks. Amongst the many bobbing heads, one in particular caught her attention. The hairstyle was achingly familiar and Jo knew immediately how soft that particular shade of brown would feel to the touch. Her heart had made the connection long before her brain and her pulse began to race. Stumbling forward, Jo followed the man as if drawn to a magnet. She bumped blindly into other shoppers as she went, the most vociferous being Steph.

'Jo, what's wrong with you? Watch where you're going!'

Jo wasn't listening; she couldn't hear a thing above the pounding of her heart and the voice inside her head telling her to come to her senses. Her fingers and toes tingled in anticipation and she began to feel warm, very warm. Her fringe was sticking to the beads of sweat prickling her brow so she tried to blow cool air on her face. Her breath caught in her throat as she drew level with the man in the next aisle and watched him reach up to grab a piece of heavy green damask. As he lifted his head Jo caught her first glimpse of his face albeit from the eyebrows up. It was enough; and with a small change in direction, Jo was no longer walking but running and didn't stop until she hit fresh air.

Standing with her back against the store window with the rain beating down on her, Jo tried to slow her breathing and calm herself but the more she tried and failed, the more panicked she became. She recognized the sensation of her heart beating so fast it threatened to burst. She had felt the same thing shortly before passing out on Bonfire Night but her memories ran much deeper. She was no stranger to anxiety attacks.

Someone took hold of her arms as if she was about to fall. 'I'll be . . . all right . . . in a minute,' Jo panted without looking up. When Steph didn't release her grip she added, 'Go back in and . . . buy the material . . . for Lauren. I'll wait . . . in the car.' She didn't want her sister watching her fall apart; she didn't want anyone watching.

'I'm not going anywhere,' Steph said levelly. 'Try to slow your breathing down.'

'What . . . do you think . . . I'm doing?' Jo snapped.

'If you're not careful, you're going to hyperventilate. Lauren, go back inside and ask for a paper bag.'

Jo lifted her head and to her dismay discovered two pairs of eyes scrutinising her. 'Yes, go,' Jo said and luckily Lauren didn't object.

Steph had the good sense not to ask questions and by the time Lauren returned with the paper bag, Jo was starting to regain her composure.

'I think I'll be OK now,' Jo said.

Steph was unconvinced. 'We need to get you to the hospital.'

'Not a chance! I started to feel a bit flustered . . . and then rushed out too quickly . . . that's all. I won't do it again.'

'I think you should go, if only for a check-up.' It was Lauren this time and if Jo didn't know better, it sounded like a veiled threat.

Jo shook her head. With each passing minute, she felt more and more able to dismiss what had just happened.

160

She refused to accept that the demons she had once battled in her adolescence had come back to haunt her. It had been different back then because her attacks had usually happened as she was drifting off to sleep. Without warning, her heart would start hammering and she had been convinced that she was suffering from some kind of heart failure. Eventually she had plucked up the courage to tell her mother, who had taken time out of her busy social life to whisk her troubled daughter off to see their GP. Liz had helpfully explained to him how Jo had just had her heart broken for the first time and so the doctor had been dismissive, quickly concluding that Jo was attention-seeking. He told Liz to come back when her daughter had decided what was wrong with her, so Jo had faced her fears alone. She had learnt to be strong and those early lessons would see her through her latest traumas.

'There's no shame in admitting you're not coping. There must be some medication the doctor can give you, even if you are pregnant.'

'I'm not going to touch any kind of drug that will mess with my mind! It's messed up enough as it is.'

'Don't be silly, Jo. If you need help, for God's sake, ask for it.'

'I can manage on my own, Steph. Now give me the car keys and I'll wait in the car while you go back inside and buy the red velvet we were looking at.'

There was no arguing with Jo, which gave Steph some reassurance. The incident had been an aftershock to David's disappearance, that was all, and Jo was back to being the sister she knew and loved.

* * *

'Don't lift that, I'll do it!' Sally rushed forward as Jo grunted, hauling a bright yellow baby bath out of the car. Sally would have pulled the offending item from Jo's hands if hers weren't already full. 'Get yourself back inside. Now!'

Sally had a strong, powerful voice and a disposition to match. It took Jo only a fraction of a second to realize that arguing was futile. She put down the bath and, checking for Sally's approval, picked up a small carrier bag. 'I'll open up the garage first. Everything can go in there until I'm ready to sort things out.'

By the time Sally had unloaded the car, Jo had a steaming mug of coffee waiting for her.

'I can't thank you enough for this, Sally,' Jo said as she slid a plate of biscuits across the dining room table towards her sister-in-law. 'And it's just a loan; you can have it all back when I'm done.'

Sally was laughing as she refused the biscuits. 'Don't bother; we won't need it. One kid is more than enough as far as Steve's concerned.'

'And one too many for his brother,' Jo said quietly as she set about arranging the untouched biscuits into a perfect circle on the plate, gathering up rogue crumbs into a neat pile as she went.

The smile that had accompanied Sally's laughter faltered. 'It just doesn't make sense,' she said. 'For all his talk about putting off having a family, David loves kids. You've seen for yourself how much he adores Luke.'

Jo visibly flinched. 'I know you mean well, Sally – but please, I don't want to hear the arguments. I only manage to get through each day because I've convinced

162

myself he's walked out on us. It might be hard to stomach, but at least it's an answer and one I could learn to live with.'

'Sorry, I just think . . .' Sally said, then pursed her lips tightly to stop herself from saying more.

'I know there are other possibilities, of course I do! I lie awake at night torturing myself with them,' Jo said, feeling that familiar mix of anger and fear gnawing away at her insides. 'Yes, he could be lying in a ditch somewhere. Yes, he could have jumped into the Mersey . . .'

Sally put her hand on Jo's before she had reduced the biscuits to a pile of crumbs. 'It's all right, Jo.'

'No, it's not all right, and it hasn't been all right for a very long time. I should have seen this coming, Sally but I was too absorbed in my own selfishness. I don't know who I should be more angry with, David or me.' *Or this baby*, she added silently.

Sally gave Jo's hand a quick squeeze before letting go. 'You shouldn't blame yourself; you made each other so happy. In fact I envied you.'

'But not now, eh?' Jo said with a trembling smile.

'Is there anything I can do to help?'

'How about changing the subject?' Jo offered. 'How are things with you and Steve?'

There was a sneer to accompany Sally's reply. 'As bad as ever, but I won't go burdening you with my troubles – you've enough on your plate.'

'Tell,' Jo ordered.

Sally sounded utterly despondent when she said, 'I'm only just starting to appreciate how much David kept Steve in check. He has absolutely no self-control and I don't know what to do about him any more. He's hardly ever home and I don't have a clue where he goes or what he gets up to. His friends try covering for him, but they're not as good at lying as he is.'

'Sorry,' Jo said, wincing as she recalled David's undoubted role in Steve's subterfuge.

'He tries to make out that he's working a lot of overtime, but I never see the benefit – the reverse, in fact. I've had to start hiding my purse.'

'Bloody moron,' Jo said under her breath, remembering too late that she was sitting in front of his wife. 'Sorry, I shouldn't have said that.'

'It's OK, Jo, I wholeheartedly agree.'

'Although he does have a good side,' Jo said. 'He's offered to paint the nursery.'

Sally's features softened and at first Jo couldn't think why. 'At least that's one thing to look forward to. Whatever the men in our lives are up to, we have our children to keep us sane.' She reached forward and, before Jo could stop her, laid a hand on Jo's belly. 'Is this one a kicker?'

Jo paled noticeably and tried unsuccessfully to ease back out of Sally's reach. 'I can't help feeling the baby might just tip me over the edge.'

'Oh, you think that now but just you wait. Maternal instinct is a powerful thing, Jo. Once that baby's in your arms he or she will become your one and only priority. You'll be able to put all this behind you and concentrate on being a mother – I promise.'

Jo wanted to believe that Sally was right but she had

put the baby first once before and that was turning out so badly that there wasn't even the slightest flicker of maternal instinct when she asked herself who she would choose if she had that choice over again.

14

By the time December arrived, Jo had completely outgrown her cashmere coat but Liz had come to the rescue with yet another bargain picked up in a charity shop in Kendal. The oversized tweed duffle wasn't exactly Jo's style but her tastes were far less demanding than they had once been. She could fasten it up and, with the weather taking a sudden turn for the worse, that was good enough for her.

The one – and perhaps only – advantage to the sudden cold snap was that the mire of a car park at the Southport site was frozen solid.

'Watch the ice,' Kelly warned. She was holding her arm out towards Jo in case she slipped.

Jo wafted the proffered hand away impatiently, her gloved fingers only just poking out from her coat sleeve. 'I'm fine, Kelly, stop fussing. I'm pregnant, not incapable,' she said, sounding harsher than she intended.

Jim was standing at the Portakabin door waiting for them. 'Morning ladies,' he said while his breath formed a cloud that temporarily obscured his smile. 'The kettle's on.'

'We shouldn't take that long,' Kelly said busily. 'And

we have another four sites to visit before the end of the day.'

The visits were a routine audit that Jo had to complete at least quarterly and involved a quick check of attendance records and accident book entries to make sure the information on each site matched that being sent through to head office. She didn't usually bring Kelly along but it had recently been agreed that she should cover some of Jo's duties while she was on maternity leave. The original plan had been to recruit someone with more experience but that had been when Jo had imagined taking a year out to immerse herself in the joys of motherhood. As things stood, she would only be dipping her toe in it before returning to work. Gary was confident that, with his close supervision, there wasn't much trouble Kelly could get them into.

'But since the kettle's on, it would be rude to say no,' Jo told Jim, overruling Kelly's not-so-subtle rebuff to his welcome.

When they stepped into the cabin, Jo discovered that they weren't the only visitors and she immediately regretted accepting Jim's hospitality. Jason was there along with a fresh-faced trainee who was plugging the gap David had left until Nelson's decided how and when to fill the vacancy. There were awkward smiles, followed by an equally awkward silence. Everyone ignored the elephant in the room as Jo unzipped her mammoth-sized coat.

'You're looking well, Jo,' Jason said.

'You too; settling down obviously agrees with you,' Jo responded, letting him know she knew almost as much about his personal life as he did about hers. Jason and

David had worked together for several years and what Jason had shared with David about his various relationships, David had of course shared with his wife. Jason was twenty-seven and had spent much of his adult life flitting from one girlfriend to the next. The lines between each relationship were often blurred, but his latest conquest had defeated him.

'He's besotted with this one,' David had told her as they lay in bed one night. 'For the first time in his life, he's not in control.'

Jo was resting her head on David's chest and she could hear the steady beat of his heart. 'He loves her more than she loves him, you mean?'

'Maybe. Not everyone can be as lucky as we are. We're the perfect match.'

'You think so?' Jo asked, unable to share her husband's confidence for reasons he wasn't yet aware of.

David lifted her face towards him. 'Don't you?' he asked as he slipped down the bed so they were nose to nose, their bodies pressed against each other. Jo's heartbeat was an echo of her husband's.

'I can be controlling.'

David smiled. 'Didn't you realize? It's only because I let you.'

'I love you, David.'

David pulled back as he recognized something akin to guilt in his wife's face. 'What have you done, Jo?'

She swallowed hard and bit her lip as she tried to summon up the courage to tell him. They had just come back from a Valentine's break to Paris and had had the most wonderful time. They had stood on the steps of the Sacré-Cœur in

168

Montmartre and repeated their wedding vows, or at least an updated version that they had made up on the spot. They had promised to love each other for ever and David had told her he would devote his life to making her happy. Taking him at his word, when they returned to England, she had started flushing her contraceptive pill down the plughole each morning rather than popping it into her mouth.

Her courage failed at the last minute and she started with a half-truth. 'What would you say if I were to stop taking the pill?'

David was still scrutinising her and didn't look reassured by what he saw. 'I'd say it's still too soon.'

She had hoped his prevarication was coming to an end and tried not to let her frustration show, asking softly, 'What are you so scared of, David?'

'Having a baby will change things between us,' he said. 'Look at what's happening to Steve and Sally. Happily married and then Luke comes along and they can't bear the sight of each other any more. I don't want that to happen to us. I just don't think we're ready yet,' he said.

'We *are* ready,' she said, simply. 'I want to have a mini-you, or a mini-me. I want to see what colour their eyes are, if they have a dimple on their chin just like yours and if they inherit your patience or my stubbornness. I want to hear that tiny little heartbeat and know that we – *we* – made a perfect human being.'

'I know.' David's words were gentle, as was the way he extricated himself from her embrace. 'And I want that too. Just not yet . . .'

'But coming off the pill doesn't necessarily mean I'll get

169

pregnant right away. Sometimes it can take years to conceive.'

It was a convincing argument and one that Jo had already used to justify her actions to herself, however David wouldn't relent – but then neither would she. Their love life had suffered a temporary setback, as if David suspected his determined wife had overruled him, but their desire for different things wasn't as strong as their desire for each other.

Jo blinked away the memory, but the guilt remained. She should have told him what she was going to do.

'We'll leave you to it,' Jason said. He had stood up and was waiting for Jo to hang up her coat so he could collect his. While he was close enough for only her to hear, he added, 'I just thought you should know. The police went through everything in the office. There was nothing to find.'

'I know.'

'And I gave them a statement, for all the good it did. Has there been any news, anything to explain what might have happened yet?'

Jo considered how much she should tell him. She had hung on to as much privacy as she could, but after seven weeks she was desperate for any breakthrough. 'I know he withdrew a fair bit of cash before he went missing. You wouldn't know anything about that, would you?'

Jason's brow furrowed, and he took his time before he answered which gave Jo hope that it would at least be a considered reply. 'Sorry, Jo,' he said, shaking his head slowly. 'Other than saving up for your holiday to America, I don't ever remember him mentioning money.'

'It's OK, never mind,' Jo said, reaching over to touch his

arm as if he were the one in need of comfort. 'I'm getting used to not having answers.'

The audit was completed in record time and Jo wasn't sure if Kelly had ploughed through the work to demonstrate how capable she was, or to prove her point to Jim that they hadn't had time for the cups of coffee that were still half-full when they left.

It was when they were leaving that they bumped into Simon Harrison, literally. He had just arrived for work and had his chin to his chest as he fought against the arctic blast that swept Jo into his path.

'Sorry, love, I wasn't looking where I was going,' he said, grabbing her arm to stop her stumbling.

'Take more care next time,' snapped Kelly, although it was unclear if her hostility was based on the near miss, or the fact he had used the term 'love', which was one of her pet hates.

Rather than look at Kelly, Simon's smiling eyes were drawn to Jo, or to be more specific, her immense bump. 'You've grown!' he said, greeting her like an old friend.

She wasn't the only one to have changed. She had visited Simon a few times when he was ill and the forty-year-old standing in front of her with broad shoulders and a square jaw bore no resemblance to the man she recalled crumpled up on his living room sofa. His eyes hadn't been smiling then, they had been empty. Whatever cocktail of drugs his doctor had plied him with had allowed him to withdraw so deeply into himself that only an outer shell had remained and his muscular frame had trembled with the effort of keeping his head upright. Neither Jo nor his ex-wife, who had temporarily returned home to care for him, had been able to break through that shell and Jo wondered if he remembered the visit at all. The gratitude written all over his face confirmed that he did.

'It's good to see you back,' Jo said. 'How are you getting on?'

'I've been to the doc's this morning, that's why I'm late,' he explained. 'Coming back to work was the right thing to do. I still have my moments but I'm getting there. One day at a time.'

'I'm glad to hear it. I really am.'

Simon hesitated then said, 'I heard about David.' There was another pause, a familiar one to Jo, where the person in front of her tried to decide whether to offer condolences or hope. 'He came to see me while I was off.'

'Yes, I know,' Jo said as she tried not to let her pain show. She didn't want to be reminded of how kind-hearted and thoughtful her husband could be. She was more than happy for the police to keep an open mind – but if she wanted to continue to function, hers needed to be closed to all possibilities except one.

'I can't believe David would leave you in the lurch, not like this,' Simon added. It was another familiar response that was starting to grate on Jo's nerves. 'The way he talked about you and the baby – he was so excited about becoming a dad.'

At first Jo was too stunned to say anything. She had watched David gradually getting used to the idea of impending fatherhood, or so she had thought, but after discovering his note, she had convinced herself that it had been an act, played out occasionally in front of others for her benefit. It was the first time she had heard of David talking about the baby so positively while she hadn't been there to be hoodwinked. Realizing her mouth was an 'Oh' of amazement she swallowed hard and said, 'Really? What did he say?'

'Well—'

'We should be going, Jo,' interrupted Kelly, who had been more interested in the dropping temperature than the conversation.

'And I need to get going too, I've got a morning's work to catch up on,' Simon said. 'But anytime you want to have a chat, give me a call. It would be nice to feel like I was doing something to repay his kindness, and yours too.'

Jo half expected him to give her a hug goodbye and when they shook hands politely it left her surprisingly disappointed.

'I still think Mr Harrison is pulling the wool over our eyes. Have you seen how many medical appointments he's attended since coming back?' Kelly said once she was in Jo's car. They were travelling together today so there was no escaping her assistant's scepticism.

'And did you also notice how he's been more than making up his hours over the rest of the week? Simon Harrison is a good man who has been through a very rough time. It happens, Kelly. There but for the grace of God and all that,' Jo said with more emotion than even she had expected. She couldn't compare what she was going through with Simon's post-traumatic stress but she certainly appreciated how little control even the strongest-minded person could have over their own thoughts and emotions.

'You can't deny that the sickness rates at this site are

way too high,' Kelly said stubbornly. 'It might be worth reviewing procedures and retraining the site supervisors.'

'Maybe.' Jo was only half listening as she checked her mobile before starting the car. She had switched her phone to silent and had missed a call. 'I won't be a minute,' she said as she dialled a number that was already stored in her directory. Jo's hands were trembling when Martin Baxter picked up after only two rings.

'Would you be able to come into the station?' he asked. 'I need you to check some CCTV footage for me.'

'New footage?'

'Someone accessed David's bank account from a cash machine yesterday.'

'David?' Jo's hand gripped the phone so tightly that it almost slipped out of her hand, which had suddenly become sweaty.

'It's not a great image so I wouldn't like to say. We need you to take a look.'

'Where? Where was he?'

'Liverpool city centre. I don't want you to build your hopes up and, like I said, the footage isn't particularly clear so even you may not be able to identify him.'

'I'm on my way,' Jo said, cutting the call and turning to Kelly who had been listening intently.

'They've found him?'

'That's what I need to find out. Do you mind if we make a detour?' Jo asked. She had already started up the engine and was putting the car in gear.

Kelly grabbed the steering wheel. 'Yes I do mind, actually.' Before Jo could give her an earful, Kelly added, 'You're in no fit state to drive anywhere. I'll do it.'

As Jo clambered out of the car and fought against the wind, she didn't notice the beads of sweat turning to ice on her brow or that her legs had turned to jelly. She was only aware of the great expanse of open space around her and in particular every window, every fence and every tree large enough to hide a grown man. David was still out there and she could feel his eyes upon her.

15

Jo was sitting at a desk covered in sticky coffee stains so she kept her hands on her lap, her fingers brushing against her bump although she didn't caress it as she had once done. She stared intently at the CCTV footage that came to life on the computer screen. The camera was pointing down towards the man standing at a cash machine although the image was so poor that he looked as if he were in the middle of a snow storm and he kept his head bowed as he keyed in his pin number.

Leaning in closer, Jo peered at the features she could only just discern. She could see the tip of the man's nose and his left hand, which could either belong to the assailant who had killed or abducted David and stolen his card, or David himself. She wasn't sure which alternative she preferred.

'I'm not expecting you to give a definitive answer – but do you *think* it's him?' Martin asked.

Jo gave a scornful laugh and when she answered, she didn't take her eyes from the screen that had been paused on the best image the policeman could manage. 'I can't honestly say I recognize the tip of his nose, but his hair's cut like David's, he moves like David, he uses his left hand like David, oh, and yes, he's wearing a Nelson's jacket, just like David.'

'Can I take that as a yes?'

She remained staring at the frozen image on screen as she said a silent plea. Look up, David, she begged. Please, just look up and remember me, remember the woman you said you would love for ever. Damn well look at me, David! Tell me how to make this right!

'Yes,' she said, surprising herself at the rush of relief she felt.

'I don't know how to feel about it,' Jo said as she gripped a couple of pins between her lips. Her brow was creased in concentration as she attached beading to the hem of Lauren's costume, the furrows deepening as she tried to find an answer to Steph's question. 'Ever since he went missing, I've kept this mental list of all the things that might have happened and how I would react. I even rated them and the last thing I wanted was for David to have come to harm but . . .'

'But then it turns out that the bastard has been living it up while you've been going through hell. And now you're wishing him dead.'

'Lauren! Language please,' Steph said.

The wicked stepmother was standing on a footstool while her mum and aunt added the finishing touches to her dress. Other than the persistent tapping on her mobile, the two sisters could be forgiven for forgetting she had even been there.

'She's right, though,' Jo admitted, adding almost casually, 'if he walked through the door right now, I would kill him.'

'And on the bright side, at least you can stop feeling guilty about hating him now you know he's alive and well,' Steph said.

'I suppose,' Jo said, not willing to admit to her sister that her first reaction was one of longing rather than loathing. Yes, she wanted to kill him but, to her shame, she also wanted him to take her in his arms and never let her go again. Recent events couldn't cancel out the past, or at least not completely. David had been her hero; a hero with faults maybe but not a villain and he was still the man she loved. 'The police think if he's already low on funds then he might make an appearance soon. They're not releasing any information about the cash withdrawal, though; they want to keep the public on his side.'

'Not that the selfish pig deserves any sympathy.'

Steph glared up at her daughter. 'Lauren, you are not being helpful. I know this is a first for me, but can you get back to messaging your friends and ignore everything else around you?'

There followed an awkward pause while Jo waited for the silent battle of wills between mother and daughter to run its course. It ended when Lauren returned her attention to her phone with a flurry of dramatic sighs and exaggerated movements. When it was safe to speak, Jo said to Steph, 'He's managed to go through £3,000 in less than two months and by my reckoning there's probably no more than £1,000 left in his account now. If I'm lucky, he could be home by Christmas! Not that I'd let him in, you understand,' she added.

'At least there's an end in sight.'

'I hope so, Steph. I really hope so,' Jo replied. 'My own finances aren't particularly rosy either. Have you seen the price of childcare these days?'

'I could leave school and look after the baby,' Lauren offered.

'Couldn't Irene help out?' Steph said, not rising to the bait her daughter had dangled in front of her.

'Even Sally didn't think it was a good idea leaving Luke with her when she went back to work.'

'Be fair, Jo – that was only because David's dad had just died.'

'I know,' Jo conceded, 'and she does look after Luke now and again, but if I'm being honest I don't want her involved so much. Since Alan died, she dithers over everything and I'd probably end up looking after her as much as the baby and I'm just not strong enough to do that.'

'That's a bit harsh, isn't it? She brought up two sons perfectly well . . .' Steph's voice trailed off. 'OK, maybe you have a point.'

But Steph was right, it *was* harsh and Jo and Irene had had a decent enough relationship once her mother-in-law had accepted that Jo was good enough for her son. And there was the real nub of the problem. As it turned out, Jo hadn't been good enough. 'It's more than that,' she admitted. 'All Irene wanted was confirmation that David was still alive and she has that. She doesn't have to deal with the sense of betrayal, the frustrations and the guilt, not to mention the financial mess.'

'She's on her own too, Jo,' Steph reminded her. 'David

is still missing from her life and I should think she'd jump at the chance of looking after the baby if only you'd ask.'

'And I can't afford to be proud,' Jo said, reading her sister's mind. 'OK, I get the message. Steve's coming over at the weekend to paint the nursery and she'll probably tag along too so I could maybe mention it then.'

'No maybes, Jo,' Steph told her firmly. 'And while it's good that Steve has magically transformed into a knight in shining armour, don't go letting him get too comfortable in David's shoes.'

When Jo laughed, she managed to prick herself with a pin. 'He has a wife and child, remember?'

'Ah, but he's the type who needs reminding of that fact now and again.'

'Seriously, Steph, don't worry. I have no intention of falling for the Steve Taylor charm.'

'I wouldn't trust him as far as I could throw him,' Lauren piped up.

Jo looked up at her and sighed. 'The sad truth is, Lauren, I don't think I could trust anyone any more.'

Jo had spent years imagining how her baby's nursery would look. She had planned a jungle theme for a boy with a large mural on one wall that, of course, she would paint herself. For a girl she would put her needlepoint skills to good use and create a magical forest full of toadstools and pixies. But when she and David had gone along to her twenty-week scan and had been asked if they wanted to know the baby's sex, David had been rendered speechless.

'Well?' Jo asked him. She too couldn't take her eyes from

180

the screen where the sonographer had frozen a perfect profile of their baby. He or she appeared to be sucking its thumb.

Jo bit down on her trembling lip. She had felt sick to the stomach for so long, worrying that she had bullied David into having a baby, but then, when he had felt the baby kick a few days earlier, she had thought she had seen a spark of excitement. Now, as she dragged her eyes away from the screen and looked at the tears welling in his eyes, she *knew* she had done the right thing.

David had to clear his throat before he spoke. 'I never imagined little FB would look so much like a baby,' he managed.

'Not just any baby, David. *Our* baby.'

He laughed and rubbed his hand hard across his face, never once taking his eyes from the image. 'It really is, isn't it?'

The sonographer, a young woman who had been waiting patiently for one of the prospective parents to answer her question, finally spoke. 'Did you think your wife had just been overeating these last five months?'

'And she's doing OK? They're both all right?' David asked.

'Yes, everything is as it should be.'

There was a sharp gasp as David had a flash of inspiration. 'Do you think it would be all right for Jo to travel? We'd talked about going on holiday to America next month. Could she still go?'

The soaring relief that had been lifting Jo's spirits dissolved into the ether. Her stomach lurched as she plummeted back to earth. 'David, don't.'

David knew immediately he had said the wrong thing. 'Sorry, I just thought, you know, one last jaunt before we settle down?'

Jo refused to accept his apology and her husband never managed to resurrect that moment of joy and relief in her ever again. It wasn't until after she had left the hospital, silent and sullen, that she realized they had forgotten to find out the sex of the baby.

The answer to that particular question would be solved soon enough, but as Jo stood in the slowly emerging nursery she felt that she couldn't care less.

'The colour will go lovely with the quilt set your mum made,' Irene told her, indicating the sunshine-yellow paint that Steve was sweeping in arcs across the magnolia wall.

Jo was standing by the window. 'I suppose so,' she said, having long since diverted her attention to the world outside. The road was all but obscured by tall hedges and trees but that didn't stop her from seeking out any signs of life. She was waiting for David to step out from behind a tree and look up at her. She could visualize him lifting a hand to his lips and blowing her a kiss. She stepped away.

Irene placed a comforting hand on her back. 'Why don't we leave Steve to it and go downstairs for a nice cup of tea.'

'Yeah, don't go worrying about me, I can manage,' complained Steve but his words had fallen on deaf ears as Irene pulled Jo away.

Jo wished she could push David from her mind but it wasn't going to be easy now Irene had her on her own. As Jo wondered how on earth she was going to navigate the conversation through the emotional minefield that had become her life, her mother-in-law decided to jump in with both feet.

'I know how difficult this must be for you,' she began once she had switched on the kettle.

'And difficult for you too,' offered Jo.

'Yes, I won't argue with that. It's a horrible time for all of us, but you're the one expecting a baby and trying to keep a roof over your head singlehandedly. Sally mentioned that you're only planning on taking a few months' maternity leave now.'

'I can't afford to be off any longer, Irene.'

'And childcare isn't cheap.'

'Extortionate.'

The tentative smile on Jo's face was enough encouragement for Irene to get to the point they were both politely sidestepping. 'I could take care of the baby,' she said.

'Wouldn't it be too much for you?'

'By that do you mean am I capable of looking after a newborn?' Irene asked, then answered her own question. 'Sally frets every time she leaves Luke with me and I will admit he can run rings around me, but he also gives me a new lease of life. Jo, I've spent my life looking after my family only to have them disappear before my eyes. You'd actually be doing me a favour by letting me help you.'

Jo wanted to say yes, but she had been avoiding Irene for a reason and that reason couldn't be ignored for the sake of civility. They needed to clear the air after Jo's outburst following the public appeal and the confession she had made. 'But I don't deserve your help, do I? I brought this on myself, you know that, Irene. I chose to become pregnant when I knew all along that David wasn't ready for that kind of burden.'

'You didn't get pregnant by yourself, Jo,' Irene answered firmly. 'And while my son might be shirking his responsibilities, I'm not.'

Still Jo fought against the generosity she didn't think she deserved. 'We're living in such uncertain times, Irene. Who knows what will happen in the coming months? I wouldn't want to rely on you if . . .'

'Come what may, the baby comes first. You know that, and I know that.'

Jo didn't know that at all, but she needed someone around who did. 'I do need you,' she said, her voice cracking with emotion. 'I can't do this on my own.'

'And you don't have to. I promise you, Jo, I won't let you down.'

Seeing the tears welling in her daughter-in-law's eyes, Irene turned away abruptly and put her hands flat against the counter to support herself. She took a couple of deep breaths and spoke quickly as if she might lose her nerve if she hesitated. 'I don't understand why he's doing this! He's fit and well enough to go to a cash machine but he can't manage to come home? In God's name, why? Because you disagreed about when to start a family? That boy was born to be a father, we could both see that! So what if he was worried about not being good enough? So what if he was afraid?' she said shaking her head. 'It's no defence and I won't even try to justify his actions, Jo, however much I want to. I'd expect Steve to pull a stunt like this but not my David. He always took his responsibilities seriously.'

'Thanks, Mum,' Steve said with a half laugh.

Irene turned around to find Steve at the door wiping his yellow stained hands on a rag. 'Oh, you know what I mean.'

'If that's the way you feel then I might disappear along with him.'

From the way he winced, Steve was already regretting his thoughtless words but it was too late. Irene had turned away again and they both watched as her body tensed. Her son came over and wrapped her tightly in his arms before kissing the top of her head. 'Sorry, Mum. That was a stupid thing to say.'

Jo felt distinctly uncomfortable as she watched the exchange between mother and son, partly because she imagined Steve's spattered overalls smearing yellow paint over his mother's cardigan but mostly because the devotion on display was something she couldn't imagine sharing with her own child, not any more. She felt impossibly disconnected from the foetus growing inside her. The only connection they shared now was the responsibility for David's disappearance.

16

'He's done a good job, I'll give him that,' Liz said.

Jo remained on the threshold while her mother stepped into the nursery, which was bathed in rare winter sunshine. The bedroom furniture wasn't new but had been transformed with a fresh coat of brilliant white paint that was almost as dazzling as the bright yellow walls. The double bed had gone, replaced by the cot Sally had given Jo. Irene had laid out the bedding and attached the mobile Liz had bought from the charity shop as a finishing touch.

'Hmm, I suppose,' Jo said, staring at the sunflowers dangling over the empty cot. Their mocking smiles seemed to know how hard she was trying not to think of the day when the room would be filled with baby smells rather than paint and turpentine.

Liz pulled open the wardrobe door. It was packed tightly with suitcases, sunhats and ski equipment. Horrified, she started pulling open the drawers to the dresser. 'You haven't cleared anything out yet! Where are all the baby things? Please don't say you haven't got anything yet, Jo.'

'Yes, of course I have. It's all in the garage.'

'You've left baby clothes in the garage to get all damp and mouldy?'

'Sally sealed them in bags and it's not like I won't wash everything beforehand.'

'Sally? You mean you're relying on hand-me-downs for everything? Have you bought *any* new clothes?'

Jo shrugged. 'Let's hope it's a boy.'

'It's not good enough, Jo. You, of all people, should be prepared by now.' Liz was shaking her head as she checked her watch. 'We've still got a few hours before the pantomime starts, why don't we cram in a bit of shopping first?'

Jo folded her arms and refused to move. 'Hand-me-downs are no different than buying things from charity shops,' she said, glancing over at the cot mobile. 'And I can't afford to go shopping, in case you've forgotten. I'm perfectly happy to make do and mend, Mum.'

Liz clenched her jaw but she couldn't hold back her opinion for long. 'I know we're all supposed to keep our thoughts to ourselves until we know exactly what's happened to David and why, but that man has a lot to answer for! He is one selfish bastard!'

Jo gasped in shock. It wasn't as if she had never heard her mother swear, but it was a rare event and she had certainly never heard her curse a member of her own family before; until recently David had been a much-loved and well-respected son-in-law. 'I expect that kind of language from Lauren but not from you,' she said.

'But doesn't it make you angry, Jo?'

'It did,' Jo admitted. 'It still does. But I don't have the energy to hold on to that kind of anger, not after two months. I'm exhausted – and besides, there's still room for doubt.'

'There's no room at all, Joanne. The police have all but stopped the search.'

'I *didn't* see his face, Mum. It might not have been David at the cash machine.'

'But it was David who withdrew £3,000 before he disappeared with his passport,' Liz reminded her.

'Yes it was, and I can't explain why he did that, but after speaking to Irene, she's made me remember the man I fell in love with, the one who wouldn't run away and do this to his family. The David I know wouldn't leave at all. So until I have absolute certainty, I'm never going to stop tying myself up in knots trying to find the answers to an endless list of questions.'

'Maybe it's time you started asking yourself some new questions, then.'

'Like?'

'Like, what can you do for the new person in your life?'

'But that,' Jo said pointing an accusing finger at her protruding stomach, 'is more than likely the reason David ran away.' She was picturing the crumpled note he had left which she was glad she hadn't mentioned to anyone. Liz would be quoting it chapter and verse by now in an effort to make her daughter despise her husband, but that would be futile. She reserved such feelings for herself and little FB. 'He couldn't face the future and I'm not sure I can either, not any more.' When Jo saw the look of alarm on her mother's face, she released a sigh of surrender. 'I will start preparing for the baby. Of course I will. I just need a little more time. Please.'

Her mum's eyes softened. 'OK, but when you're ready we're going on a spending spree – my treat.'

'So if hand-me-downs aren't good enough for your new grandchild does that mean we'll be going to proper shops?' Jo challenged.

Liz caught Jo looking at the smiling sunflowers again. 'That mobile was brand new! And you have to admit you can get some good bargains, especially baby clothes. They grow out of them long before they've had a chance to wear them out,' Liz said but stopped herself. 'OK, I admit I'm a penny pincher—'

'And then some.'

Liz chose not to notice the sharp edge to the remark and said, 'The pennies I save are put away for a rainy day and I think you'd have to agree that it's pouring down right now. I can't remember the last time you needed me, Jo. I want to help now if you'll let me, I think it would be good for us both.'

Unlike her mother, Jo could remember quite clearly the last time she had sought out her help. It was back when the doctor had failed to diagnose her anxiety attacks and accused her of attention-seeking. Perhaps Jo *had* been crying out for attention, but her mum hadn't been prepared to confront the reasons why her daughter was so desperately unhappy. Yes, Jo had just broken up with her first boyfriend, but it was her home life that was the root of her anxiety. With her dad off travelling and her mother left to her own devices, Jo had good reason to believe her parents were facing their own break-up. Her mum was never going to admit what she had been up to and so had preferred to side with the doctor and told Jo that her heart would mend of its own accord in time. Now Jo's heart was breaking again and she wished she could count on her mother's help – but she still hadn't forgiven her. 'Thanks, Mum,' she said if only to appease her.

'Good. Now, if we're not going out shopping why don't I measure up for some new curtains in here? I've got some green fabric that would work perfectly and I could add some appliqué sunflowers. Unless you wanted to . . .'

Jo could barely muster the enthusiasm to turn up for her antenatal appointments, so she had no desire to even think about the finishing touches to the nursery. 'No, your idea sounds lovely and it'll make the room just perfect,' she said with a winning smile.

Reassured, Liz set to work and sent Jo in search of a measuring tape. Jo took her time searching, even though she knew exactly where she would find it, lined up perfectly between a set of screwdrivers and a roll of duct tape in one of the kitchen drawers. But she couldn't prevaricate for ever, and eventually she dragged herself back upstairs where she could hear her mum winding up the mobile. A tinny music box started to play, 'You Are My Sunshine,' and plump bumblebees began their endless pursuit of smiling sunflowers.

Liz had her back to the door and had started humming along to the cheerful tune. Jo could remember her mum singing the song to her when she was a little girl but the words held a new, darker meaning now.

'You'll never know dear, how much I love you. Please don't take my sunshine away,' Liz sang along as the mobile turned, her soft voice faltering at the last as she too realized the poignancy of the lyrics. She turned to catch her daughter staring at her wide-eyed and teary.

Jo wanted to turn and run but her feet had been cast in cement. Liz felt obliged to talk, if only to drown out the sound of the music still playing. 'He'll come to his senses soon, Jo,' she promised. 'And if not now, then surely when the baby's born.'

Jo was shaking her head. 'No, please don't say that. I don't want to cling to false hope. I don't want to be waiting for him to turn up at the hospital with a bunch of flowers and an apology. I couldn't go through the agony of waiting for him again, I couldn't bear the pain of him not showing up. I'd rather accept now that I've lost him. He's gone, Mum, and he's never coming back.'

Lauren's first-night nerves were infectious. Jo's heart was hammering as she and Steph sneaked backstage to check her costume. There was a look of disapproval from the teacher in charge of the production, but when Jo held aloft her sewing kit and offered her services to make a last-minute repair to Cinderella's sleeve, she was allowed through the cordon. Lauren was fighting for space in front of a full-length mirror along with a gaggle of other girls. She looked stunning.

As Jo set to work on the torn sleeve of poor Cinders' dress, Steph turned to her daughter. For a heart-stopping moment, it looked as if she was going to say something embarrassing, like how beautiful she looked or how proud Steph was of her. Fortunately Lauren was saved from humiliation by her mum's inability to speak.

'Steph, could you hold this for me,' Jo asked as she tried to reattach the offending flap of material.

191

Her sister said something akin to yes and Lauren visibly relaxed. She was about to turn back to the mirror when someone else spoke.

'Oh, Lauren, you look like a supermodel,' gushed Liz.

'Mum,' Jo hissed, 'you were supposed to stay in the hall and save our seats.'

'Oh, Gerry can manage on his own and I couldn't resist coming backstage to wish my granddaughter good luck.'

Liz was too busy giving the rest of the cast the once-over to notice the looks of disapproval from her daughters or the dismay on Lauren's face. She sniffed. 'I don't understand why she didn't have the starring role,' she said but as she settled her steely gaze on her granddaughter her voice hardened. 'But then I hear from Jo you've started swearing like a trooper, so I suppose you couldn't be trusted.'

'I was joking, Mum!' Jo cried. 'And as I recall, you were the one swearing your head off at the time!' Her counter-attack was too little, too late. The damage was done and Jo could only imagine what expletives were on the tip of Lauren's tongue at that precise moment.

Jo finished the emergency repair in record time and dragged her mother and Steph away before any more harm could be done, but she couldn't help giving Lauren a piece of advice before they left. 'Hold on to that anger,' she whispered. 'You're the wicked stepmother remember. Let Cinderella feel your wrath.'

Before slipping backstage, the school hall had been practically empty but upon their return, almost every seat was taken, including the ones they had claimed at the back of the hall. 'I thought you said Gerry was saving our seats?' Jo asked her mum.

'He has. Look,' Liz said pointing to seats two rows from the front.

'But we needed to be further back so we could see the full stage. My neck will ache from there,' Jo said.

'These are the best seats in the house, Joanne. Where better to heckle from?' Liz said as she pulled along her reluctant daughter.

'There will be *no* heckling,' Steph warned her mum. 'You've upset Lauren enough for one day.'

'Me?'

As Steph and her mother continued their whispered argument, Jo squeezed down the row towards her brother-in-law. The plastic chairs looked hard and unforgiving but Jo was feeling uncomfortable even before she sat down. The skin on the back of her neck crawled and she tried not to think how someone might be watching her from the back of the hall as the lights went down and the show began.

Lauren was in the first scene and seeing her niece in her acting debut was almost enough to distract Jo from her unease. Lauren was ferocious as a stepmother and when Cinderella cowered in front of her, Jo suspected there wasn't much acting involved from either. It was only when the wicked stepmother made her dramatic exit that Jo found her mind wandering.

She started thinking about the countless meetings she had attended with David. They never sat next to each other, even after they were married, because David said he liked to watch her from afar, but knowing his eyes were upon her could be as distracting as if he was next to her, trailing a finger down her spine. David was looking at her now, she was sure of it and she began to fidget. Her hand rubbed the back of her neck as if to sweep away her husband's gaze.

'Is your back hurting?' Steph whispered.

Jo offered a smile and said she was fine but she wasn't. She pretended to stretch her neck so she could look behind and peer into the darkness, scanning the audience for a familiar face. David wouldn't have missed Lauren's performance for the world and he would have known that Jo would be here.

Taking a couple of deep breaths to settle her nerves, Jo returned her attention to the stage. Within moments, Lauren was back in the fray but Jo couldn't be distracted this time. Rather than her neck, Jo began to rub her chest, which felt tight. Her breathing was becoming shallow, more so when she realized how clammy she felt. Her hands were damp with sweat and the tide of panic she had been trying to ignore since the lights went down swelled deep within her. She had an all-consuming urge to run and checked the row of seats on both sides of her to plan her escape. Steph and her mum were to her left with at least another ten people beyond them. To her right there was Gerry and a marginally shorter route to the central aisle.

There was a chorus of boos from the audience as Lauren delivered another cutting remark. She was really building up her part, but rather than revelling in her niece's success, Jo couldn't wait for her to storm off stage again. If Lauren didn't leave soon she would be distracted by her aunt stumbling out of the hall. Jo didn't want to do that, but the growing pressure against her chest was making it almost impossible to breathe.

Jo grabbed her handbag and tensed her already taut muscles as she prepared to stand up.

'You will not go the ball!' Lauren yelled. 'Now get to work polishing every pot and pan in this kitchen. I want to be able to see my beautiful face in the bottom of them all by the time I return.'

Jo stood up without warning and had the perfect view of Lauren's back as her niece raced off stage. Jo moved just as quickly. 'I need to get some fresh air,' she said to Gerry. 'Make them stay here.'

There were mutterings and a few notes of concern as Jo shuffled down the row, trying to keep her balance with the extra weight she didn't think she'd ever get used to carrying. She kept her head down as she rushed down the aisle, only to face interminable sets of double doors before she was out. She came to a stumbling stop in the middle of the forecourt, gasping for air. Through the ghostly clouds of her own breath, Jo's eyes darted from one exit door to another, expecting someone to rush out of the school at any moment. She wasn't sure if she was more terrified of that 'someone' appearing or not appearing so she ran from her fears and hurried towards the side of the school building to huddle in a corner. Pain bloomed in her chest and stars danced across her vision. Each breath became a battle and at first she was convinced that this latest attack might be her last. She was surprised how much she wanted to survive. She still needed answers and, even though she was loath to admit it, she still needed David. She couldn't stop loving him no matter how much she wanted to hate him. He had been her anchor, the calm that would help her survive any storm. If he was out there now, she needed him more than ever.

Although Jo hadn't suffered full-blown anxiety attacks since her teens, she had come close. Those early days of travelling with David had certainly brought her to the brink, starting with their honeymoon. She had been frantically trying to pack and had a bikini clamped in one hand, a pair of flip-flops in the other when her chest began to tighten. She had stood in front of her suitcase, completely frozen by fear when David came up behind her. He had known instinctively what to do.

'Hey, it's all right,' he said, placing the palms of his hands on her diaphragm, 'there's nothing to panic about. I'm here. I'm going to keep you safe, I promise. Now take a deep breath and let it out slowly. Breathe with me, Jo.'

It may have only been the heat from her own body as she dealt with this latest assault but she felt now as if the warmth was coming from David's arms. Jo closed her eyes and imagined him rocking her gently until her breathing slowed and she was able to face the world alone . . .

'Are you all right?'

Jo peeled her eyes open slowly as if clinging on to the hope that little bit longer that it had been David speaking, but she had already recognized the man's voice.

'Hi, Gerry,' she said, deftly avoiding the question.

'I should warn you that Steph and your mum won't be too far behind unless you think you can make it back inside with me.'

Shuddering at the thought, Jo said, 'I don't think I can. It's so hot in there and I'm feeling a bit queasy. Delayed morning sickness, probably.'

'Oh, OK,' Gerry said. He looked unsure about what to

do next, but it didn't look as if leaving was an option he was considering.

Taking a deep, juddering breath, Jo straightened up, rubbed her back, and put on her best smile. 'I tell you what, why don't you go back in and calm the others down. Tell them mother and baby are doing fine but that I'd rather stay out here. I'll sit in the car and wait for you all.'

Gerry seemed reassured and when Jo promised to phone if she felt worse he handed over the keys and returned to the school hall to catch his daughter's show-stopping finale.

Sitting in the back of Gerry's four-wheel drive, Jo's body ached in much the same way as it did after an intensive workout or a long run. Her legs trembled and her lungs burned, but it was her heart that hurt the most. She was too tense to cry; that would come later when she had used up the last of her willpower to convince her family that she was well enough to be dropped off back at home and left without supervision.

17

When Jo awoke, her bedclothes were sodden. She couldn't recall the dream that had chased her through the night so concentrated instead on releasing the tension from her body as she raised herself into consciousness. Every muscle still ached from her anxiety attack the night before.

As she tried to summon the energy to get up, the radio came on and headlining the news was the dwindling shopping days left until Christmas. Jo would normally have all the presents wrapped up with neat edges and elaborate bows by now but she had given little thought to the festive season other than accepting she could afford only token gestures this year rather than the extravagant gifts she and David had enjoyed giving. Jo wondered if she should at least start writing out some Christmas cards at the weekend but the thought of that blank space where David's name should be appended to hers made her body twist in pain. She groaned and reminded herself that she wouldn't even be able to afford cards if she didn't get to work.

Jo's aches and pains intensified as she hauled herself up into a sitting position and spent a moment rubbing her stomach until the discomfort ebbed away. Fifteen minutes later, when she stepped out of the shower, her body was hit by yet another aftershock from the previous night's trauma. She ignored her ghostly reflection in the steamed-up mirror and leant against the washbasin, waiting for the dull pain running across her abdomen to ease.

Too exhausted to dress, Jo wrapped a bathrobe around her tremulous body and went downstairs to make a drink. The coffee was strong and its warmth soothed her but the house was colder than she was used to. In a cost-cutting exercise she had not only lowered the thermostat but switched off radiators in unused rooms. After years of rebelling against her mother's frugality, Jo was being forced to follow her example. This new surge of hopelessness was accompanied by another wave of pain and the cup trembled in her hand. She looked at the clock on the microwave and then forced herself to pick up the phone.

'Do you think it's too early for me to be in labour?' she asked, already feeling silly and hoping her sister would talk some sense into her.

'Why? What's happened? Are you having contractions?'

In the background, Jo could hear a clamour of familiar voices rise up in response to Steph's questions. Her mother's was loudest, adding more questions to the ones Steph had just posed. As Jo began to explain about the pains that had been slicing across her abdomen at regular intervals, snatches of her dream came back to her. She had been caught up in a gigantic spider's web. Strands of spun silk had tightened around her, pulling her into its lair. 'I think I might have been having pains during the night too. Do you think it'll be all right for me to go to work?'

'No, Jo, you most certainly cannot go to work, not until you've been checked out,' Steph said. She was doing her best to remain calm despite the commotion erupting around her. A moment later the phone was pulled from her grasp.

'I'm on my way over,' Liz said. 'Pack a bag and be ready to leave in ten minutes.'

A wave of panic washed over Jo but this wasn't like the paralysing fear of the unknown she had suffered the day before. She had a pretty good idea of what was happening and what she needed to do. She cut off the call only to dial another number and this time Gary answered.

'Don't worry, Jo, you'll be fine,' he said. 'Keep me informed when you can but otherwise don't give work a second thought.'

Jo sounded almost petulant when she asked, 'But what if I have to start my maternity leave now? I was about to start preparing for the O'Dowd case next week.' She wanted to go to work. She didn't want to give up the one part of her life that still functioned relatively normally; she didn't want things to change.

'I can manage an Employment Tribunal and Kelly will help,' he insisted. 'Your most important job now is to make sure that you and the baby are safe and well. I hope everything goes OK. I'll be thinking of you.'

After Jo had finished the call she stood still for a moment and let Gary's concern for her unborn child bleed into her consciousness. The baby was early; seven weeks early and she didn't have a clue how serious that could be. She had been wishing it away often enough in the last two months and now she could be losing it. Was this her punishment for wicked thoughts? Fear crawled down her spine and wrapped itself in a tight knot, bringing forth the now familiar pulling sensation around her abdomen.

Baby Taylor arrived in the world two days later with little more than a whimper. It was Liz who cried like the proverbial baby.

'Is everything all right?' Jo asked faintly, as a group of nurses and the doctor crowded around the small, limp body that had been delivered moments earlier.

'They're just going to give him a little help with his breathing,' the midwife said as she gave Jo's hand a comforting squeeze.

'Him? It's a boy?' Liz gulped.

'Will he be all right?' Jo asked again. During the long, slow labour, Jo's conviction that her child was being punished for his mother's sins had grown in strength, much like her contractions. She didn't know how to react to this latest development, but her heart was in her throat as she watched the team work on her baby.

The minutes ticked by and Jo held her breath, releasing it all in one dizzying rush as she heard a squawk and then a cry from a pair of tiny lungs.

The doctor brought the baby over and rested him on his mother's chest for a brief moment. 'We're going to have to give him some extra help for a while. He's weighing in at three pounds fourteen ounces which might sound small but it's good for his dates and he looks like a fighter to me.'

Jo placed a trembling lip on her son's tiny head. She couldn't believe she was holding the baby she had always longed for. He was finally here and she felt such a rush of love that she wanted to burst into tears, but the baby let out the briefest cry as he fought against his mother's embrace. He was obviously aware of her failings and Jo felt the full force of his rejection. 'I'm so sorry,' she whispered.

'Have you decided on a name yet?' Irene asked, her voice rising softly over the gentle hum of machinery that kept the tiny miracles in the special care unit safe and warm.

Jo wasn't looking at her mother-in-law. She couldn't take her eyes from the impossibly small baby lying in his incubator. There was a web of threadlike veins visible beneath his bright red, downy skin. He was fast asleep but flinched occasionally as if he sensed his mother's gaze upon him. Jo, still stunned by the fact that she had just given birth, felt that naming her child without David was beyond her. All she had to help in her deliberations was a snatch of a conversation two years earlier.

'How about Matilda for a girl or Archibald for a boy?' David had suggested back then.

'Archibald?' Jo asked, and shook her head. 'It sounds way too pompous, although I do like the sound of Archie.'

'OK, if you want something more average, how about Barry? Or Tracy for a girl?'

They were on holiday in Vietnam and had wandered off from a guided tour of a Hindu sanctuary to ramble through its scattering of ancient ruins alone. It wasn't how Jo had envisaged celebrating her thirtieth year but now they were disconnected from the realities of life back home and being immersed in the past, she thought it might be a good time to tempt David to look at the future from a safe distance.

It wasn't working. 'There's no point talking to you about babies until you're mature enough to take it seriously,' she said before hitting her husband with the palm leaf she had been using to fan herself. She had intended the strike to be playful but it had been impossible to hold back all her frustrations.

She was ready to stomp off back to the tour guide but David grabbed her hand and pulled her towards him. He slipped his arms around her waist and waited for her to stop wrestling and look at him. 'Sorry,' he said. 'I do want kids one day, honestly, Jo. But I want to get it right and that means waiting for the right time.'

'Steve and Sally had problems long before Luke came along. We're nothing like them,' she said, responding to the argument he was alluding to.

'I know and I thank God for it.'

'So?'

David relaxed his grip on her but didn't answer.

'This has something to do with your dad as well, doesn't it?'

David's dad had only been fifty-eight when he had suffered a massive stroke, severely affecting him mentally as well as physically. The larger-than-life and seemingly indestructible fireman had vanished in the blink of an eye and the dying man Irene and her sons cared for through his final months was all but a stranger to them. Alan had been frustrated and humiliated by his incapacity, devastated at the prospect of having his life cut short and angry with the world in general. Jo suspected that David had been affected more by his dad's final months than by his actual death, but the pain was still too raw for him to talk about openly.

'I just want us to squeeze all we can out of life before we settle down,' David said by way of explanation. 'That way we can give our children the perfect foundation to go on and create wonderful lives of their own.'

'We already have a perfect foundation, don't you see that, David? Look how much we enjoy looking after Luke and Lauren. Don't you want one of your own? Don't your arms feel empty when you hand Luke back, because I know mine do.' She thought she glimpsed a flicker of agreement in David's eyes but it was still annoyingly out of reach. 'I'm thirty, David,' she said, reminding him of their original plan.

David had the good grace to sound guilty but he wouldn't back down. 'A short delay is all I'm asking. Not years and years, just a little bit longer. Does that sound OK?'

Jo couldn't understand his pain but she could see it on his face and it hurt her too. She wanted so much to heal him and she knew that she could if only he would trust her. She cupped his face gently in her hands. 'I'll wait,' she promised, leaning in to kiss him and hoping that she could convince him sooner rather than later. It was fatherhood and not time that would heal him.

How wrong she had been.

'We can't keep calling him Baby Taylor,' Irene said when Jo hadn't answered.

Jo almost suggested calling him FB but she wasn't that cruel, and as she placed a tentative hand on the plastic shell that separated her from her son, she didn't understand how David could have been. 'I'm not ready yet,' she said. 'But if you're going to push me then how about Barry?' she asked, her voice dry.

'Maybe it is too soon to think about it,' Irene said hastily. 'Baby Taylor will do for now.'

In the yawning pause that followed, both women became aware of the space to the side of the incubator where David should have been standing.

'I'm sorry he isn't here for you,' Irene said and it was a testament of her strength that the tears welling in her eyes didn't fall.

'It isn't your fault, Irene.'

'And it's not yours either.'

Jo looked down at the defenceless little boy sleeping uneasily in the rigid incubator which was a poor substitute for a mother's womb. Her body's rejection of him had been inevitable given that her heart had been doing the very same thing. When she looked at her son, she felt an overwhelming sense of guilt and an obligation to care for him but there was no desire to do it. That initial rush of devotion was now a distant memory and she wondered when it was that she had turned into the kind of monster who could not love her own child. Had David seen it? Was it *Jo* he had been thinking of when he had said they weren't ready?

18

'Joanne, where are you?'

'Why, where are you?' Jo answered in a tone neither she nor her mother had heard since her teenage years.

'I'm at the hospital – where I've just been told that you've discharged yourself.'

Jo was looking out of the nursery window, her gaze following the path leading from the house to the wrought iron gate. Of the small section of Beaumont Avenue she could see, the road glistened in afternoon sunshine that was only now strong enough to melt the morning frost. Occasionally her pulse quickened as she caught a glimpse of a passer-by who would inevitably do exactly that, pass by without a second glance.

'I need to be home,' she explained, knowing it was no explanation at all. She couldn't tell her mother how she felt completely out of her depth with the baby, how she felt she was drowning under the weight of the responsibility for a new life who needed intensive care and unconditional love, neither of which she felt qualified to give. She needed David and she had come home to wait for him because that was something she was expert at.

There was a sharp intake of breath, which gave Jo enough time to move the phone an inch away from her ear before Liz began her tirade. 'You need to be here, Joanne, with your son who is doing amazingly well but would do a lot better if his mother was caring for him and not a bunch of strangers.'

'Those strangers are qualified nurses who have been giving the baby the intensive care he needs. I'll keep going in every day, but there's no point me living at the hospital, Mum. All I've been doing for the past couple of days is expressing milk like a prize cow or changing his nappy when I'm allowed to get within an inch of him.'

'Nonsense,' Liz snapped. 'I've just been feeding him.'

'They let you hold him?' gasped Jo, immediately crushed that the nurses had judged the grandmother to be more capable than the mother.

'No but I dripped a little milk into his feeding tube to help the nurse. They wanted *you* there, we all do. Now don't be silly, come back to the hospital.'

Resting her head on the cold glass, Jo closed her eyes. 'I'm not running away,' she said carefully. 'I've had things to do. I've been in touch with the police and Mary Jenkins has put together a press release to let the world know that I've had the baby and that I can't so much as give him a name yet without his father around. It's just made the midday news on the radio. I *need* to be here – in case David comes home.'

There was a pause and then Liz sounded more amenable

when she said, 'Maybe you're right. He'll know you're in hospital and might think he can come back and clear you out. Did you ever get around to changing the locks?'

It was one of the few scenarios that Jo hadn't and wouldn't consider. She was simply trying to tempt David out of the shadows and she had already decided what she would say when he appeared. She wouldn't be angry with him; he would have his reasons for running away and she would listen. She would promise him anything if only they could go back to the way they were. He didn't need to be frightened; the baby was still in hospital and, if it came down to a choice, if he didn't want the baby to come home, then maybe that was for the best. There was surely a better, more worthy set of parents out there that would give their unnamed baby the love he needed. Jo was ready to consider anything, sacrifice anything, if only she could have David back where he belonged.

But before Jo could leap to her husband's defence, something outside caught her attention. There was a man on the other side of the road, partially obscured by a tree. She couldn't see his face and had no idea how old he might be, but he was about David's height and he was standing still, facing the house. Watching.

'It'll be fine, Mum, and I'll come back in later,' Jo said. 'I have to go now. I'll phone you when I'm there.'

The call was ended before Liz had a chance to respond and then Jo took a step away from the window so she couldn't be seen from the road. For one long, heart-stopping minute she didn't move and neither did the man. She was about to rush downstairs and into her husband's arms when the watcher stepped out of his hiding place.

When Jo flung the door open, he was already halfway up the path and jumped in surprise.

'I didn't think you'd be at home,' he said.

'So what the hell are you doing here, Steve?'

Her brother-in-law made a point of scanning the length and breadth of the house and garden. 'I was passing and thought I'd better check to make sure everything was OK. You can't be too careful these days.'

'You don't have a key, do you?' Jo asked, not even trying to hide her suspicion.

'No, of course not. I was only going to check the outside. I wasn't about to break in, Jo,' he said with a nervous laugh.

'Glad to hear it,' she replied and reluctantly let him into the house.

'Is the baby home then?'

'No, I'll be going back and forth to the hospital for a while, but I – I had to come home. The news is out that I've had the baby and I thought . . .'

'That David might turn up?'

'Do you think he will?' she asked, desperately. She stared intently at Steve, looking for the slightest hint that he knew more than he was telling. There was no denying he had helped immensely since David's disappearance but Jo didn't yet understand why. Was he making up for his brother's failures or was it guilt? And if it was guilt, then whose? Could it be that Steve was a puppet and his strings were being pulled by someone else?

'It's great that you and Mum have that reassurance that Dave is out there but he's been gone two months now, Jo.'

'What are you saying?' she demanded, her voice quaking.

'Please, if you know something, anything, tell me. Please, Steve.'

Holding up his hands, Steve said, 'I don't know where he is, Jo, I swear I don't. But I can't help thinking he must have made a new life for himself and that maybe you should too. I don't blame you for wanting to cling on to the hope that he's coming back but . . . I hate to say it, but maybe it's time to let go of that dream.'

As Steve returned her gaze, the ghostly similarities between Steve and her husband were enough to make Jo shudder but it was the last words he had spoken that made her soul quake. She had heard David say the exact same thing to her earlier that year, two months after she had conceived the child of which he was still unaware.

'What do you mean, let go of the dream?' she had demanded. She had been building up to telling him about the baby and couldn't put it off any longer. He had sent her an invitation request through Outlook to take two weeks' leave in October for a trip to America and, as they lay in bed that night, he had asked her why she hadn't accepted it. She had started off subtly, reminding him of the plans that had been on hold for too long, and she certainly hadn't been prepared for his response.

'Even talking about having a baby is causing friction between us,' he said. 'Imagine what it would be like if we had one.'

Jo stifled a laugh that was too close to a sob. 'I *am* imagining it, and it looks pretty damn good to me. What are you so frightened of, David?'

'Me! I'm afraid of me!' he confessed, his voice cutting through the darkness of their bedroom where they lay, side by side but not touching. 'Having a baby will change us and I don't want to lose what we have. I don't want to lose you, Jo.'

Jo could feel the heat of his body next to her and wanted to reach out and hold him but she could hear the tension in his voice. He was wound up so tightly he might snap in two if she touched him. But it wasn't so much her touch that she was afraid might break him, as it was what she had to confess. 'And I don't want to lose you,' she said. 'But I still don't understand why you think that would happen. Tell me, David. Make me understand. I know losing your dad changed your perspective on things, but I won't believe you've reached the point where you don't want kids at all.'

'He really screwed around with my head, Jo,' David admitted as he brought his hands up and began tugging at his hair. His breathing had become ragged and it took a while, but eventually he added, 'I wish I could give you what you want.'

Jo's stomach did a somersault and her pulse raced as she prepared to reveal her secret. 'You can, David. You already have,' she whispered softly.

David fell silent. He had stopped moving and Jo couldn't even hear him breathing. She pulled herself up on to one elbow and this time couldn't stop herself from reaching out. Her fingers sliced through the darkness in search of the connection she had lost. David's body tensed as Jo took hold of his hand, but he didn't resist when she pulled it towards her. She kissed his fingers, his wrist, trailing her lips up his arm then his neck. When she kissed his cheek it was salty with the tears that had been falling

211

silently and she wasn't so delusional to think they were tears of joy. She had never seen David cry before, not even at his dad's funeral and was so shocked that she pulled away.

'I'm sorry, David. I should have told you. I should have listened to you.'

'You're pregnant?'

Jo mumbled a reply that was enough to give David the confirmation he was clearly dreading.

'But you're still . . . We talked about it, but . . .' he said stumbling over his words until his thoughts caught up with him. 'When did you come off the pill, Jo?'

His voice was flat, devoid of emotion, and Jo felt a shiver run down her spine. 'Just after our trip to Paris.' David didn't respond and silence filled the growing void between them until she dared to ask a question of her own. 'Do you hate me?' she whispered.

Turning towards her, David lifted his hand to her face and discovered the tears slipping down her cheeks, too. 'No, never.'

'I know it's a bit of a shock but this is a good thing, David. It might not be a trip to America but it's going to be a new voyage of discovery for both of us,' she said in an attempt to wring out some of the joy that was missing from the announcement. 'I love you, David.'

He didn't say anything as he pulled her towards him. He kissed her lips so softly it was barely a kiss at all. Jo was holding her breath.

'And I love you,' he said.

But he had said little else that night and they had clung on to each other a little too desperately. She had torn his dreams from his grasp and replaced them with her own and now it was her turn to know what it was like to have life taken out of her control.

'Maybe you're right,' Jo said to Steve, trying to quell the nausea her memories had inspired. 'I should let go. I can't go back and change things, however much I'd like to.'

'Why don't you concentrate on getting the baby home?' Steve said. 'That's something you can do.'

'Is it?' Jo said. He had yet to see the look of terror on her face every time she came within two feet of her son.

'He's certainly got a decent pair of lungs on him,' Heather said. She had been working in France during the whole trauma of Baby Taylor's birth and it was the first time she had seen him since he had been born a week ago.

Jo was looking down at the squirming baby she was trying to subdue and could barely hear her friend's voice above the ear-piercing cries coming from her supposed bundle of joy. Although the baby was still in hospital, he had been moved out of special care and was undoubtedly going from strength to strength, while in stark contrast his mother could scarcely summon the energy or enthusiasm to leave the house to visit him.

She felt clumsy when she tried to pick him up, frustrated when he declined to be breastfed and a complete failure when he refused to settle in her arms. He cried and cried, then cried some more and the air of confidence Jo tried to assume each time she stepped into the hospital was stripped away within moments of her son being placed in her arms. Liz had been equally unimpressed with Jo's aptitude as a new mother and at one point it looked as if she was going to move into the hospital since Jo was still refusing to stay with him. Jo appeased her to some extent by spending more time with her son than she felt entirely comfortable with, but it was Steph who finally persuaded Liz to return home so she didn't miss out on the pre-Christmas rush at the shop. But before she left, Liz reassured her daughter that she could be back within two hours if needs be. It felt more like a threat than a promise.

Unlike Liz, the midwives had reassured Jo that it wasn't all second nature or maternal instinct, that every baby was different and that every new mum had to learn along the way. But when Jo handed her screaming son over to the nearest nurse and watched them soothe him within moments, she felt her fragile confidence being eroded further.

Jo felt the shadow of a midwife looming over her now. 'He's doing so well, isn't he? That jaundice has cleared up nicely and he's feeding much better. As long as he continues to put on weight then I'd say he'll be home in a couple of days. We wouldn't want him spending his very first Christmas in hospital and I'm sure Mum wouldn't want that either.'

Jo looked up, and with the last of her depleted strength, returned the midwife's beaming smile as if the news was exactly what she had been waiting for rather than dreading. The smile didn't reach her eyes, which were stinging with tears.

'He's ready but are you?' Heather whispered in Jo's ear. 'Do you want me to try for a while?'

The moment she was unburdened, Jo fought the urge to turn tail and run, not stopping until she had left the hospital, got in the car and sped over to Nelson's head office. That was the only place where the old Jo still existed, someone who was assertive, quick-witted, self-assured and confident. But these were attributes that were beyond her reach for now, not least because when she had last phoned Gary offering to come in for a few hours between hospital visits to help with the ongoing Employment Tribunal case, he had told her in no uncertain terms that she wasn't allowed to set foot on the premises unless it was a social call. With three months' exclusion ahead of her, Jo had no choice but to face what she suspected was going to be the biggest challenge of her life: convincing her son that she was worthy of his love.

'Was Max like this?' she asked her friend. 'I don't remember him crying this much.'

Heather put the baby up against her shoulder and as she rocked him from side to side his cries began to subside. 'You weren't there at three o'clock in the morning,' she said. 'I won't insult your intelligence by telling you it won't be tough, especially on your own. It's bad enough for me as a single parent with a six-year-old, God knows how I would have coped with a newborn on my own.' For a moment the rocking motion stopped as Heather realized this wasn't the best way to prepare her friend for the challenges ahead. She gave her an encouraging smile but Jo's expression remained fixed, her eyes unblinking and her face ashen.

'There will be times when you'll think you're not coping but you will. You'll get through it,' she promised softly. 'If I've learnt one thing from being a single mum it's that you need to be organized and plan ahead. It'll be a military operation every time you have to go out and then, of course, you won't be able to leave the house once it's past baby's bedtime, no nipping out for a pint of milk or a takeaway because you're too tired to cook. But if anyone's organized, it's you.' Heather stopped to kiss the top of the baby's head which was covered in a blue woollen bonnet. He was starting to drift off to sleep but continued to open his milky blue eyes and whimper as he fought against it. 'And I promise you there will be moments when he's fast asleep in your arms and you'll just breathe him in. It may not sound like much but it'll make all the hard work worth it.'

'If you say so.'

'I do. You're going to be a wonderful mum. I don't doubt it for a second.'

Jo wanted to tell Heather that she was trying to convince the wrong person. Baby Taylor was the one judging her and so far judging her badly.

19

Jo let the emptiness wrap around her. There had been a point earlier in the day when she was convinced there wasn't enough oxygen in the house to support all the people who had squeezed into it. She had felt the walls closing in around her and her body had tensed as her unwelcome guests flapped and fussed around her. She wanted to release the scream building up inside her, wanted to tell everyone to get the hell out of her house. And yet her face didn't give even the slightest suggestion of her inner turmoil; the gentle curve of the smile on her face lifted her eyes and the mask she had assumed was becoming such a permanent feature that it felt almost natural.

There was no mask now as Jo stood in the middle of the living room and let the empty spaces stretch the house back to its proper proportions. She closed her eyes and listened to the wind howling through the trees outside, which made the calm that had settled in the house all the more reassuring. Alone at last, she thought to herself, as she took a deep breath and opened her eyes. The house was a mess but she didn't mind: here was a problem she could solve and she immediately set about putting everything back in order.

From the kitchen she grabbed a bin bag and then went through each room gathering discarded wrapping paper and abandoned scraps of food. There were even a couple of empty beer cans amongst the debris of what had somehow become a party, even though none of the visitors had been invited. She had returned from the hospital with only her mum and dad and then the whole world had descended on her.

School had broken up so Steph and Lauren had nowhere else to be on a cold and wet Friday afternoon; Irene couldn't keep away and had brought along not only Sally and Steve but Luke too. When Heather heard what was happening, she rushed over to give Jo some moral support and of course she had no choice but to bring Max with her. Next the midwife arrived, and to top it all, Mary Jenkins had turned up to reassure Jo that even though David had yet to react to the birth of his son which had now made national news, they would be following up any leads from the public; leads that so far hadn't materialized – much like her husband.

Jo couldn't help wondering why on earth her house invaders didn't have better things to do two days before Christmas and she dropped enough hints to that effect. When that didn't work, she began to feign tiredness and eventually it was her midwife who made a firm suggestion that Jo should be given some space. Even her mum and dad were persuaded to start on the long journey home, although they were the last to leave.

But it was only when the mess had been cleared and

every surface wiped down or polished that Jo was ready to slump down on to the sofa where she intended to stay for as long as she possibly could, which was all of five minutes.

The noise that disturbed Jo's longed-for peace began as tiny gasps for air, followed by the gentle whisper of cotton as the tiny form on the other side of the room began to struggle against its covers. Jo held her breath and waited for the noise to settle but next came a pitiful mewl that made her skin crawl. Panic rose like a wave and the next gasp came from Jo as she struggled to draw air into her lungs while her chest tightened.

'Shush,' she said, her words a gentle hiss that were meant to replicate the sounds she had heard others use to appease her son but the noise she made had a hint of desperation that was unique to Jo. 'Please, shush.'

Rather than stand up, Jo pushed further back against the sofa, extending the distance between herself and the bassinet, dipping her body lower so she couldn't even see over its sides. The whimpering continued and became progressively louder and more urgent. Jo put her hands over her ears and closed her eyes tightly. When that didn't work, she jumped up but rather than run to her son, she rushed out of the room.

When she reached the dining room, Jo closed the door behind her. The baby's cries were muffled as she began to pace the floor. The midwives at the hospital had warned her it might feel a little overwhelming once she brought him home. There were no specialist nurses on hand at the touch of a button to take over his care or reassure Jo that they were both doing fine. It was up to her now to keep her son warm and safe and satiated. Feeding, changing, soothing; that's all there was to it, she told herself. It was hardly rocket science. The Jo Taylor of old would have thrived on such a challenge, but that old inner calm had deserted her and the person cowering in the kitchen from a nine-day-old baby was someone Jo didn't recognize.

Gripping the kitchen counter, Jo was determined to calm herself before the sense of panic overwhelmed her. She needed to believe she still had some control over her life. Feeding off her determination, she emptied her mind and took deep, cleansing breaths. To her surprise, her pulse began to slow as she eased the tension from her body. After a couple of minutes, she slowly stood up straight and held out one of her hands in front of her; the tremble was barely noticeable.

The baby's cries were heart-rending but Jo tried not to let them unsettle her as she returned to the living room. She set down the feeding bottle she had just warmed up before picking up the writhing bundle of cotton and flesh. With one hand under her son's head, the other supporting his padded bottom, Jo scrutinized the product of the love she had once shared with her husband. Her son's face was scrunched up and wrinkly and his eyes squeezed tightly shut with the effort of expelling each lungful of air in long, piercing screeches. How could one little baby be so beautiful and yet so terrifying, she asked herself as she lifted him on to her shoulder and began to rock him.

'This isn't exactly how I imagined it would be,' she said when it seemed as if he had quietened enough to hear her voice. 'I thought your dad would be here and that we would meld naturally into the perfect family. But he isn't and I still don't understand why, not really. It wasn't as if David didn't want to be a dad, he did! He was just too scared, I suppose, and I frightened him off and now you're left with me which I know you're not happy about.'

As the delicate bundle in her arms began to relax, so did Jo. 'And here's the thing, Baby Taylor – whose mum isn't even capable of picking a name for you – after destroying my marriage so I could become a mother, it turns out that I'm not mother material after all. I'm a fraud.' She had to clear her throat before adding, 'But I brought you into this mess and it's my job to make the best of it. I know I haven't done very well so far and that it's my fault you were born too early – I should have taken better care of both of us – but I promise I won't let you down again. All I ask is that you cut me some slack and who knows? Maybe one day you'll forgive me and I'll be able to forgive myself.'

Jo lifted the baby off her shoulder so they were face to face. 'Hello, sweetheart,' she said, 'I'm your mum.'

The baby began squirm as if he objected to the idea. Jo rose above the slight and made herself comfortable in the armchair before attempting to plug the source of more whimpering with a feeding bottle. His face contorted as he stubbornly refused the teat she was attempting to thrust into his mouth. She was still supposed to make some feeble attempt at breastfeeding but she knew from experience he would reject that too and there were some battles she was happy to concede. Persevering with the bottle, Jo waited until the first cry escaped and when the baby's mouth opened wide, she inserted the teat with perfect precision. For a moment it looked as if he would suckle but then he broke free. What her son didn't know was that Jo could be stubborn too. She was prepared to repeat the process for as long as it took. Ten minutes later only a single ounce of milk had been drained from the bottle, most of which was dribbling down the side of the baby's cheek leaving a damp puddle on Jo's T-shirt, but rather than giving in to the panic that threatened to consume her again, Jo had stiffened in firm resolve. She would not be defeated by her son.

Before continuing with round two, Jo set about changing him. Baby supplies had been heaped behind one of the armchairs and Jo concentrated her mind on thinking up new storage options rather than looking at the baby's face which was bright red, the heat of his anger burning through her confidence.

She tried putting him back on her shoulder but his body was so rigid that he felt more like a plastic doll than flesh and blood. 'I know you have a right to hate me, but I'm doing the best I can. Please, sweetheart,' she said through gritted teeth that made the term of endearment sound anything but.

Jo wasn't sure how it happened, but when the baby was sleeping contentedly in his bassinet again, she felt a huge sense of relief and not a little pride. She hadn't given into her emotions and she had also fought off an anxiety attack. But it had been a hard-fought battle and one that had left her utterly exhausted. She hoped it would get easier, because she didn't know how long she could keep fighting him – or how long she could wait before giving up on the idea that she could ever love him as a real mother should . . .

* * *

Forced cheer blared from the radio as Jo set about cleaning her already pristine kitchen. As she mopped the floor she fell into the kind of robotic trance that had seen her through the first twenty-four hours at home with her new charge. She and her son seemed to have reached an understanding. If Jo could feed and change him and otherwise see to his needs without holding or pawing him too much, the baby would give her a temporary reprieve from motherly duties.

During one such break, Jo was so intent on adding another layer of sparkle to the house that the first knock at the door didn't register in her consciousness. When it became more persistent, her heart began to hammer out an echo. She had tortured herself often enough with visions of David appearing on her doorstep and what better time than on Christmas Eve? It was their favourite time of year and they had always stayed in together, sharing little pre-Christmas presents and watching cheesy films. In her imaginings, she would fling open the door ready to beat her fist against his chest while he would prepare to explain himself, but they would do neither. They would lock eyes without saying a word until the tears obscured her vision and then, terrified that he was disappearing again, Jo would wrap her arms and, for that matter, her legs around him and hold on as if her life depended on it.

Jo held on to that fantasy as she skidded across the wet kitchen floor, shoving dining chairs out of the way and bumping into the wall as she lunged towards the hall. Momentum alone kept her body moving forward long after her legs and her heart came to a juddering halt. She stumbled the last few feet to the door where she had spied the silhouette of a woman.

223

'I wasn't sure if you'd be in,' Kelly whispered. 'Am I disturbing you?'

Jo forced her features into the now familiar mask and smiled. 'No, of course not. Come in.'

With an armful of gift bags and a bouquet of flowers Kelly had to squeeze through the door that Jo was loath to open wide. 'You may have escaped the dreaded baby shower, but I come bearing gifts from everyone.'

'It's lovely to see you but it really could have waited, Kelly. I'd hate to think I'm disturbing your Christmas,' Jo said as she took the proffered bags. Her cheeks ached with the effort of the forced smile.

'It's no trouble and if it wasn't me then it would have been Gary.'

Jo obliged Kelly by agreeing she'd had a lucky escape. She didn't sound at all convincing but then she didn't need to be, Kelly wasn't paying attention. There had been an eruption of giddiness as her guest spotted the sleeping baby. 'Has he got a name yet?'

'No, still working on it,' Jo said cheerily enough even though the question was becoming almost as tiring as caring for the baby itself. When her mother rang, and she rang regularly, she started barking names down the phone before Jo had a chance to say hello. But none of the names felt right, and they never would without David's input.

'There's a baby names book in one of the bags,' Kelly said helpfully as she continued to coo over Baby Taylor. 'Oh, he's so tiny! I'd be so frightened of breaking him if I tried picking him up.'

Jo looked into the bassinet. She was afraid too. 'I've only just put him down so I'd rather leave him sleeping, if you don't mind. How about we go into the kitchen and I'll make you a hot drink while you tell me what's been happening at work?' She was hoping that talking about the one place where she didn't feel like a fraud would lift her spirits and make her smiles less forced, but Kelly wasn't there to boost Jo's ego.

'You're not going to believe this,' she began, leaning back in her chair at the dining table as she watched Jo make the drinks. Her chest was swelling with pride. 'We won the O'Dowd case.' Kelly took a moment to revel in her success before adding, 'I know you said we were up against it and we probably wouldn't win but we did, Jo.'

Jo's smile hid the grimace but only just. 'There was no "we" in it, Kelly. You and Gary deserve to take full credit. Well done.'

'Thanks, Jo, that's so nice of you to say so.'

'So is there anything else I should know about? Anything you need to talk through?' Jo said in an effort to reassert herself as her assistant's mentor and guide. There was a note of desperation in her voice.

'Nothing you need worry about, certainly not on Christmas Eve.' The smug look on Kelly's face had been replaced with one of sympathy. 'I suppose tomorrow is going to be really hard for you, thinking how things might have been if David was still around or worse still wondering what he's getting up to and with who.'

'I was trying *not* to think about it,' Jo said, wishing it had been Gary visiting.

Oblivious to Jo's irritation, Kelly scanned the room with a critical eye. If it wasn't for the baby equipment lined up carefully along the counter, the kitchen wouldn't have looked out of place in a showroom. It was all very tidy and distinctly un-festive. 'You're not spending Christmas here on your own, are you? Jo, if you're stuck for somewhere to go you can always come with me to my mum's. I'm sure she could squeeze an extra person around the dinner table and if anyone looks like they need feeding up then it's you. You're the first new mum I've seen who actually looks like she needs to put *on* weight.'

'I'm fine,' Jo said tersely. 'I'm going to my sister Steph's and then we're travelling up to the Lakes on Boxing Day to see my parents. This is the calm before the storm.'

With perfect timing, the sound of a waking baby trickled through from the other room.

'Sounds like he needs another feed,' Jo said as if she knew exactly what her baby needed from the merest grumble. She took a prepared feeding bottle from the fridge and dropped it into the bottle warmer. 'I won't be a minute.'

In the living room, Jo whispered into her son's ear as she picked him up. 'Please, little one, I need you to work with me on this. I'm begging you not to make me look like a complete incompetent, not in front of Kelly.'

To Jo's surprise, the baby was indeed hungry. He guzzled his bottle and didn't immediately object when Jo let Kelly take over for a while but it didn't take long before he was rebelling against another awkward embrace.

'I'm really not comfortable with this,' Kelly said, panic blooming on her cheeks as the newborn began to wriggle, redden and refuse his feed. For a terrifying moment, Jo thought she was going to drop the baby and her heart leapt into her mouth.

'Here, I'd better take him.'

226

With the baby safely back in her arms, Jo began to go through the motions of trying to soothe him. Kelly looked on in awe as Jo eased the grumbling infant back to sleep as if it was the most natural thing in the world.

'I don't think I'm ever going to have kids,' Kelly said.

Jo wanted to say there was nothing to it but the lie stuck in her throat.

'Thank you, sweetheart,' Jo said after she had seen Kelly to the door. Baby Taylor remained fast asleep and completely unaware of how he had mended his mother's tattered confidence, although Jo was under no illusion that it was anything but a temporary repair.

Jo would have been happy to avoid Christmas altogether and even Lauren's teenage histrionics over dinner did little to distract her from her woes for long enough to enjoy the normality of the day. She wanted to be at home where she could be her usual dysfunctional self rather than the smiling automaton who satisfied the concerns of family and friends. More importantly, she wanted to be at home, just in case . . .

But there was one more person she was obliged to visit before she could resume her vigil. Her only consolation was that it was the only other place where David's returning footsteps might be heard. If he wasn't ready to come home to her, then maybe he could find the courage to visit his mum.

'All on your own?' Jo asked as Irene welcomed her into the cosy little house that was a stark contrast to the one Jo was desperate to return to.

Irene's living room looked like an explosion in a tinsel

factory. There were enough Christmas decorations to cover a house twice the size, remnants of Christmases past that obscured the clutter normally on display. The one exception was David's photograph, which had an uninterrupted view of Jo's arrival from its prime position on the mantelpiece.

Jo had the baby carrier hooked over her arm and the sleeping baby drew Irene like a magnet. Her eyes barely left him as she spoke to Jo. 'Steve and the family came around for Christmas dinner but they didn't stay long. Luke has a new Xbox and he couldn't wait to get home to play on it with his dad. It can do all kinds of things, you can even control it by just waving at it!'

'I didn't know you were a techno geek,' Jo said. 'I wouldn't know one game console from another.'

'Hmm,' Irene answered, avoiding Jo's eye as she took the carrier from her and put it on the floor so she could free her grandson from his restraints.

'Irene?'

'I know because I was the one who bought it, but please don't tell Sally.'

Jo sighed. 'How is Steve ever going to learn to manage his own financial affairs if you keep bailing him out? David wouldn't and neither should you. He shouldn't be buying things he can't afford.'

'I know,' Irene agreed, 'but who else do I have to spend my money on?'

The slumbering baby complained briefly when she picked him up but Irene rocked him back to sleep with ease. 'Oh, don't go complaining, my little one. I have every intention of spoiling you too.'

Jo took a seat and was immediately aware of David watching her from the mantelpiece. 'Making up for your sons' failings?' she asked.

'You expect them to give you sleepless nights when they're babies, but not when they're in their thirties. I don't know where I went wrong, Jo.'

'Men in their thirties are old enough to take responsibility for their own actions,' Jo said. She was looking over at the mantelpiece, not at the image of David but searching for another treasure of Irene's that seemed to be missing. 'You and Alan gave the boys the best start in life so they have no excuse. Alan was the perfect role model for a father. A natural.'

'We were very happily married,' Irene replied in a way that suggested she was only telling half the story.

Jo eyed her beadily. 'You've taken down his photograph, haven't you?'

Irene settled on the sofa next to Jo then kissed the baby's head, leaving her lips resting gently on his scalp as she summoned the courage to speak. 'I think I might be as angry with Alan as you are with David.'

Jo's eyes widened and she couldn't hide the shock. 'Why?'

Irene's gaze was fixed on the exact spot where her husband's photograph should have been. 'I loved Alan. We had our ups and downs but we had a wonderful life together or at least I thought we did.' She paused only briefly as she considered how much to reveal. 'But you might as well know, in those last few months he said some hurtful things to me, Jo. The doctor said the changes to his personality were a result of the stroke so I put up with the abuse and tried not to take it to heart.'

'And you shouldn't,' Jo said. 'He was being pumped full of drugs too, wasn't he? He wouldn't have known what he was saying.'

'It still hurts to know that his dying words to me and his children were so full of hatred and bile.'

'Why, what did he say?' demanded Jo incredulously.

As she waited for Irene to respond, Jo's eyes were drawn to the twinkling fairy lights on the Christmas tree in the corner of the room although she was less aware of the flashes of light than she was the darkness that separated them. Of course she had known of the struggles the family were going through during Alan's illness but she had witnessed very little first-hand. Her father-in-law had kept everyone except immediate family away and that included Jo. She was aware he had become angry and depressed as he battled to come to terms with his life being cut short, but she hadn't quite appreciated how that anger might have been directed at his family. What hadn't David told her?

'I don't think I could repeat the last thing he said and certainly for the last two years, I've tried to forget it. I've tried to accept the doctor's explanations because I had absolute faith in my husband's love for me,' Irene continued.

'And now?'

'What if we were both wrong? What if David had the courage to do what his father couldn't, admit that he's not a family man and refuse to be tied down? Look at the pig's ear Steve makes of being a father. What if it's a family trait?'

Irene went on to tell Jo some, if not all, of the hurtful things that Alan had said over the course of his illness; things that Irene had put to the back of her mind because they

230

were spoken by someone who bore no resemblance to the man she had loved since she was seventeen. This imposter had deconstructed their thirty-odd year marriage piece by piece and had become obsessed with the life he could have led if he hadn't been weighed down with responsibility. Jo imagined David being forced to listen to the same kind of thing.

'He was fighting death, but he still found the energy to describe the life I'd stolen from him,' Irene said.

'The things he would have experienced instead of relying on documentaries on TV to show him what he was missing out on,' Jo said as if reading from the crumpled piece of paper she had found stuffed down a sock.

There was gasp. 'David told you what his dad said to him? He swore he never would, he was too ashamed.'

'No, he didn't tell me, though I wish he had,' Jo said. She glanced down at the sleeping baby whose only given name so far was the one his father had called him. 'I found a note he had written to his dad and I was never meant to see it. He talked about children being a *burden*.'

Irene picked up on the intonation and spoke the words her daughter-in-law had carefully edited, if only in a whisper. '*A fucking burden*. That's what he called David and Steve. That was his parting shot to them, Jo. They were his last words.'

'And David called the baby little FB. A coincidence, do you think?'

Irene's body was shaking and the tears welling in her eyes obscured her view of the missing photograph. 'I don't know, Jo. I don't believe David would be that heartless, but . . . I can't be sure of anything any more. All of those

231

treasured memories I had of Alan and our life together, the ones that were meant to keep me warm on dark, lonely nights, they've all been sullied. I can't look back without wondering if it was real or if it was an act. Was my marriage a complete sham? Was David doing the same to you?'

Neither woman spoke for the longest time. They were both edging towards the same conclusion, one that would write off both their marriages and destroy what little self-worth still survived. Jo was staring at the Christmas tree and her eyes flitted from one branch to the next as she searched out anything that would lead to a more palatable truth. There were memories attached to every bauble hanging from the tree but it was the lopsided smile on a tattered snowman that brought back to life one in particular.

It had been Luke's first Christmas and he would have been about nine months old at the time and it was also the year before Alan's stroke would poison his and his son's view of fatherhood. While the little boy's parents could be heard arguing about something and nothing in the kitchen, David preoccupied Luke with some fantastical tale about a snowman that the baby surely didn't understand but giggled just the same. They had been standing right there by the tree, Luke safe and secure in David's arms and, as the story drew to a close, the little boy had started drifting off to sleep. David's eyes were also heavy but only with pure devotion as he glanced over to Jo and mouthed, 'I want one just like this.'

Alan had been there too, and as David crossed the room, he accidently stood on the train set his dad had been busily constructing on the floor; a train set he said was for his grandson but everyone knew was for him. Chaos had erupted as Alan yelled at David for not looking where he was going and then Luke woke up and began to cry. Sally appeared soon after bringing Steve and their unfinished argument into the living room but Irene had simply looked over to Jo, the only other person in the room who had remained calm, and they had shared a contented smile. It had been a typically raucous if not entirely perfect Taylor Christmas.

Holding on to that memory, Jo wasn't sure what she was going to say until she started saying it. 'Yes, there were arguments, but with David and me it was mostly over silly things because we both liked to have the last word. But the man I remember *loved* being part of this family,' she said with a passion that frightened her. Her mouth was dry and her pulse raced as she stopped resisting where her heart was taking her. 'I don't care about the money or what he's been up to and I think he'd know that I would forgive him anything – eventually. He should be here, Irene. He *loved* Christmas and he *loved* coming over to be with you and all the family. Don't you remember? Alan was the same.'

Irene had followed Jo's gaze and strained her eyes as she searched through the tinsel-covered branches for her own memories. Then she smiled. 'Alan dressed up in my red satin pyjamas one year and tried to convince the boys he was Santa Claus,' she said with a chuckle. 'The daft sod split the pyjama bottoms and terrified the kids.'

Feeling all the more certain of her convictions, Jo said, 'They weren't men who resented family, they thrived on it. You can't spend seven years of your life keeping up that kind of pretence and you certainly can't spend *thirty* years doing it. They loved their families. They *loved* us.'

Irene shuddered as she too felt the goose bumps that were prickling Jo's skin. 'So what would stop him coming back home?' she whispered. There was desperation and fear in her voice when she added, 'I'd know if something bad had happened. I'm his mum. I'd know it in my heart.'

'And what is your heart telling you now, Irene?' Jo asked, even though she wasn't sure she was ready for the answer.

Irene kissed the baby's head again before she spoke. A tear trickled down her face and splashed his cheek. As Baby Taylor squirmed, he managed to wipe the tear away with his tiny, mitten-clad hand while his grandmother lifted her head and took a deep breath. 'It's telling me my sons are both going through a stubborn and selfish phase. It's like they've reverted back to being toddlers,' she said flippantly. They had both come too close to resurrecting their worst fears that would prove far more painful to face than betrayal and desertion and it was Irene who led the retreat. 'And it's also telling me that this child deserves a better name than FB.'

For once, Jo didn't object to opening up the never-ending debate about a name. 'I know he does, but the only names I ever remember David mentioning were Barry and Archibald. I think I actually prefer FB.'

Irene's broad smile gave her voice a certain lilt. 'Archibald was my father's name.'

Jo had thought she was beyond being shocked for one day but her jaw dropped. 'David wasn't joking then? It actually meant something to him?'

Very carefully, Irene turned the baby until he was facing them both. He yawned lazily and his flickering eyelids chased away the last of the shadows that had been creeping into the room. 'What do you think?' she asked. 'Does he suit it?'

Jo looked down at her baby's cherubic face but when her heart reached out, it yearned for David rather than their son. Why hadn't he told her what had been going on with his dad? She could have helped him work things through; she would have done things differently. Where was he? Why wasn't he here on Christmas Day?

'Well?' Irene asked when Jo still hadn't replied.

'Welcome to the world, Archie,' Jo whispered as her thoughts turned away from the past that scared her to a future that terrified her.

20

After Christmas came New Year and soon after, Jo's birthday which wasn't spent dancing around a bonfire in Iceland but at home, pretending not to listen out for approaching footsteps. And when there were no occasions left that she was obliged to celebrate, Jo was allowed to settle into as much of a routine as the baby would allow, although it felt fair to say they coexisted in the same house rather than lived together. She was still waiting for that blissful moment Heather had described where she would make that elusive connection with her son – with Archie – but although she could remember that warm rush of love when he had been born, the guilt she harboured over his conception and then his premature birth was like a dam that grew more impenetrable by the day. She loved him but she wouldn't allow herself the luxury of that love. She didn't deserve it and she had an unshakeable conviction that Archie knew that too.

Following the sage advice of family and health visitors, Jo kept Archie to a strict night-time routine of bath, bottle and bed. So after immersing her complaining son in warm water she proceeded to dry and dress him. True to form, Archie refused to co-operate and Jo could feel the heat rising in her cheeks during the struggle. The flush was undoubtedly a reaction to her exertions but the merest suggestion of a panic attack brought forth the anxiety anyway. As soon as she had fastened the last press stud on his pyjama sleeping bag, she picked the baby up and tried to soothe him but Archie fought against her. Her fraught attempt at a cuddle gave neither of them comfort and her heart was hammering by the time she put him down in his bassinet with a sigh of defeat that was all but drowned out by her son's wails.

She hurried into the kitchen to warm up a bottle. It took longer than she would like but she refused to close the kitchen door, she needed to hear her son crying. The sound was a flail to her own skin, but Archie had every right to punish her for being the incompetent mother who had brought him into this miserable world.

When she had everything ready, Jo picked up the bassinet complete with wailing child. With practised ease, she folded the stand and took everything she needed upstairs where she set the bassinet up again next to her bed. Finally there was nothing left to do but pick up her son again. He was bright red with fury and she knew from painful experience that there was little point in trying to feed him. She rested him on her shoulder and, after pacing the floor for five minutes without success, she found herself drawn to the nursery that he wasn't due to occupy for a few months yet.

'Please, sweetheart, shush,' she begged, patting his back in a slow, steady rhythm that belied her growing agitation.

The baby's cries grew louder. 'Please, Archie, please shush so I can feed you.'

Jo looked at the cot with its handmade quilt and was tempted to lay him down on it but she was terrified that if she did, she might not have the courage to pick him up again. Instead, she reached over and found herself winding up the mobile. She could barely hear the music above her son's cries.

Next, she went over to a small side table and switched on a lamp. Its warm light created sunflower-shaped shadows that danced across the wall but it was the piece of paper lying on the table that drew Jo's attention. It was Archie's birth certificate, which had found a temporary home in the nursery, perhaps because she hadn't felt ready to slot it into the rest of her life just yet.

She had been to register Archie's birth on her own and along with the baby's name, the registrar had recorded those of both his parents. She stared down at David's name in print. Would he approve? Or would he want the father's details to have remained missing, much like the man himself? Maybe he would prefer to rip the piece of paper up completely so they could start again.

Still struggling to believe such things of the husband she had adored, Jo tore her eyes away from the certificate and concentrated on her wailing son. She sat down on the rocking chair in the corner of the room, a new acquisition from one of her dad's shopping excursions. Her mum had made the cushioned seat to match the sunflower theme perfectly.

Jo began to rock Archie back and forth, the long, sweeping motion of the chair intended to relax mother and child but her tentative movements couldn't disguise her desperation and the smooth rocking quickly became disjointed and jerky. Her breathing was ragged and her ribs ached from the pounding of her heart. 'Please,' she whispered through dried, parched lips.

She wondered what David would make of her feebleness. He had been good at helping her rationalize her fears and chase away her anxieties, but her demons had never been so terrifying or so fierce. Even he would have struggled to help her conquer them now. Still, he wouldn't have left her to deal with them on her own, she told herself as she squeezed her eyes shut and imagined him appearing behind her and whispering in her ear . . .

'You can do this, Jo,' he said.

Jo stopped rocking and for a moment at least, Archie's cries eased. She could feel David's arms slip around them both, feel his breath on her cheek as he told her, 'No, keep moving. Rock him back and forth, slowly does it.'

She pushed her toes into the floor and the chair tipped gently backwards before coming forward again. Back and forth, back and forth she went in a steady rhythm that she and Archie both relaxed into. Even Jo's breathing and her pulse began to slow.

'Why don't you try to feed him now?'

Jo did as she was bidden and so did Archie. The sense of victory warmed her heart even as she felt David's arms slip away. She opened her eyes to find the room achingly empty. Above the sound of Archie's steady gulps, the music was still playing and Jo allowed the lyrics to float across her mind.

'I still love you, David,' she whispered. 'You are my sunshine and I need it back. I need you back.'

Archie's eyelids flickered open at the sound of her voice.

He blinked twice, his gaze never leaving hers as his lids grew heavier and he drifted back to sleep. It was the barest connection but it was enough to make her smile again. He had looked at her and he hadn't cried.

When January slipped into February, Irene suggested that it might be a good idea for her to get in some practice looking after Archie. She hadn't expected Jo to accept the offer so readily, but arrangements were quickly made to drop the baby off for a few hours one Saturday afternoon. There was a part of Jo that felt nervous about leaving Archie with someone else after weeks of being his sole carer, but in her heart she knew that the baby would be no worse, and possibly better off, with his grandmother.

As she sat in a small café looking out on to the high street, Jo was thinking of David. No, not thinking, that was the wrong word. She was *looking* for him, deliberately choosing a table with a view of the outside world so she could scan the faces of passers-by. She wondered if she would ever stop watching and waiting.

Tearing herself away from her hopeless search, she picked up a spoon and started to make shapes in the foam floating on her cappuccino, but David followed her in her thoughts. She breathed in coffee-scented steam and recalled the times they had sat here together. The Neighbourhood Café was only a few miles from their home and after a long walk to one of the nearby parks they would call in for brunch as their reward. She would have a healthy granola while David would indulge in a full English breakfast with extra bacon, knowing Jo would steal it from him.

There was a blast of icy air as the door opened and

when Jo looked up she fully expected to see David standing there in front of her, his beaming smile like a beacon in the darkness.

'I'm not late, am I?' Simon panted as he shrugged off his jacket and took the seat opposite Jo.

'Have you been running?'

Simon looked sheepish. 'I was in work this morning and got a bit delayed.'

Above the smell of coffee, Jo detected aftershave. 'You didn't have to get changed on my account.'

'I wouldn't want to turn up on a hot date smelling of dust and mortar,' he quipped then immediately began to squirm. 'Sorry, that was a stupid thing to say. I didn't mean anything by it. It was completely inappropriate. Sorry. Stupid of me. I'm so sorry, Jo.' When he finally stopped blustering, Jo was smiling at him.

'Yes, I might have been offended if your own reaction hadn't been quite so funny. Thank you.'

'What for?'

'For making me smile. It doesn't happen very often,' she said but then her eyes narrowed. 'But just so you know, I didn't get you here under any pretext. I still love my husband whether he deserves it or not.'

Simon lifted his hand in surrender. 'I didn't for a minute think you had any ulterior motives. If I did, I wouldn't have come out with that smart remark, honestly. And congratulations by the way, or did I say that already in my ramblings? Is the baby doing well?'

'He's doing just fine,' Jo told him, ignoring a tiny pang of guilt for the relief she had felt when she had handed him over to Irene.

While Simon placed an order for fresh coffees, Jo took in her surroundings. The café had once been a grocer's shop and it still held on to remnants of its previous life. The Victorian tiles on the walls were partly obscured by shelving that held tributes to the past rather than the wares that would once have been proudly on display. She could make out the faded lettering that clung to the window above the shop entrance, a telephone number that would no longer be answered . . . the parallels with her own life were painfully clear to her.

'So, you want to know what David and I talked about?' asked Simon, his earlier embarrassment now forgotten although the blush lingered on his cheeks.

Jo nodded tentatively. She knew that David had visited Simon only a couple of weeks before he went missing. The two men drank in the same pub and David had been tasked with passing on the best wishes of all the regulars as well as their colleagues, although Jo was more interested in what else her husband might have said. She wished she could be certain that he had disappeared of his own accord but there remained a niggling doubt that was based on nothing more than the belief she and Irene clung to that David was a decent and loving man, a doubt that Simon might be able to add weight to.

'You mentioned that David told you how much he was looking forward to having the baby.'

'Yeah, he was quite excited about it – you'd just been for the scan.'

'And he didn't seem scared about it at all? He didn't say anything that might explain why he left?'

Simon was shaking his head. 'No, he was determined to be a good dad. If he was bothered about anything, it was about that brother of his. He was frustrated that Steve wasn't facing up to his own responsibilities, which isn't exactly news to me and I'm sure it's not to you. I don't know Steve that well but whenever I bumped into them with that little boy of his, it was always David looking after him. To the casual observer, you would swear he was the dad. David was a natural which makes it so hard to believe he could have left you.'

There was a moment's pause as the waitress arrived with two cups of coffee and removed Jo's lukewarm cappuccino. 'I've lost track of the number of times people have told me that David wouldn't do this, that he wouldn't leave me, but all the evidence suggests that's exactly what happened,' Jo said and then proceeded to outline the case for the prosecution, everything except how Jo had trapped him – there were limits to how much she was prepared to share with all but close family and friends.

'It couldn't have been someone else at the cash machine?'

'Wearing David's coat? A Nelson's one?'

'It's not unique,' Simon offered.

'But his pin number is. And let's not forget his passport going missing.'

'Could someone have taken it?'

'You have no idea how spotless I keep my house,' Jo said. 'Believe me, I would know if anyone had sneaked in to take it.'

Simon rubbed his hand against his forehead as he tried to make sense of it all. Jo watched, almost enjoying the look of confusion and frustration on someone else's face instead of her own. 'So you know he left, you just don't know why,' he concluded.

'And that's the part that's tearing me up inside,' Jo confessed and the crackle of emotion in her voice took them both by surprise. She could feel her pulse starting to race and put her hand over her chest to steady her breathing. 'I don't believe it's enough to say he was simply scared of becoming a father, that just doesn't wash, does it?' When Simon shook his head, she continued, 'Maybe he did leave me, maybe he *is* out there living off the money he's taken from his account while he sorts his head out or his problems out or whatever it was that made him leave, but Archie is almost two months old now and the David I know would have been in touch, he would have come home. If it was that simple.'

Jo waited for Simon to offer a theory of his own but he could only shrug.

'Could he have been . . .' she began but was too afraid to finish her sentence. Her hand was still on her chest and she almost had to push the next words out. 'Do you think he was suicidal?'

Simon's reply was slow and measured. 'I've seen suicidal, Jo and that's not what it looks like.'

'Sorry,' Jo said.

There was a moment's awkwardness but then there was a flicker of a memory that passed like a shadow across Simon's face and Jo leapt on it. 'You've remembered something, haven't you?'

'He mentioned his dad, something about him being depressed,' Simon said although he looked to Jo for confirmation.

'He had a stroke and died a few months later. What did David say exactly?'

244

Simon scratched his head as he wracked his brain. 'It was only a passing comment; he knew I was on anti-depressants and wanted to know if I'd had any side effects.'

'And?'

'I told him that other than feeling like I'd been dropped into a vat of syrup, not much else, not that I noticed at least. Is it important?'

Jo had been leaning forward, desperate to hear the one piece of information that would make everything else fit. This wasn't it and she let her shoulders sag. 'His dad changed in those last couple of months. He said things that made his family challenge everything they thought they knew about him, and about themselves. The stroke could have affected his personality but I suspect David was trying to work out if the cocktail of drugs he was on could have played their part too . . . Anything that might give him some reassurance that the things his dad said in those last months, what he claimed to think about his family, wasn't true.'

'Sorry, I don't think I gave him that reassurance.'

Jo tried to smile. 'You have nothing to apologize for. You were dealing with your own problems. You've come a long way in the last few months, Simon.'

'And there's still a long way to go. I don't fool myself that it's all behind me, not yet, probably not ever, but today is a good day.'

As he spoke, Simon didn't break eye contact and she felt somehow envious. He had fought his battles and come through the other side while she had barely begun to understand, let alone defeat, the invisible enemies her mind conjured up to send her into a blind panic.

'How are you coping?' he asked as if he already knew the answer.

'I have good days,' she said with a weak smile.

'And today?'

The smile faltered. Today she had escaped motherhood for a few hours and she had thought she would savour every moment but she felt even more bereft than she had become accustomed to. If she didn't know better, she would say she missed Archie. 'Today will be another day I have to get through without David and without answers.'

'I wish I could have been of more help.'

Jo took a last gulp of coffee. 'Oh, don't worry about it. Every time I churn up new theories it only ever muddies the water but I have to keep trying,' she said, trying not to let her disappointment show. 'Do you mind if I make a move? I told Irene I wouldn't be long.'

'Of course,' Simon said and then went to say something else, stopped himself, but then said it anyway. 'He couldn't wait to be a dad, Jo. That's the part I don't understand.' He laughed softly to himself. 'He couldn't wait to find out if the baby would have a dimple like him.'

Jo had already stood up and when she shrugged on her coat she felt another layer of guilt weigh her down. She had looked at her son's face and seen nothing more than a crying, demanding baby who was intent on rejecting her. She hadn't seen the suggestion of a dimple in the middle of Archie's chin; she hadn't even been looking.

Jo hung around by the exit while, at his insistence, Simon paid the bill and then they both stepped out into the cold afternoon that was already draining of colour and light.

'Are you all right?' Simon asked when he realized Jo had come to a sudden halt just outside the door.

'Sorry,' she said, blinking her eyes in disbelief. She had been looking for David as always but had caught sight of someone else. 'Do you see the young girl over there with ginger hair, the one arm in arm with that boy? Well, she's my niece, and having spoken to my sister only a couple of hours ago, I know for a fact she's supposed to be over at a friend's house cramming for her mocks. And by friend, I mean *girl* friend.'

'Young love, eh?'

Jo laughed and considered, only briefly, phoning Steph to tell tales on her niece. 'Yes, young love,' she agreed.

When she and Simon parted there were no formal hand-shakes; he felt more like a friend than a colleague now and the hug seemed natural, far more natural than the butterflies that started to build in her stomach as she walked back to the car. She knew it was ridiculous to feel so nervous about picking Archie back up; she tried to remind herself that she was his mother, but another voice asked if she would ever feel worthy of such a title.

When her mobile began to ring and Irene's name appeared, Jo was half-hoping to be told that the baby was fast asleep and she should stay out longer. But at first, Irene's ramblings were unintelligible.

'What's wrong? Oh, God, Irene, is it Archie?' Jo demanded.

She could feel the searing rush of panic rising through her body, her mind collapsing in on itself as she waited for Irene to draw enough breath to speak. In those painful milliseconds while she prepared to hear the worst she quickly concluded that if she was about to lose her son as well as her husband, then her life was over. She couldn't come back from that.

Jo's body ached from the physical effort of fighting off the panic attack. She held her body taut and forced herself to breathe slowly and deeply as she drove the three miles to her mother-in-law's house where she found Archie sleeping peacefully in his bassinet. She had been able to drag enough information from Irene on the phone to reassure herself that the baby was safe – the latest Taylor crisis had something to do with Steve going missing – but as soon as she had hung up, the desire to hold her son was overwhelming and surprisingly strong enough to silence her doubts and insecurities about motherhood. She had driven to Irene's clinging on to that feeling, her knuckles white as she gripped the wheel.

But before Jo could satisfy her own needs, the trembling figure of her mother-in-law demanded her attention. It was barely two hours since she'd dropped Archie off with her and the change was remarkable. 'Tell me what's happened,' Jo asked softly.

Irene grabbed Jo's hand and squeezed the life out of it as she made her sit down next to her on the sofa. Jo stole a glance towards the bassinet but she was too low down to catch even a glimpse of her son.

'I haven't seen Steve since Tuesday, Jo, when he came over to see if he could fix the back fence,' Irene said as she struggled to resurrect the details of the last time she had seen her youngest son, knowing painfully well how precious that memory might prove to be. 'And now he's gone, just like David.'

Although Jo was at a loss to understand exactly what had sparked Irene's sudden panic, she couldn't help wondering if this new development might be a positive thing rather than the awful news Irene feared. What if the two brothers had been in league together all along? What if Steve was about to leave a fresh trail that would lead all the way to David? 'Have you spoken to him at all since then?'

'He phoned yesterday to say he'd call in at the weekend,' she said. 'Oh, why is this happening to us, Jo? Wasn't losing David bad enough? I couldn't bear to lose them both.'

With what little feeling was left in her fingers, Jo gave her mother-in-law's hand a squeeze. 'It won't come to that,' she said. It felt strange being the one offering consolation this time. A long list of platitudes came to mind but she knew only too well that they would do no good, so Jo held her tongue and concentrated on gathering the facts. 'What did Sally say? When did she last see him?'

'He stormed off at lunchtime,' she said. 'You know how difficult their relationship's been lately. One of them was bound to snap eventually.'

'Lunchtime?' Jo asked as she extracted her hand from Irene's grip of iron. 'He's only been missing since *lunchtime*?' This was the one key fact that Irene had failed to mention before. 'So, let me get this straight. Yet again, he's had an argument with his wife and yet again, he's stormed off to the pub and, judging by past experience, he'll stagger home again when he's run out of money.'

Irene was shaking her head. 'Sally's adamant and she won't listen to reason. She says she's given him enough chances and this is the last straw. They're getting divorced.'

The news was by no means a surprise to Jo; the only surprise was how Sally had put up with him for so long. 'OK,' Jo said patiently, 'if he doesn't turn up there then he'll turn up here.'

'That's what that nice policeman said.'

'You phoned the police?'

'I couldn't just sit here doing nothing,' she said, a sting of accusation in her words. 'I've phoned and phoned Steve's mobile but there's no answer.'

Jo stood up, no longer able to fight the urge to pick up Archie. He didn't even murmur as she lifted him tenderly into her arms. He calmed her heart and her thoughts enough so she could keep her voice level. 'If this had happened six months ago, you wouldn't have given it a second thought. Irene, it's happened in the past, plenty of times. I know, because it was usually David who was dragged out in the middle of the night to talk him down.'

'But David isn't here for Steve to turn to now.'

When Jo had arrived at Irene's house she had been prepared to stay for as long as she was needed. Irene had weathered plenty of heartbreak in the last few years but she had had her sons there to support her. She was on her own now and after everything she had done for her, Jo wouldn't have objected to stepping into the breach. But now that she knew all of the facts, she couldn't face the prospect of spending the evening watching Irene driving herself mad with irrational fears only for Steve to turn up drunk and unrepentant. She didn't trust herself.

'I have to go,' Jo said. 'But I promise I'll come back over tomorrow if he hasn't made an appearance.' But he will, she wanted to add, bad pennies always do. 'If I were you,

I'd make up the spare bed and have a glass of water and some paracetamol at the ready because Steve is going to be nursing a serious hangover when he does show up.'

Jo set about slipping Archie into extra layers as if preparing him for a trip to Antarctica. Only when she had strapped him into his baby carrier did she turn back to Irene who had stayed where she was, deep in her own thoughts.

'I know I'm overreacting,' her mother-in-law said. The tears she had managed to staunch were welling in her eyes and threatened to spill over.

'It's understandable, but this isn't history repeating itself. I still can't find a convincing reason why David disappeared but with Steve, I could make a list as long as your arm.'

Irene sniffed. 'I know,' she said.

'Phone me when he turns up, no matter what the time.'

Irene gave Jo a hug and kissed the top of Archie's head. 'I will,' she promised.

When Jo left, she worried about Steve for only as long as he deserved, which was about as long as it took her to take her first breath of fresh air.

Archie's eyes opened as soon as Jo stepped through the front door and switched on a light. She didn't feel the familiar flutter of panic that normally arrived when Archie awoke. She could still recall how agonized she had felt when she thought he was in danger. She had been shocked by the strength of the connection between them, a connection that she had convinced herself hadn't even existed, but it was still there now and she was desperate to hold on to it.

Jo put the dramas of the day to the back of her mind

as she concentrated on her son. Using her organisational skills to her advantage, she embarked upon his night-time routine with surprising confidence. Archie not only noticed but approved of the change in his mother and although he objected from time to time, he didn't summon up the primal fury that usually accompanied his last feed. There was no final battle of wills that would last until they were both drained of energy.

Tonight they were both winners and when Jo placed a sleeping Archie in his bassinet, she was aware of a warmth in her chest, the swell of pride and the rush of love that was all but alien to her in recent months. She had a silly, goofy grin on her face as she switched on the intercom in her bedroom so she could slip back downstairs to find some sustenance of her own – she was ravenous.

Jo was only halfway down the stairs when she caught sight of the street lights flickering outside. Her smile froze and she tried to convince herself that it was only tree branches casting spindly shadows across the window panes in the door but in the next moment they fused together and the silhouette took human form.

The faceless visitor had short-cropped hair and broad shoulders that stretched as an arm reach upwards. For a heart-stopping moment, Jo waited for the sound of a key engaging in the lock. The air in her lungs burned as she held her breath and then an electric shock zipped across every nerve in her body as a hand rapped on the window.

It was only reflex that forced her to exhale in a howling gasp. Her thumping heart expanded with each beat until it was crushing her useless lungs. She started to feel dizzy, only managing to gulp tiny mouthfuls of air. The blood had drained from her face and the sweat that had sprung to her brow felt cold. The figure knocked on the door again and the shock broke through Jo's inertia. She propelled herself towards the door where the silhouette had cupped his hand across the red and green glass panels and was peering at her. She imagined she saw the twinkle of David's eyes as he sought her out.

Jo struggled with the doorknob because her fingers had seized up but somehow she managed and flung the door open wide. With the last breath in her body she screamed in rage and hit out at the man standing in front of her who wasn't quick enough to dodge the first blow. Steve yelled too as he stumbled back a few steps before lurching forward again and grabbing both Jo's hands. She was still screaming as he pushed her back into the house, keeping hold of her as he jammed her up against the wall and held her hands aloft until her rage was spent. It took a few moments for Jo to steady her breathing enough to talk and there remained pure hatred in her eyes as she glared at her brother-in-law.

'Why couldn't you have been David? Why, Steve?' she cried. 'Have you been with him? Do you know where he is? Tell me where he is. Tell me!'

'I don't know, Jo, but if I did I swear I'd drag him home myself.' His words were slurred and yet despite the putrid stench of beer that wafted towards her, Steve didn't seem to be as drunk as Jo would have expected after one of his binges.

Her nostrils flared and her hands were still balled into fists as Jo struggled to free herself from Steve's grasp. She spat the next words out. 'I hate him! More than I've ever hated anyone or anything. I hate him with every bone in my body.'

'No you don't.'

'Yes, I do!' Jo was panting, and with each breath she released silent words that contradicted everything she had just said. Of course she loved him. She would always love him. *Come back, I love you*, each breath whispered.

Steve looked at her curiously, as if he had been eaves-dropping on her private thoughts, and Jo redirected her anger. 'And you're no better. Do you know what kind of hell you've put your mum through?'

'I know,' he said.

'Then phone her, Steve, and let her know you've managed to drag yourself out of the gutter she imagines you're lying dead in!'

'I will,' he promised. 'Is it safe to let you go first?'

Jo had still been trying to pull her hands free but she splayed out her fingers in surrender and stopped resisting.

Steve let her go but held his ground.

'Go away, Steve,' she said, wearily. 'You deserve the mess you've got yourself into and you won't get any sympathy from me. I know I've made mistakes in my time but not like you. If you've wrecked your marriage, if you've lost your son, then you have no one to blame but yourself. Go away, please.'

Her brother-in-law looked as if he was about to go but then said, 'You don't really hate Dave, do you?'

Jo wanted to tell him to mind his own business but fear nipped at her heart. What if Steve *did* have contact with David, what reports would he send back to him? Her lip trembled as she whispered, 'No, no I don't hate him. I love him and I don't care where he's been or what he's been doing, I just want him home.'

'You thought I was Dave coming home at last, didn't you?'

She nodded, then swallowed what little was left of her pride to plead with his brother. 'Please, Steve, tell me if you know anything. I won't ask anything else; just tell me he's safe.' The appeal was enough to force another eruption of emotions from Jo and she began to sob. 'Tell me there's a chance he might come home one day.'

'Sorry,' he croaked. 'I wish I could but I can't.'

'I can't bear this,' she cried and when Steve put a hand tentatively on her shoulder she fell forward into his arms despite herself.

Closing her eyes and squeezing back her tears, Jo felt his body wrap around hers and she held on as if her life depended on it. She held her breath for as long as she could, not wanting to breathe in the stale smell of beer that was Steve's trademark, that wasn't her husband's. The spell was broken with the first gasp of air and she tried to pull away from her brother-in-law but the wall behind her prevented her escape. She managed to push a little distance between them and wiped her eyes, trying to regain her composure.

'Why did you come here, Steve?' she asked.

'I thought I could stay here. I don't have anywhere else to go.'

'You can go to your mum's. In fact, she's expecting you.'

When Steve drew closer, Jo went to push him away but he took hold of her hand and held it against his chest. His face loomed in front of her. 'Don't you get lonely, Jo?' he whispered in her ear. 'I think of you here all by yourself. It's not right and if Dave can't be here then I want to help.'

His lips brushed her ear and at first she couldn't believe what was happening. She opened her mouth to scream at him to get away but Steve stifled her cry with a kiss.

The touch of his wet lips was repulsive but the adrenalin rush gave Jo the strength to lunge forward and force him away. The front door was still open and Jo didn't stop pushing until Steve tumbled back out of the door and on to the ground.

'Don't you dare touch me again!' she shouted. 'Do you really think you're some kind of replacement for your brother?'

'I only wanted to help, Jo,' Steve said as he got back unsteadily to his feet. 'I feel so damned guilty. I should be able to find Dave even if the police can't. It's eating me up.'

'You don't have to feel guilty, Steve, I'm doing enough of that for everyone. But let me make one thing perfectly clear.' Her eyes narrowed and her words had a venomous bite to them. 'It doesn't matter where David is or what he's done, it doesn't even matter if he's shacked up with someone else and never wants to come back to me: you are never going to take his place. Not ever, Steve. He will always be ten times the man that you are.'

'I know that,' Steve answered. He was crying now. 'And I know he would be here if he could. I really believe that, Jo. We should still be out looking for him. He wouldn't want us to give up.'

'So explain why someone who is perfectly capable of finding his way to the bank should still need help finding his way home?'

Jo caught herself looking to Steve for the answer but then realized how utterly useless he was. He was swaying from side to side and shivering in nothing but jeans and a T-shirt. He pulled a baseball cap from his back pocket in preparation for the hike to Irene's. Tears were streaming down his cheeks and she could still hear him mumbling about being sorry as she closed the door. She engaged all the locks before rushing upstairs to the bathroom where she scrubbed her teeth then jumped into the shower to cleanse herself. Only then did she feel ready to make a quick call to Irene to give her the wonderful news that at least one of her sons was safe and well.

When Archie woke up for his next feed, Jo lifted him gently from his bassinet and took him into the nursery where she was soon rocking her satiated baby back to sleep. The music from the mobile sliced through the emptiness enshrouding the room, and even though it was only half past nine, Jo was also ready to give in to exhaustion. The events of the last few hours had drained all her resources and she was desperate to be released from her thoughts.

As she drifted off, Jo continued to sing along to the lullaby, long after the mobile had stopped turning. In her dream, she could see sunlight streaming through the front door. She could see the perfect outline of her husband surrounded by a halo of red and green light so bright it stung her eyes. Jo's heart beat once, then soared and her fingers were bathed in sunlight as she reached towards the doorknob. But when her skin touched the metal, the icy cold shock ran through her body like a bolt of lightning before plunging the house into darkness. Overcome with dread she opened the door and found Steve standing there amongst the shadows. 'I'm sorry,' he whispered as he made a grab for her. Jo stumbled back and for one terrifying second she felt her body plummeting before waking up with a sickening jolt. Archie felt it too and began to whimper. She kissed the top of his head and gently stroked a finger down his nose, over his lips and coming to rest on the merest suggestion of a groove in his chin just like his daddy's. 'Please don't take my sunshine away,' she began to sing, and as her words echoed in the darkness, they both began to cry.

21

When Jo got up on Sunday morning, the world had returned to normal – or at least what counted for normal within the four walls of her pristine and empty house. After proving to Archie that she was as incompetent as ever by taking over an hour to feed and change him, she felt exhausted but not too exhausted to get herself dressed and ready to go out. Steph had invited her over for lunch and she was glad of the excuse to escape the confines of the house. She had mopped away the trail of footprints Steve had left at the door but the aftershock of his arrival persisted.

Archie remained fast asleep as she prepared to leave, but when she placed him in his baby carrier, his eyes flickered opened and he glared at her. She felt ridiculous, but she couldn't meet his gaze. She was determinedly holding on to the feeling she'd had the night before; of wanting to hold him and love him as a real mother should; but only just. She loved him, but she couldn't give that love freely when she was expecting her son to reject her affection in much the same way as his father had.

More desperate than ever to get away, Jo picked up the

baby carrier and turned to face the front door, but then came to a juddering halt. The sun was shining brightly through the stained glass, scattering a rainbow across the hallway like the creeping fragments of a dream. Her skin began to prickle as she raised her eyes to the doorknob and her fingers tingled with the memory of the ice-cold touch of metal. She tried to take a deep breath but her lungs refused to expand and the little air she had managed to inhale was released with a gasp, quickly followed by another. Her cheeks burned as she recalled the David-shaped silhouette that had appeared out of the shadows the night before.

Since Archie's birth, Jo had come dangerously close to having another panic attack on a few occasions, but she had always managed to regain control. This one was different. It struck without warning and her muscles began to seize up almost immediately, which only added to her distress. There was a thumping pain in her chest and her arms and legs became leaden even as her mind screamed at her to move. She was fighting a losing battle and, with the power of an avalanche beginning its slow tumble downhill, the attack fed off her rising sense of powerlessness. Jo's gaze remained fixed on the door and panic turned to terror as she realized she had become completely paralyzed.

'Help me,' she gasped.

I'm here, whispered a voice in her ear.

She closed her eyes. 'David,' she said as she leaned ever so slightly into the man standing behind her.

Her husband's hand swept down the side of her face, wiping away the tears. His fingers trailed down her neck, making her shiver and releasing some of the tension. He slipped his arms around her, placing a hand over her diaphragm. *Breathe with me*, he said.

Jo took a breath and was surprised how deeply she was able to inhale.

Slowly, let it out, he commanded.

She could feel his breath against her face as he exhaled with her. *That's good. Now, let's try that again.*

It was only when she tried to lean further into David and stumbled back a few steps that she realized she had broken through her inertia. Still holding the baby carrier, Jo started to move but instead of heading out through the door, she found herself in the living room where she waited until she could trust her voice not to tremble before picking up the phone to make her excuses to Steph.

'Why are you out of breath?' Steph demanded. She was standing on the doorstep with her arms laden with takeaway containers.

Jo shoved her shaking hands into her pockets and licked her parched lips. Steph had promised to call in after school to drop off the leftovers from Sunday lunch since Jo had been too exhausted to come over. Jo had been expecting the knock on the door, she had known it would be Steph and she had even practised opening the door a couple of times. She couldn't explain why something so simple had become such an impossible task. She managed a smile as she let her sister into the house. The door had not defeated her.

'Archie's asleep so I was busy catching up with some housework,' she said. 'Isn't Lauren with you?'

'There's a bug going around and she was looking a bit

peaky. I didn't want to chance bringing her in case she passed something on to you or the baby.'

Jo raised an eyebrow and only just stopped herself from suggesting it might be a love bug. 'That's a shame; it would have been nice to see her.'

Steph was uncharacteristically quiet as she poked her head into the living room to see her favourite nephew before heading to the kitchen to relieve herself of the mountain of food she had brought with her.

'Have you heard any more news from Irene?' she asked.

'Steve's still staying with her. Apparently Sally turned up with all his worldly goods packed into bin bags so I don't think there'll be any going back this time.'

'Hmm. Well, it's Luke I feel sorry for.'

Jo couldn't summon up the sympathy she knew the family deserved. 'There are worse things that could happen,' she said. 'And I can't help thinking Sally and Luke are better off without Steve.'

Steph was quiet for a moment. 'Do you think it has anything to do with David? You've said yourself you wouldn't be surprised if Steve knew all along where he is.'

Jo was already shaking her head. 'I don't think so. Steve and Sally had enough problems of their own to begin with and besides . . .' she said. 'Now, don't go saying I've lost it, please, Steph . . .'

Steph tried to laugh. 'I can't until you tell me what you're trying to say.'

'It's stupid, I know it's stupid.' Jo held her breath a moment before blurting out, 'I think he's dead, Steph.'

'What?'

'Maybe David did leave on purpose and maybe he was

262

involved in something I can't even begin to imagine, but he'd be back by now if he could. Even though he wasn't ready to admit it to me, he did want the baby. He wanted to be a dad and he'd come back for me and for Archie if he could. And I think he does . . .'

Steph was staring at her and when Jo sensed another 'What?' forming on her lips she closed her eyes and thought back to the recent anxiety attack and how she had got through it. 'He's here with me sometimes, I'm sure of it.'

From the living room, Archie could be heard whimpering which usually summoned dread in Jo but she felt relief at escaping the conversation she already regretted starting. 'So go on, say it. It's wishy-washy voodoo, right?'

'Well, when you put it like that . . .' Steph offered. 'But it's not surprising you want to find comfort where you can, even if it is . . . wishy-washy voodoo.'

'OK, confession over. Forget I even said anything,' Jo said. 'Now back to the real world of feeding, burping and changing babies.'

'Shall I do it?'

Jo warmed up the milk then looked on enviously as Steph managed to get Archie to accept his feed on the first attempt. 'Are you sure you're OK on your own with the baby?' Steph asked.

'We have a routine,' Jo said but chose not to expand that the said routine involved Jo tensing up, Archie tensing up, Jo pleading, Archie crying, Jo crying.

'Good,' Steph said brightly and aimed a beaming smile at her sister.

Jo tilted her head. 'Why?' When her sister tried to shrug, she added, 'What are you after, Stephanie?'

There was a pause as Steph put the baby on her shoulder to wind him. 'We've been invited to a friend's wedding next month.'

'That's nice.'

'The thing is,' Steph said slowly and deliberately as she resumed feeding the baby, 'it's a weekend affair in the Peak District. We could take Lauren with us but she doesn't want to go and, to be honest, her time would be best served at home revising.'

'So?' Jo asked. She wasn't going to make it easy for Steph to ask the favour but it wasn't because she was about to refuse. She was simply enjoying the moment. It had been a long time since she had felt of use to someone else and not a constant drain on her family.

'Would you mind? It would only involve staying over one night and I'll make sure Lauren earns her keep and I think it would be good for you to have some company.'

Jo was about to say it would be her pleasure but there was no time for her to wallow in the glowing sense of normality because the phone began to ring. It was Martin Baxter.

'There's been another withdrawal from David's bank,' he said after only a brief warning that there had been a development in the case.

Jo had stood up to take the call and as she turned to look at Steph, her face was white. She rubbed her chest hard, concentrating on the warm, comforting sensation of her hand against her skin and not the cold wave of despair crashing over her continuously battered body. 'Oh,' she managed.

'You don't sound surprised.'

Jo wasn't quite sure what the policeman had expected. If he had heard the conversation she'd had with her sister moments earlier he would understand that what she actually felt was disappointment, quickly followed by guilt. Was she sorry he wasn't dead after all? 'It's hard to get excited about something that confirms David really has abandoned me and his son.'

'You haven't had any contact with him yourself?' Martin asked, still sounding suspicious.

The derisory snort was almost manic. 'I'm apparently the last person he would want to see.'

When the policeman then asked Jo to call into the station to look at the CCTV image, she refused point-blank. Steph had been watching and listening and quickly grabbed her chance to help her sister survive this latest betrayal. 'Tell him I'll do it,' she said.

When Jo relayed this information, Martin reluctantly agreed. 'All right,' he said. 'But I'll send *you* some stills in the post. I need you to confirm it's him for the record.'

'And then?'

'I'm afraid we're quickly reaching a point where this stops being a police matter.'

As Jo's legs turned to jelly beneath her, she reflected that the only positive aspect of feeling so completely and utterly defeated was that she didn't even have the urge to cry. Even as Steph began fussing around her, Jo couldn't shake the feeling that she wasn't quite there in the room with her. She had stepped out of the picture and was looking at the impassive shell of the woman who would continue to function while the real Jo Taylor shrank away until nothing was left.

* * *

265

Jo was in the nursery, waiting for the sun to rise. The days were lengthening but there were no other signs that winter was loosening its grip. The drop in temperature overnight had given the world a sugar frosting that glistened in the lamplight, confirming that the roads would be as treacherous today as they had been the day before and the day before that.

Four days had passed since Steph had visited the police station to confirm that it was indeed David withdrawing more cash from his dwindling account and in that time Jo had left the house precisely once to take Archie to baby clinic. She had proved to herself that she could leave if she wanted to, she simply chose not to.

The feeling that David might be watching her from the shadows had returned and she wondered, as she had many times before, what would happen if they were to meet accidentally. She had once imagined beating her fists against his chest before falling into his arms and telling him she still loved him but not now. She felt as if her emotions had been peeled away like the layers of an onion. The love she had felt, the loyalty, the guilt, the anger and forgiveness had all been stripped away one by one until there was nothing left. If he were standing in front of her now she doubted she would feel anything at all. She would shake her head and simply turn away, because the thought of dealing with any of those old emotions was simply too exhausting.

The sky had turned from a molten red to soft pink while Jo continued to stare out of the window and she didn't even realize she had been humming Archie's lullaby until she stopped. She thought she heard him waking up in the next room.

Archie had been more restless than usual during the night. He had woken every couple of hours and at first had screamed as loud as ever when she tried to feed him, but as dawn approached his complaints had reduced to the kind of whimper she could hear now.

Turning from the window, Jo's eyes followed the trail of morning sun across the floor reaching towards the side table and lamp on the other side of the nursery. She was about to leave the room but something was unsettling her and she couldn't quite work out what it was. She moved closer to the table and scrutinized its clean, white-painted surface, the small drawer beneath with its silver handle and the shelf nearer the base where a stuffed giraffe stared up at her, slightly bemused. Lifting her gaze back to the table top, the shock hit her so hard she saw sparks dancing across her vision. The birth certificate was missing.

It had still been there the other day – she had even dusted it. Ignoring Archie's continued whimpers, Jo searched around the table, even lifting up the lamp and opening the drawer as if the certificate were capable of moving of its own accord. When she couldn't find it, she wracked her brain trying to remember if she had seen it since taking Archie to the baby clinic. Possibly not, she concluded with sickening dread. Had David been in the house? What other explanation could there be? Had she put the certificate away without remembering? Could she have accidentally thrown it away? She didn't think so, but if David had been there then he had disturbed nothing else, she was sure of it. But why take the birth certificate? What did it mean? What was he trying to tell her?

Her skin crawled as she imagined David watching her,

biding his time until she had finally left the house so he could sneak in and take a closer look at the life he had abandoned. Jo rubbed away the goose bumps as she went downstairs to prepare Archie's next bottle to distract herself from yet more dizzying questions, all the while glancing around the house in case she might spot other evidence that her husband had returned. She used the dead bolt on the front door before returning upstairs.

It was only when she was feeding her son that thoughts of David were abruptly pushed to the back of her mind. The baby had gulped down his feed without complaint but the moment she lifted him up to wind him, Archie threw up over both of them. For once she didn't care about the mess, only her son, who unnerved her when he didn't object to being put down on the changing mat. It was only when she stripped off his sodden Baby-gro that she noticed how hot he was to the touch. He had a temperature.

'What should I do?' she asked Steph over the phone.

'I think you should get him to the doctor.'

Jo had thought the same thing, but had been hoping Steph would persuade her that she was overreacting – she had wanted someone to give her an excuse not to step outside where David could choose to follow her or perhaps return to the house a second time. 'But the surgery won't be open yet,' she said.

'Then phone the out-of-hours service.'

The urgency in her sister's voice snaked fear down Jo's spine. 'Do you think it could be serious?'

'It's probably only a virus but you need to get him checked out, Jo. They'll be able to give you something to

268

bring down his temperature and rehydrate him. He's too little to fight it all by himself.'

'OK, I'll go,' Jo said, finally putting aside her own irrational fears for what might be a real danger to her son.

Half an hour later and Jo was in the hallway ready to leave. She hadn't stopped to draw breath since making the emergency appointment and she was panting as she shrugged into her coat. Her cheeks were glowing, surely a result of rushing around, but she could feel the beads of sweat breaking out on her forehead. Her breath juddered with the force of her hammering heart. She fought the urge to cry as she realized what was happening but she was determined to help her son and picked up the baby carrier. Archie scarcely noticed: he was becoming more and more listless by the minute. She could barely breathe for fear of losing him and yet, rather than spur her into action, her fear paralyzed her to the spot in a repeat of Sunday morning. She couldn't move towards the coloured streaks of light stretching out like monstrous fingers towards her, trying to pull her back into the nightmare that still invaded her thoughts.

Archie stared up at her through heavy lids and whimpered again, pleading with his mum to save him.

You can do this, someone whispered in her ear.

The sound of her husband's voice was only in her head but the surge of adrenalin that arrived with it brought all of Jo's fears into sharp focus; fear of David standing behind her ready to slip his arms around her and pretend he still cared; fear of him being outside somewhere watching her every move for his own sick amusement; and, God forbid, the fear that she had got it completely wrong and he wasn't there at all. Her terror was tangible, a fiery demon that sucked the air out of her lungs and yet had ice-cold hands that wrapped around her heart. Her whole body quaked and she couldn't imagine getting any closer to the door, let alone reaching up to turn the lock. She was failing Archie again.

'What's wrong with me?' she seethed. 'What does it matter if David is watching me? I have to show him he was wrong, I have to prove we *were* ready to be parents.' She felt repulsed by the wreck she had become and the scream tore from her lungs before she knew what was happening. The noise should have terrified Archie, but he remained still and quiet.

Jo lurched forward and knocked her hand hard against the doorknob as she forced her way through her inertia to fling open the door. The pain was sharp but she welcomed it. Unlike the all-consuming rush of fear that could come from nowhere, her throbbing knuckle was a sensation she could understand.

When she reached the safety of the car, she sucked her hand to ease the pain. She wanted to cry but one look at Archie reminded her that she needed to keep moving. She placed the back of her bruised hand on his cheek. He was still burning up but Jo held back the tears right until she sat down in the doctor's office and he asked her what was wrong.

22

Jo cringed every time she recalled sobbing her heart out in the doctor's surgery. The poor GP who had the misfortune of covering the out-of-hours service was a semi-retired old gent with kind eyes and a soft voice who promised that Archie was going to be just fine. He didn't sound quite so confident about the mother's prognosis.

It was a good thing then, that Jo had little time to think about her latest humiliation or any of the other trials and tribulations that constituted her life. She expected no news from the police, had no contact from work and certainly took no interest in the disintegration of Steve's marriage or the apologetic message he had left on her phone. She could even convince herself that she cared little about where David was or what he was up to. There had been no sign of him during her mercy dash to the surgery either en route or when she returned home. Jo's sole concern from that point was meeting her son's needs – and even though he was too unwell to demand her attention, she gave it willingly, as any mother would: it was the least she could do after coming so close to failing him again.

As Steph had suspected, Archie had a virus and the doctor prescribed liquid paracetamol and dehydration powders. Jo's main task was to give her son plenty of fluids and after a few days her efforts paid off and he was soon through the worst of it. She didn't need to return to the surgery and with no other reason to leave home, she cut herself off from the rest of the world, declaring the house a no-go zone to any visitors, claiming both she and Archie had the bug. Her cherished isolation lasted right up until the following Tuesday afternoon.

'You took your time,' Steph said, shaking her umbrella as she stepped into the hall with Lauren trailing behind. 'You haven't just got up, have you?'

Jo was already retreating down the hallway, her dressing gown fluttering in sympathy with her heart. She had spotted Steph's arrival from the nursery window and had wanted to pretend there was no one home but Steph's insistent hammering at the door threatened to wake up Archie who was asleep downstairs. Even so, she took her time answering the door and stopped at the mirror in the hall to check her reflection, something she hadn't done for days. Her hair was unwashed and when she tried to straighten the cow's lick in the middle of her forehead it refused to relax along with the rest of her. Her hands had been trembling when she managed to unlock and open the door, breaking the seal on her sanctuary.

'I was in the kitchen making up bottles for Archie, I didn't hear you,' she said, keeping her head down and playing nervously with her fringe. 'Why don't you check on Archie while I make us all a drink? I wouldn't be surprised if you've woken him up with all that racket you made.'

'Can I pick him up?' Lauren asked.

'Not until you've dried off and warmed up,' Steph replied, then added, 'And *I'll* make the drinks.'

'I can manage,' Jo said but she already knew that when Steph set her mind on taking control there was little point arguing.

In the living room, Lauren shook off her wet coat and peered over the bassinet to take a closer look at the baby who had woken up as Jo suspected but didn't even murmur when his cousin picked him up.

Jo sat down in one of the armchairs and rubbed her face to add some colour to her cheeks. 'So what have you been up to?' she asked as she tried to tame her hair again. It felt slick rather than shiny.

'Mum's had me under house arrest revising for my mocks,' Lauren said. Her rocking motion was a little enthusiastic but Archie looked happy enough.

'It can't be easy staying away from your friends,' Jo said with a subtle emphasis on the last word.

'You can say that again. *She* doesn't trust me at all and can't seem to understand that it actually helps having someone to study with.'

'*She*? Who's this *she* when she's at home?' demanded Steph, arriving with a tray laden with cups of coffee and a plate of biscuits.

Lauren's response was inaudible and Jo half expected Steph to ask her to stand up and share what she had just said with the rest of the class but her sister looked a little battle weary and chose to ignore her daughter. 'So how are you both?' she asked Jo.

'Archie's more or less recovered; in fact I think his appetite is better than it's ever been. He'd spend half his life feeding if I let him.' There was a hint of pride in Jo's voice. When Archie was asleep in her arms looking completely satiated, she felt a sense of fulfilment too. The rewards of motherhood were still few and far between but they were there if she looked hard enough.

'And you?' Steph asked as she shoved the plate of biscuits under Jo's nose, refusing to move until she took one.

'It may take me a while to recover from this one,' Jo answered, comfortable with the half-truth.

'Hmm,' Steph replied as if she had marked Jo's answer out of ten and wasn't impressed with the score.

'I think you should get out more,' offered Lauren. 'If you wanted to go out one night, I don't mind babysitting.'

'Really?' Jo and Steph said in unison.

Lauren chose to respond to her mum. 'Why? Don't you trust me?'

In no mood to referee, Jo said, 'Thanks Lauren, but I don't think I'm quite up to it yet.'

Jo could feel Steph watching her every move and she tried not to tense up when Archie began to cry. The only thing worse than having her son judge her, was her sister there to cast a critical eye over her performance too.

'Here, you can have him back now,' Lauren said, offering him up to Jo.

'My turn, I think,' Steph said when she noticed Jo's hesitation.

The baby settled and the conversation limped on. Jo thought she had the balance about right, somewhere between being ill enough for her guests not to overstay their welcome but not so ill that Steph would think her incapable of caring for herself or the baby.

When they had finished their drinks, Steph returned Archie to his bassinet and it looked as if she was getting ready to leave, but then she said, 'I think we need to sort out some supplies before we go. You've run out of milk and your fridge is practically empty. What food you do have is long past its best.' She tipped her head towards the plate of half-eaten biscuits.

'I do my grocery shopping online. I can manage.'

'At least let me get the basics in.'

'Honestly, Steph. I'll be fine.'

'Nonsense. Lauren won't mind.'

'Won't mind what?'

Steph silenced her daughter with a glare that held its intensity until Lauren stormed off, armed with a shopping list.

'So,' Steph said as she settled back down into her chair without relaxing a muscle, 'how are you, Jo? And I want an honest answer this time.'

Jo took too long to think up a convincing reply before Steph continued, 'You look like you've only just crawled out of bed and yet there's a full load of washing in the machine and the house is as spotless as ever. You're clearly well enough to keep a tidy house.'

Jo squirmed as she watched Steph's face become grim, her mouth opening and closing as she tried to formulate a response. Her sister's voice hardened as she added, 'You took for ever to answer the door because you said you were making up baby bottles but the only bottles I can see are ice cold in the fridge.'

Jo blinked away the unwelcome tears that had sprung

to her eyes. She was sick and tired of having her entire life under constant scrutiny and she wanted to be left alone. She didn't want to go through the shame of telling someone else she wasn't coping. Steph leant forward, placing a soothing hand on Jo's knee.

'I've seen the boxes of antidepressants, Jo.'

'I haven't taken any. The GP practically forced them on me,' she said, flushing guiltily.

'I wouldn't blame you if you did. You've been through such a lot lately and it was inevitable it would catch up with you. No one can be that strong. It's time to stop pretending you are.'

In response, a single tear trickled down Jo's cheek. She was shaking her head, silently begging her sister to stop trying to force the truth from her.

'Tell me what's wrong. Please, Jo.'

Jo's jaw clenched shut but she knew that her sister wasn't going to leave until she'd had her pound of flesh. 'I think David's been here, Steph. I can't be sure, but the birth certificate was there one minute and now it's gone and it's not anywhere else because I've looked. I've looked everywhere but then why would he take that and nothing else? OK, I burnt most of his stuff but why take that? It doesn't make sense.'

Steph managed a nervous laugh as she said, 'Neither are you making sense. Slow down, Jo.'

'Do you think I don't know I'm not making sense! I'm a complete mess, Steph!' she blurted out before she could stop herself.

'OK, one step at a time: you think David has been back in the house?'

Jo shook her head as she struggled with an answer. It wasn't as if she had a CCTV recording and in her current frame of mind, who would believe that she could be so certain of anything, especially about the whereabouts of one single piece of paper that could so easily have been misplaced. 'I don't know. I only know how I feel. I can't go out without expecting to find David lurking around every corner; I can't look out of a window without trying to catch a glimpse of him in the shadows; I can't open the door without wondering if he'll be there on the doorstep waiting for me and I can't hold my son without wondering if he's going to grow up hating me – and I wouldn't blame him if he did, because I keep letting him down, Steph. He was ill and I almost didn't make it to the doctor because I was too terrified to leave the house. What kind of mother does that make me? We would all have been better off if he'd never been born!' Jo was panting and the startled look on Steph's face was no doubt a mirror of her own. She hadn't meant to utter that last statement; she hadn't meant to even think it.

'Is it postnatal depression?' Steph asked.

Jo wrapped her arms around herself in a bid to stop trembling. 'No, I'm not depressed, Steph, I'm just unhappy – really, really unhappy and I've been that way for months, long before the baby was born. I talked it through with the doctor and he agrees too. He said that what I'm going through is a natural reaction to the pain I'm feeling. I am allowed to be unhappy, Steph,' she said, her voice breaking at the last.

'I know,' her sister said softly.

'David's taken everything from me, hasn't he?' Jo asked,

her words strangled with so much emotion that it took her breath away. 'He may not have cleared out every bank account or emptied the house but he's left me with nothing. I'm not the devoted wife any more, or the level-headed career woman and I'm certainly not the doting mother I know I could have been if he'd had the guts to stay or at least turned around to say goodbye. I'm trying, Steph, really I am, but my best isn't good enough and Archie knows it. Maybe I wouldn't be better off without him, but I don't doubt for a minute that *he'd* be better off without me.'

When Steph came over to perch on the chair and put an arm around her sister, her movements were deliberately slow as if she thought even the gentlest breeze might knock Jo down. 'Do you – God, I don't even know how to say this, Jo – should I be worried?'

Jo rested her head on her sister's shoulder. 'I'm not giving up,' she said and even though she didn't believe that was necessarily true, she hoped it was. 'It'll take time to adjust, longer still because David isn't giving me the option for closure.'

'You could divorce him.'

'I don't see what good that would do. There couldn't be any financial settlement until David appears out of the woodwork and besides, I don't need a piece of paper to tell me my marriage is over – just like I don't need a piece of paper to tell me I have a duty to Archie. What I need is an explanation.'

'If you're not going to take the medication, is there anything else the doctor can do?' Steph asked.

'There are talking therapies but the waiting list is as long as your arm. So at the moment it's a matter of heal thyself,'

Jo said as she tried to raise her head and her spirits along with it.

Steph didn't look convinced. 'Can you look after Archie?'

'Yes, of course I can. He's the only reason I have to try to build my life back up from the ground. He is worth it, Steph,' she added to contradict her previous outburst. 'He has to be.'

'Yes, he is,' Steph said, following Jo's gaze towards the sleeping infant. 'And if anyone can get through all of this crap life is throwing at you, then you can. You're the most determined, single-minded woman I know.'

Jo looked up at her sister. 'By determined, you mean stubborn, don't you?'

'Well, yes, maybe I do,' Steph confessed. 'But that's not necessarily a bad thing. Use it to your advantage, Jo. Set your sights on getting you and Archie through this, one day at a time, and you'll do it. I'll help all that I can, we all will.'

By the time Lauren returned with enough supplies to keep Jo in tea and biscuits for a month, Jo had convinced her sister that all she needed was time and a shoulder to cry on now and again. When they left, reluctantly on Steph's part, Jo wondered what her sister thought of her now. She certainly wasn't the confident, self-assured woman who everyone turned to for advice; she was someone who was needy and helpless; an object of pity. And that was, apparently, the view her mother had arrived at by the time she appeared on her doorstep unannounced the next day.

'Look at the state of you,' Liz said shaking her head. 'What the hell has that man driven you to?'

'Steph told you?' Jo asked and although the answer was obvious it was no less palatable.

Liz was weighed down with a large overnight bag and various other carrier bags that thumped into Jo as her mother forced her way in.

'I'm here to look after you for a few days – and don't worry, I've come prepared,' she said, cutting off Jo before she had a chance to argue. She dropped a bulging plastic bag at Jo's feet. 'It's an inflatable bed. I presume Archie's still sleeping in your room so I can sleep on the nursery floor.'

'You? Presume?'

Liz raised an eyebrow. 'You can't be that ill if you can still give me lip.'

'God forbid I'll ever be that bad.' Jo braved a smile but she was already wondering how much Steph had told Liz and whether there was any point in continuing to pretend that she wasn't *that bad*. It had only been the pitying look from her mother that had riled Jo enough to stop her bursting into tears the moment she discovered that the unexpected visitor on her doorstep wasn't her husband.

'Now, where's that little grandson of mine?'

Jo followed her mum like a shadow into the living room and the next few hours followed a similar vein as Liz took over without hesitation. She familiarized herself with all the baby paraphernalia so she could take care of Archie while Jo went upstairs to get showered and dressed. Jo took her time, not because she was avoiding her mum, but to her surprise, because she was actually enjoying being mothered and she felt reassured having someone else in the house with her. She was beginning to think Steph should be thanked rather than berated for sending in reinforcements, little knowing that she had been lulled into a false sense of security.

Liz nodded approvingly at her daughter's transformation when she returned downstairs in jeans and a T-shirt. She was still a shadow of her former self but at least now she had a little more substance than the ghostly apparition who had greeted her at the door. 'Right, time to get your coat on.'

Jo's heart leapt into her mouth and she had to swallow hard. 'Why?' she demanded. 'We don't need anything.'

'You need some fresh air and so does Archie.'

'Then you take him, I'm not going out.' Jo's body was starting to react as if she was outside already, looking over her shoulder, feeling eyes on the back of her head. The palpitations had arrived so quickly that she was struggling not to throw up and the tightness in her chest was making it difficult to breathe.

'I thought we could walk to the shops and pick up some fresh fruit.'

'I've ordered everything I need online,' Jo said. Her tone was reminiscent of the one Lauren used with *her* mum but, like Steph, Liz was more than capable of standing her ground. The smile on her face had lethal points that cut into her cheeks.

'That was before you knew I was going to be staying. Look, Steph told me about the missing birth certificate. I know you're worried that David might come into the house while we're out, but we won't be gone long and when we get back I'm going to call out a locksmith to change the locks – like I told you to do at the start. And if you think there's a real possibility he's stalking you, then we'll slap an injunction on him if we have to. Now,' she said as if all of Jo's problems had been solved in one fell swoop, 'will you come on, Jo.'

Realising it was an argument she wasn't going to win, Jo retreated into the corners of her mind and followed her mum's instructions. She put on her coat but her hands were shaking too badly to zip it up. Refusing to ask for help, she left it gaping while her mum opened the door.

'Ready?' Liz said all too brightly. Archie was in his pram and she was waiting for Jo to push it outside.

Jo's tongue was glued to the top of her mouth and she struggled at first to speak. 'I can't do it,' she tried again.

'Oh, for goodness' sake, Jo,' Liz said, showing the first signs that her patience was as limited now as it always had been. She herded Jo towards the pram and then out through the door as if she were a sheepdog and Jo a nervous sheep. 'Come *on*.'

Jo held on to the pram with a death grip. Her eyes were cast down as she moved forwards, concentrating on putting one foot in front of the other, pushing the pram across the threshold, then walking down the path and eventually stepping on to the pavement. The air was cold and damp but Jo's lungs burned with each breath she fought for.

She tried to reason with herself. There was nothing she could think of to justify such an intense reaction. So what if David tumbled out of the shadows? While she could accept that he still had the capacity to hurt her emotionally, she wasn't in mortal danger so why was her body reacting as if she was? She slowed down almost to a stop when she realized what it was that was terrifying her.

While she could rationalize her fears, her body had a mind of its own and was preparing for an attack of a different kind, the kind that would leave her struggling to breathe and paralysed with fear. Her body began to tense as she put all her energy into fighting off the next panic attack that would strike at any moment.

Another clash of wills ensued when Liz noticed Jo dawdling and yanked the pram from her rigid fingers. 'Hurry up or the shops will be closed at this rate.'

As her mum strode off down Beaumont Avenue, the gap between them lengthened but Jo was so absorbed in taking in enough oxygen to stop herself from fainting that she failed to notice. Slowly but surely her confidence began to grow and she thought she might be winning this latest battle. She didn't look up except to cross busy roads and refused to glance behind her. She kept her gaze fixed on the ground immediately to the front and refused to give in to the feeling that she was being followed. She was so consumed by controlling her emotions that it was her subconscious that reacted to her surroundings first. Her head snapped up and she stumbled over her own feet as she came to an abrupt halt.

Liz had taken them along a route that led past West Allerton Station and Jo found herself staring down the overgrown entrance of the shortcut that led back home. An image flashed across her mind of David slipping off down the path to shave off a few precious minutes from the final leg of his journey home from Leeds, his head bowed against the bitter wind, bare branches creaking overhead as he muttered to himself, still angry with Jo for not giving him a lift that morning, perhaps angry with himself for refusing her offer to pick him up that night. It was a false memory, but one Jo had become intimately familiar with, except it always dissolved when she tried to recreate that exact moment when David had the epiphany that would change both their lives for ever. Try as she might, Jo couldn't imagine what had made him emerge from the shadows as the kind of man who could abandon his pregnant wife. What had happened to transform him from the man Jo's heart still yearned for, into the person in the grainy image she had seen withdrawing money from a cash machine?

'Jo, hurry up!' called Liz who had only just noticed that her daughter wasn't keeping up.

Jo's eyes darted first towards her mother and then back to the path. The sudden rush of adrenalin made her gasp. Had it been shadows dancing beneath swaying boughs or had she caught a glimpse of a figure darting behind a tree? Jo's feet began to move before she had a chance to have first, let alone second thoughts. Luckily she was wearing trainers and put them to good use as she entered the path at breakneck speed. Brambles snagged and pulled at her coat, the material tearing when she refused to slow. But she wasn't pregnant any more and she didn't have the baby with her. Nothing could hold her back.

Despite her determination to face her tormentor head on, Jo couldn't catch up to the elusive shadow. She kept glancing down as she went as if expecting David to have left a trail, perhaps torn pieces of their son's birth certificate. There were no such signs and soon she was struggling to suck enough air into her burning lungs to keep up with her exertions and was forced to come to a stop at the clearing where the boys had been playing football. She took a good look around as she caught her breath. The place appeared to be deserted and the only sound came from the trees shuddering in the breeze.

'I'm here David, and I'm on my own,' she said between gasps. 'Come out and face me. Tell me why you walked out on me. Tell me why you took the birth certificate.' Her voice was growing louder and stronger. 'Are you such a coward that you can't look me in the eye and tell me why you hate me so much?'

A huge oak on the other side of the fence creaked in response, and Jo's gaze flickered feverishly around the clearing without resting on anything. Her eyes strained for even the briefest glimpse of her husband but it was her mind that created a vision of David striding away from her, dipping from view as the path curved. The sight was enough to break her spirit.

'No, don't leave me!' she cried and set off again at full pelt. If only she could run fast enough she would catch him up. She would talk to him, persuade him it was going to be all right and they could somehow get back to where they were. She pushed herself harder and in no time at all she reached the other end of the path where, rather than emerging two streets from home, she prepared to burst out into a parallel world – the one that had seduced David away from his wife. She could imagine that sense of euphoria as she fell into his arms and as she lurched into the road, her own were raised to meet him.

But of course, he wasn't there and Jo might just as well have run off a cliff. She was freefalling, her arms flailing as she crumpled to her knees.

'Sweet Jesus, are you all right, love?' an elderly gent asked. His dog whined anxiously and sniffed the strange woman kneeling on the pavement in front of him gasping for air.

Jo had her head in her hands and refused to look up, too intent on watching light and dark spots dance across her closed lids while she waited for her racing heart to slow.

'Can I call someone for you?' the man tried again.

Jo shook her head. Her chest heaved as she tried to speak but couldn't. Despite the panic still coursing through her veins there was room for an equally familiar emotion: humiliation. She attempted to get to her feet but her jelly legs weren't up to the task. When she eventually managed to stand with a little perseverance and a lot of help from her Good Samaritan, the overwhelming need to flee had left her but she remained desperate to get away and to get home.

'I only . . . live . . . down there,' she stammered. 'I'll . . . be . . . fine.'

'You don't look like you can take another step, love.'

She didn't have the breath to argue with the man but she tried her best to smile. 'Honestly. Thank you,' she said, sending him away, but both he and his dog kept glancing back down the road after they left.

On the short journey home, Jo formed an image of the black-and-white facade of her beautiful house in her mind, leaving no room for any other thoughts such as who might have receded back into the shadows to watch her. It was only when her fingers wrapped tightly around the familiar contours of the wrought iron gate that she had the courage

286

to look up. She had reached her sanctuary and her eyes travelled along the path, right up to the front door, which for once she was prepared to open without hesitation.

As her body recovered from its self-made storm, Jo imagined standing where she was on a blustery night in October. Was this where David had considered his options and chosen the brutality of the autumn gales rather than the uncertain welcome that awaited him inside? Had thoughts of his unstable and neurotic wife made him turn around and run? Jo couldn't blame him and turned as if she too could walk away from her miserable life, but there was a pram blocking her way.

There was no strength in Jo for flight but she still had some fight in her. 'You shouldn't have made me do it! You have no idea how screwed up I am but then you never did, did you, Mum? Why should now be any different?'

Rather than argue on the doorstep, Liz said, 'Let's get you into the house.' Her lip trembled and she looked as close to tears as her daughter.

Not a word was said while Liz bundled mother and baby into the house, guiding Jo down the hall and into the dining room where she sat her down and poured a glass of water. In the hall where they had left him, Archie started to complain. Jo looked to her mother.

'Don't worry, I'll see to him,' she said.

Jo's eyes flickered an acknowledgement as her mum slipped out of the room but then her gaze settled on one of the kitchen cupboards, its turquoise door gleaming with promise. When her mum returned with a bleary-eyed Archie in her arms, Jo was standing with a box of pills in her hand.

'Are they the antidepressants?'

Jo nodded. 'I was just . . . I thought . . . I don't want to take them, Mum. I want to deal with this on my own.'

'You're not on your own.'

'Aren't I?' Jo asked and then, presuming her mum wouldn't recognize the jibe, she added, 'And I don't mean because David isn't here.'

Liz didn't answer immediately but opened the door of the cupboard that Jo had removed the pills from. Leaving that one ajar, she went to the next cupboard and then the next until every door and drawer was open wide, their neatly stacked and ordered contents on display in all their symmetrical glory. 'Do you think I hadn't noticed?' she said. 'Do you think I don't remember this from before?'

Jo was surprised her mum had actually noticed, then or now. The 'before' Liz was referring to had been when Jo had her first anxiety attacks. Steph had been away at university and their dad was spending so much time on the road sourcing antiques that he was scarcely home either. Liz was left to look after her teenage daughter and run her husband's shop in Liverpool and for a while they had made quite a team. That had all changed when Jo had her heart broken in more ways than one while attempting to traverse that difficult terrain between childhood and adulthood.

She had been about Lauren's age when her first boyfriend had dumped her and she had sought solace in the nooks and crannies of her parents' antique shop, creating order out of a world she couldn't yet fathom. Jo had always assumed that her mother hadn't noticed how obsessively neat and tidy the shop was becoming, she had seemed happy enough that her daughter was keeping out of trouble and that had included not troubling her.

At the time, Liz had been spending longer in the travel agent's next door than was entirely appropriate, certainly for a married woman whose husband was away on business. And when she wasn't next door, the over-attentive travel agent was in her shop. Jo had discovered their dirty little secret when she turned up early after school one day and found them together in a less-than-chaste embrace. Liz's response had been to dismiss Jo's accusations and ignore the chaos it created in her daughter's mind. She had taken Jo to the doctor's when she had complained of chest pains, but as far as Jo was aware, Liz had refused to connect her daughter's illusory illness or her penchant for order with her emotional state. But here her mother was now, recognising that Jo's obsessions were out of the norm, not just now but back then too.

'You knew I was suffering and you just let me get on with it? Is that the kind of support I can expect from you now?' Jo asked, raising her voice enough to startle the baby.

'I know I didn't get you the help you needed, but in fairness, Jo, you didn't make it easy. You wouldn't talk to me! I didn't know what was wrong with you, not really, and neither did the doctor. He told me he thought you were attention-seeking.'

Jo was squeezing the box in her hand so hard that the top popped open and the sleeve of pills poked out. 'I didn't know what was wrong with me either. I didn't know I was having anxiety attacks, I thought I was *dying*! I wasn't looking for attention, I was looking for *help*!'

Liz pursed her lips. 'If you want me to say it was all my fault, then fine, I take full responsibility.'

The brief burst of anger had drained Jo. She shook her head and her next words came out as sobs. 'No, I don't want you to say it's your fault. I just need you to realize that I'm broken, Mum and I want you to help fix me. And for the record, changing the locks on the doors isn't going to be enough, not by a long shot.'

As Archie settled back to sleep in the crook of her arm, Liz closed all the cupboards before stepping close enough to put her hand on Jo's damp cheek. 'I will admit I thought I could come here and all I'd have to do was tell you to pull your socks up,' she said gently.

'I think that's what you said last time,' Jo offered but it failed to raise a smile from either of them.

'You scared me today, Jo – and I mean, really scared me.'

Jo had to swallow hard to hold back the tsunami of emotions that had been gathering momentum over many months. She wasn't ready to talk about her growing obsession that David was lurking nearby, nor could she explain why that idea should fill her with such terror every time she tried to leave the house, but she could make a start. When she spoke, it was the barest whisper. 'I'm scared too, Mum. I've already lost David and now it looks like I'm losing everything else, including my mind. I don't want to feel like this any more. Please, Mum, tell me what to do.'

'Will those help, do you think?' Liz said, looking at the crumpled box in Jo's hand.

Jo dropped the box on to the counter. 'I don't know. Maybe, if all else fails . . .'

'But not yet?'

Jo nodded.

'OK, then. We'll see how we get on, and when I say *we*, I mean *we*. I'll stay as long as you need me, Joanne, and I won't leave until I know you're OK.'

'Do you need me to help plan your escape?' Heather whispered.

She hadn't seen Jo for almost two weeks, having been sold the same line as everyone else to keep away in case she picked up the virus. Taking her life in her hands by calling in on her way home from work one Friday night, she wasn't surprised to find her friend tucked up in a duvet on the sofa but she hadn't expected her mum to be molly-coddling her.

'She's been looking after me,' Jo explained. 'I've needed her.'

Heather put a hand over Jo's brow. 'As I suspected, you're still feverish.'

'Maybe,' Jo said, laughing softly.

'What's going on, Jo?'

Jo's smile softened. She wanted to explain everything that had been happening but for the moment she was happy to leave the past behind her. She might only be taking baby steps, but at least they were in the right direction and she didn't want to look back. Despite being sceptical about her mum's approach to her problems, changing the locks on the doors had actually helped. It had given Jo a returning sense of control in her life, albeit with Liz riding shotgun every time she left the house. 'I'm getting better, is what's going on.'

'She's had a tough few weeks,' Liz said, arriving in the living room, laden with all the post that Jo had neatly arranged in order of envelope size and colour but had yet to open.

'I'd say she's had a tough few months,' Heather added. She was looking curiously at Jo and then at Liz, as if listening for the first time to the things that weren't being said. 'Are you sure it was a bug?'

Jo smiled. 'If I was a celebrity, they'd call it exhaustion.'

'Just wait until you get back to work, then you'll know what exhaustion is,' Heather joked, only seeing the warning look from Liz too late. She grimaced. 'Although you've got ages yet.'

'I'm due back on 10 March, which is less than a month away,' Jo said glumly.

'But she can take longer if she needs to,' Liz added.

'I've already agreed the date with Gary and I can't afford not to go back then. You know that, Mum.'

Liz sucked air through her teeth. 'Gary's told her that they've permanently filled David's old job,' she said, still speaking to Heather. 'Even if he did show up now, he wouldn't be able to give her any financial support.'

'So no more talk of me taking any longer off work,' Jo said. 'I need to stay focused. I have bills to pay.'

They all looked at the pile of unopened envelopes Liz had in her hand.

'That's what dads are for,' Liz said, only just stopping herself from glancing over to Archie who was sleeping nearby in his bassinet when she realized her faux pas. 'If you need a little extra help to see you through the next few years then we'll remortgage the house if we have to.

I don't want you worrying about money on top of everything else.'

The tears that had sprung to Liz's eyes made Jo feel warm and weepy. This was the kind of mum she had always wanted. 'It won't come to that,' Jo told her. 'I *am* getting better. Give me a few more days and I'll be behaving as rationally as the next person.'

Heather looked quizzical. 'What do you mean?'

'I think it would be a good idea if you tell Heather what's been going on. As much as I'd love to, I can't stay here for ever and when I do eventually go back home I need to know that you have a strong support network in place.'

'OK, but can you explain?' Jo said.

Liz nodded but before she said anything she heaved the pile of post she was balancing on her lap over to Jo. 'I'll do the talking while you do the sorting. There's mail in there that's been hanging around for weeks.'

Jo obediently went through the post one letter at a time as Liz proceeded to tell an increasingly dismayed Heather how her best friend had been unravelling before her eyes without her noticing. Liz threw in her own diagnoses along the way, Jo had a little agoraphobia, a little OCD and maybe even a touch of postnatal depression for good measure despite what the doctor had said. Jo didn't think she had a 'little' of anything, just an irrational fear of what might be waiting for her outside the front door coupled with the real fear that it would bring on another panic attack. But she kept quiet. She wasn't interested in dwelling on those thoughts right now; all she wanted was to get better.

By the time Liz had finished her analysis, Jo had opened all the envelopes and sorted them into piles, one for recycling and the other for action.

'I'm so sorry, Jo. I feel like I've let you down,' Heather said.

'You shouldn't feel bad. I've been fooling myself along with everyone else.'

'Well I'm telling you now; you won't fool me a second time. I'm going to be watching you like a hawk.'

'That's exactly what I wanted to hear,' Liz said.

'Me too,' Jo added.

While Heather gave Jo a tight hug, Liz got to her feet. 'How about I clear this mess and then make a start on dinner? You're welcome to stay, Heather.'

'Thanks for the offer but I'm expected back home,' Heather said, realizing a second later that she was in danger of failing Liz's first test of loyalty. 'But I'll stay if you want me to, Jo.'

Jo raised an eyebrow at her mum before smiling at her friend. 'You go home, Heather. I'm safe enough while I've got my mum fighting my corner, aren't I, Mum?'

Liz was only half listening as she said, 'Of course, sweetheart.' She had become temporarily distracted by the pile of papers Jo had said were for recycling. 'You haven't opened this one yet. It's from the police.' Without waiting for permission, she tore the flap and pulled out a photograph which had a note from DS Baxter attached. 'It's a photo of you-know-who at a cash machine,' she said with a barely disguised curl of the lip. She was holding out an image of David withdrawing money.

Pushing it away without even looking at it, Jo said,

'Please, Mum, I don't need to see it, Steph's already identified him. I don't want to look at his face.'

Jo still hoped that one day David would have the guts to step out from his hiding place so she could put her fears behind her once and for all and get the answers she deserved and needed. But by comparison, she couldn't imagine a black-and-white photograph giving her anything other than more questions, so it was returned to the envelope and pushed out of her mind.

23

Jo and her mum sat in silence. They were sitting on a wooden bench secreted away in a walled garden that was bursting with colour thanks to a carpet of crocuses, the first of the spring blooms to break through the icy layer of winter. Reynolds Park was close to home, but the journey had been a long one.

'It went better than I expected,' Jo said at last.

'At least she didn't say come back when you've worked out what's wrong with you,' her mum said cynically. Her gloved hand was playing nervously with the contours of her seat. 'But then I think I would have throttled her if she'd tried that one.'

'Dr Lawton is nothing like Dr Robertson was,' Jo said, referring to their old family GP who had so quickly come to the conclusion that Jo was nothing but an attention-seeking teenager.

'But General Anxiety Disorder, it sounds so . . .'

'Official?' Jo asked. She was still getting used to the term herself, and although her GP couldn't be conclusive, it sounded much better than her mum's description of a little bit of this and a bit of that. It was only a label, however, not the cure – and certainly not a remedy to rid her of that feeling of being watched.

'At least she seems to think therapy will help and a six-week wait isn't too bad, I suppose.'

'By the way you were badgering her, I wouldn't be surprised if an appointment came through sooner,' Jo said, keeping her tone light while she tried not to frown.

There was no doubting that she had come on by leaps and bounds since her mum's arrival. She had been sick with nerves every time she left the house; frightened in equal measure by the thought of having another panic attack and the ever-present possibility that her husband would appear out of nowhere; but she had gone outside and so far there had been no more than a wobbly moment or two. She could almost believe that one day she could leave the house and not be confronted by the hunted feeling that had pursued her for the past few weeks.

What she tried to focus on now was the doctor's conclusion that the panic attacks weren't simply a recurrence of an isolated incident that had happened fifteen years ago. Jo's battle with anxiety certainly had its roots in her teenage years but with the doctor's gentle coaxing, she had allowed herself to follow a clear path through to the present day, her life littered with all of those quirky rituals and idiosyncrasies that David had adored – or perhaps endured. She had a mental illness and *this* was what caused her shortness of breath, the crushing feeling of weight on her chest, not the possible presence of a man in the shadows, watching, waiting.

'I remember how you used to stalk the customers in our

shop,' Liz said, jolting Jo out of her inner thoughts. 'Rearranging anything they dared to pick up or move. It annoyed the hell out of me.'

'You don't have to remind me,' Jo said, but the laugh caught in her throat as she wondered if it was her annoying habits that had pushed David over the edge.

Liz couldn't share the joke either, but for different reasons, and for once, she looked in a worse state than her daughter. Her face was haunted and her eyes hollow.

'I never understood, not back then, and not even when I turned up two weeks ago. I'm ashamed to say it, but it's only just starting to sink in. I came here thinking I could fix you, Jo. I didn't realize I was the one that broke you in the first place.'

Jo closed her eyes and savoured the long-awaited revelation but only for a moment. It was a step in the right direction for their relationship, but Jo wouldn't let her mother take the burden all on her own. 'I should have spoken up, but then you were my mum and I was a teenager, so you were the last person I wanted to talk to,' she said. 'I'd worked myself up into a state because I was scared that you and dad were going to get divorced. I thought I was the expert on broken hearts and I didn't want dad to go through it too, not when it wasn't his fault. Did he know about the affair?'

Like Jo, Liz pretended it wasn't the first time they had openly acknowledged that her relationship with the travel agent had gone beyond innocent flirtation. 'I told your dad years later; long after it was all over. I needed to clear my conscience but I knew I was taking a risk and I wouldn't have blamed your dad if he'd kicked me out of the house.

298

But instead we moved on together. That was why we relocated to the Lakes. It was a fresh start for both of us.' There was a pause and then she added, 'I never imagined for a minute that you would be the one left to suffer the after-effects.'

Jo took her mum's hand in hers. 'Oh, don't go building yourself up into the villain of the piece. I've had plenty of other traumas since then. You weren't the only one to mess with my head and, at the end of the day, it's my head and my mess and you know how I love putting things back in order again.'

'What about going back to work, though? I meant what I said about supporting you if you need to take more time off.'

Jo was shaking her head. 'No, I go back in less than two weeks and I'm ready. It'll be good for me and Irene's champing at the bit to look after the baby.'

Just then Archie began to stir. 'I'll see to him,' Jo said as if to prove a point.

Archie had been sleeping in his pram to the side of the bench but Jo picked him up and cradled him in her arms. She took a long look around the garden until her eyes settled on the entrance. She couldn't stop herself from imagining David stepping through the arch, but despite the lurch inside, she wouldn't cower from that thought. If he caught sight of her now, she would look to the world like a proud new mum. One day she hoped she would *feel* like that too.

'I think it's time we all went home,' Jo said turning to her mum, a chill wind causing a shudder to run through her.

'OK,' her mum said brightly, taking a moment to realize

what her daughter meant. 'No, Jo. I couldn't leave you, not yet.'

'I need to learn to cope on my own again,' Jo insisted. Her mum had been a godsend and the thought of sending her back to the Lakes filled her with dread but, she reminded herself, her mum wasn't disappearing into thin air, nor was she running off with a travel agent.

'Maybe next week,' Liz countered. 'Besides, Steph's going away this weekend and we promised to look after Lauren.'

'*I* promised,' Jo corrected. 'And I can manage, Mum. I'm ready to stand on my own two feet again thanks to you.'

Liz stood up and before she wrapped her daughter and grandchild in her arms, she said, 'You don't have to thank me. I love you and I'd do anything for you.'

Jo caught her mum wiping her eyes as she pulled away. 'And I love you too.' Jo's lips were trembling almost as much as her mum's as they both tried to smile. 'Go home, Mum.'

Liz took a deep breath then released it through pursed lips. 'I suppose I do need to get back to see what kind of state your father's left the shop in,' she mused.

'Well, if you need someone to come and help reorganize the mess, you know where I am,' Jo said. Sensing her mum needed one final push, she added, 'You've already made Steph and Heather swear to be at my beck and call if I need them. The worst is behind us, I promise.'

Jo coped well during the first few days on her own, although she spent precious little of that time actually on her own. Steph dropped in during her lunch hours and Heather came by on her way home from work. By Friday, Jo was tired of being kept under constant scrutiny and told them to stop fussing and keep away – she was determined to have a day without worrying about anyone watching her, seen or unseen.

This morning she had risen early after a reasonable night's sleep. Archie had woken in the night only once and she was showered and dressed before he woke for his eight o'clock feed which he took with only a little resistance. He'd become used to his grandmother cosseting him throughout the day but while Jo still felt distinctly second best, he settled back down surprisingly easily.

She was feeling confident and looking forward to her first full day flying solo. She was toying with the idea of going on a shopping expedition to get some treats in for Lauren's stay that weekend – she had decided that she would rather have Lauren at her house than move herself and Archie into Steph's – when she glanced out of the living room window and spied Sally walking down the path.

The day was bright and clear, but as Jo stepped into the hall, only thin slithers of light trickled through from the outside world. The front door's brooding eye had been closed, its lid made from a patchwork of multicoloured silk. It was a parting gift from her mum who had made the blind from two dozen deconstructed neck ties she had acquired from a charity shop. It was the perfect remedy to stop Jo from feeling anxious every time she passed through the hall, expecting a figure to loom large through the glass panes.

Approaching the door, Jo became aware of her breathing, which remained steady as did her pulse. A smile crept across her face as, without hesitation, she opened the door that she no longer needed to deadbolt because only she had a key.

'Hello, Sally, this is a nice surprise,' she said, although by the look on her sister-in-law's face she wondered about that.

'I don't suppose there's been any more news from the police about David?' Sally asked once they were in the living room, having given Archie only a passing glance as he slept peacefully in his bassinet.

'The police? God no, I don't think they're even looking for him now,' Jo said. 'If there's going to be a breakthrough then it can only come from David or someone who knows more than they're letting on. If I'm honest, I was hoping that person would be Steve. That day Irene thought he'd disappeared, I was hoping he might have gone straight to David and we'd be able to track them both down.'

Sally had a look of disgust on her face. 'It's a shame it wasn't Steve who went missing in the first place! I don't think David deserves whatever it is that's happened to him – but Steve? Now there's someone who deserves everything he gets.'

'I take it there's no chance you'll let him back home then.'

'What home?' Sally asked bitterly. 'The house is on the verge of being repossessed.'

Jo was dumbfounded. She watched her sister-in-law drop down heavily on the sofa and put her head in her hands before asking, 'What's happened, Sally?'

'I've been such an idiot, Jo! Who in their right mind would let someone like Steve take control of the finances? I should have known he would go off the rails without David keeping him on the straight and narrow. In fact I *could* see it; I just let it happen. I was tired of beating my head against a brick wall and Steve's habit was definitely a brick wall.'

'Steve's habit?' Jo asked.

'His gambling habit.' Sally shook her head. 'I take it by the look on your face David didn't tell you, but then again I don't think he truly appreciated how bad it was. Neither did I until the bailiffs turned up on our doorstep. That's why I kicked him out.'

Jo stared at Sally in disbelief. She knew her sister-in-law only worked part-time and Steve's job in a car factory wasn't exactly well paid but they had always been relatively comfortable, or should have been, on paper at least.

'He has gambling debts?'

'Big ones,' Sally confirmed. 'The car's already been repossessed.'

'What will you do now?'

'I've seen a solicitor to formalize the separation but our finances are a mess. We're almost certainly going to lose the house and when that happens, I'll be moving back home with my mum. Fortunately she's more than happy if it means I'm finally shot of Steve.' She looked up, blinking rapidly as she willed away angry tears.

Jo wiped her fingers across her mouth as if to rub away the feeling of Steve's lips on hers. She had found yet another reason to find him repulsive. 'I'm so sorry, Sally, I don't know what to say. Irene was telling me he's working lots of overtime so maybe he is trying to sort things out,' she offered.

'That's what he's telling her,' Sally replied with a sniff. 'Don't take anything he says at face value, Jo.'

'I'd rather not speak to him at all, if I'm honest,' Jo said. When Sally gave her a curious look, she added, 'I've had my fill of the Taylor brothers, I think we both have.'

'Don't think too badly of David, Jo. He was a good man; we both know that in our hearts. *I* certainly owe him a lot.' Sally had her head bowed and was turning her mobile phone over and over in her hand. 'I think the police should still be searching for him,' she said, almost too quietly for Jo to hear.

Jo felt a shiver that gave her goose bumps. 'Why? What makes you say that?'

'I know you don't want to hear this and I understand how it must be easier to think he's left you rather than imagining something awful but it just doesn't make sense. We *should* still be looking for him, Jo. I don't know, maybe—'

'No, you don't know,' Jo interrupted. 'It's not wishful thinking if that's what you're trying to say. There's enough evidence to prove David's guilt, Sally.'

'Yes, but some of that evidence came from Steve and I don't believe a word of it. I don't accept that David was so afraid of becoming a father or so keen to travel the world that he would abandon you both, and you know what?' she asked, finally looking up. 'I don't think Steve believes it either. He may *talk* about David running away but he *acts* like he's never coming back, as if he *knows* he isn't coming back.'

Jo's mouth fell open in shock. 'Are you saying you think he killed him?'

'God, no, of course not! I didn't mean it to sound like that, not at all. It's just that . . . I get the feeling that Steve has reconciled himself to the fact that David must have died. He wouldn't walk out on you, Jo. I think you know that but if you've forgotten then maybe you should look at this. I came across it the other day and I knew I had to show you.' Before Jo could stop her, Sally pressed a button on her phone and turned the screen towards Jo. 'Don't you remember this? Is that the kind of man who looks terrified of becoming a father?'

Jo's eyes were wide with shock so she could see the screen perfectly. When the video started to play, the first sound she heard was the tiny squeals of delight from Luke. He was sitting cross-legged on a leather recliner looking to his left at someone out of shot of the camera. He clapped his hands and shouted, 'Again, again.'

A man's arm could be seen pulling the lever on the side of the chair to raise the leg rest. A moment later, the man came into full view. David was wearing jeans and the jumper Irene had bought him the Christmas before last, which he hated but had worn to prove how much he loved his mum. When he glanced towards the camera he winked.

'Oh, I'm so tired! I think I need to have a rest,' he said.

With a hint of amateur dramatics, he sat down on the leg rest only for it to collapse beneath him, dumping him unceremoniously on to the floor. Luke's resultant squeals verged on hysteria and then the camera started to shake. Sally could be heard laughing and Jo was there in the background too, but David's laugh was the loudest. He had grabbed hold of Luke and was tickling him.

'Stop it!' Luke cried between breaths.

'Stop it,' Jo said coldly. 'Stop it, Sally. Please.'

Sally shook her head. 'Have you forgotten what he was like?'

Of course Jo remembered. It was the last Christmas they had spent together and it had been moments like this, watching David playing with Luke, that had formed part of the justification in Jo's mind for ignoring her husband's calls to postpone having a family.

'Turn it off!' she shouted. 'What the hell are you doing, Sally? Do you really think I want to see David being the kind of father to your son that he'll never be to mine?'

Sally stood up, tears welling in her eyes. 'I'm sorry, Jo,' she said. 'I thought I was helping.'

'Helping! How on earth is this helping?' Jo said. 'David might have adored Luke, but he didn't want *my* baby. He called him little FB and do you want to know what it stands for? Fucking Burden!' Jo spat. 'David left me! He's out there, Sally! He's doing God knows what, but he's out there! I may not have cute videos, but I certainly have plenty of photos of him creeping around town taking money out of his account!'

Sally was blinking away the tears. 'He's been seen?'

'At a cash machine, twice!'

'I – I didn't know.'

'How could you not know?' Jo demanded. While the look of confusion on Sally's face told her she clearly hadn't known, it was still hard to believe. 'OK, the last time was after you and Steve split up but the first time was back in November.'

'I swear, Steve never said a word about it. I've heard you all talking as if you were sure David had left but no, I never knew why you were so sure. He's alive?' Sally asked, her relief palpable.

306

Jo wasn't sure if it was the mixture of anger or fear that made her brain make previously unthinkable connections but she couldn't stop herself. 'Why do you care so much? For that matter, why did you come here, Sally? Do you want David back for yourself? Exactly how close were you?'

Sally's jaw dropped open. 'Jo, I don't know what you're suggesting but please don't—'

Jo was already shaking her head as she recalled something Simon had said. 'David treated Luke like a son. Was he? Was that one of his dirty secrets? Is it one of yours?'

'No! Please, Jo, I know you're upset but that's ridiculous. You know David better than that! He loved you!'

It wasn't so much the things she said but the look of horror on Sally's face that brought Jo back to her senses. 'Just go,' she said quietly. When Sally didn't move, Jo raised her voice. 'Go! Get out of my house!'

After slamming the front door on Sally, Jo went through to the kitchen and locked the back door too, even though she wasn't sure any more what she was trying to keep out. Was it David, Steve, Sally – or perhaps just her inner thoughts? Returning to the hall, she bolted the front door then double-checked that it wouldn't open. Her white-knuckled hand refused to release its grip on the doorknob as she listened to the violent thump, thump, thump of her heart which all but drowned out the sound of Archie's whimpers. She had woken him up when she had been yelling at Sally.

Reminding herself how far she had come, Jo refused to move until she stilled her mind, but the thoughts she had tried to evade were there already, spiralling out of control. It was making her dizzy as she chased one scenario to the next. Was the David she knew really capable of abandoning his wife? And if he wasn't, then where the hell was he? What had kept him away? Was he being forced to take money out of his account? Was there another reason why had he sneaked back into the house?

The sound of the doorbell gave Jo a start but rather than release her grip on the doorknob, she pulled across the deadbolt with her other hand and then swung the door open so fast it startled her mother-in-law.

'How are you, love?' Irene asked, trying not to react to the look of terror on Jo's face.

Jo's mouth was bone dry when she tried to find her voice. 'Irene, what are you doing here?'

'Your mum phoned to tell me she was going home so I thought you might be missing a bit of mothering.'

As Jo let Irene into the house she tried to regain her composure. She had no idea how much her mum had told Irene about her anxiety attacks. 'I'm much better,' she said, hedging her bets.

'I told Liz you must have been completely run down the way that tummy bug knocked you for six. You still look a bit peaky.'

Irene headed straight for the living room where Archie had worked himself up into a ball of fury after being left unattended. He was in quite a state and Jo was left wondering how long she had stood by the door. It had felt like just a moment but she guessed it must have been quite some time – long enough for Irene to arrive without bumping into Sally and for Archie to get upset because his mother wasn't responding to his cries.

'Now then, what's all that noise?' Irene said, picking Archie up with practised ease, seemingly oblivious to the screams which filled Jo with terror. 'There, there, Archie, you remember me, don't you?'

Other than one brief visit when Jo had stayed in bed feigning illness, Irene hadn't seen her grandson since he had been ill, but whether he remembered her or not, he recognized the tender embrace of love. When he had calmed down a little, Irene turned to Jo and said, 'He's growing so fast, isn't he?'

'It's hard to think he should only be three weeks old now,' Jo said, surprising herself by how normal she sounded when her mind was still spinning.

'Uh-oh, I think he needs changing.'

'I'll do it,' Jo said, but the moment Archie was transferred into his mother's arms, his howling resumed. Jo could feel Irene's eyes boring into her, judging her. She tried to convince herself it was an irrational fear, as illogical as her body's response to it. Her pulse raced and showed no signs of slowing even though Archie's cries had become marginally less deafening.

Irene watched the look of horror she had seen earlier return to Jo's features. 'Here, let me,' she said softly. 'Why don't you go and make us a nice cuppa?'

Jo's body had tensed to the point that she couldn't release her grip when Irene tried to take him. Thinking she was refusing to hand the baby over, Irene stopped what she was doing. She frowned when she saw the tears slipping down Jo's face. 'Jo? What is it, love?'

Jo shook her head. 'Like you said, I'm just a bit run down. You're right, why don't you change him while I make the tea?' she said quickly, tipping Archie into Irene's arms and rushing from the room.

The kettle was boiling noisily so Jo didn't hear Irene walk in behind her a few minutes later. Jo had her hands on her chest and was slowly bringing her breathing and her pulse back under control.

'What's wrong, Jo? And no fobbing me off this time.'

When Jo turned to face her mother-in-law, two pairs of eyes were on her. Archie's were still wet with tears but he looked otherwise content in his grandmother's arms. 'I've started having panic attacks. I haven't had one for a while and I thought I was getting better, but . . .' Should she mention what had just happened with Sally or her fears about David stalking her? Wouldn't it be better to talk it through with someone? Jo hesitated. She couldn't do it. She didn't dare risk evoking that memory of David again, playing with Luke. 'I'll be all right. I just need to calm myself down.'

'Have you been to the doctor?'

Jo nodded.

Irene looked momentarily unsettled. She scanned the kitchen counter as if she would find what she was looking for. 'Did he give you anything?'

'I'd only turn to medication as a last resort,' Jo assured her, thinking of her father-in-law, as she knew Irene would be.

'You know Alan was on them?' When Jo nodded again Irene sighed before continuing. 'I'll never really know if the drugs affected Alan's personality along with the stroke but they certainly didn't help. That being said, I wouldn't judge anyone else based on that one experience.' When Jo didn't

310

look convinced, Irene actually winked then said, 'My friend Joan has taken antidepressants for years and she swears by them.'

Jo couldn't hide her surprise. 'I thought you'd disapprove.'

'Don't think I haven't been there myself, Jo. My doctor would have handed me a prescription without blinking and I really don't know how I managed without them, but I did and I still am. Talking to Joan helped. I suppose it was something as simple as knowing you're not the only one out there.'

'I'm on a waiting list for cognitive behavioural therapy to see if that helps.'

With her free hand, Irene rubbed Jo's back briefly. 'Good. I think you're doing the right thing, but if you need anything from me, you only have to ask. You do know that, don't you?'

Jo felt herself relaxing at last. She hadn't wanted to deceive Irene, not when she was about to become so involved in their daily lives once Jo returned to work, and even though Jo wasn't telling her mother-in-law everything, it was a start. 'Thanks, Irene and I'm sorry I didn't confide in you earlier.'

'Letting people think you're superwoman will only create a rod for your back and I, for one, am glad you're not. None of us is perfect and we all have our crosses to bear.'

There was a weary smile on Irene's face which made Jo think of Steve, which in turn made her think of Sally, the video, the laughter, David's face . . . A trail of tears was flowing silently down her cheeks before she even knew it.

'You are getting better, Jo,' Irene said. 'Keep telling yourself that.'

Jo watched Irene rock Archie slowly back to sleep. A gentle peace had enveloped him and Jo tried to absorb some of it. 'I will,' she said, not sounding as confident as she might have done before Sally's visit. 'I have to. I'm back at work a week on Monday.'

Irene cupped her hand on the side of Jo's face, wiping away her tears with a thumb. 'Then I'd better get some more practice in. Did you have much planned for today?'

'A bit of shopping.'

'What if I took . . .' Irene began just as Jo started to speak too.

'Could you . . . ?'

They both smiled and the plan was settled.

After helping Irene bundle Archie and his belongings into the car, Jo bent down and rested her lips on his forehead. 'I love you, Archie,' she whispered.

The baby had been dozing but when she stepped back his eyes were open and he frowned at her. Jo could feel her whole body trembling and she barely kept it together as she held her son's gaze. Love me back, she pleaded silently before shutting the car door.

Giving her daughter-in-law a hug goodbye, Irene said, 'Take some time out for you, Jo. Spend the day pampering yourself and come pick him up when you're ready.'

Jo promised she would then hurried back into the house, bolted the door and raced upstairs to the nursery to watch Irene drive off with her son. She remained at the window long after they had driven out of sight, pretending as always that she wasn't searching for a glimpse of David and longing for his return – if only he would be brave enough to step out of the shadows.

The house settled into an uneasy silence, but Jo knew what was coming; she could already hear echoes of David's laughter. Her mind was intent on replaying the video Sally had shown her even as she tried to resist. She didn't want to hear his voice or see his smile. She didn't want to remember how much she had loved him or how impossible it was that he could ever betray her. She certainly didn't want to consider how much she still loved him, even now.

Desperate to outrun her memories, Jo wound up the cot mobile and latched on to the rhythm of the lullaby as if it were a lifebuoy. But her imagination was stronger than the chimes of the music box and it began pulling her under. She sank to her knees as the image of her husband gained substance. He felt close enough to touch and, frustrated that she couldn't, Jo curled herself up into a ball and put her hands over her head. When she began to cry, it wasn't the gentle weeping that had accompanied so many long and lonely nights, nor was it the torrent of tears that had been released every time her heart had been cracked open a little further. This was a keening that grew from the pit of her stomach, becoming a howl as it ripped through her lungs and shook her whole body, again and again and again.

24

David was there in the room with her while Jo lay sleeping in bed and at first she thought she was still dreaming. She held her breath and strained her ears for the sound of the shower lurching into life, which would herald the start of the recurring dream of their last morning together. But as the seconds ticked by the bedroom remained eerily silent.

Still floating somewhere between sleep and consciousness, a shudder zipped down Jo's spine and she released her breath with a gasp. He was definitely there, but rather than a sound, it was a smell that had alerted Jo to her husband's reappearance in her life. She could smell David's aftershave and when her eyes snapped open, she knew it was no dream.

'David?' she whispered as she lifted her head from the pillow and looked urgently around the room for signs of life. But if her husband had been there watching her sleep then he had already slipped expertly back into the shadows.

The bedroom door was still closed, nothing was out of place although there was something missing. She stared at the empty space where Archie's bassinet should have been and gave herself a moment for her thoughts to come into focus. The last fingers of sleep released their grip on her and then she remembered everything, from marching Sally out of the house the day before, to phoning Irene later and asking if she could keep Archie a little longer. She hadn't been able to face the battle of going out to pick him up, having expended all her energy in allowing herself the luxury of missing her husband. She had even invited him back into her dreams by sprinkling aftershave on her pillow. But what had given her comfort the evening before had brought that familiar debilitating fear slithering into her bedroom during the night. With a sickening twist of the stomach, she realized David wasn't there after all and she was the one left feeling lost.

It had taken many gruelling weeks for Jo to pick herself up only to be knocked down again by Sally's thirty-second video; a happy scene that challenged her conviction that David had left her, a squeal of laughter that had drowned out arguments that declared her husband's guilt; a smile that insisted he loved her and would never leave her. It was evidence that told her that, if she was brave enough to listen, she should start grieving for her husband.

But this morning, with chills still running through her veins after David's latest visitation, Jo wasn't listening – her husband was still out there, somewhere. The feeling of being stalked was slowly wearing her down and now, she was barely functioning. She didn't think she would be able to pick herself up again this time, but she had no choice, not today. It was eight o'clock and Steph would be dropping Lauren off at any moment so she dragged herself out of bed, pulling the bedding with her so she could put it in

315

the washing machine and protect herself from the danger of loving memories once more.

'Are you sure you're up to this?' Steph asked half an hour later as she stood at the door looking dubiously at her sister. Jo was wearing leggings and an oversized shirt that now had damp patches on the shoulders where her soaking wet hair dripped.

'I should think Lauren will be the one looking after me rather than the other way around,' Jo said.

The throwaway comment was a little closer to the truth than Jo would have liked and she suspected her sister felt the same. Steph's only alternative would be to take her stroppy teenage daughter away with her but with Heather on her travels too, that would leave Jo completely on her own, alone and vulnerable. The solution had suited everyone.

'She knows the rules,' Steph said, looking to Lauren who had slipped away into the house as soon as she heard a lecture coming on.

'Can I make some toast, please?' Lauren asked, already halfway to the kitchen.

'Make some for Jo as well,' Steph said as she too stepped over the threshold. 'I bet you haven't eaten a thing yet, have you?' As she spoke she peeked into the living room, having already noticed the pram missing from its usual space in the hall. 'Where's Archie?'

'Irene wanted to get some practice in before I go back to work.'

'She's had him overnight?'

'They were getting on like a house on fire,' Jo said, 'and she persuaded me a good night's sleep would do me some good.'

Steph cocked her head as she listened to the lies slip effortlessly off her sister's tongue. 'So when are you going to pick him up?'

'I thought it would be nice for me and Lauren to have a girlie weekend to ourselves, and Irene doesn't mind. I've said I'll go and get him once you've collected Lauren tomorrow.' When Steph didn't look convinced, Jo smiled. 'I'm not about to abandon my own son, Steph.'

'I'm glad to hear it,' her sister said. 'And I hate to spoil your plans for a girlie night but Lauren has asked if she can go to her friend's house later to work on a project. It contributes to her exam results, otherwise I would have said no outright but I did say she'd have to check with you first.'

'Oh,' Jo said in a tone that suggested disappointment but was nearer to a sense of dread she was struggling to define. 'If she needs to go then of course she can.'

Steph raised her voice for Lauren's benefit and said, 'I've told her she has to let you know when she's leaving her friend's house. She's fine getting the bus home but she has to be back by ten at the very latest.'

Jo's stomach lurched as she imagined sitting at home waiting for someone she loved to arrive home. 'I would rather pick her up,' she said. 'I don't mind.'

'I know,' Steph said, and didn't argue. She recognized the fear in Jo's face for what it was. 'But don't let her run rings around you. Here's her friend's address and I've also written down the address and phone number of the hotel we're staying at. I'll have my mobile switched on too. If there are any problems I want you to promise you'll let me know straight away.'

They both heard the sound of a car horn from the road. Gerry was losing patience.

'I get the message! Now go before Gerry drives off without you,' Jo said, grabbing the piece of paper from her sister who still refused to move. 'Go, Steph!'

When Jo was eventually released from her sister's clutches, she followed the smell of toast that cut through the scent of disinfectant in the kitchen.

'Rule number one,' Jo said as she took in the scene of chaos that Lauren had created in a matter of minutes. 'You leave the kitchen as you found it.'

Lauren sighed heavily as she put the lid back on the jar of marmalade and returned it to the cupboard, albeit on the wrong shelf and with the label facing inwards. Jo frowned and drew her gaze away from the cupboard and towards the dusting of crumbs covering what had been a pristine countertop. Sensing her aunt's disapproval, Lauren gave a tut before stuffing half a piece of toast in her mouth and then swiping the crumbs off the counter and on to the floor.

Jo raised her hands in submission and said, 'You win! I'll clear up if you take your bags up to the nursery.'

Lauren smiled. 'Are you sure you don't want me to make you some toast first?'

'No, thank you,' Jo said and let her niece enjoy the sense of victory for a moment before she added, 'There's an inflatable bed to blow up while you're up there and when you've done that you can take the piece of paper on the dresser in the hallway and write down the *real* name and address of the "friend" you'll be visiting tonight.'

* * *

Lauren had sworn on her grandmother's grave that she would text Jo before ten to get her to come pick her up. Jo had to remind her that both her grandmothers were alive and kicking but nevertheless was still willing to put her trust in her niece. She held on to that thought as she settled down into an armchair with a hot cup of cocoa. It was nine o'clock and the next hour, or God forbid longer, was going to be a real test of nerves, despite telling herself that this wasn't history repeating itself. Lauren would be coming home, Jo knew this, and she also knew that she wouldn't hesitate when the time came to go out and pick her up: she wouldn't make the same mistake twice. While the rest of Jo's body fidgeted, she kept her breathing steady and her gaze fixed on an empty spot on the wall above the mantelpiece. Although it had been smashed to pieces, the ghost of the starburst clock still taunted her.

Jo's phone beeped and vibrated on her lap and she picked it up expecting a text from Steph but it was Lauren asking Jo to pick her up right away, with two exclamation marks. Jo was still typing the reply as she bounded out the door and within ten minutes she pulled up outside the address Lauren had given her. She exhaled slowly and deeply but the relief was short-lived when Lauren tumbled out of the house and into the car.

'Can we go?' Lauren asked when Jo made the mistake of asking if she'd had a nice time.

Jo didn't say another word until they were back in the house and Lauren was halfway up the stairs, heading for bed.

'I was having a cup of cocoa before you texted. Do you want one?'

319

Lauren's step faltered. 'No, thanks,' she muttered.

'I'll bring one up for you in two minutes,' Jo insisted.

With two steaming hot cups, Jo crept into the nursery a few minutes later. Lauren had switched on the lamp and was sitting cross-legged on the inflatable bed as she feverishly tapped away on her phone. Clearly thinking Jo's eyesight had a zoom function, she turned her body away to shield the screen. Her body language told Jo she wanted to be left alone but Jo had no intention of backing away. There was something almost liberating about seeing someone else in trouble and feeling able to help. She set the mugs down on the floor before dropping so heavily on the mattress that her niece almost bounced off.

'Man trouble?' she asked when Lauren's muted mutterings had ebbed into silence.

'I hate him!'

Jo handed her a mug of cocoa. 'Tell me about it.'

Lauren blew away a cloud of warm, chocolate-flavoured steam and took a sip. When she lifted her heavily made-up eyes to Jo, there was a glimpse of the little girl she hadn't quite outgrown. She had a chocolate moustache on her upper lip. 'He wanted sex.'

It was Jo's turn to stop herself from falling off the inflatable bed.

'I said no,' Lauren added.

'And then what?' Jo asked, her unsettled mind already thinking up all possible scenarios, none of which she wanted to dwell on too long.

'He sulked like a child.'

'How old is he?'

'Sixteen next month. He thought he could wine and dine

me and then get me into bed, but I told him right from the start that if he loved me as much as he said he did then he would have to wait. I'm not jail bait,' said the child who was doing her best imitation of the kind of sophisticated woman she would one day become.

'And where were his parents while all this was going on?'

'They've gone away for the weekend.'

'Thanks for telling me, Lauren! If I'd known what was going on then I would never have let you put yourself in that kind of situation. Anything could have happened. Apart from the fact that you were out drinking . . . What if he hadn't taken no for an answer?' Jo ran her fingers through her hair as she tried to free her mind from the images that were stampeding across it. In her other hand, her mug was slopping chocolate on to her legs. 'My God, Lauren, didn't you stop to think?'

Lauren took Jo's drink from her shaking hand and set both mugs down on the floor. 'It's all right, Jo. I'm fine. I had half a glass of red wine which was disgusting – and I know how to kick a man in the balls if I have to.'

Jo wanted to tell her that it wasn't always that easy, that it didn't matter how much you trusted someone, there was always a chance they would hurt you one day, but she chose to say nothing and accepted the hug her niece offered.

'I thought I was the one who was supposed to be consoling you?' Jo said when she finally released Lauren. 'I'm sorry he turned out to be such a scumbag. You won't be seeing him again, will you?'

'He's texted me to say he's sorry.'

Jo released a scornful laugh. 'That was very decent of him. And what did you say?'

'I haven't replied yet. I want to give him some time to think about what he's done.'

Jo let a smile break free. 'You're beginning to sound like your mum.' The thought set another in motion. 'Will you tell her?'

'Can't we just keep it between ourselves?'

'I'm not your mum, Lauren. She's the one you should be having awkward conversations with about sex and, God forbid, contraception.'

'But—'

'You should talk to your mum.' When Lauren looked as if she was about to follow her boyfriend's lead and begin to sulk, Jo felt obliged to add, 'But I'm here for advice any time you need it – and if you want my advice now, then you can do better than this guy.'

'Can I? Who else is going to be interested in a fat, ugly ginger minger?'

'You're not fat and you're not ugly! You are a beautiful young woman with an amazing figure and stunning red hair.'

Lauren looked unimpressed. 'Funny, that's not what other people see.'

'What people?'

'My boyfriend, for one. That's what he called me.'

'He called you a fat, ugly, ginger minger?'

Lauren nodded.

'Then I have two issues,' Jo said. She could feel the fight rising in her and it made her feel more alive than she had in a very long time. 'Firstly, he's your *ex*-boyfriend, and secondly, *he's* the ugly one, not you.' Jo tried to wipe away the chocolate on Lauren's face. 'So, what am

I going to have to do to make you feel better about yourself?'

Jo didn't quite know how it had happened. One minute they were planning on spending Sunday safely inside, slouching around watching soppy films and wearing mud masks and the next it was late afternoon and Steph was at the door with a look of absolute horror on her face.

'Don't you like it?' Lauren asked.

'Please don't say that's real!'

Unable to look at her a minute longer, Steph stormed past her daughter and into the house. She was searching for Jo and didn't have to look far. Her sister was peering around the living room door. 'It could have been worse. She wanted to bleach her hair,' Jo said meekly.

'You mean you went along with this?' Steph asked when she recognized the look of guilt that had been absent from her daughter's face but was painfully apparent on Jo's. 'She knows I would never allow her to get it done, not in a million years! You really thought I'd be OK with this, Jo? A nose stud! Really?'

Steph's eyes were wide with a mixture of shock and anger. Jo wanted to take a step towards her but withdrew further into the living room. 'I know it's drastic but she needed to feel good about herself; she needed to realize how beautiful she is.'

'And mutilating her body is doing that exactly how?'

'I took some convincing too, but I can see how it will make her feel more confident about herself.'

'Jo was only trying to help.'

Steph turned on her daughter. 'Go and get your things, now! We're going home!' she snapped.

As Lauren stomped upstairs, Jo tried to calm Steph down again. 'She's going through a tough time at the moment. She needs our support.'

'Really? You're in the best position to offer advice now, are you?' Steph waved a hand in front of her face as if to bat away thoughts. 'I'd better go before I say something I regret.'

'Like what, Steph? Am I not competent enough to offer an opinion? Do you think I'm so dysfunctional that I can't help Lauren?'

'Dysfunctional enough to let her get her nose pierced, yes!'

'It's not permanent, for goodness' sake! Look, I don't know what it must be like for you in your perfect world with your charmed existence, but some of us don't have it so easy! I hope Lauren inherits your luck, really I do, but if she doesn't then I want to do my damnedest to make sure she doesn't end up all alone like me!' As her voice rose, Jo could hear Lauren sobbing her way down the stairs but her eyes remained levelled on her sister.

Steph was shaking her head. 'I'm not even going to try talking to you while you're like this. Maybe you should spend less time trying to sort out Lauren's life and concentrate on your own child. Why is he with Irene, Jo? What else is going on in that—'

When she broke off, Jo finished Steph's sentence for her. 'In that twisted mind of mine?' she asked. 'You really want to know? I couldn't do it, Steph! I couldn't make myself go over to Irene's and pick him up. I stood by the door with my coat on and the car keys in my hand. All I had to do was get to the car but the more I thought about it the more I froze. I'm terrified in case David is out there watching me, judging me like everyone else seems to do! And after ten minutes, I just thought . . . What's the point? What *is* the point in bringing Archie back here? What do I have to offer him? Will I be sending him off to school in a few years' time hoping I'll still have the courage at the end of the day to pick him up again? Or do I keep him trapped in the house with me? That's if I still have a house, which isn't likely if I can't get myself to work!'

The barrage of questions had come thick and fast, Jo's voice rising higher and higher. Steph blinked in response to each but couldn't answer a single one. Jo made a strangled sound in her throat. 'I've tried, I swear I've tried, but every time I take a step forward, I'm pushed back another two. Helping Lauren helped *me*, Steph! But yet again I'm being pushed back and back and back!' she cried, only stopping when she ran out of breath.

'Let's talk about this,' Steph said, suddenly much calmer.

'No, you were right first time,' Jo said calmly and coldly. 'I think you had better go.'

In a repeat of Friday morning, Jo found herself ordering someone else out of the house. After closing the front door, she didn't dare give herself time to think so set to work tidying up, starting with the barely visible crumbs in the kitchen and working her way upwards. When she reached the nursery, Jo's first job was to wrestle with the mattress, which Lauren had deflated but not put away. She made a poor attempt at flicking it so she could lay it flat on the floor before rolling it up but in her eagerness she knocked the table and lamp over. By some miracle, the lamp didn't smash and she righted the table and placed the lamp back on top. She was about to replace the stuffed giraffe on the shelf beneath when something caught her eye. The table had a small backboard and poking out at the bottom was a piece of cream paper. She tugged at it – and pulled out the missing birth certificate.

It trembled in her hand as she stared at it. It must have slipped off the table, lifted perhaps by a draught as she closed the nursery door, before becoming wedged between the shelf and backboard. David hadn't been in the house, and maybe, just maybe, that meant he hadn't ever been watching her at all? And why would he? She was a pitiful excuse for a wife, a mother and, as Steph would agree, a sister and aunt.

With a sinking feeling in the pit of her stomach, Jo left the mattress on the floor and went into the study to put the certificate away safely with all the other import-ant documents. Then she went downstairs to the kitchen where she stood staring blankly at an open cupboard and a box of pills. She wasn't sure if she wanted to throw them in the bin, take one – or take every last one of them.

She hated who she had become and it was that self-loathing that forced her to face her worst fears. What if she had been jumping to the wrong conclusions all along? What if, as well as not being out there watching her, her husband wasn't *anywhere*? What if David was dead? What if she had been learning to hate and fear a man who had remained the devoted husband and father to the last? How would she be able to live with herself? What would be the point in carrying on simply to endure the pain of getting through one day to the next?

Standing motionless, Jo felt every last connection with her husband being severed, including the fear that had driven her to breaking point. It surprised her how much she didn't want to let it go. It was perverse, she knew that, but the fear of being watched had been a way – the only way – of keeping him in her life. He could still be out there, couldn't he? There was still the police evidence that he was alive. No, no – she wasn't ready to let him go.

And then suddenly he was there, standing behind her. She could feel the warmth from his body when he slipped his arms around her waist and she leaned into him and allowed herself to reconnect with the one person who could give her life meaning again. An image came unbidden to her mind of a little boy laughing and giggling. It wasn't a memory of Luke, this time, but a tantalising glimpse of Archie and the joy to come if only she was brave enough to fight for his love, to fight for the little boy with the dimple in his chin that was the last tenuous link to her husband.

When Jo was ready, she didn't pick the box of pills. She picked up the phone instead.

25

Jo's hands burned. It was a painful and yet comforting sensation, a complete contrast to the tingling she felt in her fingers when an anxiety attack ripped control from her grasp. She had spent all of Monday cleaning the house and the smell of bleach as she scrubbed the kitchen cupboards had stung the back of her nose as well as her bare hands. She should have worn gloves, she should have opened windows but she had thrived on the intensity of her chores, which overpowered any other feelings or thoughts including the temptation to go to Irene's and collect Archie before she was ready.

She was no nearer knowing where David was or what had happened to him, and even though she was starting to accept that he wasn't lurking in every shadow, her anxiety disorder wasn't going to release her from her fears without a fight.

Occasionally, the sound of a phone ringing intruded upon her endeavours but she refused to be distracted. It was only when the doorbell rang at six o'clock that evening that Jo was ready to consider allowing a little of the outside world in.

'Reporting for duty, ma'am,' Heather chirped but her confidence dissipated as soon as she stepped into the house. 'I think you'd better tell me exactly what's been going on, including why this house is full of fumes. I can hardly breathe.'

Jo led Heather into the living room where the smell of cleaning products was marginally less overpowering. Heather pulled a face and squeezed her nose. 'Well?' she asked.

Jo looked at her perfectly presented friend in her tailored suit with something akin to nostalgia. 'I need your help,' Jo began. 'I'm ill, Heather, and I'm sick of it.'

'Do we need to get your mum back here?'

'No, or at least not for the moment. If she comes back then she'll only mother me. I thought I was making progress but I was just following where she led. What I need is someone who can help me work things out for myself – and that's where you come in. Heather, you're the most straight-talking woman I know, please help me fight this.'

Of all the people who had been watching Jo's life unravelling, Heather was the only one who refused to treat her with kid gloves. The Jo she knew was confident and controlled so it was almost implausible to her that her friend's fears and obsessions could ever control her, and it was Heather's belief in her that Jo intended to use to her advantage. Heather was going to help her mend her broken mind by treating her normally and reminding her of the person she had been so Jo could see a way back.

'I should have come home from Portsmouth last night when you phoned. Have you actually been to bed or have you been cleaning the house for the last twenty-four hours?'

'It makes me feel better,' Jo tried.

'How are you ever going to pull yourself together, Jo if you're high on fumes?'

Jo was smoothing out the folds of her T-shirt as if she could straighten out the crumpled shell of a person sitting in her living room, occupying her place in the world. 'OK, Heather, let's get one thing straight. I have a mental illness. This isn't going to be a matter of "pulling myself together".'

'I know,' Heather said, 'but if you want some advice, stop cleaning like a lunatic.'

'Thank you for that little gem, but it's not going to be that easy,' Jo said patiently. 'I still haven't got my appointment with the therapist and even when I do, I have to be realistic. There's only a limited amount of treatment on offer on the NHS and I can't afford to go private, so that means I'm going to have to look at ways to help myself.'

'With my help?'

'Will you?'

'I'm not sure I could play at being a therapist, Jo.'

Jo laughed. 'I wouldn't dare let you inside my head, although I can certainly give you a sneak preview. I've spent the last few weeks obsessing about David being out there watching me and that's why I've been so terrified to leave the house. But I'm not so sure any more; in fact, I'm starting to believe it less and less. I've even taken the blind down off the door,' she added proudly.

'Yes, I noticed. Not one of your mum's finest creations.'

'It served its purpose, but I don't think I need it any more. What I do need though is someone who can help me rationalize my fears once and for all and tempt me back out into the world.'

'Do you want to go out for a walk now?' Heather offered.

Jo tried to ignore the flutter of her heart, which had temporarily jumped into her throat. She had wanted to go out all day, but even though she had stopped feeling as if David was watching her every move, she had another fear to contend with: she was terrified that she would have another panic attack in spite of her new-found confidence and where would that leave her? How would she ever convince herself that she was free from her fears? 'Not yet, I'll need to build myself up to that, learn how to relax, how to stay calm when I feel an anxiety attack coming on.' She had a hand on her chest and the warmth from her burning palm soothed her. 'You haven't seen me when I'm having an attack, it's not pleasant, Heather, and they can come out of nowhere.'

'You can't put me off, I'm here to help.'

'I'm glad to hear it, but I don't think you quite realize what we're up against. My mind's been in free fall these last few days.'

Heather crossed her legs, leant forward in her chair and rested her chin on a hand. 'I think you'd better tell me how this all started.'

Jo raised an eyebrow – trust Heather not to beat around the bush. Her thoughts spun round inside her head, but this was what she needed; this would help her grab hold of them. She started by telling Heather about the creeping fears she had felt since Archie was born, going into detail about how she had been convinced so many times that David had come back home only to discover it was Steve hiding behind the tree or knocking at the door. She talked about the birth certificate disappearing, about chasing shadows along the path by the station and finally about waking up in bed, convinced that David had been watching her. All of these were false alarms – she knew that, which only gave more substance to Sally's counter-argument.

'I can't help thinking Sally's right,' Jo said. 'Oh, God, what if David didn't leave me? What if—'

'But he's been *seen*, Jo. He's been caught red-handed dipping his fingers into his account. I mean, I'm certainly not about to convince you back into thinking he's been spying on you, but I do think that he's out there somewhere.'

With her hand still on her chest, Jo could feel her pulse quicken. 'You're right, of course you're right . . . But if you had seen the look on David's face when he was playing with Luke! I was there, I saw him, and he was desperate to be a dad. He was simply struggling to let go of this twisted belief that he couldn't be a good father until he had done everything else he wanted to achieve in life. It took that damned video to remind me what I already knew: he wouldn't walk away, Heather.'

Heather sighed. 'I don't blame you for wanting to think the best of him, I'm struggling to understand it myself, but he left you, Jo. He made his plans, he took his passport and his money and he left you. No. Doubt. About it,' she finished, spitting out each word.

Jo released a juddering breath as she willed herself to accept the convincing argument that was the lesser of two evils. *David wasn't dead*. 'So what I'm left with is a constant battle to convince myself that he isn't stalking me.'

'If you're that scared, then carry some pepper spray.'

'I can't do that!'

'I would,' sniffed Heather.

'I wouldn't.'

Heather looked shrewdly at her. 'So you're not *that* scared of him then?'

Jo rubbed her chest to ease the ever-present tension as she gave some thought to what Heather was trying to say in her inimitable way. 'It's not that simple. You have no idea what it's like, this fear is paralyzing. Just taking that first step outside is like jumping from a plane and not knowing if I'm wearing a parachute.'

'The step isn't *that* high,' Heather exclaimed with a twinkle in her eye.

Jo's jaw clenched. She didn't want to see the joke and wondered if Heather had been the right person to turn to after all. 'Do you think I don't know that? I'm well aware that not all my fears are rational, Heather, but it doesn't stop me reacting as if they are very real. It's like they feed off each other. Even when Archie was ill, when he needed help. What did I do? I stood in the hallway rooted to the spot. I let him down,' Jo said and closed her eyes as she relived the terror of that moment when she had been paralyzed by fear, imaginary and real.

'But you didn't let him down. You got Archie to the doctor.'

'Yes, but what about the next time? Even sitting here thinking about going outside brings me out in a cold sweat.'

The phone rang, giving Jo's already tense body a start. Heather looked back and forth from Jo's face to the phone, which her friend was refusing to pick up.

'I'm not answering it,' Jo explained. 'It's only Steph. She's been phoning constantly since last night and I think

333

she might have come over at dinner time too.' There was in fact no doubt that Steph had visited. Jo had been standing at the nursery window and had seen her arrive then leave again five minutes later when Jo refused to answer the door. Her sister might not like the sun going down on an argument but Jo was in no rush to face that particular problem just yet.

'She has a right to be angry,' Heather said after Jo explained what had happened.

'I know, but there was more to it than simply letting Lauren get a nose stud. I can't tell you and I won't tell Steph either. It's for Lauren to explain to her mum and I have to give her time to do that. But if I'm honest, I was the one who ended up the angrier one out of the two of us,' Jo said. 'She had a go at me for leaving Archie with Irene.'

Heather cleared her throat. 'And how long exactly are you planning on leaving him there?'

Jo had phoned Irene the night before and again that morning but with her self-confidence at an all-time low and Irene still worried about the state of Jo's mind and her ability to care for the baby, neither could summon up a good argument for Archie's return.

'I'm scared that I can't be the kind of mother Archie deserves.'

'Do you want to be?'

Jo looked away, avoiding Heather's eyes and the question itself. 'It's not fair on him. I've let him down time and time again.'

'So you don't want him then?'

Jo closed her eyes and immediately saw the little boy of

334

her imaginings. 'Yes, I want him. I want my son so, so much,' she said but when she opened her eyes and the image disappeared, she added, 'But if the last few days are anything to go by, he can do better.' She gulped, ready at last to consider something she had been too ashamed to fully acknowledge before. 'And what if the one thing stopping David coming home is Archie? What if it's best all round if the baby isn't here?'

Heather shook her head. 'Look, it's going to take me a while to get my head around all this anxiety business, but if you want my considered opinion then that's a load of bollocks.'

Jo's eyes widened. 'Thanks, Heather.'

'Well, it is. You told me you wanted my help, so you're going to have to put up with some straight talking. Archie's already been abandoned by his dad; he's living with his grandmother who no doubt loves him very much, but he's also under the same roof as that good-for-nothing son of hers. Or one of them, at least. Do you want Steve to be a role model in your son's life? The man who could make a pass at his missing brother's wife?'

Jo wished she hadn't mentioned the incident to Heather and was half expecting her to drag her out of the house there and then to collect her son. 'No, I wouldn't want Steve anywhere near Archie, given the choice.'

'Good, because you *do* have a choice. We're going to get Archie back here where he belongs. You cared enough about him once to get him to the doctor. So, if you love him, you'll pick him up sooner rather than later. You say you need time to prepare? OK, you have until tomorrow but you will go get him, Jo Taylor, and you'll do it because it's the best thing *all round* for you and for your son.' She stopped dictating only long enough to allow herself a smile. 'Sound like a plan?'

Playful bees chased bright yellow sunflowers in a relentless pursuit that cast long shadows across Archie's empty cot. Jo was watching from the rocking chair as she hummed along to the music. Pushing herself gently back and forth, she kept her breathing steady as she prepared herself for the epic journey to Irene's house a few miles away, a journey that would begin with one step.

Jo blinked slowly then turned to the window. The morning looked surprisingly bright but the world was still in the grip of winter and she imagined it would be deeply cold outside. She pictured herself opening the door and lifting a foot over the threshold. No one was watching her, no one was judging her, she repeated to herself but her heart still raced. She wasn't ready yet, but there was no rush, she would take her time, she would do this right. She had told Irene she would pick the baby up at midday and it was only eleven. Her pulse began to slow.

'You are my sunshine, my only sunshine,' she sang and as she did, she thought of David. He had been her sunshine and the world had been impossibly dark without him. The house was devoid of light and life and she felt his absence seeping into every nook and cranny; but here in the nursery there was dappled light playing amongst the shadows. There was hope.

Heather had filled Jo with such determination that she felt a growing sense of anticipation at the thought of being reunited with her son. 'You make me happy when skies are grey,' she continued.

When the music stopped, all she could hear was the sound of her deep, steady breaths. She stood up. David – the man who must be alive somewhere because she couldn't consider anything else – had left such a mess for her to clear up but Archie wasn't going to be part of that. He could be the shining light in the darkness if only she would let him in. Ready to face the world, Jo headed for the stairs but at the last moment changed direction. There was no need to hurry, she reminded herself.

Standing in the study, the chaos David had created was painfully apparent. There was a stack of correspondence between Jo and the countless organisations she had been forced to explain her misery to; everything ordered into neat files but with so many loose ends still to tie up. To one side of the desk an in-tray groaned under the weight of incoming mail. Her mum had opened some but more envelopes had arrived since then.

She didn't have time to go through everything but she could make a start by separating the tedious junk mail from the more demanding correspondence. It was a job that needed doing and it was far better to do it while Archie wasn't there, she told herself as she justified her latest delaying tactic.

The task didn't take long at all and soon the only envelope left in the tray was the one from the police that her mum had wafted in front of her but which Jo had refused to look at. She picked it up now, took a deep breath and removed the contents.

It was another black-and-white image of a man standing

in front of a cash machine. Because of the camera angle and the way his head was bowed, the man's face was mostly hidden by a baseball cap. It could have been David, she supposed; he was the right build and there was some sense of familiarity, particularly about the coat, which she knew would be olive green, one of Nelson's corporate colours. She was surprised how little emotion the photo evoked. With a sigh, she pulled open a drawer and took out a manila-coloured file so she could add the photo to the rest of the police evidence she had acquired. Opening the folder, she smoothed it out until her hand came to rest next to a faint smudge on the inside cover. She traced it with her finger. It was yellow paint.

Pulling out the contents of the file, Jo quickly found another smudge. The paint was the exact same shade as that in the nursery and she knew *she* would never have been so careless, but then she hadn't painted the nursery, Steve had. She turned over the smudged piece of paper and stared at another black-and-white image. This one was the first cash withdrawal and she found herself lining up both photographs side by side. Her eyes darted from one to the other. The man withdrawing cash the second time had used his right hand to take the money, not his left, as she would have expected David to do. She took a closer look at the tantalising glimpse of his face beneath the peak of his cap until her nose was almost touching the paper. She couldn't be sure, but as she sat back she let her mind summon up a third picture, the image of a man shivering against the cold in a flimsy white T-shirt and pulling a baseball cap out of his pocket. It was the same man who had stumbled into her house smelling of stale beer before taking her in his arms and telling her how sorry he was and how guilty he felt. That man was not her husband.

When Irene opened the door, she had to take a quick step back as Jo pushed past her mother-in-law into the house.

'Is Steve here?'

'He's on nights,' Irene said. 'Why? What's wrong, Jo?'

'He's in bed?'

'Jo, what's wrong? You look as if you've seen a ghost. Are you ill again? Do you want me to call the doctor?'

Jo didn't have time to explain; Irene was going to have to catch up as the drama unfolded.

Taking the stairs two at a time, Jo reached the landing and stormed straight into the second bedroom where she found Steve sprawled out on the bed in a mess of linen and limbs. Lying on his back with his mouth wide open, he had one arm dangling over the edge of the mattress, the other tucked beneath a pillow. Jo launched herself on to the bed and grabbed hold of his T-shirt. He cried out in shock and reflexively shoved away his unknown attacker. Jo almost lost her balance as Steve scrambled up so fast that he fell out of bed. He kept moving until his back thumped against the bedroom wall. Jo had been lucky his first reaction hadn't been to throw a punch.

'What the f—' he began and then recognized his assailant. 'Jo?'

'It was you!' she screamed, kneeling up on the bed with the envelope clenched in her fist.

Steve was still too groggy and confused to make any sense of the accusation. 'What was me?'

Gasping for breath, Jo struggled to open the envelope.

Her body shook so much she was in danger of toppling off the bed herself.

Irene was standing behind her. 'Jo, why don't you try to calm down so we can sort this out? I don't know what's going on but we're all here to help you. If you don't want me to phone the doctor yet then maybe I could phone your mum or your sister. They can help decide what to do.'

The gentle, sympathetic words were meant to placate Jo but instead they fuelled her anger. 'Shut *up*, Irene. I'm not going mad! Look!' She had ripped the photograph from the envelope and snapped it straight so Irene could have a clear view of her son's betrayal. 'It's Steve!'

She turned back to her brother-in-law who was wide awake now and looking just as terrified as his mother, although Jo suspected for completely different reasons.

'*You* withdrew the money! Look at the date stamp, Steve! It was the day Sally kicked you out, the night you turned up drunk at my house. Remember? You were wearing a T-shirt in the freezing cold. Where was your coat? Was it this one?' she asked waving the photo at him. 'Did you borrow David's coat that night so you could do his bidding and withdraw more money?'

'Please, Jo,' Irene was saying, 'Steve only had a T-shirt on when he arrived on my doorstep too. There was no coat. There's only one person it could be in that photo and that's David, it has to be.'

Jo ignored Irene's infuriating attempt to pacify her and continued to stare at Steve. Her eyes were wide and she could feel the sting of tears. 'What about the baseball cap! That's yours, isn't it, Steve? You've seen him, haven't you? Were you out together drowning your sorrows? Did you get David caught up in something to do with your gambling debts? Is that why he left?' Steve was shaking his head but Jo wouldn't give in. Sally was right; she couldn't take anything he said at face value. 'You've been letting us suffer all this time while you've known what happened and why he left! Where is he, Steve?'

Steve squirmed with each accusation. 'I swear to God, Jo, I don't know where he is! You're not well and you're going to make yourself worse if you carry on like this.'

'Steve's right,' Irene said. She had come closer to Jo in a bid to encourage her off the bed. 'You're not in the best frame of mind right now. I know you want answers, we all do. But screaming and shouting won't get you any nearer the truth.'

'Look at it, Irene!' Jo demanded but the fight left her with a sob.

Irene started rubbing Jo's back in much the same way as she might to soothe Archie.

'Look at it, please,' Jo begged but the tattered photograph had blurred from view and she began to cry. She had been so certain when she stood in the study looking at the photo with the sunlight streaming through the window. She hadn't stopped to think it through but had gone with her instincts just as she had done a few days earlier when she had accused Sally of an affair, and yet again, she was making outrageous accusations that were utter nonsense and made her look a fool. Why had she been so sure?

It didn't make sense, of course it didn't. Why would Steve be the one to withdraw cash if David was there? She was still crying as Irene guided her out of the room. Steve stayed where he was.

'Why don't I phone Steph?' Irene was asking. 'You shouldn't be on your own now.'

Jo wasn't listening as she made her way downstairs and into the living room where Archie had been sleeping soundly throughout his mother's latest histrionics. It was only when she began collecting up his belongings that she realized what Irene was suggesting. Her mother-in-law put her hand protectively on the bassinet. 'You can't possibly look after Archie while you're this upset.'

'I'm fine, Irene.'

'Do you really believe that after what's just happened? Please, Jo, you're not ready.'

Irene's gentle voice was hypnotic and before Jo knew what was happening, her mother-in-law had pulled Archie's changing bag from Jo's hand and guided her to the sofa. 'I'll make us a nice cuppa and then phone Steph. She can come and pick you up. I don't think you should drive in your current state.'

Or look after a baby, Jo added silently. She had failed to keep her husband and now she was losing her son. She was lost. The answers to David's disappearance eluded her like shadows in a lightless world. The police photograph had been a lone spark but now she wondered if she had only imagined it. While Irene disappeared to make the tea, Jo couldn't bear to look at the baby so took one last look at the crumpled piece of paper she had continued to clutch in her hand. She could see only the man's right arm, which was draped in deep shadow. No, something *was* wrong and she angrily wiped away the tears so she could focus on the coat sleeve. Was it really shadow or was it possible that the material had been blackened by some other means? A

342

half-formed idea blazed across her mind and more lights flickered into life. Jo jumped up and stormed back upstairs.

'It's not David's coat at all!' she yelled, launching herself at her brother-in-law for the second time. Steve had been standing in the middle of his bedroom but once again found himself pinned against the wall. Jo wasn't going to back down this time and thumped her fist against his chest before he had a chance to answer. 'You were wearing my coat! You said you threw it on the fire but you kept it so you could impersonate your brother and take his money!' The photo was balled up in her hand but she didn't need to see the charring where the sleeve had caught fire and from the look on Steve's face, neither did he.

'Don't, Jo,' Steve begged.

For a split second, Jo wanted to listen to him. If Steve had used her coat then he hadn't necessarily seen David. And if he had access to David's account to withdraw cash that second time, then why not the first? Those two sightings were the only tangible pieces of evidence she had that David was alive and well. She didn't want to do this because then she would have to face her worst fears – which by Jo's standards, would be off the scale – but she could no longer run and hide. 'You've been stealing off your own brother!'

'No!' Steve yelled back but he didn't push Jo away. 'I wouldn't take anything from Dave without his permission! I probably deserve to be hated, but not for that Jo, not for that.'

Jo was glaring at him but for a second or two she said nothing. Her mind was sharper than it had been for months and the connections she made terrified her. 'Sally told me about the bailiffs and about the house being repossessed,' she said, surprisingly calm. 'That doesn't happen overnight, Steve. You must have been in arrears for a long time. How much did you owe? Did £3,000 keep your head above water a few months longer? Was it David who bailed you out before he went missing?'

'Stop! For God's sake stop! Isn't it better to believe that he's still out there?'

Steve tried to push her away which reignited Jo's anger. 'I want the truth!' she screamed as she hit his chest again, determined to beat the confession out of him. She was within touching distance of knowing what happened if only she could hold her nerve and she had to: for her sake, for Archie and for her marriage. She wasn't sure she was going to like the answers she would find but it had to be better than living with the questions.

'I may be losing my mind but I'm not stupid, Steve! That *was* you in the photo. Did you already have David's cash card so you could withdraw the money? Did he trust you with his pin number? Of course he did, you're his brother! Why wouldn't he be that foolish? Well I'm no fool and I don't trust you,' Jo snarled. 'David gave you the £3,000 and once he wasn't there to give you any more you took it – you took the rest all by yourself. It was you, all along.' Jo's voice was trembling with emotion that exposed a vulnerability that she didn't want Steve to see. It made her all the angrier and she vented it with another blow to the chest that Steve didn't even try to deflect. 'I can't believe you've stood by and let everyone think he was safe and well. You stopped the police searching for him, you let us all abandon him!'

344

Countless memories of David flooded Jo's mind, ones she had replayed over and over again in search of hints of deceit and betrayal, but the one she clung to now was the one Sally had forced her to confront: the one of the man who had brought love, light and laughter to her world.

'You let us all hate him!' she cried, her words strangled and full of pain. 'You made me believe—' she broke off with a tortured gasp. 'You made me believe that he was still out there, that he was watching me! You made me think he didn't want Archie, and because of that I was prepared to push my child, my last link to David, away! How could you? *How could you?*'

'Stop this, Jo. Please,' he begged.

Jo shook her head. Despite knowing it was perhaps too little, too late, she was determined not to let David down now and her eyes darted across the room. Steve had been staying with his mum for over a month but he was still living out of the bin bags Sally had dumped on Irene's doorstep. Jo presumed it was to fool his mother into thinking it was only a temporary arrangement. She shoved against Steve and flew towards the bags, tearing open the nearest one and scattering clothes across the room. Steve rugby tackled her.

'Get off me!' she screamed. Her fingers clawed through the second bag she had been trying to open as Steve pulled her away, leaving a trail of black plastic ribbon and crumpled T-shirts. Unable to reach the bags any more, Jo turned on Steve and released months of pent-up anger and frustration as she punched and clawed at him.

'Steven!' a voice boomed.

Steve and Jo both froze then turned as one towards the

door. Only minutes earlier, Irene had looked at Jo with eyes brimming with sympathy, now there was only pain. She looked from one to the other and then let her gaze fall to the floor where the detritus of Steve's life lay scattered. The bin bag Steve had been pulling Jo away from lay gaping with the arm of a waterproof coat reaching out towards them, the cuff partly melted and the sleeve a mangled mess of charcoal black and olive green.

The colour drained from Steve's face as Irene stepped purposefully across the room. The sound of the slap was a thunderclap that heralded a cloudburst.

26

When Jo returned home the sun was obscured by a curtain of grey, but there was enough light left in the day to see Steph's car parked outside the house. Jo wanted time on her own to think and considered driving past and parking somewhere out of sight until her sister went away. She had been haunted for months by unfathomable questions that might explain why David had left her only to have them swept away by a single, pathetic confession. But Jo's momentary euphoria had been eclipsed by the one question that Steve couldn't answer and she asked it over and over again: if you didn't leave me, if you haven't been shadowing me all this time, then where are you, David?

As Jo pulled into the drive she was reminded of all those unremarkable car journeys they had taken together, never once considering that the drive home on the evening before David's trip to Leeds would be their last. With her eyes fixed firmly to the front, Jo began to reach a hand over to the passenger seat as if she could reconnect with the man she remembered and not the demon she had imagined him to be for far too long. Her fingers stretched tentatively towards the space he ought to occupy, the tips of her fingers electrified with desperate longing as if she was within a hair's breadth of the man she loved. He was sitting next to her and any moment now she would touch his arm, trace her hand towards his neck, comb her fingers through his hair and pull him towards her. Together again, at last . . .

Jo held her breath, anticipating that the power of her mind would give substance to her desire but her fingers sliced through emptiness. With a sob that caught in her throat, she let her hand fall but it dropped only a couple of inches before hitting rigid plastic. She trailed her fingers around the curve of the baby carrier handle until she touched lamb-soft wool. Spreading her hand wide and with barely any pressure at all, she explored the folds of the blanket until she found that long-lost connection back to her husband: Archie, David's flesh and blood.

She turned to Archie and braved a smile. 'Welcome home, sweetheart.'

Her eyes were glistening as she turned to open the car door where a shadow loomed in front of her. Jo got out of the car as if she hadn't seen it and walked to the passenger side to retrieve her son. She wondered whether or not Steph would go away if she continued to ignore her but she knew her sister too well.

'You might as well make yourself useful and help carry some of Archie's things into the house.'

Steph did as she was told without a word.

Once inside, Jo set about unwrapping each of Archie's many layers until he was snuggled only in her arms. 'So go on then,' she demanded. After the day she'd had, Jo was more than ready to face her sister's wrath. 'Get it off your chest.'

'I'm here to apologize.'

Jo's eyes narrowed. She hadn't expected that. She was, after all, the one who had corrupted her niece. It had been irresponsible to let Lauren pierce her nose, whatever the reasoning behind it. If she had been in a better frame of mind, she wouldn't have even considered it, she could see that now. She could see everything so much clearer since her confrontation with Steve. 'No, *I* should be the one apologizing. I shouldn't have done anything without your approval first.'

'Lauren told me what happened.'

'All of it?'

It was Steph's turn to narrow her eyes. 'I think so. The pathetic excuse of a boyfriend who I didn't even know existed who thought he could deflower my daughter and then proceeded to destroy her already fragile self-confidence by calling her a ginger minger?'

'Deflower?' Jo asked with a smile.

'She's my baby girl, Jo. I'm not ready to think of it in any other terms.'

Jo continued to smile as she looked down at her sleeping son. He was eleven weeks old now but no bigger than a newborn. It was impossible to imagine him as a grown man let alone how she would deal with his rites of passage. 'I understand,' she said. Where once there had been cold fear at the prospect of being responsible for such a tiny being, now she felt warmth flooding her chest.

'I see you've got him back.'

'It was a close call. Are we friends again?' Jo asked.

'You've had me worried sick for the past couple of days, Jo. After everything you've been through I was so scared that I'd tipped you over the edge. I didn't sleep at all on Sunday night and if I hadn't managed to speak to Heather last night, who reassured me that you were OK, then you might have had the police breaking down your door at one point.'

'Sorry.'

'No, *I'm* sorry and I need you to know that no matter what you do or what you say, I'll always love you. I'm never going to abandon you, Jo. I'm not David.'

Jo held her smile for a second, maybe two, and then the mask she had been presenting to her sister slowly began to crumble. Her lip trembled and the curve of her mouth dipped. 'I don't think he did abandon me, Steph.' Her voice cracked and a cold shiver ran down her spine as she considered exactly what that meant. 'I know where all the money went.'

As Jo described her confrontation with Steve, literally blow by blow, Steph's mouth fell open.

'It was meant to be a temporary loan,' Jo explained of the money David had given Steve. 'Apparently it was after David had taken me for the twenty-week scan. He told Steve he didn't need the money he'd saved for a holiday until the baby was born, so he gave him his bank card to withdraw the £3,000 to pay off his debts, or some of them at least.'

'But he carried on taking money after David went missing! How the hell does Steve justify that?'

'According to Steve, he was trying to return the card when I caught him in the study that day after David had gone missing.'

There was nothing but contempt on Steph's face when she said, 'He couldn't have tried very hard.'

Steve's confession had sickened Jo and she could barely repeat his excuses. 'He says that when he started taking out more cash, it was to help me. He used it to pay for decorating the nursery.'

'£300 for a pot of paint? I hope you're not falling for any of this. He took your coat, Jo, and kept it hidden so he could use it to creep around impersonating his brother. He even used his left hand to throw us all off the scent, for God's sake, and the only reason you caught him out was because he was too drunk the second time to remember. It's not just theft, it's callous and cruel because it gave you hope that David was still alive.'

Jo gave a broken laugh. 'He actually tried to convince me that it was an act of kindness because it made Irene and me feel better. And when I didn't fall for that one, he tried to say how his dad's death had affected him as deeply as it had the rest of the family – but I swear, Steph, if there was one person who actually agreed with Alan's last words about family being a burden, it was Steve.'

'So is he still trying to say he thinks David left of his own accord or . . . not?'

The residual anger left Jo's body with a sigh. 'I couldn't get a straight answer out of him. I think he believed what suited him at the time, but then I can hardly blame him for that.'

'You can't, but the police can. Have you phoned them yet?'

'I couldn't while I was at Irene's. She's absolutely devastated.'

'She's not taking Steve's side, is she?'

Jo shook her head. 'No, she's as desperate as I am to get the search started again. We've wasted so much time.'

'Yes, we have,' Steph said. She was already reaching for the phone.

The angelic child that Jo had brought home from his grandmother's house a few hours earlier was reacquainting himself with his vocal chords and his screams were deafening. Up until that point, she had been so proud of herself. It had been a gruelling day but one she had faced without once hesitating at the front door, not even when she had left to go to the police station to make a formal statement. While the flimsy world she had created to make sense of David's disappearance lay in ruins, Jo had somehow remained standing. But now, as she watched her son turn bright red with fury, she felt an old fear returning – how could she be a mother to this baby, the one whose conception she had been blaming for driving her husband away as much as she had blamed herself?

'I'm not falling at the last hurdle,' she told him in the gentlest of voices that belied the tremble in her throat. She patted the baby's arched back in a slow, steady rhythm and willed her pulse to do the same.

Like a bottle of soda being agitated, Jo could feel the bubbles of panic rising in her stomach so she retreated to the nursery and waited for the sunflowers to begin their merry dance before settling into the rocking chair and attempting to give her freshly bathed son his last bottle before bedtime.

'I remember the first time I ever saw your dad,' she

whispered when Archie stopped crying momentarily to explore the teat of the bottle. 'He was wearing . . .' Jo tried to summon up the image in her mind.

The meeting had been in Nelson's boardroom and Jo had chosen a seat closest to the door while David had been hemmed into the corner. All eyes were on him as he tried to explain his ideas for some project or other. He had been wearing a suit, possibly dark grey, and perhaps a white shirt. She couldn't recall, and for a moment this made her sad, but then she remembered the most important thing. 'He was wearing a smile,' she told Archie. 'Not a big cheesy one, it was more of a mischievous grin and he aimed it at me. What could I do? I cut him down and wiped that smile off his face, but your dad was a glutton for punishment. He kept coming back for more.'

When Jo returned to the present, the lullaby was still tinkling in the background but it was the long, satisfied gulps coming from Archie that took her by surprise. The baby's eyes were heavy but he was looking directly at her. 'So why didn't he come back this time?' his gaze asked.

'I don't know, Archie,' she said, 'but I really believe that he would come back to us if he could.'

The thought that something bad had happened to David ought to have terrified her as much, if not more so, than in those early days. She remembered quite vividly that sensation of having her heart torn out of her chest and ice-cold fear pumped into her veins. It was a feeling that would undoubtedly return, but for the moment she was in the eye of a storm. After months of denying her true feelings and learning to despise the husband who had abandoned her, Jo felt such a pure rush of love for the man she had given her heart and soul to, that it took her breath away.

27

'It's a straw,' Jo said, pointing out the obvious when Heather handed it to her.

They were having lunch at the Neighbourhood Café the day after Steve had made his confession. Jo had selected the same table where she had met Simon but today there was no desire to look out of the window and scan every face, no flutter of expectation that a passer-by would turn and give her that enigmatic smile. She wasn't searching for the man who was capable of turning his back on his wife and child because he didn't exist. There were, however, more practical considerations for choosing the table. It was the easiest place to park the pram. Archie had just been fed and, with a little help from Heather, was now sleeping peacefully so his mother could enjoy her own lunch in peace.

'I've come across a relaxation technique called straw breathing,' Heather told her. 'You breathe in through your nose and then out through the straw. Try it.'

'Erm, I don't think so,' Jo said with a half-smile.

Heather raised an eyebrow. 'It's to regulate your breathing.

You'll need to practice but once you're confident then whenever you feel yourself getting panicky you can use it.'

'So when I'm back at work and start to feel anxious, you really think I'm going to sit there with a straw in my mouth? Do you not think making a fool of myself will make me even more stressed?'

'It's not the only technique,' Heather said. She handed Jo a plastic folder crammed full of printouts from various websites. 'There are tons of other ideas in there, and I've also ordered a couple of self-help books that have had really good reviews.'

Jo took a sip of coffee as she mulled things over. 'I'm not sure I need them any more.' She was as sure as she could be now that whatever had happened to David, he wasn't coming home. As she let that thought settle, she held on tightly to her coffee mug and pretended not to feel the tremor coursing through her body.

'Jo, you've got to take it slowly. You said yourself that your anxiety doesn't always have to have a rational reason behind it.'

Shrugging, Jo said, 'I'm not saying I've completely got my act together, but after yesterday I feel as if I can face anything. I must have looked like a raving lunatic when I attacked Steve, but that was justifiable.'

'I don't blame you – and if anything I'm in awe of you. I don't know how you held it together.'

'I know. But I did. Enough to make it up with Steph and then go through everything Steve had told me with the police,' Jo added with a note of pride.

'And bring Archie home.'

'Ah, but that was the easy part,' Jo said as if the fraught

bedtime drama had never happened. 'I couldn't have left him there with Steve in the house and at the time Irene was in a worse shape than I was.'

'How is she?'

'Still in shock, I think. She phoned this morning to say that she's told Steve to leave. I hope she follows through with it because I don't want her looking after the baby if he's there. Not that I have any other real option if I'm going back to work next week.'

'You can't go back now!'

'I have to. My maternity leave ends and while I suppose I could get signed off sick, I wouldn't do that. I could only imagine what Kelly would make of it and besides, it's bad enough that my home life is in limbo, I can't deal with my working life being put on hold too.'

Heather didn't look convinced. 'But what about the police investigation? If they reopen the case—'

'They already *have* reopened the case,' Jo corrected.

'So things are going to be more stressful for you in the short term at least.'

Jo wanted Heather to stop there and then. She didn't want to be told that she might be asking too much of herself. Heather was the one she was relying on for encouragement. If she had wanted a dose of realism, she would have phoned her mother. Heather caught the look and responded to the unspoken plea.

'All right, maybe going back to work is a step in the right direction. It will give you something else to focus on and at least it gets you into a routine of leaving the house, but you're going to have to find some time for exercising too. It's another way to boost your mental health.'

357

Jo pulled back her shoulders to make room for her expanding confidence. 'I walked all the way here,' she said.

'So now we need to build up your energy for the walk home,' Heather said, picking up a menu.

Jo had been banking on Heather offering her a lift home but she wasn't about to admit it. 'I will,' she said, and while her friend was deciding what to have for lunch, Jo glanced out of the window. There had been a heavy downpour overnight, and although the rain was holding off, she had no idea how long the calm would last.

As Jo left the café, the sun was making a brief appearance and its smiling face reflected off the vast puddles she was so intent on dodging that she nearly knocked someone down.

'Hello there, stranger.'

Jo looked up into the smiling eyes of Simon Harrison and after the obligatory cooing over the baby, she asked, 'So how's it going back at work?'

Simon laughed softly. 'And what am I doing here in the middle of the working week? I'm not off sick again if that's what you were thinking.'

'I didn't think any such thing,' Jo said, already feeling a blush rising in her cheeks. 'I'm the one that's off, remember, so you don't have to explain your movements to me.'

'Not like that replacement of yours.'

'I presume by that you mean Kelly – and she is not my replacement. I'll be back next week.'

In the blink of an eye, Simon's laughter lines were replaced by deeper furrows. Not quite a look of sympathy, but empathy, perhaps. 'Glad to hear it.' He held the look, testing to see if she would hold his gaze and allow him to speak openly. 'How have you been?'

'Fine,' she answered a little too quickly.

'That good, eh?'

Jo shrugged. No one at Nelson's knew about her problems or at least not the ones that hadn't made the news and she wanted it to stay that way. So why she started opening up to Simon, she couldn't quite explain. 'I'll be honest, Simon, it's been hard. I lost sight of the person I was for a while.'

'I know how *that* feels.'

Trying to smile, she said, 'The good news is I think I've found her again although it's fair to say it's a work in progress.'

Simon nodded his approval and then, to answer the question Jo had been too polite to ask, he said, 'I've taken a day's leave today. It's exactly two years since Jimmy died.'

Jo needed no further explanation. Jimmy was the workmate who had been killed on site. 'You still think about him.'

'I'll never forget him or what happened. I wake up in a cold sweat some nights and, if anything, it's been getting worse in the run-up to the anniversary. I would've liked to have gone to see his wife today, but she finds it too painful. She can only imagine what I was unfortunate enough to see but she knows how it affected me and I think it scares her. Maybe she thinks that if she looks into my eyes, she'll see it too. I wouldn't wish that on anyone so I send her flowers and I visit Jimmy's grave. I was on my way there now.'

'Would you mind if I walked with you a while?'

'Only if you let me push the pram,' Simon said. The smile had returned to his face. 'I have a feeling I might be the better driver.'

Simon and Jo strolled off together and as they walked, they talked. All Saints Church was in the opposite direction to home but Jo didn't mind. She was eager to talk to someone who didn't need explanations, who wouldn't just nod in the right places but would know how she felt, how she *really* felt.

'I'm ashamed of the person I became,' Jo told him. 'It was as if it wasn't me, it was someone else inhabiting my body while I was . . . I don't know . . . somewhere else. I never thought it could happen, not to me. I thought I was so controlled – too controlled – sometimes. I thought I was stronger than that.'

'None of us are immune.'

Jo didn't look up but stared at Simon's hands, which gripped the pram tightly. They were broad hands, impossibly strong, and yet when Jo had visited Simon at home, they had been shaking uncontrollably along with the rest of his body. 'At least we're both on the mend now,' she said. 'I doubt I'll ever get back to the person I was but I'm moving forward.'

They had stopped outside the church with its sandstone wall that separated the land of the living from the graveyard. 'Can I come with you?' Jo asked. She wanted to pay her respects, but it was more than that. She had a long journey ahead of her in more ways than one and she wasn't quite ready to leave, but when Simon didn't immediately respond, she added, 'Sorry, of course not. You need to do this on your own.'

'Yes, I do need some time to myself but now you mention it, I wouldn't mind some company to get me there.'

The cemetery was on a slope that looked out across Childwall Valley and Jo couldn't think of a better spot for a final resting place. A single ray of sunshine had pierced the gunmetal-grey clouds to light up a path between heaven and earth and Jo chose to keep her head raised to the skies rather than look at the grave they were now standing beside.

She imagined the corpse of James Stevenson, a man she had occasionally laughed and joked with, lying beneath the earth waiting to be noticed, and when she did drop her gaze she noticed first the fresh flowers; deep red, velvety roses arranged carefully in a black marble urn.

'Jimmy bought his wife a bunch of roses once a month without fail, every pay day.'

'It sounds like they were happily married,' Jo said, with a sigh.

'Yes, I think they were.'

Simon turned to Jo who was deep in thought, thinking not of the man buried beneath their feet but his widow.

'You're stronger than you think, Jo. You've come a long way on your own and you'll get there.'

Jo tried to smile but her lips trembled. 'Thanks, Simon, and thank you for listening.'

'Anytime,' he said with a wink.

There was an awkward moment when neither knew how to say goodbye. 'You won't tell anyone at Nelson's, will you?'

'Your secret's safe with me,' he assured her and gave her a hug to secure the deal.

Leaving Simon to spend time on his own at his friend's

graveside, Jo pushed the pram back up the hill. Her shoulders were pulled back as she wended her way through the graveyard with its weathered headstones that marked the passage of time with partially eroded names that seemed an inadequate reflection of the lives of the long-departed and the impact they must have made on the world.

The sky above had become leaden and there was a metallic taste in the air that held the promise of a storm. Picking up her pace, Jo's eyes were drawn to a lopsided headstone. It was old and neglected and covered in lichen but the name etched into its surface was still legible. Jo drew nearer without even realizing what she was doing.

The day darkened to night and an ice-cold chill ran through her body as beads of sweat pricked the back of her neck. Her hands grew clammy and slipped on the pram handle when she tried to tighten her grip. There was a sharp intake of breath that lodged in her throat and she tried to swallow it back but her mouth was dry and her tongue stuck to the roof of her mouth. Jo took a few more breaths in quick succession until her lungs felt ready to explode. Her heart pounded and without warning she dropped to her knees, letting go of the pram in the process. It rolled a couple of feet before jamming against a neighbouring headstone.

Unable to catch her breath, Jo's mind raced and she tried desperately to remember what Heather had been telling her about relaxation. She grabbed her handbag and was rifling through it when Simon appeared at her side. He had put the brake on the pram and then knelt down beside her. Her face was white and her eyes wide as she glanced at him only briefly before returning her gaze to the headstone.

She tried to speak but Simon could make no sense of the random syllables she blurted out between desperate gasps for air.

Following her gaze, Simon muttered, 'Jesus!' under his breath as he read the name on the grave: David Taylor. He quickly turned his attention back to Jo and said, 'Look at me.'

Jo's eyes couldn't be drawn away from the grave.

'Look at me, Jo,' he said more forcefully this time, placing both hands gently on her shoulders.

She turned her head towards him.

'Breathe with me.' Simon took a slow, deep breath and waited for Jo to follow suit.

'I . . . I can't.' The pure fear welling up inside her was inescapable and she couldn't fight it. She was drowning in it.

'You can,' he said, his voice calm and steady. 'You feel like your heart's going to explode?'

Jo nodded.

'You think you're going to die?'

Jo's eyes darted from one headstone to another as they crowded around her. She nodded again.

'You're not. Nothing bad is going to happen to you, Jo and what's more, you know it isn't. The panic will ease and you'll start to relax. Give it time. All you have to do is breathe. Slowly does it.'

Jo tried again and this time she succeeded in matching Simon breath for breath. When she found a rhythm she could sustain, she resumed her search through the contents of her bag until she found what she had been looking for. She picked up the straw and held it between her teeth. Simon looked slightly bemused as Jo breathed in through her nose and out through the straw just as Heather had instructed her. She was aware of the smile appearing on Simon's face but she was too far gone to be embarrassed.

It took perhaps ten minutes, but eventually Jo was ready to stand up. 'Sorry,' she said scratchily, climbing to her feet with trembling knees.

'That's a new one on me,' he said, nodding towards the straw Jo had peeled from her parched lips.

'A friend suggested it.' Jo continued to shake while her mind was still dealing with the more difficult task of simply breathing. 'I'm not sure if it helped with the breathing but just knowing that I looked like a complete idiot was all the incentive I needed.'

The concern etched on Simon's face fell away and he didn't even try to hide his smile this time. 'Well, I didn't like to say.'

Jo tried to return the smile but it wouldn't come. She looked down at her shaking hands. They weren't as broad or as strong as Simon's but she had thought them strong enough. 'I'd convinced myself that I'd got past all of this.'

'And you will – but Jo, it doesn't happen overnight. Setbacks happen and unfortunately they can come without warning.' He paused and waited for Jo to draw her eyes away from the headstone again. 'I would never have believed that one day I'd be the one staying calm while someone else tried to outrun their fears. Your day will come too,' he promised. 'There's an old saying, "This too will pass," and it's seen me through some of the darkest hours of my life.'

'It sounds so simple.'

'Oh, it's not, not by a long shot, but that isn't the only trick you can have up your sleeve. If you can learn some breathing techniques, with or without the straw, and find a way to relax when you feel a panic attack coming on, then you're halfway there. And don't forget to keep telling yourself over and over again that nothing bad is about to happen, that you're not in immediate danger and there's nothing to run away from.'

'Except my demons.'

'Yes, and that's where the therapy will come in useful.'

'*You've* been good therapy, Simon. Thank you.'

Jo released the brake on Archie's pram and made a move to leave but Simon put one of his giant hands over hers. For a moment it stopped the tremors. 'I've never forgotten your kindness when you came to see me. I'm glad I've had the chance to return the favour.'

The warmth flooding into Jo's heart was the perfect remedy to the cold fear that had invaded her body. 'I was only doing my job,' she said.

Simon shook his head and couldn't hold back a gentle laugh. 'If you were Kelly then I'd agree, but you come from a different mould and she'll never fill your boots.'

'How's she been doing?' Jo asked.

Simon winced. 'She's had Jim running around in circles. There was nearly a walkout on site last week when she issued new instructions about— Oh, never mind. Save all of that until you're back at Nelson's.'

'Thanks, Simon. You've given me more reason than ever to get back now,' Jo said, pleased to be talking about something other than her own troubles.

'Don't run before you can walk,' he warned.

'My legs feel like jelly so there's no way I'll be running anywhere any time soon,' she said with a laugh that caught in her throat. She was looking not at Simon but the headstone inscribed to a beloved husband and father, although this particular David Taylor had died long before her own beloved husband had even been born.

It felt like an omen.

Simon had tried to persuade Jo to take a taxi home but she insisted she could manage on foot. Her legs felt wobbly at first but the pram offered some support and she hoped the walk would clear her head. It was about a half-hour trek but in the scheme of things, it was the least of the challenges that lay ahead.

However, no sooner had she set off when a spark zipped across the leaden sky, quickly followed by a deep rumble of thunder. When the heavens opened, Jo stopped only briefly to pull the waterproof cover over Archie's pram. She had no such protection for herself. Her showerproof jacket was all but useless and she was soon soaking wet. Her feet squelched inside her trainers as she strode as fast as her legs would carry her. Inside one of her pockets, her mobile phone thumped against her hip and she thought she felt it vibrate but she chose to ignore it.

The rain ought to have compounded her misery but it felt good to have her pulse racing with exertion rather than terror. She could almost believe she was outrunning the anxiety that had come back to haunt her in the graveyard, and by the time she reached Beaumont Avenue she was prepared to pick herself up, dry herself off and try again.

She had realized that her mind needed more time to heal and she was ready to accept, albeit reluctantly, that she was allowed the occasional lapse. She was glad Simon had been there for her. It wasn't just that he knew what she was going through – he had given her hope. She had seen him at his lowest and could never have imagined that one day, not only would he be well enough to return to work, but strong enough to offer someone else a helping hand.

Simon had also given her another incentive to get back to the office. She had been worrying that Kelly would do such a sterling job in her stead that Gary might not be so keen to support Jo's transition back to work, which was going to be more challenging than he expected. Kelly's success with the employment tribunal at Christmas had fed Jo's insecurities and while it wasn't fair on her assistant, Jo was glad to hear things weren't running smoothly.

With her head bowed against the heavy downpour, Jo didn't notice the car parked outside her house or the man who jumped out and rushed over to her, not until he stepped in front of the pram and blocked her way.

'Mrs Taylor?'

'Yes,' Jo said, too startled to question why he wanted to know.

'I was hoping for a statement about the latest developments?'

The first question she thought of was 'what developments?' but she had the presence of mind to go straight to the second. 'And who exactly are you?' she asked as she manoeuvred the pram past the stranger and through the gate.

The man followed her up the path as he introduced himself

as a local reporter but Jo wasted no time in telling him she had no comment to make and that he should speak to Mary Jenkins. She was as polite as she could be; the press had helped in the initial search for David and maybe they would again, but right now she needed more information and she wasn't about to comment on any developments until she knew what they were.

Jo could still see the journalist hovering on the doorstep after she closed the door. The house was cold and she shivered as she stood in indecision. She was trying to decide who to phone first when the decision was taken out of her hands. Archie began to cry.

As she dripped a trail of raindrops through the house, Jo switched the heating on and concentrated on satisfying her son's needs before her own curiosity. She cradled Archie in one arm but didn't unravel him from his winter layers. He was out of the rain but still needed protection from Jo's sopping wet clothes. Shivering, she waited for his feeding bottle to warm up, her hand trembling more than it should as she took out her mobile. There had been two missed calls, one from Irene and one from Mary. There was also a voicemail message, which she ignored. Opting to hear the news she was already dreading from a real voice rather than a recording, Jo dialled Irene's number.

28

The central heating system was still in the process of chasing away the chills when the house began to fill with warm bodies. Jo hadn't had a chance to get changed and wasn't sure if the steam curling around her came from her damp clothes or the mug of hot, sweet tea Steph had placed in her shaking hands.

'When did they say they'd be here?' Irene asked.

Jo raised her eyes to the bare chimney breast as if the missing starburst clock would tell her the time. 'Soon, I should think.'

'They'll still be beating a confession out of Steve.'

All heads snapped towards Lauren who was sitting on the floor propped up against Jo's armchair. She wriggled her nose, which looked slightly swollen with a mark where the stud had once been. Her shrug was unapologetic. 'I'm just saying.'

'Well, don't just say,' her mum replied.

There was a sigh to accompany another shrug and then Lauren returned her attention to her mobile. Other than the tap-tap of her keystrokes, the room fell silent. Jo strained her ears and imagined that the click of the phone was the tick of the non-existent clock as she stared at its invisible hands, a sight preferable to Irene's tormented form curled up tightly next to Steph on the sofa.

'He doesn't know any more than he's already told us,' Irene said at last. 'He's been arrested because he was taking money out of David's account and even I have to agree he deserves to be locked away for that – but that's all he's done.'

She had been looking to Jo for support, but even if Irene were able to see through her tears she wouldn't have found an ally. She jumped in fright when there was a knock at the door.

'I'll get it,' Steph said and Jo didn't argue. In her mind she could already see the silhouettes of the police officers standing at the front door, and it was an image that had given her too many nightmares.

'Would you like a drink?' Steph was asking as she ushered Martin Baxter and Mary Jenkins into the living room.

Martin caught the look of anticipation on everyone's face and quickly answered them. 'We've released Steve,' he said to Jo. 'We had to bring him in for questioning and he's been charged, but only in relation to theft from your husband's account. His alibi is watertight for the night in question and we have no reason to believe he had anything to do with David's disappearance.'

'Thank God!' gasped Irene.

Jo wasn't sure how she felt. There was something that might be relief because there was no bad news, no confirmation of her worst fears, but there was also a sense of disappointment. She had rejoiced in having so many answers

370

but it now felt as if she was back at square one. There was nothing to suggest David had deserted her and no evidence that he had died. She didn't know what they were meant to do next but from the way Mary was looking at Martin, she realized the police did. 'What?'

'I know it won't be pleasant having the media scrutinize your lives again but Steve's arrest has put the case back in the spotlight and I'd like to take advantage of that.'

'At least Steve's been good for something, then,' Steph said under her breath.

'I'd like to organize a reconstruction and retrace David's last known movements, starting from West Allerton station,' Martin continued.

'To where?' Jo asked, wanting to laugh at the absurdity of the idea.

'To Beaumont Avenue,' Mary answered. 'Even though we don't know how much of that route David followed, it could still trigger a memory for someone.'

'When do you want to do it?' Jo asked.

'As soon as we can, certainly within the next couple of weeks,' Mary said. 'I'll do all the liaising with the press, but we need a family member to make another public appeal.'

'Now that we know there's no suggestion that David's disappearance was premeditated, we're taking it more seriously than ever, Jo,' Martin added before she had a chance to reply.

Jo's eyes narrowed as she tried to interpret the look the policeman was giving her. Her shivering body still managed a shudder when she recognized it as sympathy. 'You think he's dead, don't you?'

'I think the chances of him disappearing of his own free will have significantly diminished. We need your help finding him.'

Jo's blood ran cold. She couldn't escape the image forming in her mind of David's body lying undiscovered somewhere. She imagined someone out there, knowing what had happened that night, and then she imagined sitting in front of a camera and making a plea to that person to put her out of her misery. Her palpitations made her stutter with fear. 'I – I w-want to – but I can't. I c-can't do it . . .'

'Could I do it?' Irene asked. She was looking at Jo.

'It would be better coming from Jo,' Martin insisted.

'I'll come with you,' Lauren said. It was an offer that was repeated by Steph a second later but it was Mary who came up with the solution that would satisfy everyone.

'If we can have the whole family there then Irene could speak on your behalf; if you can manage to sit through the press conference, Jo, that would be enough and if it got too much then you could get up and leave, it's as simple as that,' Mary said, acknowledging the look of terror on Jo's face. 'And to be brutally honest, it wouldn't do any harm if you did have to leave. It might prick someone's conscience and persuade them to pick up the phone.'

'At last, my penchant for hysteria can be put to good use,' Jo said, dryly.

29

The first fingers of sunlight stretched across the watery winter's sky and slipped through the stained glass window towards Jo as she prepared for her first day at work for more than twelve weeks. It was eight o'clock and she was standing in front of the dresser putting the finishing touches to her outfit. The folds of her scarf fell with perfect precision around her neck, the orange and brown pattern complementing her glossy auburn hair and reflecting some warmth on to her pale skin which had been draining of colour the closer she came to leaving.

The press conference had gone by in a blur both mentally and visually. With her eyes welling with tears, the enquiring faces of the press had been indistinguishable blobs and she hadn't dared look at the anxious faces of the family who surrounded her. Her mum had cradled Archie in her arms while Irene made a desperate plea for information. Jo's only contribution had been to continue to breathe through the anxiety building in her chest.

She had been annoyed and frustrated by her inability

to make any kind of coherent statement on the day. She had tried to answer questions, to add her own feelings and thoughts, but her words had stuck in her throat and nothing had come out except a sob. She supposed it was some achievement that she had held back the panic until she was out of view of the gawkers – and at least it was done.

Hooking her handbag over her shoulder, Jo picked up the baby carrier. Archie was awake and they locked eyes. His lip trembled and he seemed to be on the verge of tears too. They were going to do this, she told herself as she cast one final glance in the mirror. She took a deep breath, held it, and then released it through the bright yellow straw trembling between her dry lips. Heather's recommended breathing technique was one she had continued to practise and while Jo wasn't convinced it worked, it was the straw that occupied her mind when she exhaled her first breath of fresh air and not the empty space on the doorstep that her husband refused to occupy.

Jo was relieved to find the bottle of surface cleaner and duster still in the bottom of her filing cabinet because her first task of the day was to disinfect everything in sight. Occasionally she looked up and caught a furtive glance from one concerned colleague or another but she didn't care. They had all seen the news and had probably expected her to return a wreck. It wasn't a label she intended to keep but she wasn't ready to start that long climb back to her position as a well-respected manager until she had established solid foundations. Her office was her domain and she wanted to erase all evidence of her temporary usurper. As if on cue, the door opened and Kelly stepped in.

'Here's your coffee.' Kelly was standing in front of the desk, looking for somewhere to put it.

Jo retrieved a recently polished coaster and placed it down on the desk. It was a perfect match to the cup in Kelly's hand. The set had been a present from David and had her name printed on it with a somewhat dubious assessment of her character. Apparently *Joanne* was reckless and impulsive. David had found the description hilarious but right now, Jo thought of it as an aspiration. She was allowed to hope, wasn't she?

'Thanks, Kelly.'

'Ooh, I wouldn't mind one of those if you're offering,' Gary said looking at the steaming mug from the doorway.

Jo watched Kelly flinch and felt genuinely sorry for her. The poor girl might have questionable people skills but she was more than a coffee-maker. 'I think Janet's already on the case,' Jo said as she glimpsed Gary's PA heading off in the direction of the kitchen.

'Do you want me to stay?' Kelly asked. She was directing her question to Gary. 'I've drawn up a checklist for all the updates we need to go through with Jo. I'll just go and get it.'

Gary wafted a hand. 'We can deal with the paperwork later, Kelly. I just want to have a welcome back chat with Jo first.' Kelly looked as if she was about to respond but Gary held her gaze and the warning that went with it. She backed away and closed the door behind her.

Jo watched as Gary dropped into the visitor's chair and sighed. 'I know you're going through a really tough time,

Jo so I'm here to tell you that you shouldn't feel obliged to come back if it's too soon. You have to stop pretending you're invincible. You're not.'

'I think I've already proven that on national TV,' Jo said.

'I saw the press conference.' He shook his head. 'I'm surprised you're coping at all.'

'It's all smoke and mirrors. Beneath the surface I'm still that wailing banshee in front of the camera. Right now I'm doing a good impersonation of the old me and I can only hope that one day it will stop being an act. It's not going to be easy, though.' She took a breath and placed her hand on her chest, willing her pulse to slow. 'I need you to know that I've been having anxiety attacks and my compulsion to find some order in my life is stronger than it ever was.'

They both looked at the desk Jo was still in the process of cleaning. Gary nodded. 'Is there anything I can do to help? Maybe buy you some more polish?' he asked, managing to raise a smile from Jo's trembling lips.

'I've got some sessions lined up with a therapist so I'll need some time off to attend.'

Gary twisted in his seat; it was no more than a suggestion of a glance behind him in the general direction of Kelly. 'I'll agree to whatever it takes to get the old Jo back.'

'Good, because I'll also need some time off to deal with anything else that might come my way,' Jo added, testing his loyalties to the limit. 'The reconstruction is taking place next week so I'd like to take a couple of days off then.'

Gary nodded. 'Whatever it takes,' he said again.

Jo had been rehearsing that particular conversation over and over again in her head and, relieved it was over, began to relax for the first time that day. 'But other than that, I'm back.'

There was a lull in the conversation as Janet slipped into the office to give Gary his mug of tea. The pause gave Jo a chance to concentrate on her breathing. She picked up the yellow straw that had been sitting proud in her pen holder. Simply holding it brought a degree of comfort.

Gary was watching her. 'OK, now we've both said what needs to be said, can I just say I'm so glad you're here?' He laughed and shook his head. 'I'm no therapist but I think what you need is something to concentrate your mind on other than your private life and I have just the job for you.'

The yellow straw dropped down on to the desk and Jo picked up her pen as Gary went through a handful of documents that Kelly had somehow persuaded him to amend and issue. These were procedures that Jo had spent time developing and maybe there was room for improvement, but they had worked and Gary shouldn't have been carried away by Kelly's eagerness to impress. Fortunately for Kelly, Gary was ready to accept his own culpability and when he proceeded to list all the subsequent grievances that had been placed and the various threats from the unions, he wasn't looking for a scapegoat, he was looking for someone to get things back in order. There was a lot of work to be done repairing industrial relations. It was a mess and under different circumstances it would have horrified Jo but she had a smile on her face and she kept it for almost the entire day.

Jo had built a tower of folders on her desk with sharp corners and neat, uniform lettering describing the contents of each. In all other respects it was a complete mess. Kelly's new, improved procedures had tied everyone up in knots and, aided and abetted by some of the less experienced line managers, she had issued countless warning letters to staff who had breached one new rule or another.

Jo's most difficult task was going to be undoing everything without making it too obvious that mistakes had been made, for Kelly's sake and Gary's too. He shouldn't have given her inexperienced assistant such a free reign but Jo felt some responsibility, too. She was in charge of Kelly's development and had spent too long focusing on her strengths, hoping time alone would help her acquire the softer skills she so clearly lacked. She resolved to take a new approach, but for the moment at least, it would have to remain at the bottom of her to do list.

'Are you sure I can't help?' Kelly said when she brought in the latest set of files Jo had requested. 'I know all of these cases inside out and it might be quicker getting you up to speed if I went through them with you.'

Kelly was still under the impression that Jo was reviewing her achievements rather than undoing them. 'No, it's getting late. Why don't you go home? I won't be long myself,' Jo said.

Kelly tipped her head to one side and gave Jo her best look of sympathy. 'Are you sure you should be back? No one would question it if you went off ill and I'm sure you could persuade a GP to concoct a sick note for you.'

'Concoct?' Jo said, musing the word. 'I'm not about to start wishing myself ill, Kelly, and besides, I'm enjoying being busy. And my first challenge is seeing if there's still a thing or two I can teach you.' She held out her hand and took the files Kelly had brought in for her.

Kelly was unfazed. 'I won't hold it against you if you do.'

'Don't worry, ladies,' Jason said as he swept into the office, making them both jump. 'It's only a whirlwind visit.' His coat was buttoned up and there was a scarf tied around his neck in preparation for the blustery journey home. He had a briefcase in one hand and a folder in the other, which he offered towards Jo. 'I just wanted to give you this.'

'Another file? That's all I need,' she said, but if Kelly recognized the sarcasm, she didn't let it show.

'I was going anyway,' Kelly said. 'I'll leave you to it. Goodnight, Jo. Jason.'

'So, what is it?' Jo asked as she turned the folder over in her hand. She recognized the handwriting immediately.

'Four Corners,' Jason read out helpfully. 'I found it on one of the bookshelves in our office. It must have been missed when the police went through David's files. It's been staring me in the face for months but I only noticed it today. I heard you were back and it got me thinking about David and I started having a clear-out. At first I thought it was just an old project of his that didn't get off the ground.'

Jo snapped open the file, hopeful that Jason had stumbled upon a vital clue, but the collection of holiday brochures helped only to explain the meaning of the title David had chosen for this special project. '"The four corners of the world",' she said, and with distinctly less enthusiasm sifted through the contents. 'America, Asia, Australia. David wanted to travel the world twice over. Did you know he had a map on the wall at home with colour-coded pins stuck all over it? All the places we'd already visited and the places left to see.'

'There's some other stuff in there, too,' Jason said.

'So I can see,' Jo said. Amongst the brochures she spotted a complex chart that carefully detailed the timelines for David's plans. From a cursory glance, their trip to Vietnam to celebrate Jo's thirtieth had been the start of his world-wide voyage that went on for years. She blinked back the sting of disappointment.

'His passport's in there, Jo,' Jason said when he noticed she was about to close the file. 'It's in the brown envelope.'

Jo tore at the envelope in her haste to retrieve what had been the very first piece of damning evidence to cast David as a villain and was now the last to be dismissed. The unflattering photo of her husband left her speechless.

'I hope it helps.'

'Thanks,' she managed to reply. 'I'd better let the police know.'

Jason shuffled from one foot to the other. 'It's good to see you back, by the way,' he said. It was the same discomfort she had witnessed from other colleagues, as if one wrong word or look would send her into a spiral of despair.

Jo kept hold of the passport but closed the file on David's dreams which were destined to remain a painful juxtaposition to her own, no matter what the cause of his disappearance which looked bleaker by the day. 'Thanks, Jason. It's good to be back. So how are you?'

Jason's relief at the change of subject was obvious and his eyes lit up. 'I'm getting married,' he announced.

Jo tried to smile. 'Congratulations. It's about time.'

380

'I know – it had to happen eventually, I suppose. Anyway, I'd better go.'

Jo didn't object. Her first day at work had given her a much needed sense of purpose but she wanted to be home. After saying goodbye to Jason, Jo slipped David's passport into her bag, closed down her computer and stood up. Turning, she looked out of the window towards the horizon. The sky was darkening above the Liverpool skyline and she was reminded of a saying about it being darkest before the dawn. But dawn was still a long way off and she had an unshakeable conviction that it would get very, very dark before she could hope to bask in sunshine again. She didn't want to be alone and the need to have her husband's arms around her was unbearable. She fought the urge to cry but her heart tugged her in another direction. The feeling wasn't unpleasant; in fact, it was positively uplifting. At last she found the strength to smile when she realized how much she was missing Archie too.

30

Five months after David had stepped off the train at West Allerton and into oblivion, a young policeman followed in his footsteps. It was eight o'clock on a cool, crisp Wednesday evening in March. Notable by its absence was the howling gale that had greeted David. The storm that night had heralded a winter that was now far behind them, the gentle breeze in the air its final breath.

As he left the station, the David lookalike glanced towards Jo. She was standing with a group of curious onlookers made up of police officers, journalists and family. They made quite a crowd.

'Are you sure you want to be here?' Steph was looking intently at Jo, trying to work out how her sister was handling the sight of the man wearing a Nelson's jacket and carrying a John Lewis bag, a man who, if you squinted your eyes at just the right angle, you would swear was David.

'He doesn't look anything like him,' Jo said, dismissing the ghostly apparition that tugged at the cracks and fissures of her breaking heart.

'Don't you think?' It was Irene this time and she was less adept at hiding her feelings. Her voice quivered.

People shuffled around them and then from behind, someone spoke.

'Hi, Jo.'

When Jo turned around, Sally was squirming as if she expected her sister-in-law to send her away again with a flea in her ear and from the furtive glance she gave Irene, she was expecting the same from her. But the moment of awkwardness was swept away when Luke peaked from behind his mum. There were squeals of delight from grandmother and grandson alike and the distraction gave Sally the opportunity to talk to Jo.

'I just wanted to be here to offer my support and to say I'm so sorry for upsetting you the way I did. Steve kept me in the dark about everything. I swear I never knew what was going on with the money he took from David and I certainly never saw him with the coat he stole from you.'

'You may have been kept in the dark but you were the only one to see through Steve's lies,' Jo offered and it was her turn to look guilty. 'You were the only one to remember the real David.'

'You do know that he and I . . . We never . . .'

'Please! Forget I even said that! I don't think for a minute there was ever . . .' Jo was as unwilling as Sally to voice the unfounded accusation. 'I'm so sorry,' she continued. 'I was grasping at straws but I shouldn't have said it. I certainly hadn't been thinking it, before or since.'

Sally nodded. 'But I still want to make things right. The house is being sold and if there's any money left then we'll repay what Steve took.'

'You're losing the house?' Irene had Luke in her arms and had been listening to far more of the conversation than she had been letting on.

'I'll be moving back to my mum's in a couple of weeks.'

'Steve really has messed up this family, hasn't he?' Irene said, not needing to wait for a reply from either of her daughters-in-law. 'Sally, I'm sorry if I never gave you the support you needed but I want you to know that I'm here for you if you need me. You, Jo, and me are all single ladies now, trying to make our own way in this world. It would be so much easier if we worked together. If you ever need an extra babysitter, you know where I am.'

It was a major breakthrough for two women who had shared such opposing opinions of Steve for too many years. This felt like a new understanding, but there was no time to stand back and admire the bridge they had just built.

'Jo?' Lauren said, tugging at her arm. 'Come on or we'll lose him.'

Jo went to follow her niece but couldn't manoeuvre the pram past the throng.

'Why don't I take the baby back to the house?' Irene offered. She returned Luke to his mum with a confident smile and tried not to look at the man in the Nelson's jacket striding past them. 'I thought I could do this but . . .' Her smile wavered. 'I'm sorry, Jo.'

'I'm not sure I can either, Irene, but I'd like to try,' Jo said, handing over her house keys. 'And if I do happen to freak out, chances are I'll run so fast I'll be at the front door waiting for you.'

'Come on!' insisted Lauren.

There was only the merest trickle of daylight left from the setting sun, nowhere near enough to light their way along the overgrown path that Jo, and now the police, were convinced David would have opted for to get him home that little bit sooner, the irony of which wasn't lost on her. She felt a brief shiver as she remembered the last time she walked down this path, and the figure she had created with her mind, the one who had driven her to withdraw from the world and away from watchful eyes.

Lauren had a torch but Jo could still feel the darkness closing in around her until it was so deep it could easily swallow up an unsuspecting traveller on a lonely, wintry night. Jo tried to remind herself that the police had searched the area again only recently and found nothing. The only thing they hoped to find tonight was even just one person who might step out of the gloom and remember something.

'This is pointless,' complained Steph. 'If anyone had been walking down here they wouldn't have been able to see their hands in front of their face, let alone remember walking past David.'

'There's always a chance that something happened that night which will have stuck in someone's memory,' Mary Jenkins said. She had been corralling the journalists and camera crew who were in hot pursuit of the man who was acting as David, but she was also charged with keeping an eye on Jo. She had deliberately held back to check on her but Jo said very little as Steph and the family liaison officer discussed the relative merits of the reconstruction.

Detaching herself from her surroundings, Jo focused on

every step she took along the path as if it would lead her straight to David. Her concentration was so intense that she wasn't prepared for that path to come to an end quite so soon, and when the reconstruction spilled back out on to the road, Jo wasn't ready. Her steps faltered and she let a handful of stragglers file past her. David hadn't come out the other side, she was sure of it now more than ever. She turned back, her movements lost to her family as the crowd flowed around her.

Her progress was slower this time, the light had faded completely and there was no torchlight to help her on her way. She reached the widest section of the path at the midway point and stopped. This was the place her terror had really taken hold of her, those few short weeks ago. On her right was a distant row of houses partly obscured by trees and on her left the railway embankment sloping down twenty feet behind the tall rusted fence.

Jo held her breath and listened. At first all she heard was Mary and Steph calling out her name but then she heard something else. Rustling and whispers came from the clearing where she had seen the group of youths playing football on the day she cut her hand, the clearing where she had stood beneath the creaking oak and imagined David striding away from her and out of her life for ever. 'Who's there?' she called out.

There was more rustling. A youth, his dark hoodie over his head, emerged out of the darkness and came closer. He might have been the boy who had seen her stumble; she had no way of telling. 'What was all that about?' he asked.

'My husband went missing in October last year. It's a reconstruction.'

'The bloke with the shopping bag everyone was following – was meant to be your husband?'

'Did you recognize him? He would have come down here on his way home.' There was desperation in her voice. 'Please, if there's anything you remember about that night then you have to tell me.'

In the dim light that was barely light at all, Jo felt the boy looking at her. If he was about to say something then he didn't get the chance.

'Don't you say anything to anyone! Come on, let's go.' It was another youth, a little older or at least old enough for his voice to have broken.

'Jo?'

Steph had caught up with her and as soon as she spoke the rustling grew thunderous. Twigs snapped as the two teenagers ran off.

'No!' Jo cried and began to run after them and away from her sister and, more importantly, away from Mary in her police uniform with its reflective strips that shone like a beacon through the darkness. Jo wasn't about to let this one tenuous lead slip through her fingers and she ran as if her life depended on it.

There was a hiss and crackle behind her as Mary's radio burst into life. 'Two youths running along the path heading back to West Allerton! Somebody grab them!' she shouted but Jo was determined to get to them first.

The boys immediately deviated away from the path and plunged deeper into the undergrowth. Thorny branches clawed at Jo's clothes as she followed the sound of the boys' retreat. She was forced to scramble rather than run after them but her quarry was slowing too. She caught occasional glimpses of darting shadows but clearest in her sights was the impassable silhouette of the eight-foot fence that sectioned off the clearing from the back gardens of the neighbouring houses.

There was a crash as one of the boys hit the wooden fence running. She didn't realize he had scaled the barricade until she caught sight of a human-sized spider silhouetted against the black sky. A second later the shape disappeared with a thump as the escapee hit the ground on the other side. Jo's heart thumped too and then it skipped a beat as she heard the second boy begin his ascent.

'No, please!' Jo cried as she reached the fence. The white flash of trainers was directly in her eye line, propelling their owner upwards. She lunged at them, grabbing hold of one dangling foot and refusing to let it go even as it kicked and thrashed. There began a desperate tug-of-war and Jo used the fence as leverage, bringing all her weight to bear as she pulled at the trapped leg while fending off kicks from the free one. One kick glanced off her cheek and stars sparked across her vision but she wouldn't give up. She found purchase on the boy's clothes and began to prise him off the fence, using up every ounce of strength and pent-up frustration she had harboured for the last five months. She cried out with rage even as her superhuman powers began to fail. He was slipping through her fingers. And then he was up and out of reach, balanced on the top of the fence as effortless as a cat.

Jo fell back against the brambles, caught in its web of thorns, spent and useless. 'No! Please don't do this to me!' she cried.

As Jo forced back the tears she stared up at the silhouette

of her last, fading hope. The shadow gazed down at her for a moment and then it was gone. There was the crunch of dried bracken as the boy dropped back down to earth.

The first sob escaped as the boy's face loomed over her. 'Are you all right, love?'

Jo put her hand to her mouth and nodded to the boy who was undoubtedly the one who had come up to her all those months earlier. Her heart was hammering and her breath caught the occasional sob as she spoke but she spoke quickly, aware that time was against them. They were still being pursued by others, and the crashing of undergrowth was getting closer. 'On 16 October last year I was waiting for my husband but he never came home. I was pregnant and I was scared. I didn't know if he'd left me or if something bad had happened. I still don't know and those questions have been eating away at me and pretty soon there'll be nothing left. I can't be the person I was and I can't be the person I should be now, the mother to my son, because I don't know if I'm worth loving. I can't move on with my life until I get some answers, if not from David then from the last person who saw him that night. Was that you?'

The boy looked as if he was about to speak but the beam of a flashlight cut through the night, snaking its way along the wooden fence towards them, making him tense for flight. Jo could hear her name being called.

'This is between you and me. I'll keep them away if you promise to talk to me. Please, will you?'

The boy nodded.

'I'm over here!' Jo called out. 'I'm fine but I'm with someone. Please, let me talk to him. Stay back!'

There was a pause as collective minds tried to decide what to do. 'Are you in any danger, Jo?' It was Mary.

'No, I'm perfectly safe. Please, I just need a few minutes on my own.'

'OK, five minutes,' Mary called back.

Jo looked to the boy and waited. Her patience was eventually rewarded.

He crouched down until he was level with Jo who had remained tangled in the undergrowth. 'We play footie here all the time,' he said, 'even when it's pitch-black and teeming down. There's nothing else to do around here.'

'Or there are worse things to do.'

The boy laughed. 'Well, maybe we do a bit of that too,' he admitted although Jo preferred to believe it was only false bravado from her reluctant hero. 'Anyway, that night Reddo kicked the ball right over the railway fence. It was only stuck in some bushes, it hadn't rolled down the embankment, and everyone said we should leave it. But it was my ball; I'd only had it a few days and I knew I'd be in for all kinds of grief from my mum if I left it.'

Jo was nodding as if she understood, but all the time she was urging him to say something that would end her misery.

'There's this massive tree just on the other side of the fence and if someone can give you a bunk up, you can use it to get over and then back again when you're done. I was halfway up the fence when this bloke came along.'

Jo shuddered. She suspected the tree he was referring to was the oak that had creaked and groaned as she called out to her husband and begged him not to leave her. And there was no doubt in her mind who the man was. 'David.'

The boy shrugged. 'He was carrying a John Lewis bag full of baby stuff.'

The explosion of pain in Jo's chest took her breath away. She hadn't thought her heart could break any more. 'Baby stuff? Really?'

'He started off by telling us how dangerous it was. He wasn't having a go at us or anything, it was just a bit of banter and he gave as good as he got,' the boy said with a hint of admiration. 'That's when he started telling us how he used to do the same thing when he was a kid and we gave him a bit of a challenge.'

'David went over the fence?'

'He was pretty nifty for his age. It was Reddo who gave him a bunk up and he was up and over in no time and got us our ball back.' It was here the boy stopped as if his story had come to its end and he began to straighten up.

'Wait, what happened next? Did he get back over?' The question hung in the air and with a sickening twist of her stomach that felt like she had been punched, she had her answer. 'You left him?'

'He'd left his shopping bag on this side of the fence and Reddo decided to pinch it. We took the bag and ran.'

'You left him,' Jo repeated in a whisper but this time there was no question and she didn't even try to stop the boy as he scrambled over the fence and out of sight.

When the beam of Mary's torch eventually found her, the tears were slipping silently down Jo's face. 'Are you OK?'

Jo nodded even though she had barely heard the question.

She was listening to the silence. For the first time since she could remember, there was no background noise inside her head, no questions waiting to be answered. 'He's still there,' she said.

31

The sky was about to fall, weighed down by dark grey clouds that were ocean deep. There were dirty smears of rain on the horizon but for the moment at least, the regiment of graves looking out across Childwall Valley were bone dry.

Hoping there was still time before the cloudburst, Jo pulled back the rain cover on Archie's pram. Her son had been sleeping but his eyes flickered in confusion as he was lifted from his safe haven. He frowned only briefly before returning to his slumber in his mother's arms. Jo retrieved a small posy of flowers next and then took a step nearer the weathered headstone.

'David Taylor,' she read out loud, before turning to her son. 'That's your daddy's name, sweetheart, and you're going to grow up hearing it an awful lot. I only wish he'd had the chance to know yours – and not only your name, but the whole of you. Everything you are, Archie Taylor, and everything you're going to be. It breaks my heart that all I can do is tell you about him and oh, how I want to tell you. You're missing out on so much, Archie.'

Jo looked up to the skies and felt the wetness on her cheeks although the rain was yet to fall. 'What did you want for your son, David? Did you ever think about that? I'm trying to forget about that note you wrote to your dad. I read your last texts instead and play your voicemail message over and over again, trying to find the meaning behind your words. Was the baby I was carrying ever in the plans you wanted to tell me about? Is that why you bought some baby things? Were you ready to love him? Did you still love me?'

The only response to her questions came from the mournful cry of a seagull sailing across the ocean above her. She dropped her head and crouching down, placed the posy of purple and yellow spring flowers at the base of the headstone, which was leaning lazily to one side. She was tugging at one of the dandelions growing out of a crack in the base when she felt her phone vibrating in her pocket.

When Jo stood up her legs felt wobbly and she thought she would faint but she held on tightly to Archie and allowed him to ground her. She inhaled deeply before answering the call.

'Hello?' she asked.

'Hi, Jo, it's Martin. Where are you?'

'Why?'

'I'm at your house and you're not there.'

As Jo explained where she was she could feel the air being wrung out of her lungs. She didn't ask again why Martin wanted to speak to her but agreed to wait where she was. He would be there in five minutes.

Time slowed to a deathly pace as Jo returned Archie to

his pram and said goodbye to the old man lying six feet below as if he was an old friend. Her feet waded through an invisible mire as she made her way towards the church gate. Her mind had slowed too as she stood at the side of the road with Archie, waiting for life to catch up with her and then knock her down one last time.

The first heavy drop of rain exploded on the dry pavement as the policeman's car pulled up in front of her. Martin didn't meet Jo's eyes as he took the pram and, with surprising ease, unhooked the baby carrier from the frame and secured it in the backseat of the car. Next he collapsed the frame itself and put it in the boot.

Jo watched without a word. She realized she knew absolutely nothing about this man who was so familiar with the intimate details of her life. The questions that suddenly came to her mind were easier to voice than the more pertinent ones she refused to confront. 'Do you have children?' she asked.

'Two,' he said as he guided her to the passenger seat. 'They live with my ex-wife, but I see them every other weekend.' He closed the door and then went around to the driver's side where he took hold of the handle but didn't immediately pull open the door. He didn't want to do this either.

When the policeman finally slipped behind the driving wheel, his waterproof coat was glistening with raindrops. Somewhere in the distance, there was a rumble of thunder. Still she didn't ask.

Martin took hold of her hand in a futile attempt to halt the tremors that weren't only confined to Jo.

'We've found him.'

There was a gulp of air but no other sound as Jo swallowed back the tears that had blurred her vision, blocked her nose and closed her throat. The dark clouds she had watched approaching from the horizon had fallen with the weight of an ocean and she was drowning in it.

She had been expecting the news and so the shock slamming into her body took her by surprise. The police search had begun at first light and she had intended on staying at home, waiting for the knock on the door that wouldn't be David, not this time and not ever.

It was ironic, then, that after spending so long yearning for answers, Jo would be so eager to flee from them when the sun had risen that morning. Steph had been on her way over when Jo made her bid for freedom and it had taken some considerable effort to convince her sister that she would be all right once she was in the fresh air; another irony. Eventually, she had persuaded Steph to go over and keep Irene company; Jo wanted to be on her own with her son and her thoughts.

Foolishly, Jo had expected some kind of relief, but as she tried to breathe through the pressure that was not only constricting her chest, but had closed her ears and blackened her vision, she felt only grief. Heavy waves of it that made the sound of the policeman's voice seem further away than it should.

'There'll have to be a formal identification of the body,' Martin was saying, 'but unofficially, there's no doubt. It's him, Jo.'

Jo pulled her hand free from Martin's grasp and held on to the edges of the car seat to keep her steady. 'Do you know what happened yet?' Even her own words sounded far away.

'We still have officers at the scene gathering evidence and there's a long way to go before we put it all together, but so far everything seems to substantiate Daniel Jones's statement.'

'Daniel Jones?'

'The kid you talked to last night. It didn't take long to identify the group of lads who hang out around that path. We took him and his mates in for questioning and they all said pretty much the same thing that Daniel told you. David climbed over the fence to get their football back and then they left him stranded there. From what we've uncovered at the scene, it looks like he tried to climb a tree to get back over. It was blowing a gale that night—'

'Yes, I remember,' Jo said.

'Sorry, of course you do. There's a large broken branch close by so I'd say he fell from the tree. He landed in shrubbery, which stopped him rolling down the embankment. The debris from the storm accumulated around him, concealing his body perfectly.'

'Did he . . . Do you think . . . ?'

'Did he suffer? There'll be an autopsy and I know my opinion counts for nothing but you've waited long enough so I'm going to give it anyway. There's a significant head injury and no indication that he even tried to get back up so my guess is he sustained it in the fall, probably on another branch. Are you OK?' he asked when he noticed heavy drops of tears falling unchecked from Jo's bowed head and on to her lap. She nodded. 'I don't think it was foul play, Jo. I think he was knocked unconscious and didn't wake up again. So no, I don't think he suffered.'

Jo hung on to those words as if they were a life raft but

her mind was still trying to pull her under, weighed down by an image of David lying on the ground all alone while Jo had been at home staring at the starburst clock and watching the last minutes of his life slip away.

'I'm so sorry, Jo,' he continued. 'I'm sorry that we gave up so early on. I should have pushed for the resources I needed to do a thorough search of the area, beyond the fence rather than just the path.'

'You weren't the only one to give up too soon,' Jo said, prepared to admit her own culpability even though she wasn't yet strong enough to deal with it.

'The one thing we've yet to clear up is exactly what role Daniel and his mates played. We only have their word for it that they ran off before David fell from the tree.'

Jo looked up and when she wiped her eyes the waterproof mascara she had chosen specifically for an occasion such as this refused to smudge. She gave an undignified sniff. 'I don't think Daniel was lying,' she said. 'In fact, I'm sure of it.'

Martin took out a pack of tissues from his pocket and handed them to Jo. 'And I think I'd agree with you but you're going to have to prepare yourself for some speculation, if not from us, then from the press.' He left a pause before continuing. 'There's something else too.'

'Tell me.'

'The mystery shopping bag David was carrying. It was Daniel who ended up with it because no one else was interested.'

'And was it a present for the baby?' Jo asked. It sounded like a plea for mercy and in return she caught the beginnings of a sad smile on Martin's face as he nodded.

'He said it was full of baby toys,' Martin replied tentatively, testing Jo's reaction.

Jo gave him a trembling smile and the courage to continue.

'Daniel threw the bag over a gated entrance to one of the charity shops on Allerton Road. He described what sounded like bath toys and teething rings but the only item he could recall with any clarity was a cot mobile. It had sunflowers hanging from it.'

The smile broadened even as her pain deepened and the tears spilled down her cheeks unheeded.

'And it played, "You are my sunshine",' she added with absolute certainty.

32

The sound of a running shower lured Jo from sleep but her eyes refused to open. She could taste the soapy, damp air as the door to the en suite opened and David stepped out. Her mind turned towards him but her body remained statue-still as she listened to him dress. She could hear him moving and then the creak of the door as he prepared to leave. She tried to speak but her lips were glued tightly shut and the words she screamed could only be heard inside her head.

'Don't go, David! Please! Please stay with me; I don't want to live without you. I love you. Oh God, please listen to me! I love you so much. Don't go, don't you dare leave me!'

With her mouth sealed shut, Jo was struggling for air. Convinced she was going to suffocate, the panic began to build in her chest and she told herself to breathe slowly through her nose. The thin stream of air she managed to inhale was just enough to keep her lungs from exploding. Her ears pricked when she heard a noise. It was David moving towards her. She could smell his aftershave and then felt his warm breath on her cheek. She tried to open her eyes again and every nerve and muscle in her face strained with the effort. This was her last chance. David was going to be buried today in the graveyard with the perfect view of the valley. If she didn't open her eyes now then she would never see him again. Her closed lids were quivering as she fought through her inertia and then, without warning, she felt herself fall. Her stomach flipped and her eyes snapped open.

The room was filled with bright sunshine that lit up David's face like a halo. He smiled and the ice running through her veins melted away. He smiled and she marvelled at it. This was the very same smile that had stolen her heart – but then, she had received his heart in return. And as her loving husband trailed a finger along the side of her face, tucking away a rogue curl, Jo wondered how she could ever have doubted him.

'I love you, David.'

'And I love you, Jo,' he said.

The smile easing across Jo's face erupted into a full-blown grin that was smothered by David's lips which were warm and needy. She kissed him back hungrily and, as she did so, she made the mistake of closing her eyes again. The darkness rammed into her and forced the air out of her lungs in a gasp as she snapped her eyes back open. It was too late. He was gone, and only the darkness remained.

Her eyes darted around the room. From the green glow of the alarm clock, she could see Archie sleeping peacefully in the bassinet next to the bed and he would remain asleep for some time. It was barely five o'clock.

Jo tried to concentrate on slowing her breathing but it

was hard to ignore all the other thoughts running through her mind. Today was her last day of being David's wife. She wasn't going to think of herself as a widow, not until tomorrow. Only then would she try to start her life anew. Today she was still his wife.

When she managed a deep breath, Jo knew she was winning her latest battle. She could still detect a trace of David's aftershave in the air. It wasn't imagined, nor was it a lingering remnant of his ghostly apparition. There was no guilt or self-reproach for adding a sprinkling of his aftershave to her pillows as she had done every night since his body had been discovered ten days earlier.

Her legs were trembling when she eventually sat up and dangled them over the side of the bed. She felt defeated by the latest anxiety attack, but not surprised. The discovery of her husband's body had brought no peace and, so far, no resolution. The mystery of the past had been solved but there were still those questions that would never be answered, the what-ifs and the what-might-have-been. What would they have been doing now? Would she have been a better mother to Archie? And what would David have been like as a father? As this last thought weighed heavily on Jo's mind, Archie sighed deeply and twisted in his blankets. Grief wrapped around Jo and tried to pull her back beneath her duvet but she resisted. There was something she needed to do but she didn't work out what that was until she found herself standing in the middle of the study.

With the window blinds pulled down against a night that wasn't quite spent, Jo switched on a reading lamp which cast an arc of yellow light across the bare desk. There were no stacks of folders, not even a single letter left unfiled from the various banks, insurers, government bodies and other inflexible institutions who had once regarded her either with suspicion, pity or had simply ignored her when she had tried to manage her husband's affairs. Jo had taken no pleasure in informing them that her husband was dead, but in some ways it had been cathartic. 'Here's your answer!' she had wanted to yell at them. 'Are you happy now?'

And it hadn't only been in correspondence with faceless penpushers that Jo had felt this shift in position. Family and friends were finding it easier to express their condolences now that they knew exactly *why* they were consoling her.

Her return to work had been short-lived but there had been no question about offering Jo two weeks' compassionate leave. Gary had arrived with a bouquet of flowers and a card signed by everyone as a token of their sympathy. Clearly a bereavement card was easier to come by than the one declaring, 'Sorry your husband is missing.' Kelly had sent her own card and the message inside had been sweet and sincere. Jo had a feeling that her assistant was starting to realize she still had a lot to learn, or was that being optimistic? Jo didn't mind, a little optimism was good.

But it was Simon's card that had moved her most of all. He hadn't offered the usual platitudes. He had been honest and refreshingly blunt. He told her that he had no idea how she felt or how she would cope in the future. He had no way of knowing if the worst was over for her but he hoped it was. He was only certain of one thing. This too would pass.

Jo knew he was right but the future still frightened her.

She couldn't imagine ever being able to look at the path that lay ahead without being aware of the one running in parallel that she and David had been meant to follow together. She tried to visualize that untravelled path as she opened a filing cabinet drawer and removed a file.

She sat down and put it on the desk in front of her but she didn't open it immediately. She was listening to her body. Her pulse had barely slowed since waking and opening the file wasn't going to ease her anxiety, but she opened it anyway. She hadn't looked at the contents since Jason had handed it to her; she hadn't wanted to step into David's dreams.

Her hands were surprisingly steady as she lifted out the holiday brochures and set them to one side. A handful of loose pages slipped out from between them and Jo followed their torn edges with a finger. She had little doubt that these had been torn from the holiday brochure she had offered up as evidence to DS Baxter that David had absconded. She had been right to think the missing pages had been part of his travel plans; it was just the timing she had got completely wrong. He had talked about plans that day, plans that would surprise her, but if these were part of them, then she prepared herself for disappointment as she turned her attention to the remaining papers in the file.

David had obviously spent hours poring over the details of his secret project. She could see handwritten scribbles here and there so she presumed it had still been a work in progress. Before building up the courage to look at the future plans, Jo scanned the list of completed tasks. It was hard to believe that their trip to Vietnam had been less than two years ago. Looking closely, Jo spotted an image embedded in the description. It was a copy of the stamp on his passport; that was why he'd taken it into work, not because he had been preparing to leave at a moment's notice.

Feeling a little more encouraged, Jo skimmed over the next few lines which charted a weekend away in Venice, a winter break to Iceland and their Valentine's trip to Paris, but it was the next entry that brought back uncomfortable memories; the trip to America David had been forced to cancel when Jo became pregnant; the point at which she had shredded his plans to connect the four corners of the earth. It surprised her to see that, rather than being deleted, the holiday had only been postponed.

While David was used to working with complex charts, it took Jo some time to work out how all the individual pieces of paper fitted together so she could see the full picture. Page by page, she began piecing together David's master plan like a giant jigsaw puzzle, but this was no chocolate-box scene. The chart was two pages high and six pages wide with a list of tasks running down one side of the chart, a timeline across the top, and coloured bars in the middle to indicate what would happen when. There was only just enough room to fit everything on the desk and the last pages teetered dangerously over the edge. The reading lamp shone brightly over the centre of the chart while the outermost details of his plan remained dipped in shadows.

Squinting at the tiny writing, Jo looked first at the years along the top – all twenty-five of them, sliced into quarters – but her eyes were quickly drawn back to the list on the left-hand side. There were over thirty rows, one for each of the key events and milestones David had conjured up. She could see their Valentine's trip to Paris and quickly found a corresponding bar under the first quarter of 2013. Now concentrating on their ill-fated trip to America, Jo's eyes widened in disbelief as her finger trailed across the pages. David wasn't intending on resurrecting his plans for this trip until 2034.

'What the hell were you planning?' Jo asked.

Her eyes darted from one section of the chart to the next as she began constructing the path she had thought would always remain enshrouded in shadow and conjecture, the one they would never be able to travel together. But thanks to David's penchant for plans, they could still share it. She was about to laugh, but it caught in her throat when something drew her attention; it was only two letters, an abbreviation, but it wrenched from her an almighty sob.

A moment later, the study door creaked open. 'Jo, are you all right?'

Jo swallowed back the tears as she twisted around in her chair to find Irene standing on the threshold. Her mother-in-law had stayed over for the night, sleeping on the inflatable bed in the nursery that she had joked she would never be able to get up from.

'Sorry, did I wake you?' Jo asked.

'I heard you get up but I didn't want to disturb you. But then I couldn't bear to leave you crying in here on your own.' Irene was struggling to hold back her own tears; they were never too far from the surface these days but Jo was relying on her mother-in-law to hold it together. Irene had surprised them both by how strong she could be. It was an inner strength that had previously remained hidden and unnecessary while surrounded by the men in her life. But it was there now and Jo was grateful to have someone who would show her how to be strong. She had been more than happy when Irene suggested staying; neither wanted to be on her own the night before the funeral.

'I'm all right,' Jo said, 'but look what I've found.' Jo placed her finger so gently on one of the pages it was almost a caress.

'What is it?' Irene asked, a little unsettled by the smile on her daughter-in-law's face.

'FB.'

'Sorry?'

'Remember I told you that David had called my bump FB, and how I thought I had worked out what it meant.' Irene nodded, a look of pain crossing her face. 'Well, I was wrong.'

Jo waited for her mother-in-law to read what she was pointing at, but Irene shook her head. 'Sorry, Jo, I couldn't read that even if I did have my glasses.'

'FB is a reference David uses here. He couldn't tell me because he didn't want to share this plan with me right away. He was probably waiting until it was finished, or maybe he was making me suffer a little longer for pulling the rug from under him. Perhaps he realized I'd been proven right, that he was ready to be a dad, but he just wasn't ready to admit it to me. There are some things I'll never know, but at least I know what FB stands for now. It means First Born, Irene.' Jo gave a soft chuckle before adding, 'And there's much more. *So* much more.'

Jo stood up and moved the chair out of the way so they

could both stand in front of the desk and take in the full glory of David's plans.

'This is mine and David's life all mapped out, Irene. Like I said, he hadn't quite worked it all out yet and there are a few question marks here and there, but it's more than I could ever have hoped for . . .' Jo had to stop and swallow back the emotion that formed as a hard lump at the back of her throat. When she could talk again, she spoke softly as if she were standing in the middle of a cathedral during evensong. 'These first entries on the list are the holidays he had in mind from his original plans, but the rest is our life together – and not just me and David, but our children too, our first born and our second. It's all here, Irene, everything he wanted out of life, for him, for me and for Archie.'

Irene placed a hand reverently on the nearest page. 'What does it say?'

Jo's voice broke time and again as she explained each and every milestone, from the birth of the child he knew Jo was already carrying to the new addition he expected to follow two years later. He had assumed, correctly as it turned out, that their first born would be a boy, to be followed by the arrival of a girl to complete the set. Both he and Jo's careers would go from strength to strength, spurred on by the desire to support their growing family. There were milestones for the children too, and not only the mundane things like starting school but hobbies and other interests; football for their son and gymnastics for their daughter. Jo was laughing as she pointed out the double standards. Their son would be an adventure seeker, going off to festivals in his late teens before studying abroad.

Their daughter meanwhile wasn't going to be let out of his sight.

'He thought of everything,' Jo said. 'And when he was finally ready to let the children make their own lives, only then did he give in to his wanderlust again.'

'He would never have let them go,' Irene whispered. 'No parent does. You keep them with you always. *Always.*'

'He mentions you.'

Even in the dim light, Jo could see the goose bumps pricking Irene's bare arms. 'Really?'

'You had your work cut out,' Jo warned. 'My mum was tasked with teaching the kids how to upcycle clothes and furniture while you would teach them how to play football.'

'No!'

They were both laughing now. 'He always said you taught him far more about the game than his dad.'

'Alan *was* a bit of a couch potato,' Irene admitted.

'Yes, he was, wasn't he?' Jo said tearing her eyes from the chart to look at Irene. 'He certainly didn't come across as the kind of man who ever regretted settling down. If his life with you was all an act, Irene, it was a pretty good one.'

Irene shook her head. 'In those last few months, I know he wasn't the man I knew and loved; in fact, I find it easier thinking of him as two separate people. My Alan, the man I married, had all kinds of dreams but that's all they were. I don't think he wanted them to come true, he was happy enough sitting on the couch contemplating his navel while I was out in the garden explaining the offside rule to the boys.'

The two women turned back to David's dreams. 'So will you teach Archie?' Jo challenged.

'I think I'd displace a hip if I tried to kick a ball around these days,' Irene said staring at the pages in awe, 'but I'll give it a try.'

'I'm counting on it.'

Irene's brave face began to fray at the edges and she put her hand to her mouth to stop the sob escaping. Uncertain that she could hold back the tidal wave of emotion, her hand remained in place as she said, 'Bless you, Jo. I don't know what I'd do without you and Archie. You're giving me a reason to keep going and I promise I won't let you down. I'll do anything to keep you both in my life.'

It wasn't a throwaway comment. There was a conflict of interests between the two of them that wasn't going to go away. Steve was Irene's only surviving son and, despite his faults, he was another reason to keep her going, but she was too afraid to admit it, to Jo or to herself.

'I know you're torn in two and I know I've said I'll never forgive Steve – but I won't make you choose, Irene,' Jo said as she imagined a time not that long ago when she had wondered if she could choose between her husband and her child. 'I won't do that to you.'

'I don't think I'll ever forgive him either,' Irene said, dropping her hand from her face.

'You will, and maybe one day I will too. Only just not yet,' Jo warned, 'and probably not for a very long time, but we've lost enough family. And I don't want you going behind my back and then us falling out over it. I don't want to lose you either.'

Irene didn't try to deny the possibility; there was little

point. Steve had already been in touch with his mum to ask if he could attend the funeral. She had told him no, but when she explained to Jo what he'd said, it was clear she had been hoping Jo would overrule her. She hadn't. Emotions were still raw.

Saying nothing else, Irene took another look at the pages that tracked one amazing event to the next. David had had his own way of charting his life but he didn't have a monopoly on planning for the future. Irene had once seen her own life mapped out ahead of her. It hadn't included losing a husband for at least another couple of decades and had never, ever included losing a son. The spidery lines on David's chart that tangled up her future with his were thin and fragile, a web of ambitions that had been blown away one stormy night. She was still grasping at the gossamer threads that had been left behind, so fragile that they would disintegrate from the breath of just one wrong word.

'This has all gone now,' Irene said at last, 'and if I'm honest, Jo I can't see the future any more, not unless you count getting through to the end of another day.'

'Especially this day,' Jo concluded. She tried to straighten up, drawing strength into a body that was still recovering from the simple task of waking up that morning. 'I want to do the right thing, Irene. I want to do what's best for David. He'd be angry with Steve too but he'd want him there.'

Irene stepped away from the desk, she didn't need to see the plans any more, she was only too aware of the extent of her loss. She cupped Jo's face in her hands. 'I'll tell him to keep away from you. I'll tell him to stay at the back of the church. If he can't do that then I'll march him out so fast his feet won't touch the ground. Thank you, Jo. You're a good girl.'

'Am I?' Jo asked. It was a genuine question. Steve wasn't the only one seeking forgiveness. 'I should never have doubted David. If I'd had the kind of faith in him he deserved, if I hadn't been so quick to think badly of him, then I would never have let the police give up on the search. I know it wouldn't have changed things but I could have brought him home so much sooner. I'll never forgive myself for that.'

Irene reached up and kissed Jo on the forehead. 'He forgives you.' She dropped her hands and was ready for Jo's reaction, which was a shake of the head. 'You know David as well as anyone. Didn't you just say he would forgive Steve? He'd forgive you *anything*, Jo.'

Before Jo could object further, there was a faint whimper coming from her bedroom.

'He'd forgive you, don't ever doubt that,' Irene called as Jo left the study which held the sacred remnants of the life she had lost.

Slipping across the landing Jo noticed the door to the nursery had been left ajar. In the grey light of dawn she caught a glimpse of yellow sunshine glancing off the walls. The sunflowers hanging from the mobile were unmoved by the lullaby Jo began to hum in a bid to chase away dark thoughts of self-doubt. It was all too easy for Irene to say that David would forgive her, just as it had been easy for Jo to say that he would forgive Steve. It was what they all wanted to hear and who could prove otherwise?

But there was someone whose judgement Jo feared more

than any other's. Archie had sensed her guilt from the moment he had been born and there were times when she hadn't been able to meet his accusing gaze. And even though she knew now that she hadn't driven his father away after all, she didn't feel completely vindicated. Her performance so far, as Archie's mother, had been distinctly lacking and she wasn't sure how she was ever going to make it up to him.

As she continued the short journey to her bedroom, she could feel the shadows deepening. She had lost her sunshine, the man who had been her guiding light, and it was impossible to imagine a world without him in it. By the time she reached the door to her room she was enshrouded in a darkness that was soul deep. It was going to be a long, painful day and it started here.

She could hear Archie writhing in his bassinet, but so far his whimpering was little more than mild curiosity at the sound of his own voice. Taking a deep breath, Jo detected the faintest hint of David's aftershave and, from nowhere, his plans came to life. She had a clear image of Archie laughing as he kicked a football to his grandmother, his face full of mischief and his father's dimple all the more pronounced as he giggled. She was looking forward to seeing him grow, and that simple thought startled her. Was she actually looking forward to the future?

As she stepped closer, Archie's kicking grew more frantic. He could hear her humming and if she didn't know better, he was getting excited. The shadows were lifting and through the gloom, she could just make out tiny hands reaching up towards the person he was now expecting to appear above him at any moment. Jo made the moment stretch out as she prepared to face the little man who she had thought of as her harshest critic, but in the growing light was revealed as simply a sweet little baby, the one she had always dreamed of.

She took the last step and looked down at her son.

Their eyes locked and both their bodies stilled.

And then Archie smiled his very first smile.

The darkness retreated and the flash of light that sparked in her soul was dazzling. Jo wasn't sure if she was going to laugh or cry. Instead she said, 'Hello, my sunshine.'

Acknowledgements

I am astounded to find myself writing the acknowledgements for what is now my fourth novel. It has certainly been a difficult journey from grieving mother to published author, and one that I would never have managed without my family who are my guiding force and my greatest supporters. I would especially like to thank my daughter, Jessica, who is immensely patient and understanding during those long hours when I'm lost in my imaginary worlds. I know you're there, Jess, and I love you.

I would also thank my mum, Mary Hayes and my sister Lynn Jones for helping me care for Jessica and Nathan in those desperate months when I couldn't split myself in two between home and hospital. And special mention to my brother Chris Valentine for continuing Nathan's memory in his own way through his artwork – I wish you all the success in the world. I would also like to thank my brother Jonathan Hayes and brother-in-law Mick Jones for their immense love and support.

I am often told, although I really don't need telling, how lucky I am to have Luigi Bonomi as my agent and I thank him for his belief in me from the start and his continued support and encouragement. And of course a huge thank you to the amazing team at HarperCollins and especially Kim Young and Martha Ashby who have been incredibly supportive in helping me develop not only my novels but my career as an author too. I would also like to thank Louise Rapson at Peer Music for her help in acquiring permissions to use lyrics from 'You Are My Sunshine,' in this novel.

And finally, a big thank you to all my friends who have been with me through thick and thin, with special mention to Kate Knowles, who taught me the kind of relaxation techniques that are referenced in this book; to Pauline Walker, who is my special advisor on character names; and to Christine O'Brien, who was the inspiration behind some of the more interesting craft ideas I've used in my story.

An interview with Amanda Brooke

Where did you get your inspiration for this book from?

The idea for the story came initially from a news report about a married man who had disappeared without trace a year earlier. I began to think about how awful it must have been for his wife to have someone she obviously loved and who she presumed she knew so well, to simply walk out of her life without explanation. Jo goes through those initial feelings that I imagined any wife would experience, starting with perhaps no more than mild anxiety and uncertainty. She doesn't realise that she has just stepped into a terrifying nightmare that will see her pushed to her limits of mental endurance.

Did you know from the start what fate had befallen David or was this something you discovered as you wrote the novel?

Yes, I knew exactly what had been going on in David's life, how he felt on the day he went missing and why he didn't come home. What I hadn't worked out so clearly was how his family would react to his disappearance and that was a journey of discovery for me as much as for my characters. With each draft of the novel, I had to put myself in their shoes until I knew them well enough to know instinctively how each of them would behave and feel.

You've charted Jo's progress through the stages of grief in exquisite and agonising detail – did you find it hard to leave the emotion of this story behind when you weren't writing?

Jo's grief was a difficult one to describe because she doesn't know what it is she's grieving for. She has no way of knowing if David is dead or alive, so she can't know if she has lost a faithful and doting husband or if she has been living with a callous and conniving adulterer. The disintegration of her life and more particularly her mental health is a gradual process in spite of David's sudden departure, and because it was such a tortuous process, it did affect me. I can honestly say I spent plenty of sleepless nights wondering how Jo would be feeling as I tried to decide where I needed to take her next.

You also torture the reader with Jo's acceptance (or not) of her baby – how did you find it to write this angle?

Jo is pregnant when David goes missing and it was second nature for me to write about a character who had wanted a baby for a very long time. However, because so much has happened to Jo by the time the baby is born, I knew her feelings towards her son had to be affected. With her confidence shattered, she fears that the baby is rejecting her in the same way that his father had. It was certainly difficult to navigate my way through Jo's emotions, starting with her looking forward to the birth right through to her not wanting to bring the baby home from hospital, and while her reaction wasn't something I could relate to personally, I could understand why she felt the way she did. Jo's belief in herself and everything she held dear has been challenged, if not destroyed. She convinces herself that she won't be a good enough mother and while that's probably something many first-time mums can relate to, myself included, with Jo those feelings of self-doubt are off the scale.

Jo saw her own parents' marriage fracture, although not collapse completely, after her mother's affair. What do you think Jo brings from this experience to her own marriage? And how do you think it relates to Jo's need for control?

While I set out to make Jo a confident and self-assured career woman, there was a vulnerable side to her that was only revealed to those she trusted. In her adult life, that had been her husband but Jo had also turned to her mum as a teenager when she started suffering from anxiety attacks. Back then, she had been let down by her mum who refused to appreciate how her own behaviour was contributing to her daughter's problems, and Jo was also let down by her GP who didn't take her seriously. Jo learned to manage her anxiety on her own and took comfort from being organised which gave her a sense of control over her life and to some extent, David's too. David was a project manager so when he planned out their future, it made Jo feel secure, and their problems only began when he deviated from that plan. After he disappeared, Jo spiralled into despair and her mental health suffered as a result and it was this aspect of her life that I was most interested in as the story developed. I hope readers will be able to relate to someone who could slip from having a relatively healthy state of mind, albeit with the odd quirk of character, to someone whose mental health suffered to the extent that she wasn't able to function on a daily basis.

You write hauntingly around themes of motherhood and what it means to have children. Does this come from your own experiences?

Of all my life experiences so far, the most rewarding, demanding, challenging, life reaffirming and truly devastating have come from my role as a mother. I always wanted to have children and although being a single mum has been tough at times, the love I have for my son and daughter is such a powerful emotion and it's that kind of intense relationship between a mother and child that I love to write about. However, experience has also taught me that while a mother's love is incredibly strong, life is all too fragile, as I unfortunately discovered when my son died, and aspects of that particular emotional journey are threaded through my novels too. I'd like to think that by writing along the themes of motherhood, I'm reinforcing my love for that little boy who changed my life forever.

At the end of the book in an incredibly moving and bittersweet scene, Jo discovers David's dreams for their life together, including the growth of their family and all his plans for travelling. If you looked ahead to your own future, where would you see it going? And where would be on your 'must-see' world tour?

I'm the first to admit that I'm a bit of a home bird so it would have to be somewhere special to tempt me away. Top of my must-see list would be a trip to Iceland even though I've already been there once. The sights are stunning and the blue lagoon an experience in itself although what I'd really like to go back for are the Northern Lights which failed to appear the last time we were there. Also on my list would be trips to visit places that have a history, whether that's a landscape created by glaciers, imposing castles or ancient ruins. I love being somewhere where I can imagine what might have happened centuries or even thousands of years earlier. Oh, and I'd really, really love to go scuba diving and discover all those amazing sights beneath the ocean waves. Unfortunately, I'm a little too much like Jo and travelling does tend to stress me out and put me off – but if ever someone invents a teleporter, I'll be the first to sign up!

What would you like the reader to take away from this story?

Possibly the most important thing to take away from this novel is that life isn't as predictable or as secure as any of us would like to imagine and when we give our love to others, it has to be with a sense of hope rather than certainty.

Tell me about your writing habits – do you have to be in a certain place, listen to certain music? Do you work better at a certain time of day?

How I write varies depending upon whether it's a week day or the weekend. I still work full time so I have to squeeze in my writing where I can as if it was still a hobby, albeit one that consumes much of my free time and comes with deadlines. I'm usually home from my day job by late afternoon and fire up the computer as soon as I step through the door. There's a quick break to feed myself and my daughter and then it's back to my writing until I've finished whatever daily target I've set myself such as a specific word count. I can finish as early as 7pm but often it stretches beyond 9pm. Weekends are another matter entirely and I tend to write only in the mornings because I love being able to spend the rest of the day pottering around with the scenes I've just written still lurking inside my head – that's usually when I'll get a sudden flash of inspiration that will set me up for the next day's labours.

Can you tell us a bit about your next book?

My next novel is about Sam, who works as a gardener in Calderstones Park in Liverpool and the story opens when he falls under suspicion after a young girl goes missing. The girl in question is eight year old Jasmine who visits the park one day on a school trip. Sam is giving a guided tour and tells her class about the park's thousand year old tree, which is called the Allerton Oak. He tells them that the tree has magical powers and can grant wishes, and it's Sam's determination to make Jasmine's wishes come true that gets him embroiled in the police investigation.

Reading Group Questions

Did you believe that David had left Jo and their baby, or did you cling with Jo to the idea that something had happened to him. Why?

Discuss Jo's mental state before and after David's disappearance. Did you feel this was a realistic portrayal?

How did you feel about Jo's reluctance to care for her baby when he was first born?

How does the front door of Jo's house function as an element in the story?

What stages of grief does Jo go through and how does she cope during each stage during the novel?

Discuss the parental relationships portrayed in the novel: David and Irene, Jo and Liz, Steph and Lauren, Jo and Archie.